**About the** ████████████

**Abby Green** spent her teen~~~ ████████
romances. She then spent ma~~~ ████~~~ in the
Film and TV industry as an A████~~ Director. One
day while standing outside an actor's trailer in the rain,
she thought: there has to be more than this. So she sent
off a partial to Mills & Boon. After many rewrites,
they accepted her first book and an author was born.
She lives in Dublin, Ireland and you can find out more
here: www.abby-green.com

*New York Times* bestselling author **Maisey Yates** lives
in rural Oregon with her three children and her
husband, whose chiselled jaw and arresting features
continue to make her swoon. She feels the epic trek she
takes several times a day from her office to her coffee
maker is a true example of her pioneer spirit.

**Kim Lawrence** was encouraged by her husband to
write when the unsocial hours of nursing didn't look
attractive! He told her she could do anything she set her
mind to, so Kim tried her hand at writing. Always a
keen Mills & Boon reader, it seemed natural for her to
write a romance novel – now she can't imagine doing
anything else. She is a keen gardener and cook and
enjoys running on the beach with her Jack Russell.
Kim lives in Wales.

# Spanish Scandals

# Spanish Scandals: Ultimate Temptation

ABBY GREEN

MAISEY YATES

KIM LAWRENCE

MILLS & BOON

First Published in Great Britain 2020
By Mills & Boon, an imprint of HarperCollins*Publishers*
1 London Bridge Street, London, SE1 9GF

SPANISH SCANDALS: ULTIMATE TEMPTATION © 2020
Harlequin Books S.A.

*Claimed for the De Carrillo Twins* © 2017 Abby Green
*The Spaniard's Pregnant Bride* © 2016 Maisey Yates
*Santiago's Command* © 2012 Kim Lawrence

ISBN: 978-0-263-28213-9

**MIX**
Paper from
responsible sources
**FSC® C007454**

FSC
www.fsc.org

This book is produced from independently certified FSC™ paper to ensure responsible forest management.

For more information visit: www.harpercollins.co.uk/green

Printed and bound in Spain
by CPI, Barcelona

# CLAIMED FOR THE DE CARRILLO TWINS

**ABBY GREEN**

I'd like to thank Heidi Rice, Sharon Kendrick
and Iona Grey for all their cheer-leading,
Kate Meader, who provided counsel over
cocktails in the Shelbourne, and, Annie West,
who always provides serene and insightful advice.
And of course my editor, Sheila, who has proved
beyond doubt that she believes me capable of
anything, apart from perhaps AWAVMOT!

Thank you, all!

# PROLOGUE

CRUZ DE CARRILLO SURVEYED the thronged reception room in his London home, filled with a veritable who's who of London's most powerful players and beautiful people, all there to celebrate his return to Europe.

He felt no sense of accomplishment, though, to be riding high on the crest of his stratospheric success in North America, having tripled his eponymous bank's fortunes in less than a year, because he knew his zealous focus on work had more to do with avoiding *this* than the burning ambition he'd harboured for years to turn his family bank's fortune and reputation around.

And it killed him to admit it.

*This* was standing just feet away from him now—tall and slender, yet with generous curves. Pale skin. Too much pale skin. Exposed in a dress that left far too little to the imagination. Cruz's mouth compressed with distaste even as his blood ran hot, mocking him for the desire which time hadn't diminished—much to his intense irritation. It was unwelcome and completely inappropriate. Now more than ever. She was his sister-in-law.

Her blonde hair was up in a sleek chignon and a chain of glittering gold trailed tantalisingly down her naked back, bared in a daring royal blue backless dress. She turned slightly in Cruz's direction and he had to tense every muscle to stave off the surge of fresh desire when he saw the provocative curves of her high full breasts, barely disguised by the thin draped satin.

She looked almost vulnerable, set apart from the crowd slightly, but he knew that was just a mirage.

He cursed her. And he cursed himself. If he hadn't been

so weak he wouldn't know how incendiary it felt to have those curves pressed against his body. He wouldn't remember the way her eyes had turned a stormy dark blue as he'd plundered the sweetness she'd offered up to him that fateful night almost eighteen months ago, in this very house, when she'd worked for him as a housemaid.

He wouldn't still hear her soft, breathy moans in his dreams, forcing him awake, sweating, with his hand wrapped around himself and every part of him straining for release...aching to know the intimate clasp of her body, milking him into sweet oblivion.

*Sweet.* That was just it. There was nothing sweet about this woman. He might have thought so at one time—she'd used to blush if he so much as glanced at her—but it had all been an elaborate artifice. Because his younger half-brother, Rio, had told him the truth about what she really was, and she was no innocent.

Her seduction of Cruz had obviously been far more calculated than he'd believed, and when that hadn't worked she'd diverted her sights onto Rio, his illegitimate half-brother, with whom Cruz had a complicated relationship—to put it mildly.

A chasm had been forged between the brothers when they were children—when Cruz had been afforded every privilege as the legitimate heir to the De Carrillo fortune, and Rio, who had been born to a housemaid of the family *castillo*, had been afforded nothing. Not even the De Carrillo name.

But Cruz had never felt that Rio should be punished for their charismatic and far too handsome father's inability to control his base appetites. So he had done everything in his power after their father had died some ten years previously to make amends—going against their father's will, which had left Rio nothing, by becoming his guardian, giving him his rightful paternalistic name and paying for him to complete his education.

Then, when he had come of age, Cruz had given him a fair share of his inheritance *and* a job—first in the De Carrillo bank in Madrid, and now in London, much to the conservative board's displeasure.

At the age of twenty-one Rio had become one of Europe's newest millionaires, the centre of feverish media attention with his dark good looks and mysterious past. And he had lapped it up, displaying an appetite for the kind of playboy lifestyle Cruz had never indulged in, quickly marrying one of the world's top supermodels in a lavish wedding that had gone on for days—only for it to end in tragedy nearly a year later, when she'd died in an accident shortly after giving birth to twin boys.

And yet, much as Rio's full-throttle existence had unnerved Cruz, could he begrudge him that after being denied his heritage?

Cruz's conscience pricked. By giving Rio his due inheritance and his rightful name perhaps he'd made his brother a target for gold-diggers? Rio's first wife had certainly revelled in her husband's luxurious lifestyle, and it would appear as if nothing had changed with his second wife.

As if sensing his intense regard, his sister-in-law turned now and saw him. Her eyes widened and her cheeks flushed. Cruz's anger spiked. She could still turn it on. Even now. When he knew her real capabilities.

She faced him in that provocative dress and her luscious body filled his vision and made his blood thrum with need. He hated her for it. She moved towards him almost hesitantly, the slippery satin material moving sinuously around her long legs.

He called on every atom of control he had and schooled his body not to respond to her proximity even as her tantalising scent tickled his nostrils, threatening to weaken him all over again. It was all at once innocent, yet seductive. As if he needed reminding that she presented one face to the world while hiding another, far more mercenary one.

'Trinity.' His voice sounded unbearably curt to his ears, and he tried to ignore the striking light blue eyes. To ignore how lush her mouth was, adding a distinctly sensual edge to her pale blonde innocence.

An innocence that was skin-deep.

'Cruz...it's nice to see you again.'

Her voice was husky, reminding him vividly of how it had sounded in his ear that night. *'Please...'*

His dry tone disguised his banked rage. 'You've come up in the world since we last met.'

She swallowed, the long, delicate column of her pale throat moving. 'Wh-what do you mean?'

Cruz's jaw tightened at the faux innocence. 'I'm talking about your rapid ascent from the position of nanny to wife and stepmother to my nephews.'

That brought back the unwelcome reminder that he'd only been informed about the low-key wedding in a text from Rio.

I have you to thank for sending this beautiful woman into my life. I hope you'll be very happy for us, brother.

The news had precipitated shock, and something much darker into Cruz's gut. And yet he hadn't had any reason at that point not to believe it was a good idea—in spite of his own previous experience with Trinity, which he'd blamed himself for. Rio had been a widower, and he and Trinity had obviously forged a bond based on caring for his nephews. Cruz had believed that she was a million light years away from Rio's glamorous hedonistic first wife. *Then.*

The fact that he'd had dreams for weeks afterwards,

of being held back and forced to watch a faceless blonde woman making love to countless men, was something that made him burn inwardly with shame even now.

Trinity looked pale. Hesitant. 'I was looking for you, actually. Could we have a private word?'

Cruz crushed the unwelcome memory and arched a brow. 'A private word?'

He flicked a glance at the crowd behind her and then looked back to her, wondering what the hell she was up to. Surely she wouldn't have the gall to try and seduce him under the same roof she had before, with her husband just feet away?

'We're private enough here. No one is listening.'

She flushed and then glanced behind her and back, clearly reluctant. 'Perhaps this isn't the best time or place...'

So he'd been right. Disgust settled in his belly. 'Spit it out, Trinity. Unless it's not *talking* you're interested in.'

She blanched, and that delicate flush disappeared. Once her ability to display emotions had intrigued him. Now it incensed him.

'What do you mean?'

'You know very well what I mean. You tried to seduce me in this very house, and when it didn't work you transferred your attentions to my brother. He obviously proved to be more susceptible to your wiles.'

She shook her head and frowned, a visibly trembling hand coming up to her chest as if to contain shock, disbelief. 'I don't know what you're talking about...'

Disgust filled Cruz that she could stand here and so blatantly lie while her enormous rock of an engagement ring glinted at him mockingly. All he could see was her and her treachery. But he had to crush the recriminations that rose up inside him—it was too late for them now.

Rio had revealed to Cruz on his return to the UK a

few days before that he was on the verge of bankruptcy—
his huge inheritance all but wiped out. And Trinity De
Carrillo's name was all over nearly every receipt and
docket that had led his brother further and further into
the mire. The extent of how badly Cruz had misread her
was galling.

An insidious thought occurred to him and it made his
blood boil. 'Your innocent act is past its sell-by date. I
might not have realised what you were up to—more fool
me—but I know now. Rio has told me how you've single-
handedly run through almost every cent he has to his name
in a bid to satisfy your greedy nature. Now you're realising
his fortune isn't a bottomless pit, perhaps you're looking
for a way out, or even a new benefactor?'

Before she could respond he continued in a low, bitter voice.

'I underestimated your capacity to play the long game,
Trinity. You lulled Rio into a false sense of trust by manipulating his biggest vulnerability—his sons. I'm very
well aware of how my actions pushed you in the direction of my brother, and that is not something I will ever
forgive myself for. Needless to say if he requires financial help he will receive it, but your days of bankrupting
him are over. If you're hoping to bargain your way out
of this predicament then think again. You'll get no sympathy from me.'

Trinity was so white now Cruz fancied he could see the
blood vessels under her skin. A part of him wished she
would break out of character and get angry with him for
confronting her with who she really was.

Her hand dropped back to her side and she shook her
head. 'You have it all wrong.'

'That's the best you can come up with?' he sneered. 'I
have it *all wrong*? If I "have it all wrong" then, please, tell
me what you want to discuss.'

Cruz could see the pulse at the base of her neck beating hectically. His own pulse-rate doubled.

'I wanted to talk to you about Rio…about his behaviour. It's been growing more and more erratic… I'm worried about the boys.'

Cruz let out a short, incredulous laugh. 'Worried about the boys? You're really trying to play the concerned stepmother card in a bid to deflect attention from the fact that you're more concerned about your lavish lifestyle coming to an end?'

Bitterness filled Cruz. He knew better than most how the biological bond of a parent and child didn't guarantee love and security. Far from it.

'You're not even related to them—you've just used them as pawns to manipulate your way into my brother's bed and get a ring on your finger.'

Trinity took a step back, her eyes wide with feigned shock. He had to hand it to her. She was a good actress.

Almost as if she was talking to herself now, she said, 'I should have known he'd protect himself somehow…of course you'd believe him over me.'

A sliver of unease pierced Cruz's anger but he pushed it aside. 'I've known Rio all of his twenty-five years. I think it's safe to say I'd trust my own flesh and blood over a conniving gold-digger any day of the week.'

Heated colour came back into Trinity's cheeks. She looked at him, big blue eyes beseeching him with commendable authenticity.

'I'm not a gold-digger. You don't understand. Everything you're saying is all wrong—my marriage with Rio is not what you—'

'*There* you are, darling. I've been looking for you. Charlotte Lacey wants to talk to you about next week's charity function.'

Cruz blanched. He hadn't even noticed Rio joining

them. He'd been consumed with the woman in front of him, whose arm was now being taken firmly in her husband's hand. Rio's dark brown eyes met Cruz's over Trinity's head. They were hard. Trinity had gone even paler, if that was possible.

'If you don't mind, brother, I need to steal my wife away.'

Cruz could see it in Rio's eyes then—a familiar resentment. And shame and anger. Futility choked him. There was nothing he could do. He knew Rio would already be despising the fact that he'd allowed Cruz to see him brought so low at this woman's greedy hands.

He watched as they walked back into the crowd, and it wasn't long before they left for the evening—without saying goodbye. Rio might have shown Cruz a chink of vulnerability by revealing his financial problems, but if anything that only demonstrated how much Trinity had got to him—because he'd never before allowed his brother to see a moment's weakness. Cruz's sense that his determination to see Rio treated fairly had been futile rose up again—he had never truly bridged the gap between them.

Cruz stood at the window in his drawing room and watched his brother handing Trinity into the passenger seat of a dark Jeep in the forecourt outside the house, before he got into the driver's seat himself.

He felt grim. All he could do now was be there to pick up the pieces of Rio's financial meltdown and do his best to ensure that Rio got a chance to start again—and that his wife didn't get her grasping hands on another cent.

At the last second, as if hearing his thoughts, Trinity turned her head to look at Cruz through the ground-floor window. For a fleeting moment their eyes met, and he could have sworn he saw hers shimmer with moisture, even from this distance.

He told himself they had to be tears of anger now that

she knew she'd been found out. She was trapped in a situation of her own making. It should have filled Cruz with a sense of satisfaction, but instead all he felt was a heavy weight in his chest.

Rio's Jeep took off with a spurt of gravel.

Cruz didn't realise it then, but it would be the last time he saw his brother alive.

# CHAPTER ONE

*Three months later. Solicitor's office.*

TRINITY'S HEART STOPPED and her mouth dried. 'Mr De Carrillo is joining us?'

The solicitor glanced at her distractedly, looking for a paper on his overcrowded desktop. 'Yes—he is the executor of his brother's will, and we *are* in his building,' he pointed out redundantly.

She'd been acutely aware that she was in the impressive De Carrillo building in London's bustling financial zone, but it hadn't actually occurred to her that Cruz himself would be here.

To her shame, her first instinct was to check her appearance—which of course she couldn't do, but she was glad of the choice of clothing she'd made: dark loose trousers and a grey silk shirt. She'd tied her long hair back in a braid, as much out of habit when dealing with small energetic boys than for any other reason. She hadn't put on any make-up and regretted that now, fearing she must look about eighteen.

Just then there was a light knock on the door and it opened. She heard Mr Drew's assistant saying in a suspiciously breathless and awestruck voice, 'Mr De Carrillo, sir.'

The solicitor stood up, immediately obsequious, greeting Cruz De Carrillo effusively and leading him to a seat beside Trinity's on the other side of his desk.

Every nerve came to immediate and tingling life. The tiny hairs on her arms stood up, quivering. She lamented her uncontrollable reaction—would she ever *not* react to him?

She sensed him come to stand near her, tall and effort-lessly intimidating. Childishly, she wanted to avoid look-ing at him. His scent was a tantalising mix of musk and something earthy and masculine. It was his scent now that sent her hurtling back to that cataclysmic evening in his house three months ago, when she'd realised just how badly Rio had betrayed her.

The shock of knowing that Rio obviously hadn't told him the truth about their marriage was still palpable, even now. And the fact that Cruz had so readily believed the worst of her hurt far worse than it should.

It had hurt almost as much as when he'd looked at her with dawning horror and self-disgust after kissing her to within an inch of her life. It was an experience still seared onto her brain, so deeply embedded inside her that she sometimes woke from X-rated dreams, tangled amongst her sheets and sweating. Almost two years later it was be-yond humiliating.

Trinity dragged her mind away from that disturbing labyrinth of memories. She had more important things to deal with now. Because three months ago, while she and Rio had been driving home from Cruz's house, they'd been involved in a car crash and Rio had tragically died.

Since that day she'd become lone step-parent to Mateo and Sancho, Rio's two-and-a-half-year-old twins. Miracu-lously, she'd escaped from the accident with only cuts and bruises and a badly sprained ankle. She had no memory of the actual accident—only recalled waking in the hospi-tal feeling battered all over and learning of her husband's death from a grim and ashen-faced Cruz.

Gathering her composure, she stood up to face him, steeling herself against his effect. Which was useless. As soon as she looked at him it was like a blow to her solar plexus.

She'd seen him since the night of the accident—at the

funeral, of course, and then when he'd called at the house for brief perfunctory visits to check that she and his nephews had everything they needed. He hadn't engaged with her beyond that. Her skin prickled now with foreboding. She had a sense that he'd merely been biding his time.

She forced herself to say, as calmly as she could, 'Cruz.'

'Trinity.'

His voice reverberated deep inside her, even as he oozed his habitual icy control.

The solicitor had gone back around his desk and said now, 'Espresso, wasn't it, Mr De Carrillo?'

Trinity blinked and looked to see the older gentleman holding out a small cup and saucer. Instinctively, because she was closer and because it was good manners, she reached for it to hand it to Cruz, only belatedly realising that her hand was trembling.

She prayed he wouldn't notice the tremor as she held out the delicate china to him. His hand was masculine and square. Strong. Long fingers…short, functional nails. At that moment she had a flash of remembering how his hand had felt between her legs, stroking her intimately…

Just before he took the cup and saucer there was a tiny clatter of porcelain on porcelain, evidence of her frayed nerves. *Damn.*

When he had the cup she sat down again quickly, before she made a complete fool of herself, and took a quick fortifying sip of her own cup of tea. He sat down too, and she was aware of his powerful body taking up a lot of space.

While Mr. Drew engaged Cruz De Carrillo in light conversation, before they started discussing the terms of Rio's will, Trinity risked another glance at the man just a couple of feet to her left.

Short dark blond hair gave more than a hint of his supremely controlled nature. Controlled except for that momentary lapse…an undoubtedly rare moment of heated insanity with someone he'd seen as far beneath him.

Trinity crushed the spike of emotion. She couldn't afford it.

Despite the urbane uniform of a three-piece suit, his impressive build was apparent. Muscles pushed at the fabric in a way that said he couldn't be contained, no matter how civilised he might look.

His face was a stunning portrait of masculine beauty, all hard lines and an aquiline profile that spoke of a pure and powerful bloodline. He had deep-set eyes and a mouth that on anyone else would have looked ridiculously sensual. Right now though, it looked stern. Disapproving.

Trinity realised that she was staring at him, and when he turned to look at her she went puce. She quickly turned back to the solicitor, who had stopped talking and was now looking from her to Cruz nervously, as if he could sense the tension in the room.

He cleared his throat. 'As you're both here now, I see no reason not to start.'

'If you would be so kind.'

Trinity shivered at the barely veiled impatience in Cruz's voice. She could recall only too well how this man had reduced grown men and women to quivering wrecks with just a disdainful look from those glittering dark amber eyes.

The half-brothers hadn't been very alike—where Rio had been dark, with obsidian eyes and dark hair, Cruz possessed a cold, tawny beauty that had always made Trinity think of dark ice over simmering heat. She shivered… she'd felt that heat.

*'Mrs De Carrillo…?'*

Trinity blinked and flushed at being caught out again. The solicitor's impatient expression came into focus. He was holding out a sheaf of papers and she reached for them.

'I'm sorry.' It still felt weird to be called Mrs De Carrillo—it wasn't as if she'd ever *really* been Rio's wife.

She quickly read the heading: *Last will and testament of Rio De Carrillo*. Her heart squeezed as she thought of the fact that Mateo and Sancho had now lost both their parents, too prematurely.

As bitter as her experience had been with Rio in the end, after Trinity had been sickened to realise just how manipulative he'd been, and how naive she'd been, she'd never in a million years have wished him gone.

She'd felt a level of grief that had surprised her, considering the fact that their marriage had been in name only—for the convenience of having a steady mother figure for the boys and because Rio had wanted to promote a more settled image to further his own ambitions.

Trinity had agreed to the union for those and myriad other reasons—the most compelling of which had to do with her bond with the twins, which had been forged almost as soon as she'd seen them. Two one-year-old cherubs, with dark hair, dark mischievous eyes and heart-stopping smiles.

Her heart had gone out to them because they were motherless, as she had been since she was a baby, and they'd latched on to her with a ferocity that she hadn't been able to resist, even though she'd known it would be more professional to try and keep some distance.

She'd also agreed because Rio's sad personal story—he had been all but abandoned by his own parents—had again chimed with echoes of her own. And because he'd agreed to help her fulfil her deepest ambitions—to go to university and get a degree, thereby putting her in a position to forge her own future, free of the stain of her ignominious past.

Rio hadn't revealed the full extent of *his* ambitions until shortly before the accident—and that was when she'd realised why he'd taken such perverse pleasure in marrying her. It had had far more to do with his long-held simmering resentment towards his older half-brother than any real desire to forge a sense of security for his sons, or to shake off his playboy moniker...

The solicitor was speaking. 'As you'll see, it's a relatively short document. There's really no need to read through it all now. Suffice to say that Mr De Carrillo bequeathed everything to his sons, Mateo and Sancho, and he named you their legal guardian, Trinity.'

She looked up. She'd known that Rio had named her guardian. Any concerns she'd had at the time, contemplating such a huge responsibility had been eclipsed by the overwhelmingly protective instinct she'd felt for the twins. And in all honesty the prospect of one day becoming their guardian hadn't felt remotely possible.

She realised that she hadn't really considered what this meant for her own future now. It was something she'd been good at blocking out in the last three months, after the shock of the accident and Rio's death, not to mention getting over her own injuries and caring for two highly precocious and energetic boys. It was as if she was afraid to let the enormity of it all sink in.

The solicitor looked at Cruz for a moment, and then he looked back to Trinity with something distinctly *uncomfortable* in his expression. She tensed.

'I'm not sure how aware you are of the state of Mr De Carrillo's finances when he died?'

Trinity immediately felt the scrutiny of the man to her left, as if his gaze was boring into her. His accusatory words came back to her: *'You've single-handedly run through almost every cent my brother has to his name in a bid to satisfy your greedy nature. Now you're realising Rio's fortune isn't a bottomless pit...'*

She felt breathless, as if a vice was squeezing her chest.

Until the evening of Cruz's party she hadn't been aware of any such financial difficulty. She'd only been aware that Rio was growing more and more irrational and erratic. When she'd confronted him about his behviour, they'd had a huge argument, in which the truth of exactly why he'd married her had been made very apparent. Along with his *real* agenda.

That was why Trinity had wanted to talk to Cruz—to share her concerns. However, he'd comprehensively shut that down.

She said carefully now, 'I was aware that things weren't…good. But I didn't know that it was linked to his financial situation.'

Mr. Drew looked grim. 'Well, it most probably was. The truth is that Rio was bankrupt. In these last three months the sheer extent and scale of his financial collapse has become evident, and it's comprehensive. I'm afraid that all he left behind him are debts. There is nothing to bequeath to his children. Or you.'

Trinity hadn't married Rio for his money, so this news didn't have any great impact on her. What did impact her, though, was the realisation that Cruz must have been putting money into the account that she used for day-to-day necessities for her and the boys and Mrs Jordan—the nanny Rio had hired once Trinity had married him, when her job had changed and she'd been expected to accompany him to social functions. Something she'd never felt comfortable doing…

The solicitor said, 'I'm sorry to deliver this news, Mrs De Carrillo, but even the house will have to be sold to cover his debts.'

Before she could absorb that, Cruz was standing up and saying, in a coolly authoritative tone, 'If you could leave us now, Mr. Drew, I'll go over the rest with my sister-in-law.'

The solicitor clearly had no issue with being summarily

dismissed from his own office. He gathered some papers and left, shutting the door softly behind him.

Trinity's mind was reeling, as she tried to take everything in, and revolving with a sickening sense of growing panic as to how she was going to manage caring for the boys when she didn't have a job. How could she afford to keep Mrs Jordan on?

Cruz walked over to the floor-to-ceiling windows behind the large desk, showcasing an impressive view of London's skyline.

For a long moment he said nothing, and she could only look helplessly at his broad shoulders and back. Then he turned around and a sense of déjà-vu nearly knocked her off her chair. It was so reminiscent of when she'd first met him—when she'd gone to his house in Holland Park for an interview, applying for the position of maid in his household.

She'd never met such an intimidating man in her life. Nor such a blatantly masculine man. Based on his reputation as one of the world's wealthiest bankers, she had assumed him to be older, somewhat soft... But he'd been young. And gorgeous. His tall, powerful body had looked as if it was hewn from pure granite and steel. His eyes had been disconcertingly unreadable...

*'Miss Adams...did you hear my question?'*

She was back in time, caught in the glare of those mesmerising eyes, his brows drawn into a frown of impatience. His Spanish accent had been barely noticeable, just the slightest intriguing inflection. She'd felt light-headed, even though she was sitting down.

'I'm sorry...what?'

Those eyes had flashed with irritation. 'I asked how old you are?'

She'd swallowed. 'I'm twenty-two. Since last week.'

Then she'd felt silly for mentioning that detail—as if

one of the richest men in the world cared when her birthday was! Not that she even knew when her birthday was for sure…

But she'd survived four rounds of intense interviews to be there to meet the man himself—evidence of how he oversaw every tiny detail of his life—so Trinity had gathered her fraying wits, drawn her shoulders back and reminded herself that she had hopes and dreams, and that if she got this job she'd be well on her way to achieving a life for herself…

'I have to hand it to you—you're as good an actress as you were three months ago when you first feigned ignorance of Rio's financial situation. But you must have known what was coming down the tracks. After all, you helped divest my brother of a small fortune.'

The past and present meshed for a moment, and then Trinity realised what Cruz had just said.

She clasped her hands tight together on her lap. 'But I didn't know.'

'Did the accident affect your memory, Trinity?' His voice held more than a note of disdain. 'Do you not recall that illuminating conversation we had before you left my house on that fateful night?'

She flushed, remembering it all too well. 'I don't have any memory of the accident, but, yes, I do recall what you said to me. You're referring to your accusation that I was responsible for Rio's financial problems.'

Cruz's mouth compressed. 'I think *ruin* would be a more accurate word.'

Trinity stood up, too agitated to stay seated. 'You're wrong. It's true that Rio spent money on me, yes, but it was for the purposes of—'

Cruz held up a hand, a distinct sneer on his face now. 'Spare me the details. I looked into Rio's accounts after he died. I know all about the personal stylist, the VIP seats to every fashion show, the haute couture dresses, private jet travel, the best hotels in the world... The list is endless. I curse the day that I hired you to work for me—because, believe me, I blame myself as much as you for ruining my brother.'

At that damning pronouncement Trinity felt something deep inside her shrivel up to protect itself. She had not been prepared for Cruz's vitriolic attack.

But then, this was the man who had wiped her taste off his mouth and looked at her with disgust when he'd realised that he'd lowered himself to the level of kissing his own maid.

Trinity bitterly recalled the intimate dinner party he'd hosted the following evening—when the gaping chasm between them had been all too apparent.

Cruz had welcomed a tall and stunningly beautiful brunette, kissing her warmly on both cheeks. As the woman had passed her fur coat to Trinity, not even glancing in her direction, Trinity had caught an expressive look from Cruz that had spoken volumes—telling her to forget what had happened. Telling her that this woman was the kind of woman he consorted with, and whatever had happened between them must be consigned to some sordid memory box, never to be taken out and examined again.

That was when she'd been unable to hold her emotions in, utterly ashamed that she'd let her crush grow to such gargantuan proportions that she'd let him actually *hurt* her. And that was when Rio, Cruz's half-brother, who had also been a guest that night, had found her outside, in a hidden corner of the garden, weeping pathetically.

He'd come outside to smoke and had sat down beside her, telling her to relax when she'd tried to rush back inside, mortified. And somehow...she still wasn't sure how... he'd managed to get her to open up, to reveal what had happened. She hadn't told him of her burgeoning feelings for

Cruz, but she probably hadn't had to. It must have been emblazoned all over her tearstained face.

'Tell me what your price is for signing away your guardianship of my nephews?'

Trinity blinked and the painful memory faded.

As she focused on his words she went cold all over. 'What did you just say?'

Cruz snapped his fingers, displeasure oozing from his tall, hard body. 'You heard me—how much will it take, Trinity, for you to get out of my nephews' lives, because I don't doubt you have a price.'

Horror curdled her insides at the thought of being removed from Mateo and Sancho. Only that morning Sancho had thrown his arms around her and said, *'I love you, Mummy...'*

She shook her head now, something much hotter replacing the horror. 'There is no price you could pay me to leave the boys.'

'I am their blood relation.'

'You've only met them a handful of times!'

Cruz snorted. 'Are you trying to tell me that you could care for them more than their own flesh and blood? You've just been using them as a meal ticket. And now that Rio's left nothing behind they're your only hope of keeping your nest feathered—presumably by extorting money out of me.'

Trinity gasped. 'I would never—'

Cruz lifted a hand. 'Spare me.'

Trinity's mouth closed as she struggled to process this. All her protective hackles were raised high now, at the suggestion that she would use her stepchildren for her own ends. She would never leave them at the mercy of a cold-hearted billionaire who didn't even really know them, in spite of that flesh and blood relationship.

Impulsively she asked, 'What qualifications could you

possibly have for taking on two toddlers? Have you ever even held a baby? Changed a nappy?'

Cruz's jaw clenched. 'I do not need qualifications. I'm their uncle. I will hire the best possible staff to attend to their every need.'

His gaze narrowed on her so intently she fought against squirming under it.

'What possible qualifications could *you* have? When you came to work for me you'd left school after your A-levels with not much work experience.'

His remark went right to the heart of her and stung— badly. It stung because of the way she'd longed to impress this man at one time, and had yearned to catch his attention. It stung because of the very private dreams she'd harboured to further her education. And it stung because in all the foster homes where she'd lived through her formative years she'd instinctively found herself mothering any younger foster children, as if drawn to create what she didn't have: a family.

She pushed down the hurt at Cruz's sneering disdain now, cursing her naivety, and lifted her chin. 'I've been caring for them since they were a year old. No one is qualified to be a parent until they become one. From the moment I married Rio I became their step-parent, and I would never turn my back on them.'

'Very noble indeed. But forgive me if I don't believe you. Now, we can continue to go around in these tiresome circles, or you can just tell me how much it'll take.'

He gestured to the table and she looked down to see a chequebook.

'I will write a cheque for whatever you want, Trinity, so let's stop playing games. You've done it. Your impressive act of caring for children that aren't your own is over. You can get on with your life.'

The sheer ease with which Cruz revealed his astounding cynicism angered Trinity as much as it shocked her.

She balled her hands into fists by her sides. 'I am not playing games. And those boys are as much mine as if I'd given birth to them myself.' It hit her then—the enormity of the love she felt for them. She'd always known she loved them, but right now she'd lay her life down for them.

The thought of Cruz taking the boys and washing his hands of them the way Rio had done—abdicating all responsibility to some faceless nanny—made her feel desperate. She had to try and make him believe her.

She took a deep breath. 'Please listen to me, Cruz. The marriage wasn't what you think... The truth is that it was a marriage of convenience. The twins were primarily the reason I agreed to it. I wanted to protect them.'

Trinity could feel her heart thumping. Tension snapped between them.

Then, showing not a hint of expression, Cruz said, 'Oh, I can imagine that it was very convenient. For you. And I have no doubt that my nephews were front and centre of your machinations. I know my brother was no saint—believe me, I'm under no illusions about that. But, based on his first choice of wife, it stretches the bounds of my credulity that he would turn around and marry a mere nanny, for convenience's sake. He was a passionate man, Trinity. You are a beautiful woman. I can only imagine that you used every trick in the book to take it beyond an affair between boss and employee. After all, I have personal experience of your methods. But, believe me, the only "convenience" I see here is the way you so *conveniently* seduced your way into his bed and then into a registry office, making sure you'd be set for life.'

Trinity ignored Cruz's *'you're a beautiful woman'* because it hadn't sounded remotely complimentary. She longed to reveal that no such affair had taken place, but she felt suddenly vulnerable under that blistering gaze, all her anger draining away to be replaced with the humiliation she'd felt after that *'personal experience'* he'd spoken of.

She found the words to inform him that Rio hadn't been remotely interested in her lodging in her throat. The reality was that one brother had rejected her and another had used her for his own ends. And the fact that she was letting this get to her now was even more galling. She should be thinking of Mateo and Sancho, not her own deep insecurities.

She stood tall against the biggest threat she'd ever faced. 'I'm not going anywhere. I am their legal guardian.'

Cruz folded his arms. 'I won't hesitate to take you to court to fight for their custody if I have to. Do you really want that to happen? Who do you think the courts will favour? Their flesh-and-blood uncle, who has nothing but their best interests at heart and the means to set them up for life, or their opportunistic stepmother who systematically spent her way through her husband's wealth? Needless to say if you force this route then you will receive nothing.'

Trinity felt her blood rush south so quickly that she swayed on her feet, but she sucked in a quick breath to regain her composure before he could see it. 'You can't threaten me like this,' she said, as firmly as she could. 'I'm their legal guardian, as per Rio's wishes.'

Cruz bit out, 'I told you before—I'm not interested in playing games.'

'Neither am I!' Trinity almost wailed. 'But I'm not letting you bully me into handing over custody of Matty and Sancho.'

Cruz looked disgusted. *'Matty?* What on earth is that?'

Trinity put her hands on her hips. 'It's what Sancho has called him ever since he started talking.'

Cruz waved a hand dismissively. 'It's a ridiculous name for an heir to the De Carrillo fortune.'

Trinity went still. 'What do you mean, heir? Surely any children *you* have will be the heirs…'

Cruz was close to reaching boiling point—which wasn't helped by the fact that his libido seemed to be reaching boiling point too. He was uncomfortably aware of how Trinity's breasts pushed against the fabric of her seemingly demure silk shirt. It was buttoned to her neck, but it was the most provocative thing he'd ever seen. It made him want to push aside the desk and rip it open so he could feast his gaze on those firm swells…

Which was an unwelcome reminder of how he'd reacted that night when he'd found her in his study—*supposedly* looking for a book—testing the very limits of his control in not much more than a vest and sleep shorts, with a flimsy robe belted around her tiny waist.

It *had* broken the limits of his control, proving that he wasn't so far removed from his father after all, in spite of his best efforts.

Cruz had had her backed up against the wall of shelves, grinding his achingly hard arousal into her quivering body, his fingers buried deep in slick heat and his mouth latched around a hard nipple, before he'd come to his senses…

Cursing her silently, and reining in his thundering arousal, Cruz said, with a coolness that belied the heat under the surface, '*Mateo* and Sancho will be my heirs, as I have no intention of having any children.'

Trinity shook her head. 'Why would you say such a thing?'

Already aware that he'd said too much, Cruz clamped down on the curious urge to explain that as soon as he'd heard Rio was having children he'd felt a weight lift off his shoulders, not having been really aware until then that he'd never relished the burden of producing an heir for the sake of the family business.

He'd learnt from a young age what it was to have to stand by helplessly and watch his own half-brother being treated as nothing just because he was the result of an affair. He'd experienced the way parents—the people who were meant to love you the most—sometimes had scant regard for their offspring. Cruz might have been the privileged legitimate heir, but he'd been treated more like an employee than a loved son.

He'd never felt that he had the necessary skills to be a father, and he'd never felt a desire to test that assertion. However, his nephews had changed things. And the fact that Rio was no longer alive *really* changed things now. And the fact that this woman believed she could control their fate was abominable.

Cruz was aware that he barely knew his nephews—every time he saw them they hid behind Trinity's legs, or their nanny's skirts. And until Rio had died he hadn't felt any great desire to connect with them...not knowing *how* to, in all honesty. But now an overwhelming instinct to protect them rose up in him and surprised him with its force. It reminded him of when he'd felt so protective of Rio when he'd been much smaller, and the reminder was poignant. And pertinent. He hadn't been able to protect Rio, but he could protect his nephews.

Perhaps Trinity thought she'd get more out of him like this. He rued the day she'd ever appeared in his life.

Curtly he said, 'I'll give you tonight to think it over. Tomorrow, midday, I'll come to the house—and trust me when I say that if you don't have your price ready by then, you'll have to prepare yourself for a legal battle after which you'll wish that you'd taken what I'm offering.'

# CHAPTER TWO

ON THE BUS back to Rio's house near Regent's Park—Trinity had never considered it hers—she was still reeling. She felt as if someone had physically punched her. Cruz had...except without using fists...and the reminder that she'd once fancied herself almost in love with him was utterly mortifying now.

The full enormity of his distrust in her was shocking—as was his threat that he would take her to court to get the boys if he had to.

She didn't need Cruz to tell her that she wouldn't fare well up against one of the world's wealthiest and most powerful men. As soon as his lawyers looked into her background and saw that she'd grown up in foster homes, with no family stability to her name, she'd be out of Matty and Sancho's lives.

It didn't even occur to her to consider Cruz's offer—the thought of leaving the twins in his cold and autocratic care was anathema to her.

Being in such close proximity to him again had left her feeling on edge and jittery. Too aware of her body. Sometimes the memory of that cataclysmic night in Cruz's study came back like a taunt. And, no matter how much she tried to resist it, it was too powerful for her to push down. It was as vivid as if it had just happened. The scene of her spectacular humiliation.

The fact that Cruz obviously hated himself for what had happened was like the lash of a whip every time she saw him. As if she needed to be reminded of his disgust! As if he needed another reason to hate her now! Because that much was crystal-clear. He'd judged her and condemned her—he hadn't even wanted to hear her defence.

Trinity tried to resist thinking about the past, but the rain beating relentlessly against the bus windows didn't help. She felt as if she was in a cocoon...

She'd been working as Cruz's housemaid for approximately six months, and one night, unable to sleep, she'd gone down to the study to find a new book. Cruz had told her to feel welcome to read his books after he'd found her curled up in a chair reading one day.

Trinity had been very aware that she was developing a monumentally pathetic crush on her enigmatic boss—she'd even read about him in one of his discarded copies of the *Financial Times*.

She'd loved to read the papers, even though she hadn't understood half of what they talked about, and it had been her ambition to understand it all some day. She'd finally felt as if she was breaking away from her past, and that she could possibly prove that she didn't have to be limited by the fact that her own parents had abandoned her.

Cruz had epitomised success and keen intelligence, and Trinity had been helplessly impressed and inspired. Needless to say he was the kind of man who would never notice someone like her in a million years, no matter how polite to her he was. Except sometimes she'd look up and find him watching her with a curious expression on his face, and it would make her feel hot and flustered. Self-conscious...

When she'd entered the study that night, she'd done so cautiously, even though she'd known Cruz was out at a function. She'd turned on a dim light and gone straight to the bookshelves, and had spent a happy few minutes looking for something to read among the very broad range he had. She'd been intrigued by the fact that alongside serious tomes on economics there were battered copies of John Le Carré and Agatha Christie. They humanised a very intimidating man.

She'd almost jumped out of her skin when a deep voice had said, with a touch of humour, 'Good to know it's not a burglar rifling through my desk.'

Trinity had immediately dropped the book she was looking at and turned to see Cruz in the doorway, breathtakingly gorgeous in a classic tuxedo, his bow tie rakishly undone. And her brain had just...melted.

Eventually, when her wits had returned, she'd bent down to pick up the book, acutely aware of her state of undress, and started gabbling. 'I'm sorry... I just wanted to get a book...couldn't sleep...'

She'd held the book in front of her like a shield. As if it might hide her braless breasts, covered only by the flimsiest material. But something in Cruz's lazy stance changed as his eyes had raked over her, and the air had suddenly been charged. Electric.

Her eyes had widened as he'd closed the distance between them. She'd been mesmerised. Glued to the spot. Glued to his face as it was revealed in the shadows of the room, all stark lines and angles. He'd taken the book she was holding out of her hand and looked at it, before putting it back on the shelf. He'd been so close she'd been able to smell his scent, and had wanted to close her eyes to breathe it in even deeper. She'd felt dizzy.

Then he'd reached out and touched her hair, taking a strand between two fingers and letting it run between them. The fact that he'd come so close...was touching her...had been so unlikely that she hadn't been able to move.

Her lower body had tightened with a kind of need she'd never felt before. She'd cursed her inexperience in that moment—cursed the fact that living in foster homes all her life had made her put up high walls of defence because she'd never been settled anywhere long enough to forge any kind of meaningful relationship.

She'd known she should have moved…that this was ridiculous. That the longer she stood there, in thrall to her gorgeous boss, the sooner he'd step back and she'd be totally exposed. She'd never let anyone affect her like this before, but somehow, without even trying, he'd just slipped under her skin…

But then he'd looked at her with a molten light in his eyes and said, 'I want you, Trinity Adams. I know I shouldn't, but I do.'

He'd let her hair go.

His words had shocked her so much that even though she'd known that was the moment to turn and walk out, her bare feet had stayed glued to the floor.

A reckless desire had rushed through her, heady and dangerous, borne out of the impossible reality that Cruz De Carrillo was looking at her like this…saying he wanted her. She was a nobody. She came from nothing. And yet at that moment she'd felt seen in a way she'd never experienced before.

It had come out of her, unbidden, from the deepest part of her. One word. *'Please…'*

Cruz had looked at her for a long moment, and then he'd muttered something in Spanish as he'd taken her arms in his hands and walked her backwards until she'd hit the bookshelves with a soft *thunk*.

And then he'd kissed her.

But it had been more like a beautifully brutal awakening than a kiss. She'd gone on fire in seconds, and discovered that she was capable of sudden voracious desires and needs.

His kiss had drugged her, taking her deep into herself

and a world of new and amazing sensations. The feel of his rough tongue stroking hers had been so intimate and wicked, and yet more addictive than anything she'd ever known. She'd understood it in that moment—what the power of a drug might be.

Then his big hands had touched her waist, belly, breasts, cupping their full weight. They'd been a little rough, unsteady, and she hadn't expected that of someone who was always so cool. In control.

The thought that she might be doing this to him had been unbelievable.

He'd pulled open her robe so that he could pull down her vest top and take her nipple into his mouth, making Trinity moan and writhe like a wanton under his hands. She remembered panting, opening her legs, sighing with ecstasy when he'd found the naked moist heat of her body and touched her there, rubbing back and forth, exploring with his fingers, making her gasp and twist higher and higher in an inexorable climb as he'd spoken low Spanish words into her ear until she'd broken apart, into a million shards of pleasure so intense that she'd felt emotion leak out of her eyes.

And that was when a cold breeze had skated over her skin. Some foreboding. Cruz had pulled back, but he'd still had one hand between her legs and the other on her bared breast. He'd been breathing as harshly as her, and they'd looked at each other for a long moment.

He'd blinked, as if waking from the sensual spell that had come over them, and at the same time he'd taken his hands off her and said, 'What the hell…?'

He'd stepped away from her so fast she'd lurched forward and had to steady herself, acutely aware of her clothes in disarray. She'd pulled her robe around herself with shaking hands.

Cruz had wiped the back of his hand across his mouth

and Trinity had wanted to disappear—to curl up in a ball and hide away from the dawning realisation and horror on his face.

'I'm sorry... I—' Her voice had felt scratchy. She hadn't even been sure why she was apologising.

He'd cut her off. '*No*. This was *my* fault. It should never have happened.'

He'd turned icy and distant so quickly that if her body hadn't still been throbbing with the after-effects of her first orgasm she might have doubted it had even happened—that he'd lost his control for a brief moment and shown her the fire burning under that cool surface.

'It was an unforgivable breach of trust.'

Miserable, Trinity had said, 'It was my fault too.'

He'd said nothing, and then, slightly accusingly, 'Do you usually walk around the house dressed like that?'

Trinity had gone cold again. 'What exactly are you saying?'

Cruz had dragged his gaze back up. His cheeks had been flushed, hair a little mussed. She'd never seen anyone sexier or more undone and not happy about it.

'Nothing,' he'd bitten out. 'Just...get out of here and forget this ever happened. It was completely inappropriate. I *never* mix business with pleasure, and I'm not about to start.' He'd looked away from her, a muscle pulsing in his jaw.

Right then Trinity had never felt so cheap in her life. He obviously couldn't bear to look at her a moment longer. She'd felt herself closing inwards, aghast that she'd let herself fall into a dream of feeling special so easily. She should have known better. Cruz De Carrillo took beautiful, sophisticated and intelligent women to his bed. He didn't have sordid fumbles with staff in his library.

The divide between them had yawned open like a huge dark chasm. Her naivety had slapped her across the face.

Without saying another word, she'd fled from the room.

Trinity forcibly pushed the memory back down deep, where it belonged. Her stop came into view and she got up and waited for the bus to come to a halt.

As she walked back to the huge and ostentatious house by Regent's Park she spied Mrs Jordan in the distance with the double buggy.

Her heart lifted and she half ran, half walked to meet them. The boys jumped up and down in their seats with arms outstretched when they spotted her. She hugged each of them close, revelling in their unique babyish smell, which was already changing as they grew more quickly than she knew how to keep up with them.

Something fierce gripped her inside as she held them tight. She was the only mother they'd ever really known, and she would not abandon them for anything.

When she stood up, Mrs Jordan looked at her with concern. 'Are you all right, dear? You look very pale.'

Trinity forced a brittle smile. She couldn't really answer—because what could she say? That Cruz was going to come the next day and turn their world upside down? That lovely Mrs Jordan might be out of a job? That Trinity would be consigned to a scrap heap somewhere?

The boys would be upset and bewildered, facing a whole new world...

A sob made its way up her throat, but she forced it down and said the only thing she could. 'We need to talk.'

The following day, at midday on the dot, the doorbell rang. Trinity looked nervously at Mrs Jordan, who was as pale as she had been yesterday. They each held a twin in their arms, and Matty and Sancho were unusually quiet, as if sensing the tension in the air. Trinity had hated worrying the older woman, but it wouldn't have been fair not to warn her about what Cruz had said...

Mrs Jordan went to open the door, and even though Trinity had steeled herself she still wasn't prepared to see Cruz's broad, tall frame filling the doorway, a sleek black chauffeur-driven car just visible in the background. He wore a three-piece suit and an overcoat against the English spring chill. He looked vital and intimidating and gorgeous.

He stepped inside and the boys curled into Trinity and Mrs Jordan. They were always shy around their uncle, whom Matty called *'the big man'*.

'Mr De Carrillo, how nice to see you,' Mrs Jordan said, ever the diplomat.

Cruz looked away from Trinity to the older woman. There was only the slightest softening on his face. 'You too, Mrs Jordan.'

They exchanged pleasantries, and Mrs Jordan asked if he wanted tea or coffee before bustling off to the kitchen with Sancho. Trinity noticed that he'd looked at his nephews warily.

Then he looked at her with narrowed eyes. 'I presume we can talk alone?'

She wanted to say no, and run with the boys and Mrs Jordan somewhere safe. But she couldn't.

She nodded jerkily and said, 'Just let me get the boys set up for lunch and then I'll be with you.'

Cruz just inclined his head slightly, but he said *sotto voce*, as she passed him to follow Mrs Jordan to the kitchen, 'Don't make me wait, Trinity.'

Once they were out of earshot, Matty said in an awe-struck voice. 'Tha's the big man!'

Trinity replied as butterflies jumped around her belly. 'Yes, sweetie. He's your uncle, remember…?'

'Unk-*el*…' Matty repeated carefully, as if testing out the word.

Trinity delayed as much as she dared, making sure the

boys were strapped securely into their high chairs, but then she had to leave.

Mrs Jordan handed her a tray containing the tea and coffee, and looked at her expressively. 'I'm sure he'll do what's right for the boys and you, dear. Don't worry.'

Trinity felt shame curl through her as she walked to the drawing room with the tray. She'd been too cowardly to tell Mrs Jordan the truth of Cruz's opinion of her. The woman believed that he only wanted custody of his nephews because he was their last remaining blood relative.

Stopping at the door for a second, she took a breath and wondered if she should have worn something smarter than jeans and a plain long-sleeved jumper. But it was too late. She balanced the tray on her raised knee, then opened the door and went in. Her heart thumped as she saw Cruz, with his overcoat off, standing at the main window that looked out over the opulent gardens at the back of the house.

She avoided looking at him and went over to where a low table sat between two couches. She put the tray down and glanced up. 'Coffee, wasn't it?'

Cruz came and sat down on the couch opposite hers. 'Yes.'

No *please*. No niceties.

Trinity was very aware of how the fabric of his trousers pulled taut over his powerful thighs. She handed over the coffee in a cup, grateful that this time her hands were fairly steady. She sipped at her own tea, as if that might fortify her, and wished it was something slightly stronger.

After a strained moment Trinity knew she couldn't avoid him for ever. She looked at him and blurted out, 'Why are you doing this now? If you're so sure I'm… what you say I am…why didn't you just step in after Rio's death?'

Cruz took a lazy sip of his coffee and put the cup down,

for all the world as if this was a cordial visit. He looked at her. 'I, unlike you, grieved my brother's death—'

'That's not fair,' Trinity breathed.

Okay, so Rio had made her angry—especially at the end—and theirs hadn't been a real marriage, but she had felt a certain kinship with him. They hadn't been so different, as he'd told her—both abandoned by their parents. But then he'd betrayed her trust and her loyalty.

Cruz continued as if she'd said nothing. 'Once the state of Rio's finances became apparent, there was a lot of firefighting to be done. Deals he'd been involved in had to be tied up. I had to search for his mother to let her know what had happened—'

'Did you find her?' Trinity's heart squeezed as she thought of the impossible dream she never let herself indulge in: that some day she'd find *her* mother.

Cruz shook his head. 'No—and yes. She died some years ago, of a drug overdose.'

'Oh,' she said, feeling sad.

'I knew when the reading of the will would be taking place, and I wanted to see your face when you realised that there was nothing for you. And I'd been keeping an eye on you, so I knew what you were up to and how my nephews were.'

Trinity gasped. 'You had us followed?'

Cruz shrugged minutely. 'I couldn't be sure you wouldn't try to disappear. And you're the very public widow of a man most people still believe was a millionaire, with two small vulnerable children in your care. It was for your protection as much as my surveillance.'

Before she could fully absorb that, he went on, with palpable impatience.

'Look, I really don't have time for small talk, Trinity. Tell me how much you want so that I can get on with making the necessary arrangements to have my custody of my nephews legalised.'

His words were like a red rag to a bull—having it confirmed that he'd just been biding his time. That she'd never really registered on his radar as anyone worth giving the benefit of the doubt to.

She put her cup down with a clatter on the tray and glared at him. 'How dare you? Do you really think it's that simple? They are not pawns, Cruz. They are two small human beings who depend on structure and routine, who have lost both their parents at a very vulnerable age. Mrs Jordan and I are the most consistent people in their lives and you want to rip them away from that?'

She stood up then, too agitated to keep sitting down. Cruz stood too, and Trinity immediately felt intimidated.

He bit out, 'I want to take them away from a malignant influence. *You*. Are you seriously telling me you're prepared to go up against me? You know what'll happen if you do. You'll lose.'

*'No!'* Trinity cried passionately. 'The twins will lose. Do you know they've only just stopped asking for their *papa* every night? Because that's usually when he came to see them, to say goodnight. Their world has been turned upside down and you want to do it again. Who will be their primary carer? Don't tell me it's going to be *you*.' Trinity would never normally be so blunt or so cruel, but she felt desperate. 'Have you noticed how they look at you? They're intimidated by you. They hardly know who you are.'

Clearly unaccustomed to having anyone speak to him like this, Cruz flashed his eyes in disapproval. 'If anyone has been these boys' primary carer, I'd wager it's been Mrs Jordan. There's no reason why she can't remain as their nanny. But you have no claim on these boys beyond the legal guardianship you seduced out of Rio in a bid to protect your own future.'

Trinity's hands balled into fists. Her nails cut into her palms but she barely noticed. She wondered how she'd ever felt remotely tender about this man. 'That is *not* true. I love these boys as if they were my own.'

Cruz let out a curt laugh. 'I *know* that's not true.'

His smile faded, and his face became sterner than she'd ever seen it.

'And do you know why? Because Rio and I both learned that the people who are meant to love you the most *don't*. There's no such thing as an unbreakable bond.'

The fire left Trinity's belly. She felt shaky after the rush of adrenalin. Rio had told her about the way he'd been treated like an unwelcome guest in his own father's home. How his mother had abandoned him. It had played on all her sympathies. Now she wondered about Cruz's experience, and hated herself for this evidence that he still got to her.

'Not all parents were like yours or Rio's.'

Cruz arched a brow. 'And you know this from personal experience, when you grew up in a series of foster homes? Your experience wasn't too far removed from ours, was it, Trinity? So tell me how you know something I don't.'

Trinity went very still. 'How do you know that?'

He watched her assessingly. 'I run background checks on all my staff.' His lip curled. 'To think I actually felt some admiration for you—abandoned by your parents, brought up in care, but clearly ambitious and determined to make something of yourself. I seriously underestimated how little you were actually prepared to work to that end.'

The unfairness of his assessment winded her when she thought of the back-breaking work she'd done, first as a chambermaid in a hotel, then as a maid in his house, before becoming nanny to two demanding babies. And then Rio's *wife*.

Feeling seriously vulnerable upon finding out that Cruz

had known about her past all this time and had mentioned it so casually, she said, 'My experience has nothing to do with this.'

*Liar,* said a voice. It did, but not in the way Cruz believed.

'I love Matty and Sancho and I will do anything to protect them.'

Cruz was like an immovable force. 'You have some nerve to mention love. Are you seriously trying to tell me you loved Rio?'

Feeling desperate, she said, 'I told you—it wasn't like that.'

He glared at her. 'No, it wasn't. At least you're being honest about that.'

Trinity shivered under his look. His anger was palpable now. She said then, 'I did care for him.'

Before Cruz could respond to that there was a commotion outside, and Mrs Jordan appeared in the doorway with a wailing Sancho, who was leaning out of her arms towards Trinity, saying pitifully, *'Mummy...'*

Everything suddenly forgotten, she rushed forward and took him into her arms, rubbing his back and soothing him.

Mrs Jordan said apologetically, 'Matty hit him over the head with his plastic cup. It's nothing serious, but he's fractious after not sleeping well again last night.'

Trinity nodded and Mrs Jordan left to go back to Matty. She was walking up and down, soothing a now hiccupping Sancho, when she realised Cruz was staring at her with an angry look on his face.

He said almost accusingly, 'What's wrong with him?'

Suddenly Trinity was incredibly weary. 'Nothing much. He had a bug and he hasn't been sleeping, so he's in bad form. Matty just wound him up.' When Cruz didn't look appeased she said, 'Really, it's nothing.' She felt exposed under Cruz's judgemental look. 'Let me settle him down for a nap. That's all he needs.'

\* \* \*

Cruz watched Trinity walk out of the room with Sancho in her arms, his nephew's small, chubby ones wrapped tight around her neck, his flushed face buried in her neck as if it was a habitual reflex for seeking comfort. He had stopped crying almost as soon as he'd gone into her arms.

Cruz had felt a totally uncharacteristic sense of helplessness seeing his nephew like that. It reminded him uncomfortably of his own childhood, hearing Rio cry but being unable to do anything to help him—either because Rio would glare at him with simmering resentment or his father would hold him back with a cruel hand.

Sancho's cries hadn't fazed Trinity, though. In fact she'd looked remarkably capable.

Feeling angry all over again, and this time for a reason he couldn't really pinpoint, Cruz turned back to the window. He ran a hand through his hair and then loosened his tie, feeling constricted. And he felt even more constricted in another area of his anatomy when he recalled how his gaze had immediately dropped to take in the provocative swell of Trinity's bottom as she'd walked away, her long legs encased in those faded jeans that clung like a second skin.

Damn her.

Witnessing this little incident was forcing Cruz to stop and think about what he was doing here. It was obvious that not only had Trinity seduced Rio for her own ends, she'd also ensured that the boys would depend on her...in case of this very scenario?

Cruz thought of pursuing his plans to take Trinity to court to fight her for custody, but he'd already seen what a good actress she was. If someone were to come to the house and see her interacting with his nephews they wouldn't be able to help being swayed by her *apparent* love and concern. As he had just been.

And did he really want to court a PR frenzy by pitting himself against the grieving widow of his brother? He knew she wasn't grieving—she wasn't even pretending. But no one else would see that. They'd only see him, a ruthless billionaire, protecting his family fortune.

It had taken him since his father's death to change the perception his father had left behind of a failing and archaic bank, blighted by his father's numerous high-profile affairs. Did he really want to jeopardise all that hard work?

Something hardened inside him as he had to acknowledge how neatly Trinity had protected herself. She was potentially even worse than he'd thought—using his nephews like this, manipulating them to need her.

She'd lived a quiet life since Rio's death—she'd only moved between the house, the local shops and the nearby park. No shopping on Bond Street or high-profile social events.

When she'd been with Rio, Cruz had seen countless pictures of them at parties and premieres, so she had to be approaching the end of her boredom threshold.

He thought again of her assertion that she loved the boys... He couldn't countenance for a second that she loved these children who weren't even her own flesh and blood.

A memory of his own mother came back with startling clarity—he'd been a young teenager and he'd confronted her one day, incensed on her behalf that his father had been photographed in the papers with his latest mistress.

She'd just looked at him and said witheringly, 'The only mistake he made, Cruz, was getting caught. This is how our world works.' She'd laughed then—nastily. '*Dios mio*, please tell me you're not so naive as to believe we married because we actually had *feelings* for one another?'

He'd looked at his mother in shock. No, he'd never laboured under the misapprehension that any such thing as *affection* existed between his parents, but he'd realised in that moment that some tiny part of him that hadn't been obliterated after years of only the most perfunctory parenting had still harboured a kernel of hope that something meaningful existed... Shame had engulfed him for being so naive.

She'd said then, with evident bitterness, 'I was all but packaged up and sent to your father, because our two families belong to great dynasties and it was a strategic match. I did my duty and bore him a son, and I put up with his bastard son living under this very roof, and his mistresses—because, no matter what he does, this family's legacy is safe with you, and *I* have ensured that. That is all that matters in this life Cruz. Cultivating our great name and protecting it. One of these days your father will die, and as far as I'm concerned it can't come soon enough. Because then *you* will restore this family's reputation and fortune. That is your duty and your destiny, above all else.'

She'd died not long after that speech. The memory of her had faded but her words hadn't. *Duty and destiny.* There was no room for emotion, and he'd had to acknowledge the enormity of what he stood to inherit. He'd become a man that day, in more ways than one, leaving behind any childish vulnerabilities and misconceptions.

And because he'd stepped up to that responsibility he now had something solid to pass on to his nephews. They aroused something in him that he'd only felt before for Rio—an urge to protect and forge a bond. He'd become Rio's guardian while he'd still been underage, and he wanted to do the same for his vulnerable nephews. He vowed now that they would not go the way of their father. By the time they came of age they would know how to handle their legacy...he would make sure of it.

When Cruz had realised that he hadn't been named as guardian after Rio's death he'd felt inexplicably hurt, even though he'd known that he was hardly in a position to take

on two small children he barely knew. It had been like a
slap from beyond the grave, and he'd had to wonder if the
rapprochement he'd believed to be present in his relationship with Rio had actually been real.

Or, as he'd come to suspect, was it more likely to have
been someone else's influence?

Cruz had looked at Trinity, dressed in black on the other
side of Rio's grave at the funeral, as his brother had been
lowered into the ground. Her face had been covered in a
gauzy veil, her body encased in a snug-fitting black suit.
And that was when he'd vowed to do whatever it took to
make sure her influence over his nephews was thwarted.
He wanted them under his protection—away from a gold-
digging manipulator.

Suddenly an audacious idea occurred to him. He immediately thrust it aside—appalled that he'd even thought it.
But it wouldn't go away. It took root, and as he looked at
it analytically it held a kind of horrific appeal.

He stared out over the gardens without really seeing
them, and finally had to acknowledge grimly that there
was really only one option where Trinity was concerned—
but was he prepared to go to those lengths?

His gut answered him. *Yes.*

As if fate was contriving to make sure he didn't have
time to change his mind he heard a noise and turned around
to see Trinity coming back into the room. Her hair was
pulled back into a low ponytail, but loose tendrils curled
around her face. He noticed for the first time that there
were delicate smudges of colour under her cornflower-blue
eyes. Evidence of fatigue.

He ruthlessly pushed down a very curious sensation he'd
never felt in relation to a woman before—and certainly not
one he welcomed for this one: *concern.*

He faced her and saw how she tensed as she came towards him, folding her arms in a defensive gesture. Her chin tilting towards him mutinously.

With not a little relish, Cruz said, 'I have a solution which I think will work for both of us, my nephews and Mrs Jordan.'

He could see Trinity's arms tighten fractionally over her chest and he focused on her treacherously beautiful face. Even now she looked as innocent as the naive twenty-two-year-old who had come to work for him. Except, of course, she hadn't been naive. Or innocent. And she was about to face the repercussions of her actions.

'What solution?'

Cruz waited a beat and then said, very deliberately, 'Marriage, Trinity. You're going to marry me.'

# CHAPTER THREE

For a moment all Trinity heard was a roaring in her ears.
She shook her head but Cruz was still looking at her with
that expression on his face. Determined.

She asked weakly, 'Did you just say marriage?'

'Yes, I did.'

Trinity's arms were so tight across her chest she was
almost cutting off her air supply. 'That is the most ridiculous thing I've ever heard.' And yet why was there an
illicit shiver deep in her belly at the thought of being married to this man?

Cruz started to stroll towards her and Trinity had a very
keen sense that he was a predator, closing in on his prey.

'Even though I know I'd win in a courtroom battle for
the twins, I don't really have the inclination to invite un-
necessarily adverse PR in my direction by pitting myself
against my brother's widow. And from what I've seen it's
evident to me that Mateo and Sancho are clearly attached
to you.'

'Of course they are,' she said shakily. 'I'm all they've
known as a mother since they were one.'

He stopped within touching distance and Trinity's
breath hitched at his sheer charisma. She forced herself
to fill her lungs. She couldn't afford to let him distract her.

'Why on earth would you suggest marriage?'

He grimaced, 'You are legally my nephews' guardian,
and I don't trust you not to exert your right to do something drastic. Marriage will make me their legal guardian too, and I'm not prepared to settle for anything less to
ensure their protection.'

Trinity shook her head and took a step back, hating

herself for it but needing some space. 'You're crazy if you think I'll agree.'

With lethal softness he said now, 'Who do you think has been funding your existence these past few months?'

'You,' she said miserably.

'If you were to walk out of this house with my two nephews that allowance would be stopped immediately. How on earth do you think you would cope without a nanny?'

Desperation clawed upwards. 'I could get a job.'

Cruz was scathing. 'You'd be happy to lower yourself to Mrs Jordan's status again? Because that's all you're qualified for—either working as a maid or as a nanny.'

Trinity refused to let him intimidate her. 'Of course—if I had to.' A voice screamed at her—how on earth could she work with two small children in tow?

Cruz was obdurate, and Trinity knew with a sinking feeling that one way or the other he wasn't leaving until he'd got what he wanted. Her. And his nephews.

'It's very simple. I don't trust you not to take advantage of your position. And you seem to be forgetting a very pertinent fact.' He looked at her.

Eventually, with extreme reluctance and the sensation of a net closing around her, she said, 'What fact?'

'Since Rio's death those boys have had nothing but their name. The only way they will receive their inheritance now is through me, and I'm not going to let that happen unless you marry me.'

The net closed around Trinity as the full significance of that sank in. She would be responsible for not letting Matty and Sancho receive their inheritance?

'That's blackmail,' she breathed, astounded at his ruthlessness.

Cruz all but shrugged, supremely unperturbed. 'Their legacy is considerable, and as such I have a responsibility to see that it, and they, are protected.'

Affront coursed through her. 'I would never touch what's theirs.'

Cruz's lip curled. 'And yet you managed to divest Rio of a small fortune within less than a year of marriage?'

Trinity opened her mouth to defend herself again but from the look on Cruz's face she knew it would be pointless to say anything. Not in this emotive atmosphere.

She whirled away from that mocking look in his eyes and took refuge by a solid object—the couch. When she felt relatively composed again, she turned back to face him.

'There has to be some other way.' She seized on an idea. 'I can sign something. A contract that says I have no claim to their inheritance.'

Cruz shook his head and moved, coming closer. 'No. Marriage is the only option I'm prepared to consider. I've decided to move back to the De Carrillo ancestral home in Spain, near Seville. The bank is flourishing here in the UK, and in America. Its reputation has been restored. It's time to build on that, and presenting a united family front will only strengthen the business and in turn my nephews' legacy.'

Rendered speechless, Trinity could only listen as Cruz went on.

'Locking you into a marriage with me is the only way they'll get their inheritance and I'll be satisfied that you're not going to prove to be a threat to my nephews. And as it happens a convenient wife will suit my needs very well. But I'm afraid I can't offer you the bling of married life with Rio. You might have been keeping a low profile since my brother died, but I would estimate that once the reality of living in a remote *castillo* hits you'll be climbing the walls and looking for a divorce before the year is out…which I'll be only too happy to grant once I've got full custody of my nephews.'

The extent of his cynicism shocked her anew. She'd

surmised from Rio's account of his early life that things probably hadn't been idyllic for Cruz either, but she'd never imagined that he carried such a deep-rooted seam of distrust.

Trinity hated it that it aroused her empathy and curiosity—again. She cursed herself. She'd felt empathy for Rio and she'd let him manipulate her. If it hadn't been for Mateo and Sancho she'd tell Cruz where to shove his autocratic orders and storm out.

But how could she? He was threatening to withhold their very legacy if she didn't comply. And there was no way she was leaving her boys in his cold and cynical care alone. She was all they had now.

Surely, she thought quickly, if she said yes he'd realise what he was doing—marrying someone he hated himself for kissing—and agree to make some kind of compromise? Trinity shoved down the betraying hurt that Cruz would never even be suggesting such a thing if she didn't have something he wanted. His nephews.

She called his bluff. 'You leave me no choice. Yes, I'll marry you.'

She waited for Cruz to blanch, or for realisation to hit and for him to tell her that he'd only been testing her commitment, but he showed no emotion. Nor triumph. After a beat he just looked at his watch, and then back at her, as cold as ice.

'Good. I'll have my team draw up a pre-nuptial agreement and organise a fast and discreet civil wedding within the next few weeks, after which we'll leave directly for Spain.'

He had turned and was walking out of the room before the shock reverberating through Trinity subsided enough for her to scramble after him—clearly he was not a man who was easily bluffed. He was deadly serious about this.

His hand was on the doorknob when she came to a

stumbling halt behind him, breathless. 'Wait a minute—
you don't really want to marry me. What about falling in
love?'

Cruz turned around with an incredulous look on his
face, and then threw his head back and laughed so abruptly
that Trinity flinched. When he looked at her again his eyes
glittered like dark golden sapphires.

'*Love?* Now you really are over-acting. Choice in marriage and falling in love are best left to the deluded. Look
where infatuation got my brother—driven to fatal destruction. I have no time for such emotions or weaknesses. This
marriage will be one in name only, purely to protect my
nephews from your grasping hands, and you will fulfil
your role as my wife to the best of your ability.'

Trinity tried one more time. 'You don't have to do this.
I would never harm my stepsons, or take their inheritance
from them.'

Cruz's eyes gleamed with stark intent. 'I don't believe
you, and I don't trust you. So, yes, we *are* doing this. You'll
need to see if Mrs Jordan is happy to stay in my employment and come to Spain. If not, we'll have to hire another
nanny. The sooner you come to terms with this new reality
and start preparing the boys for the move the easier it will
be for me to make the necessary arrangements.'

For long minutes after he'd walked out Trinity stood
there in shock. What had she just done?

True to his word, just over two weeks later Trinity stood
beside Cruz De Carrillo in a register office. He was dressed
in a sleek dark grey suit, white shirt and matching tie. She
wore an understated cream silk knee-length sheath dress
with matching jacket. Her hair was up in a smooth chignon, her make-up light.

In the end resistance had been futile. No matter which
way she'd looked at it, she'd kept coming back to the fact

that she wasn't prepared to walk away from Mateo and Sancho after all they'd been through—as well as the fact that the thought of leaving them made her feel as if someone was carving her heart out of her chest.

By agreeing to marry Rio she'd at least felt that she could offer them some permanence, which she'd never had. She hadn't wanted them to go through the same insecurity…and now she was in exactly the same position. So it had come down to this: she had nowhere to go, and no one to turn to.

When she'd put Cruz's plan to Mrs Jordan, the woman had thought about it, consulted with her son who was at university in Scotland, and then agreed to stay with them as long as she could be guaranteed regular visits home. Trinity had felt emotional, knowing that at least she'd have Mrs Jordan's quiet and calm support.

She was acutely conscious now of Cruz's tall, hard body beside her as the registrar spoke the closing words of the ceremony. She was all but a prisoner to this man now. The perfect chattel. She looked at the simple gold band on her finger that marked her as married for the second time in her life. This time, though, she thought a little hysterically, at least she wasn't remotely deluded about her husband's intentions.

*'I now pronounce you husband and wife. Congratulations. You may kiss your wife, Mr De Carrillo.'*

Slowly, reluctantly, Trinity turned to face Cruz. She looked up. Even though she wore high heels, he still towered over her.

Cruz just looked at her for a long moment. Trinity's breath was trapped in her throat like a bird. Was he going to humiliate her in front of their small crowd of witnesses—largely made up of his legal team—by refusing to kiss her?

But then, just when she expected him to turn away

dismissively, he lowered his head and his mouth touched hers. Firm. Cool. His lips weren't tightly shut, and neither were hers, so for a second their breaths mingled, and in that moment a flame of pure heat licked through her with such force that she was hurled back in time to that incendiary kiss in his study.

Before she could control her reaction, though, Cruz was pulling back to look down at her again with those hard, glittering eyes. They transmitted a silent but unmistakable message: he would do the bare minimum in public to promote an image of unity, but that was as far as it would go.

Trinity was humiliated by her reaction, by the fact that he still had such a devastating effect on her. And terrified at the prospect of him realising it. She tried to pull her hand free of his but he only tightened his grip, reminding her of how trapped she was.

She glared up at him.

'Smile for the photos, *querida*.'

Trinity followed Cruz's look to see a photographer waiting. Of course. This was all part of his plan, wasn't it? To send out a message of a family united.

Aware that she must look more like someone about to be tipped over the edge of a plank than a besotted bride, Trinity forced a smile and flinched only slightly when the flash went off.

Cruz could hear his nephews chattering happily as they were fed at the back of the plane. Then he heard softer, lower tones… Trinity's… He tensed. Any sense of satisfaction at the fact that he'd achieved what he'd set out to achieve was gone. He cursed silently. Who was he kidding? He'd been tense since he'd left her standing in that room in Rio's house, with her eyes like two huge pools of blue, and a face leached of all colour.

It should have given him an immense sense of accomplishment to know he'd pulled the rug from under her feet, but he'd walked away that day with far more complicated emotions in his gut—and a very unwelcome reminder of when he'd seen a similar look of stunned shock on her face...the night he'd kissed her.

She'd been the last person he'd expected to see when he'd walked into his study that night, weary from a round of engaging in mind-numbingly boring small-talk. And fending off women who, up until a few months before, would have tempted him. His mind had been full of...*her*. And then to find her there, stretching up, long legs bare and exposed, the lush curve of her bottom visible under the short robe and the even more provocative curve of her unbound breasts... It was as if she'd walked straight out of his deepest fantasy...

He could still recall the second he'd come to his senses, when he'd realised he was moments away from lifting her up against his shelves and finding explosive release in her willing body, all soft and hot and *wet*. No other woman had ever caused him to lose it like that. But she'd been his *employee*. Someone he'd been in a position of power over.

The stark realisation that he was following in his father's footsteps in spite of every effort he'd made to remove the shadow of that man's reputation had been sickening. He was no better after all.

He'd been harsh afterwards...angry at his reaction... demanding to know what she was doing there as if it had been her fault. He'd felt like a boor. Little had he known then that she'd obviously been waiting until he got home and had made sure he found her...

It was galling. A sign of weakness. Cruz scowled. Trinity had no power over his emotions. She represented a very fleeting moment in time when he'd forgotten who he was.

The reality of his situation hit him then—in marrying Trinity he was consigning himself to a life with a woman he would never trust. But the sacrifice would be worth it for his nephews' sake.

At least now she was under his control and his watchful eye.

He'd felt anything *but* watchful earlier, though, when she'd turned to face him in that sterile register office and everyone had waited for their kiss. He'd had no intention of kissing her—it would show her how it would be between them. And prove that he could control himself around her... But for a split second his gaze had dropped to that lush mouth and every cool, logical intention had scattered, to be replaced with an all too familiar desire just to take one sip, one taste...

So he'd bent his head, seeing the flash of surprise in her eyes, and touched his mouth to hers. And he'd felt her breath whisper over his mouth. It had taken more effort than he liked to admit to pull back and deny himself the need he'd had to take her face in his hands, angle her mouth for better access so he could explore her with a thoroughness that would have made him look a complete fool...

Cruz only became aware that he was being watched when the hairs went up on the back of his neck, and he turned his head from brooding out of the small window. He had to adjust his gaze down to see that one of his nephews—he couldn't tell which—was standing by his chair with small pudgy hands clutching the armrest.

For a second time was suspended, and his mind went blank. Two huge dark eyes stared up at him guilelessly. Thick, dark tousled hair fell onto a smooth forehead and the child's cheeks were flushed. Something that looked like mashed carrot was smeared around his mouth. And then he smiled, showing a neat row of baby teeth. Something gripped Cruz tight in his chest, throwing him back in time to when he'd looked at an almost identical child, six years his junior.

'*Matty*, don't disturb your uncle.'

That low, husky voice. Gently chiding. Two slender pale hands came around his nephew to lift him up and away. Trinity held him easily with one arm, against her body. The small face showed surprise, and then started to contort alarmingly just before an ear-splitting screech emerged.

Cruz noted that she looked slightly frayed at the edges. Her hair was coming loose and she had smears of food on her jacket. He looked down and saw pale bare feet, nails painted a delicate shade of coral, and he felt a surge of blood to his groin. Immediately he scowled at his rampant reaction and Trinity backed away.

'Sorry, I didn't realise he'd slipped out of his chair.'

She was turning to walk back down the plane when Cruz heard himself calling out, 'Wait.'

She stopped in her tracks and Cruz saw Mrs Jordan hurrying up the aisle, reaching for Mateo to take him from Trinity. The indignant shouting stopped as the older woman hushed him with soothing tones.

Trinity turned around and Cruz felt something pierce him as he acknowledged that, *in*convenient wedding or not, most brides were at least given a meal before being whisked away after their nuptials.

They'd gone straight from his solicitor's office, where Trinity had signed the pre-nuptial agreement, to the register office and then to the plane. He'd expected her to pore over the pre-nuptial agreement, but she'd just glanced through it and then looked at him and said, 'If we divorce then I lose all custody of the boys, is that it?'

He'd nodded. Aware of his body humming for her even while they were surrounded by his legal team. She'd just muttered something under her breath like, *Never going to happen*, and signed. Cruz had had to include some kind of a severance deal for her if they divorced, so Trinity would always be a wealthy woman, but he knew she could have fought him for a better deal.

*So why hadn't she?* asked a voice, and Cruz didn't like the way his conscience smarted. He wasn't used to being aware of his conscience, never doubting himself in anything—and he wasn't about to start, he told himself ruthlessly. For all he knew Trinity's actions thus far were all an act to lull him into a false sense of security.

'Have you eaten yet?' he asked abruptly, irritated that she was making him doubt himself.

She looked at him warily and shook her head as she tucked some hair behind her ear. 'I'll eat when the boys have eaten.'

Cruz gestured to the seat across the aisle from him. 'Sit down. I'll get one of the staff to take your order.' He pressed the call button.

Trinity looked towards the back of the plane for a moment. Her visible reluctance was not a reaction he was used to where women were concerned.

'Sit before you fall. They're fine. And we have some things to discuss.'

She finally sat down, just as an attentive air steward appeared and handed her a menu. Trinity's head was down-bent for a moment as she read, and Cruz found it hard to look away from that bright silky hair.

When the air steward had left Trinity felt uncomfortable under Cruz's intense gaze. It was as if he was trying to get into her head and read her every thought. Just the prospect of that made her go clammy—that he might see the effect his very chaste kiss had had on her.

In a bid to defuse the strange tension, she prompted, 'You said we have things to discuss...?'

Cruz blinked and the intensity diminished. Trinity

sucked in a breath to acknowledge how attuned she felt to this man. It was disconcerting—and unwelcome.

'As soon as you're settled at the *castillo* I'll organise interviews for another nanny to help Mrs Jordan. You're going to be busy as my wife.'

*The castillo.* It even sounded intimidating. She said, as coolly as she could, as if this was all completely normal, 'Maybe this would be a good time for you to let me know exactly what you expect of me as your wife.'

*Maybe*, crowed a snide voice, *it would have been a good idea for you not to get so attached to two babies that aren't yours in a bid to create the family you never had.*

Trinity gritted her jaw.

Cruz said, 'My calendar is already full for the next three months, and I should warn you that my social events are more corporate-orientated than celebrity-based... I'll expect you on my arm, looking the part, and not scowling because you're bored.'

Trinity boiled inside. Clearly he was expecting her to last for about two weeks before she ran for the hills. And he was obviously referring to Rio's predilection for film premieres or events like the Monte Carlo Grand Prix, which Trinity had found excruciating—all she could remember of that particular event was the overwhelming diesel fumes and the constant seasickness she'd felt while on some Russian oligarch's yacht.

Rio had invariably paraded her in public and then promptly dropped her once the paparazzi had left—which had suited her fine. She'd usually been in her own bed, in her own separate room, by the time he'd finished partying around dawn. But she could just imagine telling Cruz that, and how he'd merely shut her down again.

Then she thought of something. 'What do you mean, "looking the part"?'

He swept an expressive look over her, and at that moment she was aware of every second of sleep she hadn't got in the past couple of years. *And* the fact that today was probably the first day she'd worn smart clothes and actually put on make-up in months.

Compounding her insecurity, Cruz said, 'As *my* wife you'll need to project a more…classic image. I've already arranged for you to be taken shopping to buy new clothes.'

Trinity tensed at the barb. 'But I have clothes.'

His lip curled. 'The kind of clothes you wore around my brother will not be suitable and they've been donated to charity.'

Her face grew hot when she recalled seeing Cruz again, for the first time since her marriage to Rio, three months ago. His effect on her had been instantaneous—a rush of liquid heat. And then he'd looked at her as if she was a call girl. How could she blame him? She'd felt like one.

Rio's sense of style for women had definitely favoured the 'less is more' variety. He'd handed her a dress to wear for that party that had been little more than a piece of silk. Skimpier than anything she'd ever worn.

She'd protested, but he'd said curtly, 'You're working for me, Trinity. Consider this your uniform.'

It hadn't been long after their row and her finding out exactly why he'd married her. Rio had been acting more edgily than usual, so Trinity hadn't fought him on the dress and had assured herself that she'd talk to Cruz that night—seek his help. Except it hadn't turned out as she'd expected. She'd been a fool to think she could turn to him.

The memory left her feeling raw. She averted her eyes from Cruz's now and said stiffly, 'It's your money—you can spend it as you wish.'

The air steward came back with Trinity's lunch, and she focused on the food to try and distract herself from a feeling of mounting futile anger and impotence. But the fact that she was destined to dance to the tune of another autocratic De Carrillo man left the food in her mouth tasting of dust.

She gave up trying to pretend she had an appetite and pushed her plate away. Cruz looked up from the small laptop he'd switched his attention to. He frowned with disapproval at how little she'd eaten—it was an expression that was becoming very familiar to Trinity, and one she guessed was likely to become even more familiar.

Her anger rose. 'Was this marriage really necessary?' she blurted out, before she could censor her tongue.

*A bit late now*, whispered that annoying voice.

As if privy to that voice, Cruz mocked, 'It really is futile to discuss something that's already done. But by all means, Trinity, feel free to seek a divorce whenever you want.'

And leave Matty and Sancho at this man's mercy? Never, vowed Trinity.

Just then a plaintive wail came from the back of the plane.

*'Mummy!'*

She recognised the overtired tone. Seizing her opportunity to escape, Trinity stood up and tried not to feel self-conscious in her creased dress and bare feet.

'Excuse me. I should help Mrs Jordan.'

She walked away with as much grace as she could muster and tried her best not to feel as though her whole world was shrinking down to the size of a prison cell—even if it was to be the most luxurious prison cell in the world.

A few hours later Trinity shivered, in spite of the warm Spanish breeze. They'd driven into a massive circular courtyard and she was holding a silent and wide-eyed Sancho in her arms, thumb stuck firmly in his mouth. Mrs Jordan was holding a similarly quiet Matty. They were still a little groggy after the naps they'd had on the plane.

Her instinct about the *castillo* being intimidating had

been right. It was massive and imposing. A mixture of architecture, with the most dominant influence being distinctly Moorish. Cruz had explained that they were about midway between Seville and a small historic town called El Rocio, which sat on the edge of a national park. But there was nothing around them now except for rolling countryside; he hadn't been lying about that.

Cruz was greeting some staff who had appeared in the imposing porch area. They were all dressed in black. Trinity caught Mrs Jordan's eye and was relieved to see that the older woman looked as intimidated as she felt.

Mrs Jordan said brightly, 'Well, my word, I don't think I've ever seen anything so grand. I'm sure it's bright and airy on the inside.'

But when they went in, after a whirlwind of introductions to several staff whose complicated names Trinity struggled to imprint on her brain, it wasn't bright and airy. It was dark and cool—and not in a refreshing way.

The stone walls were covered with ancient tapestries that all seemed to depict different gruesome battles. Then there were portraits of what had to be Cruz's ancestors. She could see where he got his austere expression. They all looked fearsome. There was one in particular whose resemblance to Cruz was uncanny.

She hadn't even noticed that she'd stopped to stare at it for so long until a cool voice from behind her said, 'That's Juan Sanchez De Carrillo—my great-great-grandfather.'

Unnerved, in case he might guess why she'd been momentarily captivated by the huge portrait, Trinity desisted from saying that she thought it looked like him. Instead she asked, 'So is this where you and Rio grew up?'

For a moment he said nothing, and Trinity looked at him. She caught a fleeting expression on his face that she couldn't read, but then it was gone.

He led her forward, away from the portrait, as he said

smoothly, 'Yes, we were both born in this *castillo*. But our circumstances couldn't have been more different.'

'I know,' Trinity said cautiously. 'Rio told me that his mother was a maid here, and that she blackmailed your father for money after their affair and then left Rio behind.'

In spite of everything that had happened, she *still* felt sympathy. These dark corridors and austere pictures only confirmed that Cruz's experience couldn't have been much happier here. That treacherous curiosity to know more rose up again, much to her disgust. She was a soft touch.

But Cruz was clearly not up for conversation. He was moving again, leaving the long corridor, and she had to follow or be left behind. He opened a door to reveal an enclosed open-air courtyard and Trinity automatically sucked in a deep breath, only realising then how truly oppressive the *castillo* had felt.

They'd lost Mrs Jordan and the other staff somewhere along the way. Afraid that Cruz suspected she was angling for a personal tour, she shifted Sancho's heavy and now sleeping weight on her shoulder and hurried after his long strides.

'You don't have to show me around—there'll be plenty of time for that.'

*A whole lifetime,* whispered that wicked voice.

Cruz just said brusquely, 'This isn't a tour. We're just taking another route to your quarters.'

Trinity felt a childish urge to poke her tongue out at his back. *Your quarters.* She shivered a little.

He led them back into the *castillo* on the other side of the surprisingly pretty courtyard. The sensation of the walls closing around her again made her realise that this was *it*. Hers and the boys' home for the foreseeable future. The prospect was intimidating, to say the least.

Trinity vowed then and there to do everything she could to ensure Matty and Sancho's happiness and security in such a dark and oppressive atmosphere. After all, she'd chosen to be their protector and she had no regrets.

Cruz helped himself to a shot of whisky from the sideboard in his study on the other side of the *castillo*. He took a healthy sip, relishing the burn which distracted him from the uncomfortable feeling that lingered after walking away from Trinity, Mrs Jordan and the boys, all looking at him with wide eyes, as if they'd just been transported to Outer Mongolia.

He didn't like the way his nephews fell silent whenever he approached them, looking at him so warily, clinging on to Trinity. His urge to protect them had grown exponentially since he'd decided marriage was the only option— thanks to which he was now their legal guardian too.

While the jury was still very much out on Trinity—her easy signing of the pre-nup had thrown up questions he wasn't eager to investigate—he had to admit grudgingly that so far it didn't look as if his nephews were being adversely affected by her.

Cruz had been surprised to discover that Rio had told her the full extent of his mother's treachery.

When he and Rio had been younger they'd never been allowed to play together, and on the few occasions Cruz had managed to sneak away from his nanny to find Rio his younger half-brother had always looked at him suspiciously.

One day they had been found together. Cruz's father had taken Rio into his study, and he could still remember the shouts of humiliation as his father had beaten him. Rio had eventually emerged with tears streaking his red face, holding his behind, glaring at Cruz with a hatred that had been vivid.

Their father had appeared in the doorway and said to Cruz, 'That's what'll happen if you seek him out again. His is *not* your real brother.'

Cruz had felt so angry, and yet so impotent. That was the moment he'd vowed to ensure that Rio was never denied what was rightfully his...much good it had done his brother in the end.

He realised now for the first time that the knowledge that he was his nephews' legal guardian had soothed something inside him. Something he never could have acknowledged before, while Rio had held him at arm's length. It was the part of him that had failed in being able to protect his brother when they were younger. He was able to do this now for his nephews in the most profound way. It made emotion rise up, and with it futile anger at Rio's death.

Cruz's mind deviated then, with irritating predictability, back to his new wife. He'd expected something more from her by now—some show or hint of defiance that would reveal her irritation at having her wings clipped. But there was nothing. Just those big blue eyes, looking at him suspiciously. As if he might take a bite out of her... That thought immediately made him think of sinking his teeth into soft pale flesh.

What the hell was wrong with him? He would not fall into that pit of fire again. She disgusted him.

A little voice jeered at him. *She disgusts you so much that your blood simmers every time she's close?*

Cruz shut it down ruthlessly.

Trinity would not tempt him again. This situation was all about containment and control and ensuring his nephews were in his care and safe. That was all that mattered—their legacy. As soon as she realised how limited her life would be she'd be begging for a divorce, and that day couldn't come soon enough.

# CHAPTER FOUR

A WEEK LATER Trinity felt as if she were on a slightly more even keel. She and the boys and Mrs Jordan had finally settled, somewhat, into their palatial rooms. Decorated in light greys and soft pinks and blues, with contemporary furniture and a modern media centre, they made for a more soothing environment than the rest of the dark and brooding *castillo*, which was not unlike its owner.

Mrs Jordan had an entire apartment to herself, as did Trinity, and they were both connected by the boys' room, which was light and bright but other than that showed no indication that it was home to two small boys with more energy than a bag of long-life batteries.

They took their meals in a large sunny dining room, not far from their rooms, that led out to a landscaped garden. Trinity and Mrs Jordan spent most of their time running after Matty and Sancho, trying to stop them pulling the very exotic-looking flowers out of the pristine beds.

Trinity sighed now, and pushed some hair behind her ear as she contemplated the two napping toddlers who looked as exhausted as she felt. She'd have to talk to Cruz about modifying their bedroom and installing something more practical outside that would occupy their vast energy and satisfy their need to be stimulated. Otherwise the head gardener was going to be very upset, and the boys were going to grow more and more frustrated.

The staff they'd seen so far—a taciturn housekeeper who spoke no English and a young girl who looked terrified—hardly inspired confidence in it being a happy household where she could get to know people and let the boys run free. It was very obvious that Cruz believed he had corralled them exactly where he wanted them and had now all but washed his hands of her, in spite of his decree that she be available as his social escort.

Mrs Jordan had had the morning off, and was going to keep an eye on the boys this afternoon when they woke, so Trinity took the opportunity to go and see if Cruz had returned from his trip to Madrid yet—she'd managed to ascertain that he'd gone from the shy maid.

She refused to give in to a growing feeling of helplessness but while making her way from their wing of the *castillo*, back through the pretty courtyard, she could feel her heart-rate increasing. She told herself it was not in anticipation of seeing Cruz after a few days. What was wrong with her? Was she a complete masochist?

As she walked past the stern portraits of the ancestors she didn't look up, not wanting to see if their eyes would be following her censoriously, judging her silently.

Just at that moment a door opened and a tall hard body stepped out—right in front of Trinity. She found herself slamming straight into the man who so easily dominated her thoughts.

Big hands caught her upper arms to stop her lurching backwards. All her breath seemed to have left her lungs with the impact as she stared up into those tawny eyes.

Somehow she managed to get out the words, 'You're back.'

Cruz's hands tightened almost painfully on Trinity's arms. 'I got back late last night.'

Tension was instant between them, and something else much more ambiguous and electric. She tried to move back but she couldn't.

Panic that he might see her reaction to him spiked. 'You can let me go.'

Cruz's eyes widened a fraction, as if he'd been unaware he was holding her, and then suddenly he dropped his hands as if burnt. Trinity stepped back, feeling sick at the expression crossing his face—something between disgust and horror. She'd seen that look before, after he'd kissed her.

She said quickly, 'I was looking for you, actually.'

After a silent moment Cruz stepped aside and gestured for her to go into the room he'd just left. She stepped inside, still feeling shaky after that sudden physical impact.

Cruz closed the door and walked to his desk, turning around to face her. 'I'll call for some coffee—or would you prefer tea?'

'Tea would be lovely, thank you.'

So polite. As if he *hadn't* just dumped her and her stepsons in his remote intimidating home and left them to their own devices. Maybe he thought she would have run screaming by now?

When Cruz turned away to lean over his desk and pick up the phone Trinity had to consciously drag her gaze away from where his thin shirt stretched enticingly over flexed and taut muscles. She looked around the room, which was huge and obviously his home office.

Dark wood panelling and big antique furniture gave it a serious air. Floor-to-ceiling shelves dominated one whole wall, and Trinity felt a wave of heat scorch her from the inside out as the memory of another wall of shelves flashed back, of how it had felt to have Cruz press her against it so passionately.

'Do you still read?'

Trinity's head snapped back to Cruz. She hadn't even noticed that he'd finished the call. She was mortified, and crushed the memory, hoping her cheeks weren't flaming.

She shook her head, saying with a slightly strangled voice, 'I haven't had much time lately.' She was usually so exhausted when she went to bed now that her love of reading was a thing of the past. A rare luxury.

'Well? You said you were looking for me?'

He was looking at her expectantly, one hip resting on his desk, arms folded. Formidable. Remote. Her ex-employer, now her husband, but a stranger. It struck her then that even though they'd shared that brief intimacy, and she'd had a glimpse of what lay under the surface, he was still a total enigma.

She shoved down her trepidation. 'Yes. I wanted to talk to you about the boys.'

A light knock came on the door, and he called for whoever it was to come in as he frowned and said, 'What's wrong? Are they okay?'

The maid, Julia, appeared with a tray of tea and coffee, distracting Trinity. She noticed how the girl blushed when Cruz bestowed a polite smile on her and said thank you. Trinity felt humiliation curl inside her. She'd used to blush like that when she'd worked for him. It felt like a lifetime ago.

When the girl had left Cruz was still looking at Trinity, waiting for her answer. Feeling exposed under that laser-like intensity, she said, 'Nothing is wrong with them—they're fine. Settling in better than I'd expected, actually.'

Some of the tension left Cruz's shoulders and she felt a dart of unexpected emotion—what if he really did care about the boys?

He deftly poured tea for her and coffee for him and handed her a cup. 'Sit down.'

She chose a chair near the desk and cradled her cup, watching warily as he took a seat on the other side of his desk. He took a sip of his coffee and arched one dark golden brow, clearly waiting for her to elaborate.

She put the cup down on the table in front of her and sat up straight. 'The rooms...our rooms...are lovely. And very comfortable. But the boys' room isn't exactly tailored for children their age. It could do with brightening up, being made more cheerful—somewhere they can play and where they'll want to go to sleep. Also, they've been playing in the gardens—which they love—but again it's not exactly suitable for them. Your head gardener has already had to replant some of his flowerbeds.'

Cruz's conscience pricked as he acknowledged that he'd not even had the courtesy to stick around for one day and make sure that Trinity and his nephews and their nanny were comfortable.

He knew that the *castillo* was dated in parts, but the rooms he'd given to them had been those used by his mother before her death, so they were the most up-to-date. But evidently not up-to-date enough.

It hadn't even occurred to him to make the space child-friendly, and that stung now. What also stung was the fact that he had to acknowledge that his trip to Madrid had been less about business and more about putting some space between him and this new domestic world he'd brought back to Spain with him.

He was distracted by Trinity's very earthy clean-faced appeal. A look he had thought she'd eschewed as soon as she'd married Rio. Certainly any pictures he'd seen of them together had shown her to have morphed into someone who favoured heavy make-up and skimpy clothes.

And yet where was the evidence of that now? Her hair was pulled back into a low, messy bun. She was wearing soft jeans and a loose shirt, with a stain that looked suspiciously like dried food on her shoulder—as unalluring as any woman who had ever appeared in front of him, and yet it didn't matter. Cruz's blood sizzled over a low-banked fire of lust.

'So, what are you suggesting?' he asked, irritated at this reminder of how much she affected him.

Trinity swallowed, making Cruz notice the long slim column of her throat. Even that had an effect on him. *Damn it.*

'I'd like to make the boy's room more colourful and fun. And with regards to the garden... I'm not saying that that's not enough for them—your grounds are stunning— but they're bright, inquisitive boys and they're already becoming frustrated with being told they can't roam freely and touch what they want. Perhaps if they had something that would occupy their energy, like swings... They loved the children's playground in Regent's Park.'

All of what she'd just said was eminently reasonable, yet Cruz felt a tide of tension rising up through his body.

'Anything else?'

As if she could sense his tension, something flashed in her eyes. Fire. It sent a jolt of adrenalin through Cruz. She certainly wasn't the shy girl who'd come for that job interview a couple of years ago. More evidence of her duality, if he'd needed it.

She lifted her chin. 'Yes, actually. I don't know how the school systems work here, but if it's anything like in the UK I'll—' She stopped herself and flushed slightly. 'That is, *we'll* have to think about enrolling them in a local school. Also, I'd like to investigate playschools in the area—they should be around other children their own age. Surely you weren't expecting to them to never go beyond the *castillo* gates?'

He'd never been allowed beyond the *castillo* gates until he'd gone to boarding school in England.

He reacted testily to the fact that she was showing a level of consideration for his nephews that he'd never expected to see. 'Are you sure you're not just looking for opportunities to spread your own wings beyond these walls? You're not a prisoner, Trinity, you can leave any time you want. But if you do the boys remain here.'

She paled dramatically, any bravado gone, but seconds later a wash of bright pink came into her cheeks. Cruz was momentarily mesmerised by this display of emotion—he was used to people disguising their natural reactions around him. It had intrigued him before and he was surprised that she still had the ability.

She stood up. 'I'm well aware that I am here because I have little or no choice—not if I want to see my stepsons flourish and be secure—but I will never walk away from them. Not while they need me. I will do whatever it takes to ensure their happiness and wellbeing.'

Her blue eyes blazed. *Dios*, but she was stunning.

'So if you're hoping to see the back of me it won't be any time soon, I can assure you.'

With that, she turned on her heel and stalked out of the room, the heavy door closing with a solid *thunk* behind her. Cruz cursed volubly and stood up, muscles poised to go after her. But then he stopped.

He turned to face the window, which took in the breathtaking vista of the expanse of his estate. He couldn't allow Trinity to distract him by fooling him into thinking she'd changed. Because the moment he dropped his guard she'd have won.

'What on earth did you say to him?'

Trinity was too shocked to respond to Mrs Jordan's question as she took in the scene before her. Building was underway on a playground for the boys...an exact replica of the playground in Regent's Park.

At that moment the atmosphere became charged with a kind of awareness that only happened around one person. *Cruz.*

Mrs Jordan reacted to his presence before Trinity did. 'Mr De Carrillo, this really is spectacular—the boys will love it.'

He came to stand beside Trinity and his scent tickled her nostrils, earthy and masculine. Her belly tightened and she flushed. Superstitiously she didn't want to look at him, as if that might make his impact less.

He answered smoothly, 'Please, Mrs Jordan, call me Cruz… Trinity was right—the boys need somewhere they can expend their energy safely.'

Matty and Sancho were currently playing with big toy building bricks in an area that had been cordoned off for them by the builders. They were wearing small hard hats and jeans and T-shirts and they looked adorable, faces intent, trying to keep up with the real builders just a few feet away.

Mrs Jordan turned to Cruz more directly and said, with an innocent tone in her voice, 'We were just about to bring the boys in for lunch—won't you join us?'

Trinity glanced at the woman, aghast, but Mrs Jordan was ignoring her. Fully expecting Cruz to refuse, she couldn't believe it when, after a long moment, he said consideringly, 'Thank you. That would be lovely.'

Mrs Jordan smiled. 'I'll ask Julia to add another place.'

She disappeared with a suspicious twinkle in her eye before Trinity could say anything. She supposed she couldn't really blame the woman for taking the opportunity to meddle gently when it arose.

When Trinity glanced up at Cruz she almost expected him to look irritated at the thought of spending lunch with them, but he was staring at the boys with an enigmatic expression on his face. Uncertainty?

Then, as if he sensed her watching him, the expression was gone and he looked down at her. 'You haven't said anything—are the plans all right?'

Against her best intentions to remain impervious to this man's pull, something inside her melted a little at his thoughtfulness. She forced a smile. 'They're perfect. I didn't expect you to take my words so literally.'

He frowned. 'But you said they loved that playground, so naturally I would try to recreate it for them.'

Trinity desisted from pointing out that only a billion-aire would think along such lavish lines and just said dryly, 'It's extremely generous, and they will love it. Thank you.'

Cruz looked away from her to the boys and another curi-ous expression crossed his face. She'd seen it before when he looked at them: something between fear and longing. Trinity cursed herself for not reading it properly till now. This man scrambled her brain cells too easily.

She said, 'They won't bite, you know. They're as curi-ous about you as you are about them.'

Without taking his eyes off them Cruz said gruffly, 'They always seem to look at me as if they don't know what I am.'

Trinity felt something weaken inside her at this evi-dence of rare vulnerability. 'They don't really know you yet, that's all. Once they become more used to you they'll relax. Why don't you help me get them in for lunch?'

She moved forward before he could see how easily he affected her.

'Matty! Sancho!' she called out when she came near to where they were playing so happily. 'Time to go in for lunch.'

Two identical faces looked up with predictable mulish-ness—and then they spied Cruz and immediately put down what they were playing with to come to Trinity. She bent down to their level and took their hats off, ruffling their heads, feeling the heat from their small, sturdy bodies. Even though they were in the shade the Spanish spring was getting warmer every day.

Cruz was towering over them in one of his trademark pristine suits. No wonder he intimidated the boys. He intimidated her. Softly she said, 'It might help if you come down to their level.'

He squatted down beside her and the movement made her uncomfortably aware of his very potent masculinity. She closed her eyes for a second. What was wrong with her? Until she'd shared that incendiary moment with him in his study she'd had no great interest in sex. And yet a couple of days in Cruz's company again and all her hormones seemed to have come back to life.

She focused her attention on her boys, who were huddled close, brown eyes huge. 'Matty, Sancho...you know this is your Uncle Cruz's house, where we're going to live from now on?' She ignored the pang inside her when she said that, and the thought of a life stretching ahead of her as a wife of inconvenience.

'Man. The big man,' Matty observed.

Trinity bit back a smile at the innocent nickname. 'Yes, sweetie—but he's also your uncle and he wants to get to know you better.'

Sancho said nothing, just regarded his uncle. Then he said imperiously, 'Play with us.'

Matty jumped up and down. 'Yes! Play!'

Sensing things starting to unravel, Trinity said firmly, 'First lunch, and then you can play again for a little while.'

She scooped up Matty and handed him to Cruz, who took him awkwardly and rose to his feet. She then picked up Sancho and started to walk inside, almost afraid to look behind her and see how Matty must be tarnishing Cruz's sartorial perfection.

He was saying excitedly, 'Higher, Unkel Cooz...higher!'

Seeing his brother in the arms of the tall, scary man who now wasn't so scary was making Sancho squirm to get free from Trinity's arms. 'I want higher too!'

They walked into the bright dining room where Mrs Jordan was waiting for them. Trinity didn't miss the gleam of approval in the woman's eyes when she saw Cruz carrying one of his nephews.

Trinity thought again of that rare chink of vulnerability Cruz had revealed outside. She realised belatedly that this had to be hard for him—coming from such a dark and dour place with only a half-brother he'd never been allowed to connect with properly. And yet he was making a real effort.

A rush of tenderness flooded her before she could stop it.

She tried to hide her tumultuous emotions as she strapped Sancho into his high seat. When she felt composed again she looked up to see Mrs Jordan showing Cruz how to strap Mateo into his. He looked flummoxed by such engineering, and it should have emasculated the man but it didn't. It only made that tenderness surge again. Pathetic.

Cruz sat down at the head of the table. The boys were seated one on each side beside Trinity and Mrs Jordan. Staff scurried in and out, presenting a buffet of salads and cold meats, cheese and bread. The boys were having chopped up pasta and meatballs. They ate with their habitual gusto, insisting on feeding themselves and invariably spraying anyone in close proximity with tiny bits of pasta and meat.

Trinity sneaked another glance at Cruz to see if this domestic milieu was boring him, but he was watching his nephews, fascinated.

'How do you tell them apart?' he asked, during a lull when small mouths were full.

Trinity nodded her head towards Mateo on the other side of the table. 'Matty is a tiny bit taller and leaner. He's also a little more gregarious than Sancho. Where he leads, Sancho follows. She scooped some of Sancho's food back onto his plate and said with a fond smile, 'Sancho is more watchful and quiet. He's also got a slightly different coloured right eye—a tiny discolouration.'

Cruz leaned forward to look and Sancho grinned at the attention, showing tiny teeth and a mouth full of masticated food.

When he pulled back, Cruz said a little faintly, 'Rio had the same thing...one eye was slightly lighter in colour.'

'He did...?' Trinity had never noticed that detail.

Cruz sent her a sharp glance and she coloured and busied herself cleaning up Sancho's tray, feeling absurdly guilty when she had no reason to. It wasn't as if she'd spent any time looking deep into Rio's eyes. Not that Cruz would believe that. She wondered if he ever would.

It didn't escape her notice that Mrs Jordan had excused herself on some flimsy pretext. Trinity sighed inwardly. She wouldn't put it past the woman, who subsisted on a diet of romance novels, to try and matchmake her and Cruz into a real marriage.

The thought of that was so absurd that she coloured even more for a moment, as if Cruz might see inside her head.

The very notion of this man looking at her with anything other than suspicious disdain was utterly inconceivable.

*But he looked at you differently once before,* said a little voice.

Trinity blocked it out. Cruz wouldn't touch her again if his life depended on it—of that she was sure. And that suited her just fine. If he ever discovered how susceptible she still was—*and* how innocent she still was, in spite of his belief that her marriage to Rio had been a real one... The thought sent a wave of acute vulnerability through her.

Cruz's comprehensive rejection of her had left a wound in a deeply private feminine space. The thought of opening herself up to that rejection again was terrifying.

Cruz cleared his throat then, and said, 'I've arranged

for you to be taken to a local boutique tomorrow morning, where a stylist will help you choose a wardrobe of clothes. Think of it as a trousseau.'

Trinity put down the napkin and looked at him. She felt raw after her recent line of thinking. She hated to be so beholden to him. It made her feel helpless and she didn't like that. She saw the look in his eye, as if he was just waiting for her to show her true avaricious nature.

'There's not just me to think of,' she said testily. 'I need to get the boys some new clothes too, more suitable for this warmer climate. They're growing so fast at the moment that they've almost outgrown everything.'

Cruz inclined his head, only the merest glint in his eye showing any reaction to her spiky response. 'Of course. I should have thought of that. I'll see to it that the stylist takes you to a suitable establishment for children also.'

The boys were starting to get bored now, having eaten enough and grown tired of the lack of attention and activity. Sancho was already manoeuvring himself to try and slip out of his chair and Trinity caught him deftly.

She took advantage of the distraction. 'I'll let them play some more while their lunch digests and then it'll be time for their afternoon nap.'

Without asking for help, Cruz stood and plucked a clearly delighted Matty, little arms outstretched, out of his seat. It irked her no end that Cruz was already holding him with an ease that belied the fact that it was only the second time he'd held one of his nephews in his arms.

It suited him. Matty looked incredibly protected in those strong arms and a sharp poignancy gripped her for a moment as she realised that he was already charming them. They'd gone from looking at him as if he was about to devour them whole, to looking at him with something close to awe and adoration. Their tiny minds were obviously cottoning onto the fact that this tall person might become an important ally and be able to do things that Trinity and Mrs Jordan couldn't.

Sancho was whingeing—he wanted to be in the big man's arms too.

Cruz held out his other arm, 'I can take him.'

After a moment's hesitation Trinity handed him over, to see Cruz expertly balance Sancho in his other arm. And then he walked out of the room, two glossy brown heads lifted high against his chest. The twins were delighted with themselves, grinning at her over those broad shoulders.

And just like that Trinity knew she'd started to lose them to Cruz... And, as wrong as it was, she couldn't but help feel a tiny bit jealous at how easily he accepted the innocence of his nephews when he would never ever accept the possibility of Trinity's. Not while he was so blinded by his loyalty to his deceased brother.

The next few days passed in a blur for Trinity. She was taken to cosmopolitan and beautiful Seville by Cruz's driver, to a scarily exclusive boutique where she lost track of the outfits she tried on. Then she was taken to a department store that stocked children's clothes, where she picked up everything she needed for the boys.

Their bedroom had been refurbished, and once again Cruz's efficiency had been impressive. An interior designer had taken her ideas on board and now, with murals of animals and tractors and trains on the walls, it was a bright and inviting space for two small boys. And they each had a bed, built in the shape of a car.

For a moment, when she'd seen it transformed and the way the boys had stood there in wide-eyed awe, she'd felt ridiculously emotional. They would have so much more than she'd ever had...or even their father.

She would have thanked Cruz, but he hadn't been

around much in the last few days. He hadn't joined them for lunch again, and the boys had been asking for him plaintively.

Trinity folded up the last of Sancho and Matty's new clothes and put them in the colourful set of drawers, chastising herself for the constant loop in her head that seemed to veer back to Cruz no matter how hard she tried to change it.

She was about to push the drawer closed when a deep voice came from behind her. 'Where are the boys?'

She jumped and whirled around to see Cruz filling the doorway, dressed in jeans and a shirt open at the neck. Irritation at the way she'd just been wondering about him, and the effortless effect he had on her, made her say waspishly, 'They're outside, playing with Mrs Jordan.'

Her irritation only increased when she found herself noticing how gorgeous he looked.

'They've been asking for you, you know. If you're going to be in their lives you need to be more consistent. They don't understand why you're there one day but not the next...it confuses them.'

Her conscience pricked. What she really meant was that it put *her* on edge, not knowing where or when he was likely to turn up...

His gaze narrowed on her and he slowly raised one brow. Clearly the man wasn't used to having anyone speak to him like this. Well, tough, she told herself stoutly. She was no longer in awe of her scarily sexy stern boss. She folded her arms.

'I understand that you've had your wardrobe replenished, as well as my nephews'?' Cruz drawled.

Trinity flushed. She immediately felt churlish and unfolded her arms. 'I wanted to say thank you for the bedroom—it worked out beautifully, and the boys love it. And, yes, we got clothes... But more clothes were delivered from the boutique than I ever looked at or tried on…it's too much.'

Cruz shook his head slowly, a hard light in his eye. 'Still with the act? I'm impressed. I thought you would have cracked by now and shown your true colours—but perhaps you're saving yourself for a more appreciative audience.'

She just looked at him. This evidence of his continued mistrust hurt her and, terrified to look at why that was, and not wanting him to see her emotions, she focused on the last thing he'd said. 'What do you mean, *audience?*'

'I have a function to attend in Seville tomorrow night. It'll be our first public outing as husband and wife.'

Panic gripped her. 'But Mrs Jordan—'

Cruz cut her off. 'Has already agreed to babysit. And we're rectifying that situation next week. I've organised with a local recruitment agency for them to send us their best candidates for another nanny. It'll free you up to spend more time with me, and Mrs Jordan will have more of her own free time.'

'Is that really necessary?' she asked, feeling weak at the thought of more time with him.

'Yes.' Cruz sounded impatient now. 'I'll have social functions to attend and I expect you to be by my side. As discussed.'

Trinity's irritation flared again. and she welcomed it. 'As I recall it was more of a decree than a discussion.'

Cruz's jaw clenched. 'You can call it what you want. We both know that, thanks to Rio's dire financial state when he died, you had no way of offering independent support to my nephews without me. The sooner you accept this as your new reality, the easier it will be for all of us.'

And evidently Cruz still believed that state of financial affairs to be *her* fault, based on her alleged profligate spending of her husband's money.

For a moment Trinity wanted to blurt out the truth—that

Rio had hated Cruz so much he'd wanted to ruin him—but Cruz wouldn't believe her, and she found that the impulse faded quickly. First of all, it wasn't in her to lash out like that, just to score a point. And she also realised she didn't want to see the effect that truth would have on him, when he clearly believed that his brother had been flawed, yes, but inherently decent.

And that shook her to the core—knowing that she resisted wanting to hurt him. Even as he hurt her.

She had to take responsibility for the fact that she'd agreed to the marriage of convenience with Rio. She really had no one to blame but herself.

And, as much as she hated this situation and being financially dependent, she couldn't deny the immutable fact that Matty and Sancho were in the privileged position of being heirs to this great family legacy and fortune. She didn't have the right to decide on their behalf, even as their legal guardian, that she was going to fight to take them away from all this and turn their lives into something it didn't have to be.

The silence grew between them almost to breaking point, a battle of wills, until eventually Trinity said, 'Fine. What time do I need to be ready?'

There was an unmistakable gleam of triumph in Cruz's eyes now and he said, 'We'll leave at six. It's a formal event, so wear a long gown. I'll have Julia show you to the vaults so you can pick out some jewellery.'

*Jewellery...vaults...* Not wanting him to see how intimidated she was, or how easily he affected her emotions, she just said coolly, 'Fine. I'll be ready by six.'

# CHAPTER FIVE

THE FOLLOWING EVENING Cruz paced back and forth in the entrance hall of the *castillo* and looked at his watch again impatiently. He forced himself to take a breath. It was only just six o'clock so Trinity wasn't actually late *yet*. Just then he heard a sound and looked to where she stood at the top of the main stairs.

For a long second he could only stare, struck dumb by the glittering beauty of the woman in front of him. She was refined…elegant. Classic. Stunning.

Her dress was long—as he'd instructed—and a deep blue almost navy colour. It shone and glistened and clung to those impossibly long legs, curving out to her hips and back in to a small waist. It shimmered as she came down the stairs. It clung everywhere—up over her torso to where the material lovingly cupped full, perfectly shaped breasts. All the way to the tantalising hollow at the base of her throat.

Cruz was dimly aware that he'd possibly never seen less flesh revealed on a woman, and yet this dress was sexier than anything he'd ever seen in his life. Her hair was pulled back at the nape of her neck, highlighting the delicate slim column of her throat and her bone structure.

She gestured to herself and he could see that she was nervous.

'What is it? Is the dress not suitable?'

Cruz realised he was ogling. He felt a very uncharacteristic urge to snap, *No, the dress is entirely unsuitable*. And yet that would be ridiculous. The dress effectively covered her from head to toe and he was reacting like an animal in heat—how the hell would he react when he saw some flesh? As it was, all the blood in his body was migrating from his brain to between his legs with alarming speed.

Any delusion he'd been under that he could successfully block out his awareness of this woman was laughable. She was under his skin, in his blood, and he couldn't deny it. His intellect hated this desire for her but his body thrummed with need.

Calling on all the control and civility he possessed, Cruz locked eyes with Trinity's—not that that helped. The colour of the dress only made her bright blue eyes stand out even more. They were like light sapphires, stunning and unusual.

'It's fine,' he said tightly. And then, goaded by thoughts of how she'd dressed for Rio, he said provocatively, 'Or perhaps you'd feel more comfortable in less material?'

To his surprise he saw the faintest shudder pass through her body. 'No. I never felt comfortable in the clothes Rio wanted me to wear.'

He looked at her. For some reason that admission only made him feel more conflicted.

Tersely he said, 'The driver is waiting—we should go.'

He indicated for her to precede him out of the *castillo* and his gaze tracked down her back and snagged on the enticing curves of her buttocks. He cursed himself. He was behaving as if he'd never seen a beautiful woman before in his life.

The driver helped her into the back of the luxury Jeep and Cruz got in the other side. As they were pulling out of the *castillo* courtyard his gaze swept over her again and he noticed something. 'You're not wearing any jewellery. Didn't you go to the vaults?'

She looked at him and Cruz saw a flush stain her cheeks. 'I did, but everything was so valuable-looking I was afraid to take anything.'

Something dark pierced him—was this finally evidence of her avaricious methods? Was this how she angled for more?

'Perhaps you'd have preferred something from Cartier or Tiffany's?'

She shook her head, eyes flashing. 'No, I wouldn't prefer that.' She held out her hand. 'I'm wearing the wedding band—isn't that enough? Or maybe you'd prefer if I wore a diamond-studded collar with a lead attached so no one is mistaken as to whom I belong?'

Irritation vied with frustration that she was so consistently refusing to conform to what he expected. He curtly instructed his driver to turn around and go back to the *castillo*.

'Why are we going back?' Trinity asked.

Cruz looked straight ahead. 'We're going back to get you an engagement ring.'

'I don't need one,' she said stubbornly.

He looked at her. 'It's not a choice. People will expect you to have a ring.'

She rounded on him, tense and visibly angry. 'Oh, and we can't have anyone suspecting that this isn't a real marriage, can we? Do you really think an engagement ring will convince people that you fell in love with your brother's widow?'

Cruz wanted to laugh at her suggestion of anyone in his circle ever being convinced that people married for love, but for some reason the laugh snagged in his chest.

'Don't be ridiculous,' he breathed, his awareness of her rising in an unstoppable wave in the confined space. 'No one would expect that. They'll know I'm protecting what's mine—my heirs.'

'And I'm just the unlucky pawn who got in your way.'

The bitterness in Tiffany's voice surprised him. Anger spiked at the way his control was starting seriously to fray at the edges. 'You put yourself in the way—by seducing my brother. By inserting yourself into my nephews' lives so they'd come to depend on you.'

She went pale and looked impossibly wounded. 'I've told you—that's not—'

Before she could issue another lie Cruz's control snapped and he acted on blind instinct and need. He reached for Trinity, clamping his hands around her waist, and pulled her towards him, vaguely registering how slender and light she felt under his hands.

He only had a second of seeing her eyes widen with shock before his mouth crashed down onto hers, and for a long second nothing existed except this pure, spiking shard of lust, so strong that he had no option but to move his mouth and haul Trinity even closer, until he could feel every luscious curve pressed against him.

And it was only in that moment, when their mouths were fused and he could feel her heart clamouring against his chest, that he could finally recognise the truth: he'd been aching for this since the night he'd kissed her for the first time.

Trinity wasn't even sure what had happened. A minute ago she'd been blisteringly angry with Cruz and now she was drowning and burning up at the same time. The desire she'd hoped she could keep buried deep inside her was shaming her with its instant resurrection. Brought back to life by a white-hot inferno scorching along every artery and vein in her body.

Cruz's mouth was hot and hard, moving over hers with such precision that Trinity couldn't deny him access, and when his tongue stroked hers with an explicitness that made heat rush between her legs her hands tightened around his arms, where they'd gone instinctively to hang on to something…anything…so she wouldn't float away.

His hands were still on her waist and one started moving up her torso, until it came tantalisingly close to the side of her breast, where her nipple peaked with need, stiffening against the sheer material of her underwear and her dress. She remembered what it was like to have his mouth on her there…the hot sucking heat…the excruciating pleasure of his touch.

A voice from the past whispered through the clamour of her blood—his voice. *'It should never have happened.'* It was like a slap across the face.

Trinity jerked backwards away from Cruz. She was panting as if she'd just run a race. Mortification was swift and all-consuming. He'd barely had to touch her before she'd gone up in flames. Any hope of convincing him she didn't want him was comprehensively annihilated. It wasn't even a comfort to see that his hair was dishevelled and his cheeks were flushed.

Those amber eyes glittered darkly. He muttered, 'I told myself I wouldn't touch you ever again, but I can't *not* touch you.'

She took her hands off him, but he caught them and held them tightly. The recrimination on his face was far too painfully familiar. She was angry and hurt.

'So now it's justifiable for you to kiss me, even if you still hate yourself for it? Because I'm your wife and not just a lowly maid?'

She pulled her hands free and balled them into fists in her lap.

Cruz frowned, 'What the hell are you talking about— justifiable?'

Trinity tried not to sound as emotional as she felt. 'You rejected me that night because you couldn't bear the thought that you'd kissed your maid. I saw the kind of women you took as lovers, and you don't need to tell me that I was nowhere near their level—socially, economically or intellectually.'

Cruz clamped his hands around her arms, his face flushing. He was livid. 'You think I stopped making love to you because I was a snob? *Dios* Trinity, that was *not* the case. I had to stop because you were my employee and I had a duty of care towards you. I put you in a compromising situation where you might have felt too scared to say no.'

His mouth twisted.

'My father was renowned for his affairs—some of which were with willing and impressionable staff members at the *castillo*. I vowed that I would never follow his footsteps—not least because I'd seen the destruction one of his affairs cost us all. He slept with Rio's mother, who took advantage of the situation, only to then abandon her son.'

Trinity was speechless for a moment as she absorbed this. 'You think,' she framed shakily, 'that I'm like Rio's mother, then? That I'm no better...?'

Cruz's wide, sensual mouth compressed. 'I didn't think so at first—not that night. I hated myself for losing control like that, but I didn't blame you. Since then...let's just say any illusions about your innocence I may have had have been well and truly shattered.'

An awful poignancy gripped Trinity at the thought that for a short while Cruz *had* seen the real her...and respected her. But even the memory of her naivety and humiliation couldn't stop her saying bitterly, 'It would only have ever been a mistake, though, wouldn't it? I mean, let's not fool ourselves that it would have developed into anything... more...'

*More.* Like the kind of more that Cruz had once hoped existed until any such notion was drummed out of him by his mother and her bitter words? Since then he'd never been proved wrong—any woman he'd been with had only confirmed his cynicism. Not least this one. And yet... when he'd first laid eyes on her he'd never seen anyone who looked so untouched and innocent.

And she was looking at him now with those huge eyes, taunting him for his flight of fancy. It was as if she was reaching inside him to touch a raw wound.

He was unaware of his hands tightening on her arms, knew only that he needed to push her back.

'More…like what?' he all but sneered. 'Hearts and flowers? Tender lovemaking and declarations of undying love? I don't *do* tender lovemaking, Trinity, I would have taken you until we were both sated and then moved on. I have no time for relationships—my life isn't about that. It never was and it never will be. I have a duty of care to my nephews now, and you're here only because I'm legally bound to have you here.' His mouth twisted. 'The fact that I want you is a weakness I'm apparently not capable of overcoming.'

A veritable cavalcade of emotions crossed Trinity's face, and then a look of almost unbelievable hurt—it had to be unbelievable—superseded them all. She shrank back, pulling herself free, and he only realised then how hard he'd been holding her. He curled his hands into fists and cursed himself. What was it about this woman that made his brain fuse and cease functioning?

In a low voice that scraped along all of Cruz's raw edges she said, 'I wasn't looking for anything more than a book that night, no matter what you choose to believe.'

Cruz still felt volatile, and even more so now at this protestation of innocence and her stubborn refusal to reveal her true nature. He ground out, 'Maybe if I'd taken you as I'd wanted to, there against the bookshelves, we wouldn't be here now and Rio would still be alive.'

Trinity had thought he couldn't hurt her much more than he already had, but he just had—even as a lurid image blasted into her head of exactly the scenario he mentioned…his powerful body holding her captive against a wall of books while he thrust up, deep into her body.

She held herself rigid, denying that hurt, and blasted back, 'So you would have thrown over that elegant brunette beauty for me? Am I supposed to be flattered that you would have been happy to conduct an affair on your terms, only to discard me by the wayside when you were done with me?'

A muscle ticked in Cruz's jaw but he just said tersely, 'We're back at the *castillo*, we should get the ring. We've wasted enough time.'

*Wasted enough time.*

Trinity was still reeling as she followed Cruz's broad tuxedoed form down stone steps to the vaults, holding her dress up in one hand. The depth of his cynicism astounded her all over again, and she hated it that he'd hurt her so easily.

She blamed his interaction with Matty and Sancho. It had made her lower her guard against him and he'd punished her for it, reminding her that he was not remotely someone to pin her hopes and dreams on... She scowled at herself. Since when had she ever entertained those notions herself? It wasn't as if she'd ever been under any delusions of *more*.

*More* existed for people who weren't her or Cruz. Who had grown up with normal, functioning, loving families. And yet she couldn't deny that when she'd worked for him for a brief moment she'd entertained daydreams of him noticing her...wanting her...smiling at her—

Trinity slammed a lid on that humiliating Pandora's box.

She wasn't sure what was worse—finding out that Cruz hadn't dismissed her because she was a nobody all those years ago, or believing that if he'd taken her *until they were both sated* he could have averted Rio's destruction. Right now, she hated Cruz with a passion that scared her.

But not far under her hatred was something much more

treacherous. A very illicit racing excitement at the knowledge that he still wanted her. And that he'd rejected her because he'd felt he'd taken advantage of his position, not because he'd been horrified to find himself attracted to her...

Once in the vault, Trinity welcomed the change of scenery from the heightened and heated intensity of the back of the Jeep even as she shivered in the cold, dank air.

She hated herself for it, but found herself instinctively moving closer to Cruz's tall, lean form because the place gave her the creeps. She could imagine it being used as a location for the Spanish Inquisition, with its dark stone walls and shadowy cavernous corridors.

She thought, not a little hysterically, that if they'd been back in medieval times Cruz might have just incarcerated her down here in a cell.

He had pulled out a velvet tray of rings from a box in the wall and stood back. 'Choose one.'

Trinity reluctantly stepped forward. Almost immediately one ring in the centre of the tray caught her eye. It was one of the smallest rings, with an ornate gold setting and a small square ruby in the middle.

Cruz followed her gaze and picked it up. 'This one?'

She nodded. He took her hand and held it up and slid the ring onto her finger. It was a perfunctory gesture, so it shouldn't feel in any way momentous but it did. The ring fitted like a glove and, bizarrely, Trinity felt emotion rising when emotion had no place there—especially not after what had just passed between them.

Swallowing the emotion with effort, Trinity was unprepared when Cruz took her chin in his thumb and forefinger, tipping it up. The look in his eyes burned.

'As much as I'd like to be able to resist you, I don't think I can.'

Her heart thumped—hard. The thought of Cruz touching her again and seeing right through to where she was most vulnerable was anathema.

She jerked her chin out of his hand. 'Well, I can resist you enough for both of us.'

He smiled urbanely and stood back, putting out a hand to let her go ahead of him up the stairs and out of the vaults. 'We'll see,' he said with infuriating arrogance as she passed him, and she had to stop herself from running up the stairs, away from his silky threat.

This was Cruz's first social appearance back in Seville. His return was triumphant, now he had tripled his family's fortune and restored the reputation of the once great bank. Now no one would dare say to his face or behind his back the things they'd used to say when his father had been alive.

And yet he could not indulge in a sense of satisfaction. He was too keyed-up after that white-hot explosion of lust in the back of the Jeep, which had proved to him that where Trinity was concerned he had no control over his desires.

His body still throbbed with sexual frustration. And he was distracted by their exchange, and how it had felt to see her with that ring on her finger down in the vaults. It had affected him in a place he hadn't welcomed. As if it was somehow *right* that she should wear one of his family's heirlooms.

Down in that vault it had suddenly been very clear to him that he couldn't fight his desire for her—so why should he? He might not like himself for his weakness but she was his wife, and the prospect of trying to resist her for the duration of their marriage was patently ridiculous.

But something niggled at him—why wasn't she using his desire for her as a means to negotiate or manipulate? Instead she'd looked almost haunted when she'd fled up the steps from the vault. She was still pale now, her eyes huge. Irritation prickled across Cruz's skin. Maybe now that she knew he wanted her she was going to play him in a different way, drive him mad…

'What is it?' he asked abruptly. 'You look paler than a wraith.'

She swallowed, the movement drawing Cruz's gaze to that long, slender column. Delicate. Vulnerable. Damn her. She *was* just playing him. He was giving in to his base desires again and—

'I'm fine. I just… Events like this are intimidating. I never get used to it. I don't know what to say to these people.'

Cruz's recriminations stopped dead. If she was acting then she was worthy of an award. He had a vivid flashback to seeing her standing alone in the crowd at that party in his house, the night of the accident, her stunning body barely decent in that scrap of a dress.

Cruz had been too distracted by the rush of blood to his extremities to notice properly. He'd hated her for making him feel as if he was betraying his brother by still feeling attracted to her. But the memory jarred now. Not sitting so well with what he knew of her.

Almost without registering the urge, Cruz took his hand off her elbow and snaked it around her waist, tugging her into his side. It had the effect of muting his desire to a dull roar. She looked up at him, tense under his arm. Something feral within him longed for her to admit to this attraction between them.

'What are you doing?'

'We're married, *querida*, we need to look it. Just follow my lead. most of the people here are committed egotists, so once you satisfy their urge to talk about themselves they're happy.'

'You don't count yourself in that category?'

Her quick comeback caused Cruz's mouth to tip up.

Suddenly the dry, sterile event wasn't so…boring. And she had a flush in her face now, which aroused him as much as it sent a tendril of relief to somewhere she shouldn't be affecting him.

He replied dryly, 'I find it far more fruitful to allow others to run their mouths off.'

Cruz's hand rested low on Trinity's hip and he squeezed it gently.

She tensed again, as someone approached them, and he said, 'Relax.'

*Relax…*

It had been the easiest thing and the hardest thing in the world to melt into his side, as if she was meant to be there. It was a cruel irony that she seemed to fit there so well, her softer body curving into his harder form as if especially made for that purpose.

Cruz hadn't let her out of his orbit all night. Even when she'd gone to the bathroom as soon as she'd walked back in to the function room his eyes had been the first thing she'd seen, compelling her back to his side like burning beacons.

It had been both disconcerting and exhilarating. In social situations before she'd invariably been left to fend for herself, Rio being done with her once their initial entrance had been made.

Trinity sighed now and finished tucking Matty and Sancho into their beds—she'd come straight here upon their return from the function, all but running away from Cruz, who had been lazily undoing his bow tie and looking utterly sinful.

The boys were spreadeagled, covers askew, pyjamas twisted around their bodies. Overcome with tenderness for these two small orphaned boys, she smoothed back a lock of Sancho's hair and sat on the side of Matty's bed, careful not to disturb him. Resolve filled her anew not to bow under Cruz's increasingly down-and-dirty methods to disturb her—that incendiary kiss in the back of his Jeep, his words of silky promise in the vault...

After this evening things had changed. Cruz had obviously given himself licence to seduce her. And she knew if he touched her again her ability to resist would be shamefully weak.

She looked at the ring on her finger—heavy, golden. A brand. And an unwelcome reminder of the emotion she'd felt when Cruz had pushed it onto her finger.

She hated it that he believed whatever lies Rio had told him about her so easily. She wasn't remotely mercenary or avaricious. She had remonstrated with Rio countless times over the amounts of money he was spending on her. But he hadn't wanted to know. He'd told her that they had a certain standard to maintain, and that she needed to educate herself about fashion, art, et cetera.

The prospect of a future in which Cruz refused to listen to her and wore down her defences until he found out about her innocence in the most exposing way possible filled Trinity with horror.

She stood up and left the room decisively. She had to at least try to make Cruz see that she wasn't who he thought she was. She would appeal to him rationally, without emotion and physical desire blurring the lines between them.

Above all, she had to make him see that the twins were and always had been her priority.

It was time to talk to her husband and make him listen to her.

'Come in.'

Trinity nearly lost her nerve at the sound of that deeply authoritative voice, but she refused to give in to it and pushed the door open. Cruz was sitting behind his desk, jacket off, shirtsleeves rolled up and the top of his shirt undone. There was a glass of something in his hand. He epitomised louche masculine sensuality.

He looked up from the papers he'd been perusing and immediately sat up straight and frowned when he saw it was her. 'What's wrong? Is it the boys?'

His instant concern for his nephews heartened something inside her. Some fledgling and delicate hope that perhaps she *could* appeal to him. In spite of all the evidence so far to the contrary.

She shook her head. 'No, they're fine. I just checked on them.'

'Well, is it something else?'

Trinity came further into the room, suddenly aware that Cruz was looking at her with a very narrow-eyed assessing gaze and that she was still in the dress. She cursed herself for not having changed into something less...dramatic.

Cruz stood up. 'Would you like a drink?'

She shook her head, thinking that the last thing she needed was to cloud her brain. 'No, thank you.'

He gestured to a seat on the other side of the table and as she sat down he said, 'I noticed you didn't drink much earlier—you don't like it?'

She shook her head. 'Not really. I never acquired the taste.' As soon as she said that, though, she regretted not asking for some brandy—she could do with the Dutch courage.

'So? To what do I owe the pleasure of this late-night visit?'

Trinity looked at Cruz suspiciously. Something about the tone of his voice scraped across her jumping nerves. Was he mocking her for having exposed herself so easily earlier, when he'd kissed her? His expression was unreadable, though, and she told herself she was imagining things.

She took a breath. 'I just...wanted to talk to you about

this arrangement. About going forward, making a practical life together.'

Cruz took a sip of his drink and lowered the glass slowly again. 'Practical? I seem to recall events earlier which would turn the "practical" aspects of this relationship into far more pleasurable ones.'

Trinity immediately stood up, agitated. He *was* mocking her. 'I did not come here to talk about that.'

Totally unperturbed, and like a lazy jungle cat eyeing its prey, Cruz just sat back and said, 'Pity. What did you want to talk about, then?'

She ploughed on before this far more disturbing and *flirty* Cruz could make her lose her nerve.

'I know that I won't be able to continue with this sham marriage while you believe the worst of me and don't trust me. It'll start to affect the boys. They're too young to pick up on the tension now, but they're intelligent and inquisitive and it'll soon become apparent. That kiss earlier…it was unacceptable and disrespectful of my boundaries. This is meant to be a marriage in name only. You will either need to learn to deal with your antipathy for me or…' she took a breath '…we can move on from the past.'

Cruz went very still and then he put his glass down. He stood up and put his hands on the table, his eyes intense. A muscle ticked in his jaw. 'You think that kiss was a demonstration of my antipathy? That kiss was the inevitable result of our explosive mutual desire and proof that you want me as much as I want you.'

Trinity sucked in a breath, mortification rushing through her, and in a desperate bid to deny such a thing she blurted out, 'You gave me no time to respond. I was in shock.'

He arched a brow. 'So your response was down to shock?'

He stood up straight and started to move towards her.

Trinity panicked, stepping away from the chair. She should never have come in here. This had been a terrible idea.

'Yes,' she said desperately. 'Of course it was shock. And you can't do that... Just...manhandle me when you feel like it.'

Cruz stopped in his tracks. Trinity's words hung starkly in the air between them. Anger raced up his spine. No, *fury*. He had to control himself, because he was very close to *manhandling* her into admitting that their kiss had been very mutual.

But she was looking at him with wide eyes, as if he was some kind of wild mountain lion. He felt wild, and he was *not* wild. He was civilised.

He bit out, 'For someone being *manhandled* your response was very passionate.'

He saw her throat move as she swallowed and the pulse beating frantically at the base of her neck. Right now he knew with every cell in his body that if he was to touch her they would combust. But something held him back—some sense of self-preservation. He couldn't trust that she wasn't just baiting him on purpose.

When they did come together it would be on his terms, and he wouldn't be feeling these raw, uncontrolled urges pushing him to the limits of his control.

'Look,' she said, 'I'm here because there are things I want to talk to you about. Important things.'

Cruz kept his gaze up, away from her tantalising curves in that amazing dress. He would put nothing past her. One thing was for sure, though. She wasn't going to see how his blood throbbed just under the surface of his skin. He wouldn't lose it twice in one evening.

He leant back against his desk and folded his arms, as if that might stop him from reaching for her. 'Well, no one is stopping you from talking now, Trinity. I'm all ears.'

She swallowed visibly, and Cruz saw that she was nervous. Once again she could be taking advantage of this situation, seducing him, but she wasn't. It irritated him.

'All that stuff Rio told you about me being a gold-digger...none of it is true. He lied to you.'

Cruz went cold. She didn't have to come here and seduce him—she was smarter than that. She just had to come and mess with his head.

He stood and closed the distance between them and her eyes widened. He stopped just short of touching her. 'How dare you use the fact that my brother is silenced for ever as an excuse to further your own cause?'

'I'm not,' she said fiercely, tipping up her chin. 'You need to listen to me. You need to know the real truth of my marriage to Rio...'

A dark emotion was snapping and boiling inside Cruz at the thought of *the truth* of her marriage to Rio. Sharing his bed. The thought that his brother had got to fully taste what she'd offered up to Cruz so enticingly before he'd stopped her.

Did he want to hear about that? *No.* He wished that thoughts of her with Rio would make him turn from her in disgust, but the fire inside him only burnt brighter as he battled a primal urge to stake a claim that reduced him to an animal state.

He caught her arms in his hands and hauled her into his body, so he could remind her of where she was and with whom. *Him.*

He ground out, 'When will you get it that I will never trust a word you say? From now on if you want to try to manipulate me I'd prefer if you used the currency you use best...your body. At least that way we'll both get pleasure out of the interaction and it'll be a lot more honest.'

'*Cruz...*'

That was all he heard before he stopped Trinity's poisonous words with his mouth.

The kiss was an intense battle of wills. Cruz's anger was red-hot, thundering in his veins. But then she managed to break free, pulling back, her hands on his chest, breathing heavily. If Cruz had been able to call on any rationality he would have been horrified. No woman had ever driven him to such base urges. To want to stamp his brand on her.

They stared at each other, tension crackling. But then, as he looked down into those blue eyes, swirling with something he couldn't fathom, the intense anger dissipated to be replaced by something far less angry and more carnal.

He curled an arm around her waist, drawing her right in, close to his body, until he saw her cheeks flush with the awareness of his erection against her soft flesh. It was torture and pleasure all at once. With his other hand he reached around to the back of her head and undid her hair, so that it fell around her shoulders in a golden cloud.

He could feel her resistance melting. Even though she said, 'Cruz…don't…'

'Don't what?' he asked silkily. 'Do this?' And he touched her jaw, tracing its delicate line, then cupped her cheek, angling her head up.

She spread her hands on his chest and he thought she was going to push him away, but she didn't. Something inside him exulted. This time when he bent his head and kissed her there was an infinitesimal moment of hesitation and then her mouth opened to him and his blood roared. There was just *this,* and this was all that mattered right now.

# CHAPTER SIX

TRINITY WAS RUNNING down the long, dark corridors of the *Castillo*. The stern faces of all those ancestors were staring down at her, each one silently judging her. The footsteps behind her were getting closer…her heart was in her throat, thumping so hard she could hardly breathe…

There was an open door on the left. She ducked in and slammed the door shut, chest heaving, sweat prickling on her skin. And then she heard it. The sound of breathing in the room…

Terror kept her frozen in place, her back to the door as the breathing got closer and closer. And then out of the gloom appeared a face. A very familiar, starkly beautiful face. Amber eyes hard. Stern. Angry. *Hot.*

Hands reached for her and Trinity knew she should try to escape. But suddenly she wasn't scared any more. She was excited… And instead of running she threw herself into Cruz's arms…

The disturbing dream still lingered, and Trinity shivered in the bright morning sunlight of another beautiful day. She didn't have to be a psychologist to figure out where it had come from. When Cruz had kissed her after that angry exchange in his study at first she'd resisted, but then something had changed…and when he'd touched her again she'd responded against her best intentions.

All the man had to do was touch her, look at her, and she wanted him. And with each touch and kiss it was getting harder to resist… She'd finally had the sense to pull back and step away last night, but it had taken every last shred of control she had.

Shakily she'd said, 'I didn't come here for this.'

'So you say,' Cruz had answered, with infuriating insouciance, looking as if he hadn't just kissed her so hard she could barely see straight. It had been particularly galling, because just moments before he'd demonstrated that once again any attempt to defend herself or tell the truth would be met with stubborn resistance.

A sense of futility made her ache inside. How could she continue like this? With Cruz blatantly refusing to listen to her? Maybe this was how he'd drive her away…by stonewalling her at every turn…

Matty shouted, 'Mummy, look! Unkel Cooz!'

Sancho jumped up, clapping his hands. 'Play, play!'

Trinity tensed all over as a long shadow fell over where she was sitting cross-legged in the grass; the boys were playing nearby. With the utmost reluctance she looked up, shading her eyes against Cruz's sheer masculine beauty as much as against the sun. Matty and Sancho—not scared of him at all any more—had grabbed a leg each, looking up at their new hero.

He lifted both boys up into his arms with an easy grace that annoyed her intensely. The fact that he was dressed down, in faded jeans and a dark polo shirt that strained across his chest muscles, was something she tried desperately not to notice. But it was hard when his biceps were bulging enticingly, reminding her of how it felt when they were wrapped around her.

She stood up, feeling at a disadvantage.

Cruz said, 'I came to tell you that I've been invited to another function this evening. We'll leave at seven.'

His autocratic tone sliced right into her, as did the scary prospect of countless more evenings like the previous one, when she'd reveal herself more and more. When he might *touch* her again.

She folded her arms and said coolly, 'I'm not going out this evening.'

The boys were squirming in Cruz's arms, growing bored already, and when he put them down they scampered off to the nearby sandpit. Trinity saw how his eyes followed them for a moment, making sure they were all right, and his concern made her feel warm inside until she clamped down on the sensation. This man evoked too much within her.

He looked back at her. 'I don't recall you being offered a choice.'

Irritation spiked at her reaction as much as to his tone. 'I'm not just some employee you can order around. It would be nice if you could pretend you're polite enough to *ask* if I'd like to come.'

'You're my wife,' Cruz offered tersely.

Something poignant gripped Trinity—if she was his wife for *real* then presumably they'd have a discussion about this sort of thing… She might agree to go because he'd tell her he'd be bored, or that he'd miss her if she didn't. The thought of that kind of domesticity made a treacherous shard of longing go through her before she could stop it.

Where had that illicit fantasy come from? One of the reasons she'd agreed to marry Rio—apart from her concern for the boys—was because after years of being an outsider in other people's homes as a foster child it had been easier to contemplate a marriage of convenience than to dare dream that she might one day have a real family of her own…

The prospect of Cruz ever seeing that deeply inside her made her go clammy all over.

Her arms tightened. 'I'm not going out this evening because I think the boys are coming down with something and I want to observe them for twenty-four hours to make sure they're okay. Sancho still isn't over his bug completely.'

Cruz glanced at the boys and back to her. 'They look fine to me.'

'They were off their food at breakfast, which isn't like them.'

'Mrs Jordan can watch them, and call us if she's worried.'

Exasperated, Trinity unfolded her arms and put her hands on her hips. 'You don't get it, do you? I'm worried about them, and even if it's only a niggle then I will put them first. *I* am the one they need if they're not feeling well.'

Scathingly, Cruz said, 'So you're not above using my nephews as an excuse?'

Hurt that he should think her capable of such a thing she said, 'Their welfare comes first, so I don't really care what you think.'

Cruz's jaw clenched, and then he just said, 'Seven p.m., Trinity. Be ready.' And then he turned and walked away.

To her shame she couldn't stop her gaze from dropping down his broad back to where his worn jeans showed off his powerful buttocks. Disgusted with herself, she whirled around and went over to the boys who, she had to admit, would look fine to most observers but not to her, who knew all their little habits and foibles.

Something wasn't quite right and she wasn't going to let Cruz bully her.

Later that evening Cruz's blood was boiling. No one had ever stood him up. Certainly not a woman. But Trinity had. Julia, looking terrified—*was he really that scary?*—had come with a note when he'd been waiting for Trinity in the hall.

*Sorry, Cruz, but I'm just not certain the boys aren't coming down with something. I'm not coming. T.*

The note was crumpled in his palm now, as he strode along the dark corridors to the wing Trinity and the boys occupied. Something about the oppressiveness of the *castillo* scraped along his nerves, when it never really had before. It was as if having Trinity and the boys here was throwing everything into sharp relief…

When he was near the boys' bedroom he could hear fractious cries and Trinity's tones, soothing. He stopped in the doorway to see her changing a clearly cranky Sancho into his pyjamas.

Mateo was running around in his nappy. As soon as he saw Cruz he sped over. 'Come play, Unkel Cooz!'

Cruz's chest felt tight. He bent down. 'Not now, *chiquito.* Tomorrow.'

He put his hand to Mateo's head and it felt warm. He looked up to see Trinity standing in front of him, still wearing the jeans and shirt she'd had on earlier. She really wasn't coming.

He straightened up and a determined expression came over her face. 'I meant it, Cruz, I'm worried about the boys. They've been off their food all day and they're both running slight temperatures. They also didn't nap today, so they're overtired now. It's probably nothing serious, but I'm not leaving them. I've given Mrs Jordan the evening off so she can take over in the morning.'

Cruz was slightly stunned yet again to think that she wasn't even their mother. Right now, with the boys in the room behind her, he had the distinct impression of a mother bear guarding her cubs from danger. He couldn't figure out what she could possibly be gaining from this if she *was* playing some game.

To his surprise something dark gripped his gut, and it took him a moment to acknowledge uncomfortably that it was jealousy—and something else…something more ambiguous that went deeper.

Jealousy of his nephews, who were being afforded such care and protection—the kind of protection he'd vowed to give them but which now he realised he was too woefully inexperienced to give.

The something deeper was a sharp sense of poignancy that his own mother had never cared for him like this. *Dios*, even his nanny hadn't shown this much concern.

Feeling very uncharacteristically at a momentary loss, he recognised that for the first time in his life he would have to back down.

'Call me if they get worse, or if you need anything. Maria the housekeeper has the number of my doctor.'

Trinity nodded, shocked that Cruz was conceding. She'd half expected him to insist on dressing her himself and dragging her out of the *castillo*.

He stepped away and said, 'I'll check on you when I get back.'

The thought of him coming in later, with his bow tie undone and looking far too sexy, made her say quickly, 'There's no—'

He looked at her warningly. 'I'll check on you.'

'Okay.'

For a moment something seemed to shimmer between them—something fragile. Then Cruz turned and left and she breathed out an unsteady breath. She turned around to focus on the boys and told herself that she'd just been imagining that moment of softening between them. Wishful thinking.


When Cruz returned later that night he went straight to the boys' room, where a low light leaked from under the door. He ruminated that he hadn't enjoyed one minute of the function—not that he usually did, because he considered these events work—and he realised now with some irritation that he'd missed having Trinity at his side. Seeing her reaction to everything. Having her close enough to touch.

He opened the door softly and stepped in. His eyes immediately tracked to the two small figures in their beds and he went over, finding himself pulling their covers back over their bodies from where they'd kicked them off. Something turned over in his chest at seeing them sprawled across their beds, dark lashes long on plump cheeks, hair tousled. They looked so innocent, defenceless. Once again he was overcome with a sense of protectiveness.

Then he looked up and saw another figure, curled in the armchair near the beds. Trinity. She was asleep, her head resting on her shoulder. A book lay open on her thigh and he looked at it: *The A-Z of Toddlers.*

For a moment he felt blindsided at this evidence of her dedication. That sense of poignancy he'd felt earlier gripped him again, and it was deeply disturbing and exposing.

Something else prickled under his skin now. If she was playing a game then it was a very elaborate one.

He recalled her coming into his office last night and her words: *'All that stuff that Rio told you about me being a gold-digger...none of it is true.'*

Cruz's rational mind reminded him that there was evidence of her treachery. Her name on receipts. Demands she'd made. Rio's humiliation. Maybe this was her game— she was trying to convince him she was something she wasn't and would wriggle under his skin like she had with Rio until he too felt compelled to give her everything...

'Cruz?'

She was awake now, blinking up at him. She sat up, looking deliciously dishevelled, compounding the myriad conflicting emotions she evoked.

His voice was gruff when he spoke. 'Go to bed, Trinity. I'll sit up with them.'

She looked flustered. 'No!' She lowered her voice. 'You don't have to do that. It's fine... I think they're okay now, anyway. Their temperatures were normal last time I checked.'

'Go to bed. I'll let you know if anything happens.'

She looked up at him helplessly and he offered ruefully, 'I'm going to have to get used to doing this kind of thing. I'm their uncle, and I don't intend to treat them like guests in my home.'

For the first time since Rio had died it struck Cruz forcibly that he hadn't really thought about how taking responsibility for his nephews would affect him until now. And this was what it meant, he realised with a kind of belated wonder. Being concerned. Sitting up all night to watch over them if need be.

Trinity eyes were wide, and even in this light Cruz could see the smudges of fatigue under them. From this angle he could also see down her shirt to the bountiful swells of her breasts. His body reacted.

He gritted out, 'Just go.'

She stood up jerkily, as if her muscles were protesting. 'You'll let me know if they wake?' She sounded uncertain.

Cruz nodded and took her place on the chair, stretching out his long legs and picking up the book. He gestured with it for her to go.

Feeling more than a little discombobulated at having woken to find Cruz standing over her, looking exactly like the sexy fantasy she'd envisaged earlier, Trinity eventually moved towards her own room, glancing back to see Cruz tipping his head back and closing his eyes, hands linked loosely across his flat abdomen.

Her footsteps faltered, though, as she was momentarily transfixed by the fact that he had insisted on staying. Emotion expanded in her chest at the domestic scene—dangerous emotion—as she thought how incongruous he looked here, yet how *right*.

His willingness to forge a bond with his nephews made that emotion turn awfully poignant... She had a vision of going over to him, smoothing his hair back...of him looking up at her and reaching for her, smiling sexily as he pulled her down onto his lap...

Shock at the vividness of this fantasy made her breathless. And at how much she yearned for it. When it was only his nephews he cared about. Not her.

Without opening his eyes, Cruz said softly, 'Go to bed, Trinity.'

And she fled before he might see any vestige of that momentary fantasy on her face.

When Trinity woke the following morning it was later than she'd ever slept since she'd started looking after the twins. And they were her first thought.

She shot out of bed and went into their room, to see that their beds were empty and their pyjamas were neatly folded on their pillows.

She washed quickly and got dressed in jeans and a T-shirt, pulling her hair back into a low ponytail as she went down to the dining room, where she found Mrs Jordan and the twins.

'*Mummy!*' they both screeched in unison when they saw her, and her heart swelled.

She went over and kissed them both. She looked at the older woman. 'You should have woken me.'

Mrs Jordan waved a hand. 'Cruz wouldn't hear of it. He insisted that you sleep in and I agreed. You've been looking tired lately.'

Trinity's heart skipped. She still felt raw after that moment of insanity when she'd wished for a domestic idyll that would never exist.

'He was still there this morning?'

She sat down and helped herself to coffee, noting with relief that the boys seemed to be making up for their lack of appetite the previous day, with their mouths full of mushy cereal.

Mrs Jordan nodded and a look of unmistakable awe came over her face. 'He was changing them when I went in this morning, and apart from putting Sancho's nappy on back to front he didn't do a bad job at all…'

Trinity choked on her coffee, spraying some out of her mouth inelegantly, and the boys went into paroxysms of giggles.

'Funny, Mummy…do it again!'

She distracted them for a minute, playing aeroplanes with their spoons as she fed them, and avoided Mrs Jordan's far too shrewd gaze. She almost felt angry with Cruz for blurring the boundaries like this and inducing disturbing fantasies. And then she felt awful—she should be happy that he was intent on connecting with his nephews in a real and meaningful way.

After the boys had finished their breakfast, and Mrs Jordan had taken them outside to play, Trinity sipped her coffee, recalling again how dangerously intimate it had felt to share that space with Cruz last night. And how seductive.

Just then a sound made her look up and her heart stopped at the sight of the object of her thoughts standing in the doorway, dressed in a three-piece suit, looking so gorgeous it hurt.

He came in and Trinity still felt a little raw, unprepared to see him. It made her voice stiff. 'Thank you for watching the boys last night.'

Cruz poured himself a cup of coffee and took a seat opposite her. He shook his head minutely. 'Like I said, I'm going to be in their lives in a meaningful way.'

Feeling absurdly shy, she said, 'Mrs Jordan told me you changed them.'

Cruz's eyes gleamed with wry humour and it took Trinity's breath away. 'I won't ever again underestimate the ability of a two-and-a-half-year-old to create a toxic smell to rival the effluent of a chemical plant. Or the skill it takes to change one of those things.'

Cruz took a sip of his coffee and put down the cup. 'I've arranged for some potential nannies to come later today, for you and Mrs Jordan to interview.'

'Do you really think that's necessary?'

'Yes.' The wry gleam was gone from his eyes now. 'I've been invited to an event at the newly refurbished opera house in Madrid this Friday night, and I have meetings to attend in the afternoon. Barring any unforeseen events, I am asking you to attend the function with me in Madrid. We'll be gone until Saturday. It'll be a good opportunity for the new nanny to start and get used to the boys under Mrs Jordan's supervision.'

Two things were bombarding Trinity at once. Namely he fact that he was *asking* her, even if it was slightly mocking, and that she'd be away for a whole night with Cruz.

'But I've never left the boys for that long before.'

His tone was dry. 'I think they'll survive less than twenty-four hours without you, and with two nannies in attendance. I spoke with Mrs Jordan about it earlier—she's fine.'

Of course she was, thought Trinity churlishly. Mrs Jordan was his number one fan.

'Tell me, Trinity,' Cruz asked silkily, 'is the reason you're reluctant because you fear maintaining the lie that you don't want me? Are you afraid that you won't be able to control your urges if we're alone? I don't think it's out of concern for the boys at all—I think it's much more personal.'

She felt shamed. He was right. She *was* scared—scared of her reactions around this man. Scared of what might happen if he touched her again. Scared to have him see underneath to where her real vulnerabilities lay. Scared of what he would do if he were faced with the ultimate truth of just how deeply Rio had loathed him. Her guts twisted at the thought in a way that told her she was far more invested in this man than she liked to admit.

But as Cruz looked at her, waiting for her response, she knew she couldn't keep running. She could resist him. She had to.

Coolly she ignored what he'd said and replied, 'Friday should be fine. What time do we leave?'

A few days later Trinity risked looking at Cruz from where she sat in the back of the chauffeur-driven limousine that had picked them up at Madrid airport, but he was engrossed in his palm tablet on the other side of the car, seemingly oblivious to her. She'd just had a conversation on her mobile phone with Mrs Jordan, to check on her and the boys and the new nanny, who were all fine.

As if reading her mind, Cruz put down his tablet and looked at her, that golden amber gaze sweeping down her body and taking in the very elegant and classic sheath dress and matching jacket she'd put on that day in a bid to look presentable.

His gaze narrowed on her assessingly, and she had to fight not to squirm self-consciously. 'What is it?'

She was half raising a hand to check her hair when Cruz answered simply, 'You're a good mother to them.'

If there'd been a grudging tone in his voice Trinity would have hated him, but there hadn't. He'd sounded... reluctantly impressed. She desperately tried to ignore the rush of warmth inside her that signified how much she wanted his approval.

'I love them, Cruz, even though they're not mine.' Impulsively she asked, 'Why is that so hard for you to believe? Is it because of your upbringing?'

He smiled, but it wasn't a nice smile. 'You could say that. Rio wasn't the only one neglected in the *castillo*. Once she'd had me, my mother considered her maternal duty taken care of. She didn't love me, and she didn't love my father either. Their marriage was a purely strategic one, bringing two powerful families together as was the tradition in my family for centuries.'

Cruz's eyeline shifted over Trinity's shoulder just as the car came to a smooth halt on a wide tree-lined street.

'We're here,' he said, leaving Trinity's brain buzzing with what he'd just shared.

She looked out of the window on her side, saw a scrum of men with cameras waiting for them and instantly felt nervous. She'd always hated the way Rio had wanted to court as much media attention as possible.

Cruz said tersely, 'Wait in the car. I'll come round to get you.'

Trinity would have been quite happy if the car had turned around and taken them straight back to the airport.

When Cruz appeared outside the car the scrum had become a sea of flashing lights and shouting. Her door was opened and his hand reached in for her. She took it like a lifeline. He hustled her into the foyer of the gleaming building and within seconds they were in the elevator and ascending with a soft *whoosh*.

It was the hushed silence after the cacophony of sound that registered first, and then Trinity became burningly aware that she was pressed from thigh to breast into Cruz's body. His free arm was around her shoulder and her other hand was still in his, held over his taut belly.

She couldn't be any closer to him if she climbed into his very skin.

She scrambled apart from him, dislodging his arm and taking her hand from his. She couldn't look at him. For a split second before she'd come to her senses she'd loved the sensation of his strength surrounding her, and for someone who'd long ago learnt to depend on herself it was scary how easy it had felt just to…give in.

Thankfully the lift doors opened at that moment, and the sight that greeted Trinity took her breath away. She stepped out into a huge open space dominated on all sides by massive glass windows which showcased the breathtaking view of one of Europe's most beautiful and stately cities.

She walked over to one of the windows and could see a huge cathedral soaring into the blue sky.

'That's the Almudena Cathedral, infamous for taking five hundred years to complete.'

Cruz's voice was far too close, but Trinity fought the urge to move away and instead turned around to take in the penthouse apartment. It was unmistakably a bachelor pad, every inch of every surface gleaming and pristine. But it was also cultured—low tables held massive coffee table books on photography and art. Bookshelves lined one entire interior wall. Huge modern art canvases sat in the centre of the few walls not showcasing the view.

'Let me show you around.'

Trinity followed Cruz as he guided her through a stunning modern kitchen that led into a formal dining room, and then to where a series of rooms off a long corridor revealed themselves to be sumptuous en-suite bedrooms and an office.

When they were back in the main open-plan living and dining area, she felt a little dazed. 'Your apartment is stunning.'

'But not exactly toddler-proof.'

She looked at Cruz, surprised that he'd articulated the

very thing she'd just been thinking in her head: it was beautiful apartment but a potential death trap for small energetic boys.

He glanced at her and she quickly closed her open mouth, looking around again. 'No. Not exactly.'

'I will ensure this place is made child-friendly for when the boys come to visit. I intend on my nephews becoming familiar with their capital city. This is where the seat of the main De Carrillo bank has been since the Middle Ages. This is where their legacy resides, as much as it does in Seville.'

*Their capital city.* It had been said with such effortless arrogance. But the truth was that Cruz was right—he was undoubtedly a titan of this city. Probably owned a huge swathe of it. And the twins would one day inherit all this.

It was mind-boggling to contemplate, and for the first time Trinity felt a sense of fear for the boys and this huge responsibility they'd have one day.

She rounded on Cruz. 'What happens if Matty and Sancho don't want any of this?'

His gaze narrowed on her and something flashed across his face before she could decipher it. Something almost pained.

'Believe me, I will do what's best for my nephews. They will not be forced to take on anything they can't handle or don't want. I won't let that happen to them.'

Trinity's anger deflated. She'd heard the emotion in Cruz's voice. Almost as if he was referring to someone who *had* taken on something they couldn't handle. Was he thinking of Rio and the irresponsible and lavish way he'd lived?

Cruz looked at his watch. 'I have to go to meetings now, but I'll be back to get ready for the function this evening. We'll leave at six p.m.'

Before he left he took something out of his inner pocket. He handed her a black credit card.

She took it warily. 'What is this? A test?'

His face was unreadable, but she wasn't fooled. She knew he'd be assessing her every reaction.

'You'll need access to funds. Do what you want for the afternoon—a driver will be at your disposal downstairs.'

He left then, and for a long minute Trinity found herself wondering if he *had* been talking about Rio not being able to handle things...

Then, disgusted with herself for obsessing like this, she threw the credit card down on a nearby table and paced over to a window. When she looked down to the street far below she could see Cruz disappearing into the back of another sleek Jeep.

It pulled into the flow of traffic and she shivered slightly, as if he could somehow still see her. He was so all-encompassing that it was hard to believe he wasn't omnipresent.

She sighed and leaned forward, placing her hot forehead against the cool glass. It felt as if every time they took a step forward they then took three backwards. Clearly the credit card was some kind of a test, and he expected her to revert to type when given half a chance.

Cruz was standing with his back to the recently emptied boardroom on the top floor of the De Carrillo bank, loosening his tie and opening a top button on his shirt. Madrid was laid out before him, with the lowering sun leaving long shadows over the streets below where people were leaving their offices.

He hated himself for it, but as soon as the last person had left the room he'd pulled out his phone to make a call, too impatient to wait.

'*Where* did she go?' he asked incredulously, his hand dropping from his shirt.

His driver answered. 'She went to the Plaza Mayor, where she had a coffee, and then she spent the afternoon in the Museo Del Prado. She's just returned to the apartment.'

'And she walked,' Cruz repeated flatly, not liking the way the thought of her sightseeing around Madrid on her own made him feel a twinge of conscience. As if he'd neglected her. 'No shopping?'

'No, sir, apart from two cuddly toys in the museum shop.'

Cruz terminated the call. So Trinity hadn't spent the day shopping in Calle de Serrano, home to the most lavish boutiques. He had to admit that the credit card *had* been a test, and a pretty crude one at that. But once again either she was playing a longer game than he'd given her credit for...or he had to acknowledge that she had changed. Fundamentally. And in Cruz's experience of human nature that just wasn't possible.

Cruz didn't deal in unknowns. It was one of the driving motives behind his marrying Trinity—to make sure she was kept very much within his sphere of *knowns*.

Suddenly he wasn't so sure of anything any more.

But *how* could he trust her over his own brother?

He could still see the humiliation on Rio's face when he'd had to explain to Cruz that that his own wife had tipped him over the edge. Cruz knew that Rio's lavish lifestyle and his first wife had undoubtedly started the process of his ultimate destruction, but Trinity had finished it off. And, worse, used his nephews to gain privileged access.

But then he thought of her, standing between him and his nephews the other night, so adamant that they came first. And he thought of how he'd found her, curled up asleep in the chair… He shook his head angrily and turned away from the window. *Merda*, she was messing with his head.

Cruz blocked out the niggles of his conscience. He would be the biggest fool on earth if he was to believe in this newly minted Trinity De Carrillo without further evidence. She was playing a game—she had to be. It was that simple. And he had no choice but to go along with it for now…

Because eventually she would reveal her true self, and when she did Cruz would be waiting.

# CHAPTER SEVEN

A COUPLE OF hours later Cruz's mind was no less tangled. The woman beside him was drawing every single eye in the extravagantly designed and decorated open-air court-yard of the new opera house. When he'd arrived back at the apartment she'd been in her room getting ready, so he'd been showered and changed before he'd seen her, waiting for him in the living area of the apartment.

The shock of that first glimpse of her still ran through his system, constricting his breath and pumping blood to tender places. She wore a strapless black dress that was moulded to every curve. Over one shoulder was a sliver of chiffon tied in a bow.

She wore no jewellery apart from the engagement ring and her wedding band. Her nails were unpainted. Minimal make-up. And yet people couldn't stop looking at her. *He* couldn't stop looking at her.

Very uncharacteristically, Cruz wanted to snarl at them all to look at their own partners. But he couldn't, because he could see what they saw—a glowing diamond amidst the dross. She appealed to this jaded crowd because she had an unfashionable air of wonder about her as she looked around, which only reinforced the shadow of doubt in his mind...

Just then her arm tightened in his and he looked down to see a flush on her cheeks. She was biting her lip. Irritated at the effect she had on him, he said more curtly than he'd intended, 'What is it?'

She sounded hesitant. 'I shouldn't have put my hair up like this. I look ridiculous.'

Cruz looked at her hair, which was in a sleek high ponytail. He didn't consider himself an expert on women's hair-styles, but he could see that the other women had more complicated things going on. Another reason why Trinity stood out so effortlessly. She looked unfussy—simple and yet sexy as sin all at once.

'Someone left a fashion magazine on the table in the café earlier and I saw pictures of models with their hair up like this. I thought it was a thing…'

The shadow of doubt loomed larger. He thought of how she'd shrunk back from the paparazzi earlier. She certainly hadn't been flaunting herself, looking for attention. Anything but. She'd clung to him as if terrified.

He took her arm above the elbow and she looked up at him. He could see the uncertainty and embarrassment in her eyes. It was getting harder and harder to see her as the cold-hearted mercenary gold-digger who had willingly fleeced his brother.

His voice was gruff. 'Your hair is absolutely fine. They're looking because you're the most beautiful woman here.'

Trinity was disorientated by Cruz's compliment. He'd barely said two words to her since he'd got back to the apartment and they'd left to go out again, and he'd just looked at her suspiciously when he'd asked her what she'd done for the afternoon.

Cruz was staring at her now, in a way that made her heart thump unevenly. But then a low, melodic gong sounded, breaking the weird moment.

He looked away from her and up. 'It's time for the banquet.'

Breathing a sigh of relief at being released from that intensity, and not really sure what it meant, she followed Cruz into a huge ballroom that had the longest dining table she'd ever seen in her life. Opulent flowers overflowed from vases and twined all along the table in artful disarray. A thousand candles flickered, and low lights glinted off the solid gold cutlery. She sighed in pure wonder at the scene—it was like a movie set.

And then she spotted Lexie Anderson, the famous actress, and her gorgeous husband, Cesar Da Silva, and felt as if she'd really been transported into a movie. The stunning petite blonde and her tall husband were completely engrossed in each other, and it made something poignant ache inside her.

'Trinity?'

She blushed, hating it that Cruz might have caught her staring at the other couple, and sat down in the chair he was holding out for her.

When she was seated, Trinity saw Cruz walking away and she whispered after him. 'Wait, where are you going?'

He stopped. 'I've been seated opposite you—beside the president of the Spanish Central Bank.'

'Oh, okay.' Trinity feigned nonchalance, even though she was taking in the vast size of the table and realising he might as well be sitting in another room.

Of course he couldn't resist the opportunity to mock her. He came back and bent down, saying close to her ear, 'Don't tell me you'll miss me, *querida*?'

'Don't be ridiculous,' she snapped, angry that she'd shown how gauche she was. She turned away, but hated it that her stomach lurched at the thought of being left alone to fend for herself in an environment where she'd never felt comfortable.

She couldn't take her eyes off him as he walked around to the other side of the table, being stopped and adored by several people on his way. One of them was Cesar Da Silva, who got up to shake Cruz's hand, and the two tall and ridiculously handsome men drew lots of lingering looks. He even bent down to kiss Lexie Anderson on both cheeks, and it caused a funny twisting sensation in Trinity's stomach, seeing him bestow affection so easily on anyone but her.

No, what he'd bestow on *her* was much darker and full of anger and mistrust.

Determined not to be intimidated, Trinity tried talking to the person on her left, but he couldn't speak English and she had no Spanish so that went nowhere. She had more luck with an attractive older gentleman on her right, who turned out to be a diplomat and did speak English, and who put her at ease as only a diplomat could.

Finally she felt herself relax for the first time in weeks, chuckling at her companion's funny stories of various diplomatic disasters. With Cruz on the other side of the very large and lavishly decorated table she relished a reprieve from the constant tension she felt around him, even if she fancied she could feel his golden gaze boring into her through the elaborate foliage. She resisted the urge to look in his direction. She'd already given far too much away.

After the coffee cups had been cleared away her dinner partner's attention was taken by the person on his other side. Trinity risked a look across the table and saw that Cruz's seat was empty. And then she spotted him—because it would be impossible to miss him. He was walking towards her with that lean animal grace, eyes narrowed on her, this time oblivious to people's attempts to get his attention.

The tension was back instantly. Making her feel tingly and alive as much as wary. When he reached her he didn't even have to touch her for a shiver to run through her body.

'Cold?' The tone of his voice was innocuous, but the expression on his face was hard.

Trinity shook her head, feeling a sense of vertigo as she looked up, even though she was sitting down. 'No, not cold.'

'Enjoying yourself?'

Now his words had definite bite in them, and she saw his eyeline shift over her head. 'Nice to see you, Lopez,' he drawled. 'Thank you for keeping my wife amused.'

The man's smoothly cultured voice floated over Trinity's shoulder.

'The pleasure was all mine, De Carrillo. Trinity is a charming, beautiful woman. A breath of fresh air.'

Trinity watched, fascinated, as Cruz's face darkened and a muscle ticked in his jaw. 'Then I'm sorry that I must deprive you of her presence. I believe the dancing has started.'

She barely had time to get a word out to say goodbye to the other man before Cruz was all but hauling her out of her chair and onto the dance floor, where a band was playing slow, sexy jazz songs. His arm was like steel around her back and her other hand was clasped in his, high against his chest.

He moved around the floor with such effortless expertise that Trinity didn't have time to worry about her two left feet. To her horror, though, she felt absurdly vulnerable, reminded of how lonely she'd felt during the day even while she'd appreciated the beautiful majesty of Madrid.

She'd missed Matty and Sancho and she'd felt a very rare surge of self-pity, wondering if this would be her life now—forever on the periphery of Cruz's antipathy.

It was a long time since she'd indulged in such a weak emotion and it made her voice sharp. 'What do you think you're doing?'

Cruz's mouth was a thin line. 'I'm not sure. Maybe you want to tell me? Sebastian Lopez is a millionaire and renowned for his penchant for beautiful young women—maybe you knew that and saw an opportunity to seek a more benevolent benefactor?'

Trinity fought to control her breathing and her temper, and hated it that she was so aware of every inch of her body, which seemed to be welded against his.

'Don't be ridiculous,' she hissed. 'He's old enough to be my father and there was nothing remotely flirtatious about our conversation.' She tilted her head back as much as she could so she could look Cruz dead in the eye. 'But do you know what? It was nice to talk to someone who doesn't think I'm one step above a common thief.'

Terrified that Cruz would see emotion she shouldn't be feeling, she managed to pull herself out of his embrace and stalked off the dance floor, apologising as she bumped into another couple. She walked blindly, half expecting a heavy hand on her shoulder at any moment, but of course Cruz wouldn't appreciate that public display of discord.

She made it out to the marbled foyer area, where a few people milled around, and walked out to the entrance. She sucked in a breath to try and steady her heart. Night was enfolding Madrid in a glorious velvet glow but it couldn't soothe her ragged nerves.

It wasn't long before she felt Cruz's presence. The little hairs all over her body seemed to stand up and quiver in his direction. She refused to feel foolish for storming off. He'd insulted her.

He came to stand beside her, but said nothing as his car arrived at the front of the building with a soft sleek purr. Trinity cursed the fact that she hadn't been quicker to call a cab. Cruz held open the back door and she avoided his eye as she got in, not wanting to see the undoubtedly volcanic expression on his face.

As the driver pulled into the light evening traffic Trinity said frigidly, 'You don't have to leave. You should stay. Your brother soon learned that it made more sense to let me leave early.'

\* \* \*

Cruz was in the act of yanking at his bow tie and opening his top button, wanting to feel less constricted. But now his hand stilled and the red haze of anger that had descended over his vision during the course of the evening as he'd watched Trinity talking and laughing with that man finally started to dissipate.

'What did you just say?' he asked.

Trinity was staring straight ahead, her profile perfect. But she was tense—her full lips pursed, jaw rigid.

It slammed into him then—the truth he'd been trying to deny. He was insanely jealous. He'd been jealous since the day she'd walked out of his house and got into Rio's car to go and work for him.

At that moment she looked at him, and he could feel himself tipping over the edge of an abyss. Those huge blue eyes were full of such...*injury.*

Her voice was tight. 'I said that your brother soon learned that I don't fit into those events well. I'm not from that world, and I don't know what to do or say.'

She clamped her mouth shut then, as if she'd said enough already.

Cruz reeled. His impression had been that Rio had taken her everywhere and that she'd loved it and milked it, but something in the tightness of her voice told him she wasn't lying, and that revelation only added to the doubts clamouring for attention in his head.

He tried and failed to block out the fact that when she'd pulled free of his arms on the dance floor and stalked away he'd thought he'd seen the glitter of tears in her eyes.

She turned her head away again and he saw the column of her throat working. His gaze took in an expanse of pale skin, slim shoulders, delicate clavicle, the enticing curve of her breasts under the material of the dress, and heat engulfed him along with something much more nebulous:

an urge to comfort, which was as bewildering as it was impossible to resist.

He reached across and touched Trinity's chin, turning her face towards him again. 'I'm sorry,' he said. 'You didn't deserve that. The truth is that I didn't like seeing you with that man.'

The shock on her face might have insulted Cruz if he hadn't been so distracted by those huge eyes.

Her mouth opened and the tense line of her jaw relaxed slightly. 'I…okay. Apology accepted.'

That simple. Another woman would have made the most of Cruz's uncharacteristic apology.

His thumb moved back and forth across Trinity's jaw, the softness of her delicate skin an enticement to touch and keep touching.

'What are you doing?'

He dragged his gaze up over high cheekbones, perfect bone structure. 'I can't *not* touch you.' The admission seemed to fall out of him before he could stop it.

Trinity put a hand up over his. The car came to a smooth stop. Cruz knew that he had to keep touching her or die. And he assured himself that it had nothing to do with the emotion that had clouded his judgement and his vision as he'd watched her at ease with another man, and everything to do with pure, unadulterated lust.

Trinity was locked into Cruz's eyes and the intensity of his gaze. One minute she'd been hurt and angry, and then he'd apologised…once again demonstrating a level of humility that she just wouldn't have expected from him. And now… Now she was burning up under his explicit look that told her that whatever they'd just been talking about was forgotten, that things had taken a far more carnal turn.

She felt a breeze touch her back. She blinked and looked

around to see the driver standing at the door, waiting for her to get out. They'd arrived back at the apartment building and she hadn't even noticed.

She scrambled out inelegantly, feeling seriously jittery. It was as if some kind of silent communication had passed between them, and she wasn't sure what she'd agreed to.

The journey up to the apartment passed in a blur. The lift doors opened and they stepped into the hushed interior of Cruz's apartment. He threw off his jacket and Trinity's mouth dried as she watched the play of muscles under the thin silk of his shirt.

He glanced back at her over his shoulder. 'I know you don't really drink, but would you like something?'

Trinity was about to refuse, but something in the air made her feel uncharacteristically reckless. She moved forward. 'Okay.'

'What would you like?'

She stopped, her mind a blank. Embarrassment engulfed her—she was no sophisticate.

Cruz looked at her. 'I've got all the spirits. What do you like?'

Trinity shrugged one shoulder. 'I'm not sure...'

He looked at her for a long moment and then turned back to the drinks table, doing something she couldn't see. Then he turned and came towards her with two glasses. One was large and bulbous, filled with what looked like brandy or whisky. The other glass was smaller, with an orange liquid over a couple of ice cubes.

He handed her the second glass. 'Try this—see what you think.'

After a moment's hesitation she reached for the glass and bent her head, taking a sniff. Cruz was waiting for her reaction, so she took a sip of the cool liquid and it slid down her throat, leaving a sweet aftertaste. She wrinkled her nose, because she'd been expecting something tart or strong.

She looked at him. 'It's sweet. I like it—what is it?'

A small smile played around the corner of Cruz's mouth. 'It's Pacharán—a Spanish liqueur from Navarre. Very distinctive. It tastes sweet, but it packs quite the alcoholic punch. Hence the small amount.'

Before he could suck her under and scramble her brain cells with just a look Trinity went and sat down at the end of one couch, bemused by this very fragile cessation in hostilities. Cruz sat too, choosing the end of a couch at right angles to hers. He effortlessly filled the space with his muscled bulk, long legs stretched out, almost touching hers.

Trinity felt unaccountably nervous, and a little bewildered. She was so used to Cruz coming at her with his judgement and mistrust that she wasn't sure how to navigate these waters. He sat forward, hands loose around his glass, drawing her attention to long fingers.

'Tell me something about yourself—like your name. How did you get it?'

She tensed all over. Every instinct within her was screaming to resist this far more dangerous Cruz. 'What are you doing? You're not interested in who I am...you don't have to ask me these things.'

'You were the one,' he pointed out reasonably, 'who said we need to learn to get along.'

And look how that had ended up—with him kissing her and demonstrating just how weak she was. What could she say, though? He was right.

Hating it that she was exposing her agitation, but needing space from his focus on her, Trinity stood up and walked over to one of the windows, holding her glass to her chest like some kind of ineffectual armour.

Looking out at the view, she said as lightly as she could,

'I was called Trinity after the church where I was found abandoned on the steps. The Holy Trinity Church in Islington.'

She heard movement and sensed Cruz coming to stand near her. She could feel his eyes on her.

'Go on,' he said.

Night had descended over Madrid, and the skyline was lit up spectacularly against the inky blackness.

'They think I was just a few hours old, but they can't be sure, and it wasn't long after midnight, so they nominated that date as my birthday. I was wrapped in a blanket. The priest found me.'

'What happened then?'

Trinity swallowed. 'The authorities waited as long as they could for my biological parent, or parents, to come and claim me. By the time I was a toddler I was in foster care, and there was still no sign of anyone claiming me, so they put me forward for adoption.'

'But your file said you grew up in foster homes.'

Trinity was still astounded that he'd looked into her past. She glanced at him, but looked away again quickly. 'I did grow up in foster homes. But I was adopted for about a year, until the couple's marriage broke up and they decided they didn't want to keep me if they weren't staying together.'

She shouldn't be feeling emotion—not after all these years. But it was still there…the raw, jagged edges of hurt at the knowledge that she'd been abandoned by her own mother and then hadn't even managed to persuade her adoptive parents to keep her.

'Apparently,' she said, as dispassionately as she could, 'I was traumatised, so they decided it might be best not to put me through that experience again. That's how I ended up in the foster home system.'

'Were you moved around much?'

'Not at the start. But when I came into my teens, yes. I was in about six different foster homes before I turned eighteen.'

'Your affinity with Mateo and Sancho… You have no qualification in childcare, and yet you obviously know what to do with small children.'

Trinity felt as if Cruz was peeling back layers of skin. It was almost physically painful to talk about this. 'For some reason the small children in the foster homes used to latch on to me… I felt protective, and I liked mothering them, watching over them…'

But then the inevitable always happened—the babies and toddlers would be taken away to another home, or put up for adoption, and Trinity would be bereft. And yet each time it had happened she'd been helpless to resist the instinct to nurture. Of course, she surmised grimly now, a psychologist would undoubtedly tell her she'd been desperately trying to fulfil the need in herself to be loved and cared for.

And the twins were evidence that she hadn't learned to fill that gap on her own yet.

'Did you ever go looking for your parents?'

Trinity fought to control her emotions. 'Where would I start? It wasn't as if they'd logged their names anywhere. I could have investigated pregnant women on record in the local area, who had never returned to give birth, but to be honest I decided a long time ago that perhaps it was best to just leave it alone.'

The truth was that she didn't think she could survive the inevitable rejection of her parents if she ever found either one of them.

She felt her glass being lifted out of her hands, and looked to see Cruz putting it down on a side table beside his. He turned back and took her hand in his, turning it over, looking at it as if it held some answer he was looking for. The air between them was charged.

'What are you doing?' Trinity asked shakily.

Their eyes met and she desperately wanted to move back, out of Cruz's magnetic orbit, but she couldn't.

'You're an enigma,' he said, meeting her eyes. 'I can't figure you out and it bothers me.'

Feeling even shakier now, she said, 'There's nothing to figure out. What you see is what you get.'

Cruz gripped her hand tighter and pulled her closer, saying gruffly, 'I'm beginning to wonder if that isn't the case.'

It took a second for his words to sink in, and when they did Trinity's belly went into freefall. Was he…could he really listen to her now? And believe her?

But Cruz didn't seem to be interested in talking. His hand was trailing up her arm now, all the way to where the chiffon was tied at her shoulder.

With slow, sure movements, and not taking his eyes off hers, Cruz undid the bow, letting the material fall down. He caressed her shoulder, moving his hand around to the back of her neck and then up, finding the band in her hair and tugging it free so that her hair fell down around her shoulders.

Trinity was feeling incredibly vulnerable after revealing far more than she'd intended, but Cruz was looking at her and touching her as if he was burning up inside, just as she was, making her forget everything. Almost.

She couldn't let him expose her even more…

It was the hardest thing in the world, but she caught his hand, pulling it away. 'We shouldn't do this…'

He turned her hand in his, so he was holding it again, pulling her even closer so she could feel every inch of her body against his much harder one.

'Oh, yes, we should, *querida*. It's inevitable. The truth is that it's been inevitable since we first kissed.'

Cruz wrapped both hands around her upper arms. Trinity's world was reduced down to the beats of her heart and the heat prickling all over her skin. Surely his mention of that cataclysmic night should be breaking them out of this spell? But it wasn't…

A dangerous lassitude seeped into her blood, draining her will to resist. Cruz bent his head close to hers, his breath feathering over her mouth.

'Tell me you want this, Trinity. At least this is true between us—you can't deny it.'

She was in a very dangerous place—feeling exposed after her confession and the tantalising suggestion that Cruz might be prepared to admit that he was wrong about her… All her defences were snapping and falling to pieces.

As if sensing her inner vacillation, Cruz touched her bare shoulder with his mouth and moved up to where her neck met her shoulder. He whispered against her skin. 'Tell me…'

Unable to stop herself, she heard the words falling out of her mouth. 'I want you…'

He pulled back, a fierce expression on his face. Triumph. It made her dizzy. She didn't even have time to think of the repercussions before Cruz's mouth was on hers and suddenly everything was slotting into place. She didn't have to think…she only had to feel. It was heady, and too seductive to resist.

The intimacy of his tongue stroking roughly along hers made blood pool between her legs, hot and urgent. Pulsing in time with her heart.

Time slowed down as Cruz stole her very soul right out from inside her. A fire was taking root and incinerating everything in its path.

His hands landed on her waist, hauling her right into him, where she could feel the solid thrust of his arousal just above the juncture of her legs. Any warning bells were lost in the rush of blood as her own hands went to Cruz's wide chest and then higher, until she was arching into him and winding her arms around his neck.

When his mouth left hers she gasped for air, light-headed, shivering as he transferred his attention to her neck, tugging at her skin gently with his teeth before soothing with his tongue.

Air touched her back as the zip of her dress was lowered. The bodice loosened around her breasts and she finally managed to open her eyes. Cruz's short hair was dishevelled, his eyes burning, as he pulled the top of her dress down, exposing her bare breasts to his gaze. The cut of the dress hadn't allowed for a bra.

'So beautiful,' he said thickly, bringing a hand up to cup the weight of one breast in his palm.

Trinity felt drunk...dazed. She looked down and saw her own pale flesh surrounded by his much darker hand. Her nipple jutted out, hard and stark, as if begging for his touch. When he brushed it with his thumb she let out a low moan and her head fell back.

Her arms were weakening around his neck and her legs were shaking. There was so much sensation on top of sensation. It was almost painful. And then suddenly the ground beneath her feet disappeared altogether and she gasped when she realised that Cruz had picked her up and was now laying her down on the nearby couch.

Her dress was gaping open and she felt disorientated yet hyper-alert. Cruz came down on his knees beside her supine body and pulled her dress all the way down to her waist, baring her completely.

She couldn't suck in enough air, and when he lowered that dark golden head and surrounded the taut peak of her breast with sucking heat her back arched and she gasped out loud, funnelling her hands through his hair...

She ignored the part of her whispering to stop this

*now*…she couldn't stop. She wasn't strong enough. She'd never felt so wanted and connected as she did right in that moment, and for Trinity that was where her darkest weakness lay. Still…

Cruz was drowning…in the sweetest, softest skin he'd ever felt or tasted in his life. The blood thundering through his veins and arteries made what he'd felt for any other woman a total mockery. It was as if he'd been existing in limbo and now he was alive again.

One hand was filled with the flesh of Trinity's breast, the hard nipple stabbing his palm, and he tugged the sharp point of her other breast into his mouth, his tongue laving the hard flesh, making it even harder. She tasted of sweet musky female and roses, and she felt like silk.

He wasn't even aware of her fingers clawing into his head so painfully. He was only aware of this pure decadent heaven, and the way she was arching her body at him so needily.

He finally let go of the fleshy mound of her breast and found her dress, pulling it up over her legs. He needed to feel her now, feel how ready for him she was. He wanted to taste her… His erection hardened even more at that thought.

He found her heat, palpable through the thin silk of her panties, and lifted his head, feeling animalistic at way she throbbed so hotly into his palm.

Trinity stopped moving. Her eyes opened and Cruz wanted to groan when he saw how sensually slumberous she looked, golden hair spread around her, breasts moving up and down, nipples moist from his touch. Mouth swollen from his kisses.

Giving in to his base needs, he moved down, pulling her dress up higher. Her panties were white and lacy and he pulled them off, heedless of the ripping sound, dropping them to the floor.

'Cruz...what are you doing...?'

She sounded breathless, rough. Needy. And there was some other quality to her voice that Cruz didn't want to investigate. Something like uncertainty.

'I need to taste you, *querida*.'

Her eyes widened. 'Taste me...? You mean like...?'

Cruz touched her with his finger, sliding it between soft silken folds. She gasped and tried to put her hand down, but he caught it and stopped her. He explored the hot damp seam of her body, pressing into the fevered channel of her body and exerting pressure against her clitoris.

He took his finger away, even though he wanted to thrust it all the way inside, and brought it to his mouth, taking the wet tip into his mouth. His eyes closed...his erection jumped. For the first time since he was a teenager Cruz was afraid he'd spill before he even got inside her.

The taste of her musky heat on his tongue...

He opened his eyes and she was looking at him, shocked. Two spots of red in her cheeks. A thought drifted across the heat haze in his brain... Why was she looking so shocked? Surely she'd...? But he batted the thought away, not wanting images of what she'd done with previous lovers—*his brother*—to intrude.

There would only be one lover now. Him. She was here and she was *his*.

He said in a rough voice, 'I need to taste you...like that.'

She said nothing. He saw her bite her lip. She looked feverish, and then she gave an almost imperceptible nod. Cruz pushed her legs apart, exposing the blonde curls covering her slick pink folds...slick for him.

There was none of his usual finesse when he touched her. He licked her, sucked and tasted, until he was dizzy and drunk. He thrust two fingers inside her heat, moving them in and out. He felt her hips jerk, her back arch. Heard soft moans and gasps, felt hands in his hair.

Her thighs drew up beside his head and her whole body tensed like a taut bow, just seconds before powerful muscles clamped down tight on his fingers and her body shuddered against his mouth.

She was *his*.

# CHAPTER EIGHT

TRINITY WAS BARELY CONSCIOUS, floating on an ocean of such satisfaction that she wondered if she might be dead. Surely this wasn't even possible? This much pleasure? For her body to feel so weighted down and yet light as a feather? She could feel the minor contractions of her deepest muscles, still pulsing like little quivering heartbeats...

She finally came back to some level of consciousness when she felt a soft surface under her back and opened her eyes. She was on a bed, and Cruz was standing before her, pulling off his shirt and putting his hands on his trousers, undoing them, taking them down.

She saw the way his erection tented his underwear, and watched with avid fascination as he pulled that off too, exposing the thick stiff column of flesh, moisture beading at the tip.

'If you keep looking at me like that—' He broke off with a curse and bent down, hands on the sides of her dress, tugging it free of her body.

Trinity was naked now, and yet she felt no sense of self-consciousness. She was so wrapped in lingering pleasure and so caught up in this bubble of sensuality that she ignored the persistent but faint knocking of something trying to get through to her...

Cruz reached beside the bed for a condom and rolled it onto his erection, the latex stretched taut. Incredibly, as he came down onto the bed and moved over her, she felt her flesh quiver back to life. Her pulse picked up again and she no longer felt like floating...she wanted to fly again.

Cruz's hips pushed her legs apart and he took himself in his own hand, touching the head of his sex against hers, teasing her by pushing it in slightly before drawing it out again, her juices making them both slick. She felt as if she should be embarrassed, but she wasn't.

Between her legs she could feel her flesh aching for Cruz, aching for more than his mouth and tongue and fingers…aching for more.

She arched up. 'Please, Cruz…'

Was that ragged voice hers? She didn't have time to wonder, because with one feral growl and a sinuous move of his lean hips he thrust deep inside her. His whole body went taut over hers, and the expression on his face was one of pure masculine appreciation.

But Trinity wasn't seeing that. It had taken only a second for the intense need and pleasure to transform into blinding hot pain. She couldn't breathe, couldn't make sense of what she was feeling, when seconds ago she'd craved for him to do exactly this…

'*Dios,* Trinity…' he breathed. 'You're so tight…'

Cruz started to pull back, and Trinity's muscles protested. She put her hands on his hips and said, as panic mounted through her body along with the pain, 'Get off me! I can't…breathe…'

Cruz stopped moving instantly, shock in his voice. 'I'm hurting you?'

Her eyes were stinging now, as she sobbed while trying to push him off, '*Yes,* it hurts!'

He pulled away and Trinity let out a sound of pain. Cruz reared back, staring at her, and then down at something on the bed between them.

'What the hell—?'

She was starting to shiver in reaction and she looked down. The cover on the bed was cream, but even in the dim light she could see the spots of red—blood.

Her head started to whirl sickeningly as what had just happened sank in and she scrambled to move, almost falling off the bed in her bid to escape. She got to the bathroom and slammed the door behind her.

Cruz paced up and down after pulling on his trousers. There was nothing but ominous silence from the bathroom. His mind was fused with recrimination. He simply could not believe what her tight body and the evidence of blood told him. That she was innocent. That she was a virgin. It was like trying to compute the reality of seeing a unicorn, or a pig flying across the sky.

It simply wasn't possible. But then his conscience blasted him… He'd never been so lost in a haze of lust—he'd thought she was there with him, as ready as he was.

He wanted to go after her, but the sick realisation hit him that he was probably the last person she wanted to see right now. Nevertheless, he went and knocked softly on the door. 'Trinity?'

*Silence.*

Just when Cruz was about to try and open the door she said, 'I'm fine. I just need a minute.'

Cruz's hand clenched into a fist at the way her voice sounded so rough. He took a step back from the door and then he heard the sound of the shower being turned on. His guts curdled. Was she trying to wash him off her?

He'd never been in this situation before. He'd never slept with a virgin before…

And then his mind went on that disbelieving loop again—how was it even possible? She'd been his brother's *wife*!

Cruz sat down on the end of the bed and a grim expression settled over his features as he waited for Trinity to come out of the bathroom and explain what the hell was going on.

Trinity sat on the floor of the shower stall, knees pulled into her chest, arms wrapped around them and her head resting on the wall behind her, eyes closed as the hot water sluiced down over her skin. She couldn't stop shivering, and all she could see was the shock on Cruz's face.

Between her legs it still stung slightly, but the red-hot pain had gone. And yet along with that pain Trinity had felt something else—something on the edges of the pain, promising more—but the shock of realising that Cruz was witnessing her ultimate exposure had eclipsed any desire to keep going.

She opened her eyes and saw nothing but steam. In the heated rush of more pleasure and sensations than she'd ever known, maybe she'd hoped that Cruz wouldn't realise…

But he had. And what she'd experienced before when he'd rejected her was nothing compared to the prospect of how he would look at her now.

When Trinity emerged a short time later, wrapped in a thick towelling robe, Cruz stood up from where he'd been sitting on the end of the bed. He looked as pale as she felt, and something quivered inside her.

His chest was bare, and it was if she hadn't really seen it the first time he'd bared it. She'd been so consumed with desire. It was wide, with defined musculature and dark golden hair covering his pectorals, leading down in a line between an impressive six-pack to arrow under his trousers. A glorious example of a masculine male in his prime.

'Trinity…?'

She looked at his face and saw an expression she'd never seen before—something between contrition and bewilderment.

'I'm sorry,' she said, her voice husky.

Now something more familiar crossed his face—irritation. 'Why the hell didn't you tell me that you were still a virgin?'

She wanted to curl up in a corner, but she stood tall. 'I didn't think you'd notice.'

He frowned. 'How could I not have noticed?'

He seemed to go even paler for a second, as if he was remembering what it had been like to breach that secret and intimate defence. And that only made Trinity remember it too—the pain and then that other tantalising promise of pleasure...hovering on the edges. How amazing it had felt up to that point. How lost she'd been, dizzy with need and lust. Forgetting everything. Forgetting that she needed to protect herself from this...

She went to move past him. 'I don't really want to talk about this now.'

He caught her arm as she was passing. 'Wait just a second—'

'Look, I *really* don't want to talk about this right now.' She felt flayed all over, and way too vulnerable.

Cruz's hand tightened on her arm. 'I deserve an explanation. *Dios*, Trinity, I *hurt* you. And you were married to my brother—how the hell are you still a virgin?'

Her heart slammed against her ribs. This was it. The moment when Cruz would *have* to listen to her. Because of the irrefutable physical humiliation she'd just handed him on a plate.

She turned to face him and looked up. Her voice was husky with emotion. 'I've been trying to explain to you all along that it wasn't a real marriage, Cruz, but you didn't want to hear it. It was a marriage of convenience.'

There was silence for a long moment. The lines of Cruz's face were incredibly stark and grim. He said, 'I'm listening now.'

Trinity's legs felt wobbly and she sat down on the edge of the bed, seeing the stain of her innocence on the sheets in her peripheral vision.

Her cheeks burning, she gestured with her hand. 'I should do something with the sheet—the stain—'

'Can wait,' Cruz said with steel in his tone. 'Talk, Trinity, you owe me an explanation.'

Anger surged up, because if he'd been prepared to listen to her weeks ago they could have avoided this scene, but it dissipated under his stern look. In truth, how hard had she really tried to talk to him? Had she been happy just to let him think the worst so she could avoid him seeing how pathetic she really was? Contriving to make a home out of a fake marriage with children who weren't even her own?

'Okay,' Cruz said, when the words still wouldn't come. 'Why don't we start with this: why did you go to work for Rio? I hadn't fired you.'

She looked up at him. 'How could I have stayed working for you after what had happened? I was embarrassed.' Realising that she'd reached peak humiliation, she said bitterly, 'I had a crush on you, Cruz. I was the worst kind of cliché. A lowly maid lusting after her gorgeous and unattainable boss. When you rejected me that night—'

'I told you,' he interrupted. 'I did not reject you. I hated myself for crossing a line and taking advantage of you.'

Trinity stood up, incensed. 'You asked me if I regularly walked around the house in my nightclothes, as if I'd done it on purpose!'

A dull flush scored along Cruz's cheekbones. 'I didn't handle the situation well. I was angry... But it was with myself. Not you—no matter how it sounded.'

Refusing to be mollified, Trinity said, 'The following night you gave me that look as you greeted the beautiful brunette... You were sending me a message not to get any ideas. Not to forget that what had happened was a huge mistake.'

Cruz ran his hands through his hair impatiently, all his

muscles taut. 'I don't even remember who that was. All I could see was you and that hurt look on your face.'

Trinity's cheeks burned even hotter. She'd been so obvious.

She continued, 'At one point during the evening I went outside. Rio was there, smoking a cigarette. He saw that I was upset and he asked me why…so I told him. He seemed nice. Kind. And then…then he told me that he was looking for a new nanny. He asked me if I'd be interested… and I said yes. I couldn't imagine staying in your house knowing that every time you looked at me it would be with pity and regret.'

Cruz's eyes burned. 'And yet after six months you were his wife?'

Trinity sat down again on the bed. 'Yes.'

Cruz was pacing back and forth now, sleek muscles moving sinuously under olive skin. Distracting.

He stopped. 'So do you want to tell me how you went from nanny to convenient wife?'

She'd wanted this moment to come, hadn't she? And yet she felt reluctant. Because she knew she'd be revealing something of Rio to Cruz that would tarnish him in his eyes, and even after everything she was loath to do that.

But she didn't have a choice now.

She took a breath. 'I'd gone out to the cinema one night. Rio had assured me he had no plans and that he'd be home all evening. When I got back the twins were awake in their room and hysterical. Their nappies were soaking and I don't think they'd been fed. It took me a couple of hours to calm them down, feed them and put them down again. Frankly, it terrified me that they'd been in that state. I went downstairs and found Rio passed out over his desk, drunk. I managed to wake him up and get some coffee into him… but it was clear then that he was in no fit shape to be left alone with his sons—ever.'

Cruz looked shocked. 'I know Rio liked to indulge, but I never would have thought he'd do it while looking after his sons.'

Trinity sucked in a breath. 'I threatened to tell the police…even call you…but Rio begged me not to. He said it was a one-off. I told him I couldn't stand by and let him neglect his children and he begged me to listen to him before I did anything. He told me what had happened to him as a child. He told me he wasn't a perfect father but that he didn't want his boys to be taken into care.'

Trinity looked at Cruz.

'He knew about my past…where I'd come from. I'd told him not long after I started working for him.' Her mouth compressed at the memory of her naivety. 'He seemed to have an ability to unearth people's secrets. And he used that to make me feel guilty for even suggesting that I'd report him. That I would risk subjecting his sons to the same experience I'd had.'

Cruz interjected. 'I would never have let that happen.'

'You were on the other side of the world,' Trinity pointed out. 'And Rio didn't want me to tell you what had happened. I knew you weren't close, so how could I go behind his back?'

She stood up, feeling agitated. Pacing back and forth, aware of Cruz's preternatural stillness.

'But then suddenly he was offering me a solution—to marry him. It was crazy, ridiculous, but somehow he made it seem…logical.'

She stopped and faced Cruz.

'He promised that it would be strictly in name only. He told me he'd hire a nanny to help. He said he wanted to appear more settled, to prove to people that he wasn't just a useless playboy. He said that in return for taking care of the boys and going to some social functions with him I could name my price. Whatever I wanted…'

Something gleamed in Cruz's eyes. 'What was it, Trinity? What did you want?'

She hated it that even now Cruz seemed to be waiting for her to expose herself. She lifted her chin. 'I told him I'd always wanted to go to college. To get a degree. And so he promised to fund my course once the boys were a little older and in a more settled routine.'

Cruz looked at her for a long moment and then shook his head. 'I don't get it. Even with the promise of fulfilling your college dream, why would you agree to a marriage like that unless you were going to get a lot more out of it? Evidently you didn't sleep with Rio, but did you want to? Did you plan on seducing him? Making the marriage real?'

Disappointment vied with anger. 'You will never believe me, will you? Even when you have to admit that I'm not a gold-digger, your cynicism just won't let you...'

She went to walk out of the room, but Cruz caught her arm. She stopped and gritted her jaw against the reaction in her body.

Cruz pulled her around to face him, but before he could say anything, she inserted defensively, 'Of course I wasn't planning on seducing Rio. I had no interest in him like that, and he had no interest in me.'

She looked down for a moment, her damp hair slipping over one shoulder, but Cruz caught her chin between his thumb and forefinger, tipping it back up. Not letting her escape. There was something different in his eyes now—something that made her heart flip-flop.

He just said, '*Why*, Trinity?'

She felt as if he could see right down into the deepest part of her, where she had nothing left to hide.

She pulled her chin away from his hand and said, 'I felt a sense of affinity with him...with the fact that in spite of our differences we had a lot in common.' Her voice turne~ husky. 'But the largest part of why I agreed was becaus~

come to love Matty and Sancho. They needed me.' Afraid that the next thing she'd see on Cruz's face would be pity, Trinity said, 'I'm well aware that my motivations had a lot to do with my own experiences, but I'm not afraid to admit that. They had no one else to look out for them, and I believed I was doing the right thing by them.'

She tried to pull her arm free of Cruz's grip but it only tightened.

She glared at him, hating him for making her reveal so much. 'Just let me go, Cruz. Now you know everything… and I know that after what just happened you won't want a repeat performance…so can we just put it behind us? *Please?*'

He frowned. 'Won't want a repeat performance?'

He pulled her closer. Her breath hitched and her heart started pounding.

'I hurt you, Trinity. If I'd known it was your first time I would have been much more gentle.'

She looked away, humiliation curdling her insides. 'You really don't have to pity me, Cruz. You came to your senses after kissing me that first time. I was unsuitable before and now I'm *really* unsuitable.'

Trinity had managed to pull her arm free and take a couple of steps towards the door when Cruz acted on blind instinct and grabbed her waist and hauled her back, trapping her against him with his arms around her body.

He was reeling from everything that had just transpired—the sheer fact of Trinity's physical innocence was like a bomb whose aftershocks were still being felt. He didn't like to admit it, but the knowledge that her marriage to Rio hadn't been real… It eclipsed everything else at that moment, making a ragged and torn part of him feel whole again.

Trinity put her hands on his arms and tried to push,

but he wouldn't let her go. *Not now. Not ever*, whispered a voice. Base desires were overwhelming his need to analyse everything she'd just said. *Later*. When his brain had cleared.

She said in a frigid voice, 'Let me go, Cruz.'

He turned her so she was facing him. Her face was flushed, eyes huge. He felt feral as he said, 'Believe me when I say that the last thing I feel for you is pity, Trinity. Or that you're unsuitable. And you're wrong, you know...'

'Wrong about what?' She sounded shaky.

Looking down at her now, some of the cravening need Cruz was feeling dissipated as his chest tightened with an emotion he'd never expected, nor welcomed. But this woman evoked it effortlessly, especially after the shattering revelations of her innocence, and in more ways than one.

He shook his head, honesty compelling him to say, 'I haven't come to my senses since that night. You've bewitched me, Trinity.'

'What do you mean?'

Cruz knew that he'd never before willingly stepped into a moment of emotional intimacy like this. No other woman had ever come close enough to precipitate it. After everything that had just happened he felt exposed and raw, in a way that should have been making him feel seriously claustrophobic, but what he *was* feeling was...a kind of liberation.

'What I mean is that I haven't looked at another woman since that night.' His voice turned rough as he admitted, 'I haven't *wanted* another woman since I touched you.'

Her eyes widened. Her mouth closed and then opened again. Finally she said, 'You're not just saying this?'

Her vulnerability was laid bare, and Cruz wondered bleakly how he'd blocked it out before now.

*Because he'd wanted to. Because it had been easier to believe the worst rather than let himself think for a second that she could possibly be as pure as he'd believed from the start. Because then he'd have had to acknowledge how she made him feel.*

He shook his head. 'No, I'm not just saying this. You're all I want, Trinity. I hated thinking of you and Rio together... I was jealous of my own brother.'

Trinity felt breathless at Cruz's admission. She could see how hard it was for him to open up like this, even as it soothed a raw hurt inside her. And with that came the heavy knowledge that he was beating himself up now over feeling jealous of Rio—and that was exactly the result Rio had wanted to achieve. To mess with Cruz's head.

Loath to shatter this fragile moment, Trinity pushed that knowledge down deep, like a coward, and said, 'We were never together...not like that.' Feeling absurdly shy, she said, 'No other man has ever made me feel like you did. After...that night... I couldn't stop thinking about you... about how it would have been...'

'If we hadn't stopped?'

She nodded jerkily.

He gathered her closer and a tremor ran through her body. The air shifted around them, tension tightening again. 'We don't have to stop now...'

Trinity couldn't battle the desire rising inside her—not after what he'd just told her. She was already laid bare. Nowhere to hide any more. And she wanted this—wanted to fulfil this fantasy more than she wanted to take her next breath.

She looked up at him and fell into molten amber heat. 'Then don't stop, Cruz. Please.'

He waited for an infinitesimal moment and then lowered his head, touching his firm mouth to her softer one with a kind of reverence that made emotion bloom in her chest. To counteract it, because she wasn't remotely ready to deal with what it meant, she reached up and twined her arms around his neck, pressing closer, telling him with her body what she wanted...

He deepened the kiss, stroking into her mouth with an explicitness that made her groan softly, excitement mounting again. His hands moved around to her front, unknotting her robe. He pushed it apart and spread his hands on her hips, tracing her curves, before she broke away from the kiss, breathing raggedly.

He pulled back and looked at her, before pushing her robe off completely. Without looking away, he opened his trousers and pushed them down, kicking them off. Now they were both naked. Trinity looked down and her eyes widened. That stiff column of flesh jerked under her look, and a sense of very feminine wonder and sensuality filled her at the thought that she could have an effect on him like this.

He took her hand and brought it to his hard flesh, wrapping her fingers around him. Slowly, gently, he guided her, moving her hand up and down... It was heady, the way her skin glided over steely strength...

Cruz felt beads of perspiration pop out on his forehead as Trinity's untutored touch drove him to the edge of any reason he had left. It was a special kind of torture...and before she could reduce him to rubble he took her hand from him and led her to the bed.

He wanted to consume her until she was boneless and pliant and *his*.

When he laid her down on the bed and came down alongside her she reached out a tentative hand and touched his chest.

He sucked in a breath. 'Yes...touch me.'

His eyes devoured her perfect curves, slender and yet lush all at once. An intoxicating mix. Innocent and siren.

*Innocent.*

She laid her hand flat on his pectoral, and then bent her head and put her tongue to the blunt nub of his nipple. Cruz tensed. He'd never even known he was sensitive there. Small teeth nibbled gently at his flesh and his erection grew even harder at the certainty that she would be a quick study…that she would send him to orbit and back all too easily.

A fleeting moment of vulnerability was gone as she explored further and took him in her hand again, moving over his flesh with more confidence.

He groaned and put his hand over hers. She looked at him—suddenly unsure—and it made his chest squeeze. 'If you keep touching me like that I won't last…and I need to.'

'Oh,' she said, a blush staining her cheeks.

Cruz cupped her chin and said roughly, 'Come here.'

She moved up and his arm came around her. He hauled her into him so that she half lay on him, breasts pressed against his side. Her nipples scraped against his chest. Cruz pressed a hot kiss to her mouth, his tongue tangling lazily with hers, revelling in the lush feel of her body against his and the taste of her.

When he could feel her moving against him subtly, he gently pushed her back so that he was looking down at her. Her sheer beauty reached out and grabbed him deep inside, transcending the physical for a moment. Her eyes were wide and her pupils dilated. Her cheeks were flushed and her hair was spread around her head like a golden halo.

She was perfection. And everything she'd told him, if it was true— Cruz shut his mind down. He couldn't go there now.

He explored her body with a thoroughness that made her writhe against him, begging and pleading. But there was no way he wasn't going to make sure she was so ready for him that when they came together there would be no pain. Only pleasure.

He smoothed his hand over her belly, down to where her legs were shut tight. He bent his head again, kissing her deeply, and as he did so he gently pushed them apart and felt her moist heat against his palm.

He cupped her sex, letting her get used to him touching her there, and explored along the seam of her body, releasing her heat, opening her to him with his fingers. He moved his fingers in and out. He could feel her body grow taut, and then he lifted his head to look down at her.

'Come for me, Trinity...'

And as if primed to do his bidding, she did, tipping over the edge with a low, keening cry. He had to exert extreme control to stop himself from spilling at the stunning beauty of her response.

Her hand was gripping his arm, and he could feel her body pulsating around his fingers. He looked at her for a long moment and said, 'If you don't want to go any further now, that's okay.'

Her eyes opened and it seemed to take her a second to focus on him. She shook her head. 'No, I'm okay. Keep going...'

Cruz sent up a prayer of thanks to some god he'd never consulted before. He reached over her to get protection from the drawer. When he was sheathed, he came up on his knees between her legs, pushing them apart, hands huge on her thighs.

Cruz came forward, bracing himself on one hand on the bed beside her, and with his other hand notched the head of his erection against her body, using her arousal to ease his passage into her. He teased her like this until she started panting a little, and arching herself towards him.

Unable to wait a second longer, slowly, inch by inch, he sank into her body, watching her face. She stared up at him, focused, and something inside him turned over even as all he could think about was how perfect it felt to have his body filling hers.

And then, when Cruz was so deep inside her that he could barely breathe, he started to move in and out, with achingly slow precision. She wrapped one of her legs around his waist and he had to clench his jaw as it deepened his penetration.

'I'm okay...' she breathed. 'It feels...good.'

He couldn't hold back. The movements of his body became faster, more urgent. Trinity was biting her lip, her pale skin dewed with perspiration. Cruz reached under her and hitched her hips up towards him, deepening his thrusts even more. Trinity groaned.

'That's it, *querida*, come with me.'

When she shattered this time it was so powerful that he shattered with her, deep inside her, his whole body curving over hers as they rode out the storm together.

Trinity woke slowly from a delicious dream, in which she had arms wrapped tight around her and she was imbued with an incredible sense of acceptance, belonging, safety, home.

*Trust.*

As soon as that little word reverberated in her head, though, she woke up. She was in Cruz's bedroom, amongst tangled sheets, and her whole body was one big pleasurable ache.

And she was alone.

When that registered it *all* came back.

Trinity's sense of euphoria and well-being faded as she recalled telling Cruz *everything*.

*She'd trusted him with her deepest vulnerabilities.*

*Trust.* Trinity went even colder as the magnitude of that

sank in. She'd let Cruz into a space inside her that had been locked up for as long as she could remember.

Trust was not her friend. Trust had got her where she was today. First of all she'd trusted herself to follow her instincts and allow Cruz to kiss her that night. Then she'd trusted Rio, believing his motives for hiring her and marrying her were transparent and benign. Instead he'd manipulated her into becoming a tool of destruction against Cruz.

And now that urge was whispering to her again…to trust Cruz just because he'd made her body weep with more pleasure than she'd ever known could be possible. And because he'd admitted that he hadn't been with another woman since that night in his study. Since he'd kissed her.

Just remembering that now made her chest grow tight all over again. She'd never expected him to say that. What if it had just been a line, though? To get her back into bed? And she, like the fool, had believed him…

Feeling panicky now, at the thought of Cruz suddenly appearing and finding her when she felt so raw, she got out of bed and slipped on a robe. She picked up her severely crumpled dress, her face burning.

There was no sign of him as she went back to her room, and after a quick shower and changing into clean clothes she went into the main part of the apartment. She was very conscious of her body—still tender in private places—and it only made her feel more vulnerable. As if Cruz had branded her.

She knew he wasn't there even before she saw that it was empty and an acute sense of disappointment vied with relief. What had she wanted? To wake up with his arms around her? *Yes*, whispered a voice, and Trinity castigated herself. Men like Cruz didn't indulge in such displays of affection.

Her phone pinged from her bag nearby just then, and Trinity took it out to see a text from Cruz. Instantly her heart skipped a beat. Scowling at herself she read it.

I had an early-morning meeting and some things have come up so I'm going to stay in Madrid for another day/ night. My driver is downstairs and he will take you to the airport where the plane is waiting whenever you are ready. Cruz.

Trinity dithered for a few minutes before writing back.

Okay.

She almost put an automatic *x* in the text, but stopped herself just in time.

A couple of minutes later there was another ping from her phone. She put down the coffee she'd just poured to read the text.

Just okay?

Feeling irritated at the mocking tone she could almost hear, she wrote back.

Okay. Fine.

*Ping.*

How are you feeling this morning?

Trinity's face was burning now. She would bet that Cruz didn't text his other lovers like this. They'd know how to play the game and be cool.

She wrote back.

Totally fine. Same as yesterday.

*Ping.*

Liar.

She responded.

I thought you had meetings to go to?

*Ping.*

I'm in one. It's boring.

Trinity was smiling before she stopped herself and wrote back.

Okay, if you must know I'm a little tender, but it feels nice.

She sent it before she had time to change her mind, feeling giddy.

*Ping.*

Good.

Not knowing how to respond to that smug response, Trinity put the phone down and took a deep breath. Her phone pinged again and she jumped.

Cursing Cruz, she picked it up.

We'll talk when I get back to the castillo.

The giddiness Trinity had been feeling dissipated like a burst balloon. She went cold. Of course they would talk. He'd had a chance to process what she'd told him now, and she could imagine that he didn't appreciate her telling him those less than savoury things about Rio.

That wasn't even the half of it. He didn't know the full extent of just how much Rio had despised him.

Trinity wrote back.

Okay.

Cruz didn't respond. She left the coffee untouched and put her arms around herself as the full enormity of what had happened the previous night sank in. She walked to the huge window in the living room and stared out, unseeing.

The prospect of Cruz going over what she'd told him and digging any deeper than he'd already done, finding out the true depth of hatred that Rio had harboured for him, made her go icy all over. She couldn't do that to him.

And that was the scariest revelation of all. The intensity of the emotion swelling in her chest told her she was in deep trouble. The walls she'd erected around herself from a young age to protect herself in uncaring environments were no longer standing—they were dust.

First two small brown-eyed imps had burrowed their way in, stealing her heart, and now—

She put a hand to her chest and sucked in a pained breath. She could no longer claim to hate Cruz for what he'd done in forcing her into this marriage—if she ever truly had.

From the start she'd been infatuated with him, even after what she'd perceived to be his rejection of her. And then she'd seen a side to him that had mocked her for feeling tender towards him. But hadn't he shown her last night that he could be tender? Achingly so.

And, as much as she was scared that he'd just spun her a line about there being no women since he'd kissed her, just to get her into bed, she realised that she *did* trust him. He was too full of integrity to lie about something like that. He didn't need to.

And that left her teetering on the edge of a very scary precipice—although if she was brutally honest with herself she'd fallen over the edge a long time ago. Right about the time when Cruz had insisted on her going to bed so that he could sit up with the twins and she'd found herself yearning to be part of that tableau. *A family...*

She whirled away from the window, suddenly needing to leave and get back to the *castillo*—put some physical space between her and Cruz. One thing was uppermost in her mind—there couldn't be a repeat of last night. She wasn't strong enough to withstand Cruz's singular devastating focus and then survive when he got bored or decided to move on—which he would undoubtedly do.

For the first time, shamefully, Trinity had to admit to feeling unsure of her ability to sacrifice her own desires for the sake of Matty and Sancho. And she hated Cruz for doing this to her. Except...she didn't.

She loved them all and it might just kill her.

# CHAPTER NINE

TRINITY HATED FEELING so nervous. She smoothed her hand down over the linen material of her buttoned shirt-dress. She'd changed after Julia had come to tell her that Cruz was back and wanted to see her.

She hated that she wondered if it was a bad omen that Cruz hadn't come looking for her himself. If not for her, then for the boys, who'd been asking for him constantly.

Cursing her vacillation, she lifted her hand and knocked on his study door, feeling a sense of déjà-vu when she heard him say, 'Come in.'

She went in and saw Cruz was behind the desk. He stood up, his gaze raking her up and down, making her skin tingle. She was conscious of her bare legs. Plain sandals. Hair tied back.

She closed the door behind her.

Cruz gestured to a chair. 'Come in…sit down.'

His voice sounded rough and it impacted on her.

She walked over and took the seat, feeling awkward. Not knowing where to look but unable to look away from those spectacular eyes and that tall, broad body. Remembering how it had felt when he'd surged between her legs, filling her—

Cruz sat down too. 'How are the boys?'

Trinity fought against the blush she could feel spreading across her chest and up into her face. Sometimes she really hated her colouring.

'They're fine… They were asking for you, wondering where you were.'

An expression that was curiously vulnerable flashed

across Cruz's face. 'I'll go and see them later,' he said. 'How are you?' he asked then.

Trinity fought not to squirm. 'I'm fine.'

An altogether more carnal look came across his face now. 'No...soreness?'

Trinity couldn't stop the blush this time. 'No.'

The carnal look faded and suddenly Cruz stood up again, running a hand through his hair. Trinity's gaze drank him in, registering that he must have changed when he got back as he was wearing soft jeans and a polo shirt.

When he didn't say anything for a moment she dragged her gaze up to his face and went still. He looked tortured.

She stood up, immediately concerned. 'What is it?'

He looked at her. 'I owe you an apology...on behalf of me *and* my brother.'

She went very still, almost afraid to say the words. 'You believe me, then...?'

Cruz paced for a moment, and then stopped and faced her again. He looked angry, but she could recognise that it wasn't with her.

'Of course I do.'

She sat down again on the chair behind her, her legs suddenly feeling weak. She waited for a feeling of vindication but it didn't come. She just felt a little numb.

Cruz shook his head. 'After Rio died I took everything his solicitor told me for granted. The truth was that I was in shock...grieving. Based on what he'd told me, I believed you deserved to be the focus of my anger and resentment, so I didn't do what I should have done—which was to investigate his finances with a fine-tooth comb. I've started to do that now,' he said heavily, 'and I had my own legal team haul in his solicitor for questioning yesterday. That's why I stayed behind in Madrid.'

Trinity's throat moved as she swallowed. 'What did you find?'

'Did you know he was a chronic gambler?'

She shook her head, shocked. 'No, of course not… He was away a lot. And worked odd hours. He never really explained himself.'

Cruz was grim. 'He hid it very well. It seems that as soon as he knew what was happening he spent even more money, and he started putting your name on things—like authorising the redecoration of the house, ordering credit cards in your name but using them himself…'

Trinity breathed in, feeling sick. 'So *that* was the trail directly back to me?'

Cruz nodded. 'He made sure you were seen out and about, at fashion shows and events, so if anyone ever questioned him he could point to you and say that you'd been instrumental in his downfall.' Cruz continued, 'You shouldn't feel like he duped you too easily—he did it to countless others along the way. Including me. If I hadn't been so blinkered where Rio was concerned, and had looked into his affairs before now—'

'Then you wouldn't have felt obliged to marry me because you'd have known I wasn't a threat,' Trinity said quickly.

She was avoiding his eye now and Cruz came over.

'Look at me,' he commanded.

After an infinitesimal moment she did, hoping her emotions weren't showing.

'I'm Matty and Sancho's uncle, and I'm going to be in their lives. You are the only mother my nephews have known and I was always going to come back here. Marriage was the best option.'

Trinity felt herself flinch minutely. *Marriage was the best option.* Suddenly feeling exposed under that amber gaze, she stood up and stepped around the chair in a bid to put some space between them. He was too close.

'We haven't finished this conversation,' he said warningly.

Her need to self-protect was huge. 'I think we have. You've said sorry and I accept your apology.'

'There's more, though, isn't there?' he asked now, folding his arms. 'That night—the night of the party at my house—you wanted to tell me something but I shut you down. What was it, exactly?'

Trinity felt panicky and took a step back towards the door. 'It was just my concerns about Rio—he'd been acting irrationally and I was worried, and we'd had that row—' She stopped suddenly and Cruz seized on it.

'You had a row? What about?'

She cursed her mouth and recognised the intractability in Cruz. He wouldn't let this go. He'd physically stopped her leaving before, and if he touched her now...

Reluctantly she said, 'I'd confronted him about being so...erratic. He was spending no time with the boys. He was drinking. And I'm sure he was doing drugs. I threatened to call you and tell you I was worried.'

Rio had sneered at her. *Go on, run to lover boy and cry on his shoulder and you'll see how interested he still is. Cruz doesn't care about you, or me. He only cares about the precious De Carrillo legacy. The legacy that's mine!*

'What did he say?'

Trinity forced herself out of the past. 'He said that if I did anything of the sort he'd divorce me and never let me see Matty or Sancho again, and that he'd ruin any chances for my future employment, not to mention my chances of going to college.'

Cruz said, 'That must have been just after I'd returned to London. I'd asked to meet him—I'd been alerted by our accountants that he was haemorrhaging money. That's when he told me those lies about you and blamed you for pretty much everything. I had no reason not to believe him when there were all those receipts and the evidence of your social lifestyle...'

Trinity felt unaccountably bitter to hear Cruz confirming all this. She was also shocked at one person's ability to be so cruel. Without thinking, she said, 'He used me because he wanted to get back at you. He wanted to make you jealous because he—' She stopped suddenly, eyes fixed guiltily on Cruz.

What was wrong with her? It was as if she physically couldn't keep the truth back.

'Because he *what*?' Cruz asked, eyes narrowed on her flaming face.

She backed away, feeling sick. 'Nothing.'

Cruz was grim as he effortlessly reached for her, caught her by the hands and pulled her back, forcing her back down into the chair and keeping her hands in one of his.

'Tell me, Trinity. I know there's more to it than just the fact that Rio was going off the rails. He'd been going off the rails ever since he got his inheritance and, believe me, I know that's my fault.'

She looked up at him, momentarily distracted. Anger rushed through her because Cruz felt such irrational guilt over someone who didn't deserve it. Especially when that guilt had blinkered him to Rio's true nature and crimes.

She pulled her hands back, resting them on her lap. 'That wasn't your fault, Cruz. I lived with him for a year and a half, so I should know. Rio was selfish and self-absorbed, and all that inheritance did was highlight his flaws.'

Cruz looked at her carefully. 'There's still more.'

She shook her head, desperately wishing he'd drop it. 'No, there's not.'

He grabbed a nearby chair and pulled it over to sit down right in front of her, all but trapping her. Their knees were touching and she was very conscious of her bare legs under the dress. It didn't help when his gaze dropped momentarily to her chest.

He looked up again and arched a brow. She scowled at him. 'You can't force me to talk.'

'You'll talk, Trinity, and if you don't want to talk then we'll find other ways to occupy our time until you do.'

He put a hand on her bare knee, sliding it up her thigh until she slapped her hand down on his. He gripped her thigh and she felt a betraying pulse throb between her legs.

'Your choice. Either way, you're talking.'

She was between a rock and a hard place. If Cruz touched her she'd go up in flames and might not be able to hold back her emotions. But if she told him the truth about Rio, and he realised why she'd been so reluctant to tell him...

But he deserved to know—however hard it was. However much she wished she didn't have to.

She blurted out, 'I don't want to tell you because I don't want to hurt you.'

Cruz looked at her. Trinity couldn't have said anything more shocking. No one had ever said such a thing to him because no one had ever cared about hurting him before. Certainly not a lover, because he was always very careful not to give them that power.

But right now he could feel his insides contracting, as if to ward off a blow. Instinctively he wanted to move back, but he didn't. 'What are you talking about?'

Her eyes were like two blue bruises.

'Rio set me up way before he needed to use me to blame for his money problems.' She felt her face grow hot as she admitted, 'He offered me the job because he saw an opportunity to distract you, to make you jealous. He told me when we had the row that he'd hated you for as long as he could remember, but that he'd managed to make you believe he was grateful for the hand-outs he said you gave him.'

Cruz forced himself to say, 'Go on.'

'His ultimate ambition was to take you over—to use the marriage and his sons as evidence that he was the more stable heir. That he could be trusted. He wanted to see you humiliated, punished for being the legitimate heir. He never got over his resentment of you, Cruz.'

He realised dimly that he should be feeling hurt, exactly as Trinity had said. But it wasn't hurt he was feeling. It was a sense of loss—the loss of something he'd never had. And that realisation was stark and painful.

Trinity was looking at him and he couldn't breathe. He took his hand off her thigh and moved back, standing up. A sense of inarticulate anger rushed up...that awful futility.

Trinity stood too, and she was pale, and it made his anger snap even more. An irrational urge to lash out gripped him. A need to push her back to a safe distance, where it wouldn't feel as if her eyes could see right down to the depths of his very soul.

'You have to admit,' he said now, 'things worked out for you remarkably well, considering. You still managed to elevate yourself from humble maid to nanny to wife. You may have proved your physical innocence, but can I really trust that you weren't the one who saw your opportunity that night when you spoke to Rio? Maybe you followed him into the garden?'

'No!'

She shook her head, and now there was fire in her eyes as well as something far more disturbing. Something that twisted Cruz's guts.

'*No*. I was hurt, and I was naive enough to let him see it...and he took advantage of that.'

All Cruz could see was her. Beautiful. Injured. *His*

*fault.* The desire to push her back faded as quickly as it had come on.

Acting on instinct, he went over to her, chest tight. The desk was behind her—she couldn't move. Cruz took her face in his hands, lifting it up. 'Who are you, Trinity Adams? Is it really possible that you're that wide-eyed naive girl who turned up in my office looking for a chance? Full of zeal and a kind of innocence I've never seen before?'

Cruz's character assessment of her chafed unbearably, and Trinity balled her hands into fists at her sides.

'Yes,' she said, in a low voice throbbing with pain. 'I was that stupidly naive girl who was so starved for a sense of belonging that at the first sign of it she toppled right over the edge.'

She hated it that his proximity was making her melt even as hurt and anger twisted and roiled in her gut.

She took his hands down off her face. 'Just let me go, Cruz… There's nothing more to discuss. There's nothing between us.'

She felt his body go rigid and saw his eyes burn.

'You're wrong. There isn't nothing—there's this.'

His mouth was over hers before she could take another breath and Trinity went up in flames. Panic surged. She couldn't let this happen.

She tore her mouth away. 'Stop, Cruz, this isn't enough.'

'It's more than enough, *querida,* and it's enough for now.'

He started undoing the buttons of her shirt-dress, exposing her breasts in her lacy bra, dragging one cup down and thumbing her nipple. She wanted to tell him to *stop* again, but it was too late. She was tipping over the edge of not caring and into wanting this more. Anything to assuage the ache in her heart.

He lifted her with awesome ease onto the side of his

desk. She heard something fall to the floor and smash, but it was lost in the inferno consuming them. He was yanking open her dress completely now...buttons were popping and landing on the floor.

He captured her mouth again as he pushed the dress off her shoulders and down her arms, pulling her bra down completely so her breasts were upthrust by the wire and exposed. The belt was still around her waist—the only thing keeping her dress attached to her body.

He palmed her breast as he stroked his tongue along hers, thrusting, mimicking a more intimate form of penetration. Trinity groaned into his mouth, instinctively arching her back to push her breast into his palm more fully, gasping when he trapped a hard nipple between his fingers before squeezing tightly.

She blindly felt for his T-shirt, pushing it up until they had to break apart so he could lift it off. He dropped it to the floor and Trinity reached for his jeans, snapping open the top button, aware of the bulge pressing against the zip. Heat flooded her—and urgency.

She was hampered when Cruz bent down and tongued a nipple, his hand going between her legs, spreading her thighs and pushing aside her panties to explore along her cleft. He pulled her forward slightly, so that she was on the edge of the desk, feet just touching the ground.

He slowly thrust one finger in and out, while torturing her breasts with his mouth and tongue. She was throbbing all over, slick and ready. The previous emotional whirlwind was blissfully forgotten in this moment of heated insanity.

'Please, Cruz...'

He looked up, his face stark with need. He undid his jeans and pushed them down and his erection sprang fee. Trinity took it in her hand, the moisture at the tip wetting her palm.

Cruz settled himself between her legs, the head of his

erection sliding against her sex, and it was too much. She was ready to beg when he tipped her back and notched himself into her heat. They both groaned, and he rested his forehead on hers for a moment.

Then he said, 'Wrap your legs around my waist.'

She did, barely aware that her sandals had fallen off. Cruz pulled her panties to one side and with one earth-shattering movement thrust into her, deep enough to steal her breath and her soul for ever.

He put an arm around her and hauled her even closer as he slowly thrust in and out, each glide of his body inside hers driving them higher and higher to the peak. She wrapped one arm around his neck, the other around his waist, struggling to stay rooted.

'Look at me,' he commanded roughly.

She opened her eyes and tipped back her head. The look on his face made a spasm of pure lust rush through her. It was feral. Desperate. Hungry. *Raw.*

Their movements became rougher...something else fell to the floor.

Cruz pushed her back onto the table, lying her flat, and took her hands in one of his, holding them above her head as he kept up the relentless rhythm of their bodies. She dug her heels into his buttocks, biting her lip to stop from screaming as the coil of tension wound so tight she thought she couldn't bear it any longer. But just at that moment he drew her nipple into his mouth, sucking fiercely, and the tension shattered to pieces and Trinity soared free of the bond that had been holding her so tight.

Cruz's body tensed over hers and she felt the hot burst of his release inside her.

Cruz took her to his room in his arms, because her legs were too wobbly to hold her up. She'd buried her face in his shoulder, eyes closed, weakly trying to block out the storm that had just passed but had left her reeling and trembling.

Her head hurt after too many confessions and an overload of pleasure. And too many questions that she didn't want to answer now. Or ever, maybe.

His room was dark and austere. There was a four-poster bed with elaborate drapes. This was very evidently the old part of the *castillo*.

He put her down on the side of his bed and she felt shell-shocked when he disappeared into what she presumed to be the bathroom. She heard the sound of running water and a few minutes later he appeared again and took her into the en-suite.

The bath smelled amazing. Like Cruz. Musky and exotic. He helped her out of her dishevelled clothes and into the hot water. She sank down and looked at him warily. He wore nothing but his jeans, slung low on his hips. She wished she had the nerve to ask him to join her, but she also wanted time to herself, to try and take in everything without him scrambling her brain to pieces.

As if reading her mind, he said, 'I'll be waiting outside,' and walked out, leaving her alone with thoughts she suddenly didn't want to think about.

*Coward.* She wanted to sink down under the water and block everything out, but she couldn't.

She let out a long, shuddering breath. It really was as if a storm had taken place down in Cruz's study, whipping everything up and then incinerating it in the fire that had blown up between them, white-hot and devastating. But a very fragile sense of peace stole over her as she lay there, even as she had to acknowledge that she wasn't sure where she stood now. And wasn't sure if she wanted to find out.

Aware that the water was cooling rapidly, and Cruz was waiting, she washed perfunctorily, stiffening as a jolt of sensation went through her when she touched the tenderness between her legs.

When she finally emerged, in a voluminous towelling robe with the sleeves rolled up her arms, Cruz was standing at the window. He turned around and she could see that he'd changed into dark trousers and a long-sleeved top and his hair was damp. So he'd gone to another room to shower. Because he'd wanted to give her space, or because he couldn't bear to spend more time with her?

Trinity gritted her jaw against the sudden onset of paranoia.

He came forward. 'How are you?'

She nodded. 'I'm okay.'

He was looking at her with a strange expression on his face, as if he'd never seen her before. In spite of the explosive intimacies they'd just shared Trinity felt as if a chasm yawned between them now.

'I'm sorry,' she said impulsively, thinking of the look on his face when she'd revealed the depth of Rio's hatred.

A muscle ticked in Cruz's jaw. 'You're sorry? For what? It's me who should be apologising to you for all but forcing you into this marriage, and for what my brother put you through to get back at me.'

His belief in her innocence didn't make her feel peaceful now—it made her feel sick. If he really believed that she had just been a pawn in Rio's game what future was there for them? Her heart lurched. *None.* Because he had to be regretting this marriage, which had been born out of an erroneous belief that he couldn't trust her and that he needed to protect his nephews.

It was the last question she wanted to ask, but she had to. 'What happens now?'

He smiled, but it was mirthless. 'What happens now? What happens now is that you could be pregnant. We didn't use protection.' He cursed volubly. 'I didn't even think of it.'

Trinity sank down onto the side of the bed nearest to her as her legs gave way. 'Neither did I,' she said faintly. She'd felt it…the hot rush of his release inside her…and she'd conveniently blocked it out.

She stared at Cruz's grim countenance as the significance of this sank in. The full, horrifying significance.

If she was pregnant then he wouldn't be able to disentangle himself from this marriage—and she didn't need to be psychic to intuit that that was exactly what he wanted. He was angry.

'There was two of us there,' she pointed out, feeling sick. 'It wasn't just your oversight.'

His mouth twisted. 'As much as I appreciate your sentiment, I was the one who should have protected you.'

*You.* Not *us.*

Panic galvanised Trinity at the prospect of Cruz resenting her for ever for a moment of weakness.

She calculated swiftly and stood up. 'I'm sure I'm not pregnant. It's a safe time for me. And even if it happened, by some miracle, it doesn't mean anything. We don't have to stay married—we could work something out.'

'That,' Cruz said coolly, fixing his amber gaze on her, 'would never be an option in a million years. If you are pregnant then we stay married.'

'But if I'm not…?'

'Then we will discuss what happens. But for now we wait. I have to go to Madrid again in two weeks. I'll set up an appointment with my doctor and we'll go together. That should be enough time for a pregnancy test to show up positive or negative…'

Feeling numb, Trinity said, 'We could just wait. I'll know for sure in about three weeks.'

Cruz shook his head. 'No, we'll find out as soon as possible.'

Trinity really hated the deeply secret part of her that hoped that she might be pregnant, because that was the only way she knew she'd get to stay in Cruz's life. But if she wasn't... The sense of desolation that swept over her was so acute that she gabbled something incoherent and all but ran out of the room to return to hers.

Cruz didn't come after her, or try to stop her, which told her more eloquently than words ever could how he really felt about her.

Cruz stood in the same spot for a long time, looking at the door. He'd had to let Trinity go, even though it had taken nearly everything he possessed not to grab her back. But he couldn't—not now. Not after the most monumental lapse in control he'd ever experienced.

He started to pace back and forth. He'd fallen on her in his study like a caveman. Wild. Insatiable. Filled with such a maelstrom of emotions that the only way he'd known how to avoid analysing them was to sink inside her and let oblivion sweep them away. But he couldn't avoid it now.

He'd been angry with her for revealing the extent of Rio's antipathy—but hadn't he known all along, really? And she'd just been the reluctant messenger.

He'd felt anger at himself for indulging in that delusion in a bid to forge some meagre connection with his only family. And he'd felt anger that Trinity had been so abused by Rio *and* him. He hadn't deserved her purity and innocence after all he'd put her through, and yet she'd given it to him with a sensuality and abandon that still took his breath away.

He stopped. Went cold. He'd actually had a tiny moment of awareness just before he'd come that there was no protection. But he'd been so far gone by then that to have pulled away from Trinity's clasping heat would have killed him… Cruz knew that there was no other woman on this earth who would have had that effect on him.

The insidious suspicion took root… Had he subconsciously wanted to risk getting her pregnant? Because he was aware that after what she'd told him he could no longer insist they stay married if she was innocent of everything he'd thrown at her?

Cruz sank down heavily on the end of the bed. If that was what had happened then he was an even sicker bastard than Rio.

When he thought of how he'd treated Trinity…how he'd shoved the past down her throat at every opportunity without giving her a chance to defend herself or explain…he deserved for her to walk away without a second glance.

But if she was pregnant then she would stay. And Cruz would be aware every day of his life that he had trapped her for ever.

That moment when she'd said so emotionally, *'I don't want to tell you because I don't want to hurt you,'* came back to him. Its full impact.

The fact that she'd actually been willing to keep it from him—the full extent of Rio's ambition and hatred—made him feel even worse. At best she pitied him. At worst she would come to resent him, just as Rio had, if she was pregnant and had no choice but to stay…

By the time Trinity came down for breakfast with the boys the following morning, feeling hollow and tired, she knew that Cruz was no longer in the *castillo*. And sure enough Julia appeared with a note for her.

*I have to go to Madrid for a couple of days and then New York. I'll return in time for the doctor's appointment. Cruz.*

It couldn't be more obvious that he didn't want to have anything to do with her until they knew if she was pregnant and then he would *deal* with it.

Even Mrs Jordan seemed to sense that something was going on, because she kept shooting Trinity concerned looks. She did her best to project as happy a façade as possible, and suggested that Mrs Jordan take the opportunity to go to Scotland for a few days to see her son, telling her that she'd just need her back for when she would be going to Madrid.

She also, if she was honest, wanted time alone with the boys to lick her wounds.

She filled their days with activities, wearing herself and the boys out so comprehensively that she could sleep. But that didn't stop the dreams, which now featured her running through the *castillo*, going into every room, endlessly searching for Cruz.

And each night before she went to sleep she forced herself to remember what he'd said in London, when she'd asked him about marrying for love: *'I have no time for such emotions or weaknesses...'*

*Two weeks later...*

Trinity was standing on Harley Street, having just come out of the doctor's office, in the bright spring sunshine. Cruz had brought her to London instead of Madrid at the last minute, because there had been something urgent he had to attend to at the UK bank.

She felt raw now, being back here. Where it had all started. And she felt even more raw after her appointment with the doctor...

A sleek car pulled up just then, and stopped. Trinity saw a tall figure uncoil from the driver's seat. *Cruz*. He'd timed his meeting so that he could meet her after the doctor's appointment.

He held the passenger door open for her to get in, saying nothing as she did so, just looking at her carefully. When he was behind the wheel he looked at her again.

Feeling too brittle at that moment, Trinity said, 'I'll tell you when we get to the house.'

They were staying overnight.

A muscle pulsed in Cruz's jaw, but he said nothing and just drove off. Trinity felt a little numb as she watched the streets go by outside, teeming with people engrossed in their daily lives.

When they got to the Holland Park house her sense of déjà-vu was overwhelming. The door closed behind them, echoing in the cavernous hall. Trinity's heart was thumping and she could feel clammy sweat breaking out on her skin. She sensed Cruz behind her, watching her, waiting, and slowly turned around.

She knew she had to say the words. She opened her mouth and prayed to sound cool and in control. Not as if she was breaking apart inside. She looked at him.

'I'm not pregnant, Cruz.'

He said nothing for a long moment. Trinity was expecting to see relaxation in the tense lines of his body. Eventually he said, 'We should talk, then.'

She recoiled at the thought of doing it right now. 'Can we do it later, please? I'm quite tired.'

Cruz nodded once. 'Of course. Whenever you're ready. I'll be in my study.'

'Okay,' Trinity said faintly, and turned to go up the stairs to the bedrooms. Calling herself a coward as she did so. She was just staying the execution. That was all.

# CHAPTER TEN

AFTERNOON PASSED INTO dusk and evening outside Cruz's study, but he was oblivious. Two words echoed in his head: *not pregnant...not pregnant.* He'd felt an unaccountably shocking sense of loss. When he had no right.

Trinity would get pregnant one day, and create the family she'd always wanted. And she deserved that. There was no reason for him not to let her go now. If anything, *he had to.* It was time for him to make reparation.

It had come far too belatedly—the realisation that Rio's deep hatred of Cruz hadn't irreparably damaged his ability to care. That his mother's even deeper cynicism hadn't decimated the tiny seed of hope he'd believed to have been crushed long ago—hope for a different kind of life, one of emotional fulfilment and happiness. One not bound by duty and destiny and a desire to protect himself from emotional vulnerability at all costs.

He'd never wanted more because he'd never really known what that was. Until he'd seen Trinity interact so lovingly and selflessly with his nephews and had found himself sitting up in their room all night, watching them sleep and vowing to slay dragons if he had to, to keep them safe.

The thought of family had always been anathema to him, but now—

He heard a sound and looked up to see his door open. *Trinity.* She'd changed and was wearing soft faded jeans and a long cardigan, which she'd pulled around herself. Her hair was down and a little mussed, and her face was bare of make-up. Her feet were bare too.

For a second Cruz thought he might be hallucinating... even though she wasn't wearing the same clothes as that night… Past and present were meshing painfully right now. Mocking him with the brief illusory fantasy that perhaps there could be such a thing as a second chance.

He stood up as she came in and shut the door behind her.

Her voice was husky. 'I'm sorry. I slept far later than I wanted to.'

On automatic pilot, Cruz asked, 'Are you hungry? Do you want to eat?'

She shook her head and smiled, but it was tight. 'No, thanks—no appetite.'

A bleakness filled Cruz. No doubt she just wanted to sort this out and be gone. Back to the life he'd snatched out of her hands.

'Please, sit down.'

Again, so polite. Trinity came in and sat down. The weight of their history in this room was oppressive. She'd told a white lie about sleeping—she hadn't slept a wink all afternoon, was too churned up. She'd spent most of her time pacing up and down.

After an initial acute sense of loss that she wasn't pregnant she'd felt a sense of resolve fill her. She wasn't going to give up without a fight. She knew Cruz had an innate sense of honour and decency, so even if that was all she had to work with she would.

Cruz sat down. His shirt was open at the top and his shirtsleeves were rolled up.

'You said that part of the deal with Rio was that he would pay for you to do a degree?'

Trinity blinked, taken by surprise that he'd remembered that. 'Yes, he did.'

'Do you still want to do it?'

She felt as if she was in an interview. 'Well, I haven't had much time to think about it lately, but yes…at some point I think I'd like to.'

Cruz nodded. 'I'll make sure you get a chance to do your degree, Trinity, wherever you want to do it.'

'Cruz...' She trailed off, bewildered. 'I presumed we were going to talk about what happens next—not my further education and career options.'

His voice was harsh. 'That is what happens next. You get to get on with your life—the life you would have had if you hadn't had the misfortune to meet me and my brother.'

He stood up then, and walked to the window which overlooked the park. It was still light outside—just.

Trinity stood up too, anger starting to sizzle. 'You do not get to do this, Cruz—blame yourself for what happened. Even Rio can't be apportioned blame either...not really.'

She came around the desk and stood a few feet away from him.

'I was just as much to blame. I shouldn't have been so hurt after what had happened between us that I spilled my guts to Rio with the slightest encouragement. You might not have handled it very well, but you didn't take any liberty I wasn't willing to give. It was the most thrilling moment of my life up to that point.'

Cruz turned around. Trinity saw his gaze drop and widen, and colour darken his cheeks. She didn't have to look down to know that her cardigan had fallen open, revealing her flimsy vest top and braless breasts underneath. She could feel her nipples peak under his gaze, and her heart thumped hard. She couldn't deny that she'd hoped to provoke a reaction from him.

'And there's this, Cruz.' She gestured between them, where tension crackled. 'This hasn't gone away...has it?'

His gaze rose and his jaw clenched. 'It's not about that any more. It's about you getting a divorce and moving on.'

*Divorce.*

Trinity's heart started thumping. She pulled the cardigan around herself again, feeling exposed. 'I told you before that I won't abandon Matty and Sancho—that hasn't changed.'

Cruz's voice was tight. 'The fact that you stepped in and protected and nurtured my nephews went above and beyond the call of duty.'

Trinity felt even more exposed now. 'I told you—I explained why—'

'I know,' Cruz said, and the sudden softness in his voice nearly killed her. 'But they're not really your responsibility. You have a life to live. And I won't be responsible for stopping you. We can work out a custody arrangement. I wouldn't stop you from being in their lives. But they're in good hands now.'

For a second Trinity wondered how she was still standing…how she wasn't in a broken heap at Cruz's feet. Whatever pain she'd experienced in her life didn't come close to the excruciating agony she felt right now.

Yet something dogged deep within her forced her to ask hoarsely, 'Do *you* want a divorce, Cruz?'

His eyes were burning. 'I want you to have your life back, Trinity. And I will support you and your relationship with the boys however you want.'

She folded her arms across her chest and Cruz's gaze dropped again to where the swells of her breasts were pushed up. Something came to life in her blood and belly. The tiniest kernel of *hope*.

'You didn't answer me. Do *you* want a divorce?'

His eyes met hers and she saw something spark deep in their golden depths before it faded. Something cold skated across her skin. A sense of foreboding.

'What I want,' Cruz bit out, 'is for my life to return to where it was before I ever met you.'

Trinity looked at him blankly for a long moment. And then, as his words impacted like physical blows, she sucked in a pained breath. Her fight drained away and her arms dropped heavily to her sides.

She might have fought Cruz if she'd thought there was half a chance. But there wasn't. He wanted her to have her life back. But he wanted his back too. She'd been a fool to think they had a chance. To think that she could persuade him by seducing him...

She whirled around to leave, terrified he'd see how badly he'd hurt her. The door was a blur in her vision as she reached for the knob, just wanting to escape.

She heard a movement behind her and then Cruz said hoarsely, 'Stop. Do not walk out through that door, Trinity.'

Her hand was on the knob. Her throat was tight, her vision blurring. She wouldn't turn around. 'Why?' she asked rawly.

His voice came from much closer. He sounded broken. 'Because I let you go through it once before and it was the worst mistake of my life.'

He put his hands on her shoulders and turned her around. She didn't want him to see the emotion on her face. But this was Cruz, who demanded and took, so he tipped her face up and cursed.

She looked at him and her heart flip-flopped. The stark mask was gone and he was all emotion. Raw emotion. And it awed her—because she realised now how adept he'd been at holding it all back for so long.

He'd been so controlled. But no more.

'I'm sorry,' he said, cupping her face, thumbs wiping at tears she hadn't even realised were falling. 'I didn't mean what I just said. It was cruel and unforgivable. I only said it because in that split second I thought going back to the life I had before I knew you was preferable to the pain of opening up. I thought I was doing the right thing...forcing you out of my life...'

Trinity whispered brokenly, 'I don't want you to force me out of your life.'

Cruz's whole body tensed. 'Do you mean that?'

She nodded, heart thumping. She put her hands on his and repeated her question. 'What do you want, Cruz?'

His eyes glowed with a new light. He said roughly, 'I want you. For ever. Because I know there can never be anyone else for me. I want to stay married to you and I want a chance to show you how sorry I am—for everything.'

Trinity just stared at him. Wondering if she was hallucinating.

He went on. 'I want to create a family with you—the kind of family neither of us had. Nor Rio. Maybe through his sons we can give him that finally. But,' he said, 'if you want a divorce...if you want to walk away...then I won't stop you. As much as I wanted you to be pregnant, I'm happy you aren't because I couldn't have borne knowing that you'd never had a choice... Now you do have a choice.'

Trinity's vision blurred again. 'I choose you, Cruz. I would always choose you.'

'I love you,' Cruz said fervently.

Trinity blinked back her tears and sucked in a shuddering breath. 'I came down here this evening prepared to fight and make you see, and then you said—'

Cruz stopped her mouth with his in a long soulful kiss. When they broke apart they were both breathing heavily, and Trinity realised that her back was against the wall of shelves. Cruz's body was pressed against hers, the unmistakable thrust of his arousal turning her limbs to jelly and her blood into fire. With an intent look on his starkly beautiful face he pushed her cardigan off her shoulders and pulled it off.

Euphoria made Trinity's heart soar. 'What are you doing?'

But Cruz was busy pulling down the straps of her vest top and exposing her breasts to his hungry gaze. Hoarsely he said, 'I'm taking care of unfinished business—if that's all right?'

As he made short work of undoing her jeans and pulling them down excitement mounted, and she said breathily, 'I have no objections.' She kicked her jeans off completely.

Cruz stopped for a moment and looked at her, all teasing and sexy seductiveness gone as the significance of the moment impacted on them. 'I love you.'

Trinity nodded, biting her lip to stave off more emotion. 'I love you too...'

But then their urgency to connect on a deeper level took over again.

Cruz stepped out of his clothes. She reached up and wound her arms around his neck, revelling in the friction of her body against his, and when Cruz picked her up she wrapped her legs tight around his hips and together they finished what they'd started, soaring high enough to finally leave the past behind and start again.

# EPILOGUE

'CAREFUL, BOYS, YOUR little sister is not a doll,' Cruz admonished Matty and Sancho, who were tickling their four-month-old sister where she lay in her pram in the shade. The fact that she was their cousin and not really their sister was something they could wrap their heads around when they were older.

The boys giggled and ran away, chasing each other down the lawn, dark heads gleaming in the sunlight.

Cruz watched them go. They'd grown so much in the two years since he and Trinity had officially adopted them—turning their legal guardianship into something much more permanent and binding.

One day, not long after the adoption had come through, they'd both suddenly started calling him Papa. As if they'd taken a private mutual consultation to do so. The day it had happened he'd looked at Trinity, unable to keep the emotion from filling his eyes and chest. She'd reached out and taken his hand, her eyes welling up too as they'd realised what had just happened.

They were a family.

He shook his head now, marvelling that he couldn't even remember a time before these two small boys existed. He would die for them. It was that simple. It was bittersweet to know that he was finally able to show his love for Rio by protecting and nurturing his nephews like this.

A happy gurgle made Cruz look down again to see his daughter, Olivia—who was already being called Livvy—smiling gummily and waving her arms and legs. She had the bright blue eyes of her mother and a tuft of golden curls on her head, and she had Cruz so wrapped around her tiny finger that he could only grin like a loon and bend down to pick her up.

'Hey,' protested a sleepy voice, 'you're meant to be getting her to sleep.'

Cruz looked to where Trinity was lying in a gently rocking hammock between two trees. Her hair was loose and long around her shoulders and she was wearing short shorts and a halterneck top that showed off her lightly golden skin and luscious curves. An indulgent smile made her mouth curve up, telling Cruz that he was *so* busted where his baby daughter was concerned.

Whatever he felt for his children expanded tenfold every time he looked at this woman, who filled his heart and soul with such profound grace and love he was constantly awed by it.

In spite of their busy lives she was already one year into a three-year degree in business and economics at the University of Seville, and loving it.

The *castillo* was almost unrecognisable too, having undergone a massive renovation and redecoration. Now it was bright and airy, with none of the darkness of its tainted past left behind.

Cruz devoured her with his eyes as he walked over, holding his precious bundle close. Trinity's cheeks flushed as their eyes met and desire zinged between them. Everpresent. Everlasting.

She made room for him on the family-sized hammock and then settled under the arm he put behind her, her hand over Livvy where she was now sleeping on his chest, legs and arms sprawled in happy abandon.

The boys were shouting in the distance—happy sounds. Cruz could hear Mrs Jordan's voice, so he knew they were being watched. He took advantage of the brief respite and tugged Trinity closer into his chest. She looked up at him, her mouth still turned up in a smile that was halfway between innocent and devilishly sexy.

Emotion gripped him, as it so often did now, but instead of avoiding it he dived in. 'Thank you,' he said, with a wealth of meaning in his words.

*Thank you* for giving him back his heart and an emotional satisfaction he would never have known if he hadn't met her and fallen in love.

And even though he didn't say those words he didn't have to, because he could see from the sudden brightness in her eyes that she knew exactly what he meant.

She reached up and touched her lips to his—a chaste kiss, but with a promise of so much more. And she whispered emotionally against his mouth, 'I love you, Cruz. Always.'

'Always,' he whispered back, twining his fingers with hers where they rested over their daughter.

Trinity rested her head in the spot made for her, between his chin and his shoulder, and the future stretched out before them, full of love and endless days just like this one.

\* \* \* \* \*

# THE SPANIARD'S
# PREGNANT BRIDE

**MAISEY YATES**

To everyone who said "You shouldn't" and "You can't" you gave me a reason to prove that I should, and I could.

# CHAPTER ONE

HE WAS DEATH come to take her away. At least, that was what he looked like as he descended the sweeping stairs of the Venetian ballroom, his black cloak billowing behind him, his blunt fingertips brushing the elegant marble banister. Allegra felt it like a touch against her skin, and for the rest of her life she would wonder at the strength of it.

He was masked, like everyone else in attendance, but that was where the similarity between him and anyone else—or indeed, him and any mortal—ended.

He was not wearing the bright silks of many of the men there, rather he was dressed all in black. The mask that covered his face some sort of glittering midnight material, cut into the shape of a skull. His skin must have been painted a deep charcoal beneath it, because she could catch no sight of man or even a trace of humanity in the small spaces between the intricately fashioned metal.

She wasn't the only woman to be struck dumb by his appearance—a ripple ran through the room. Resplendent, silk-wrapped creatures were all quivering in anticipation of a look, a glance. Allegra was no exception. Her identity hidden behind the beautiful painted designs on her face, she allowed herself the indulgence to look at him.

The party, being held in one of the most beautiful and historic hotels in Venice, was hosted by one of her brother's business associates. It was one of the most sought-after invitations in the world, and those attending were the elite.

Italy's oldest, wealthiest families. Old money and new. Eligible heiresses who held whole rooms captive with a saucy glance.

She supposed she was part of them. Her father was old money and new. Nobility with a lineage that could be traced back to the Renaissance. But unlike his father before him, he'd taken that position and spun it into gold. Had taken crumbling, inherited properties and reinvigorated them as his business, pushing him to the height of the social and financial stratosphere.

Her brother, Renzo, had only brought the Valenti family higher, taking her father's company global and increasing their wealth by leaps and bounds.

Still, Allegra didn't feel like she was one of these women. Didn't feel seductive or vibrant. She felt…caged.

But this was supposed to be her chance. Her chance to lose her virginity to a man that she chose, rather than to the prince that she was promised to marry, who did nothing to heat her blood or fire her imagination.

Perhaps such a sin would send Allegra straight to hell. Though, who better to take her there than the devil himself? He was here, after all. And with his entrance into the room he had affected her more deeply, more profoundly, than her arranged fiancé ever had.

She started to take a step toward the staircase, and then stopped. Her heart was pounding so hard she thought she might be sick. Who did she think she was? She was not the kind of woman to approach a strange man at a party.

To approach him and flirt and ask him to—

She had no idea what she'd been thinking.

Allegra turned away from the stranger. She wasn't going to court Death at this party, in all the ways that term applied. Yes, she had the fantasy that she might find someone tonight. Someone she wanted. But when push came to shove, she simply didn't have the courage.

Anyway, her brother had brought her to this party under sufferance, and if she caused any trouble, he would probably burn the place to the ground. Renzo Valenti was not known for his quiet temperament. Allegra, however, had learned to curb hers.

As a child she had been a trial, according to both of her parents. But she had allowed them to teach her. With lessons in deportment and carriage and all other manner of things designed to make her the sort of lady who would make something of herself.

And it had paid off. At least, from the point of view of her parents. Renzo's close friendship with Cristian Acosta—a Spanish duke her brother had been friends with since his years in private school—had made an introduction between her father and Prince Raphael DeSantis of Santa Firenze.

From that introduction, at the urging of *dear* Cristian—who Allegra wanted to dunk into the sea—had come a marriage agreement that saw Allegra promised to a prince. A triumph in her parents' eyes.

She should be ecstatic, so she'd been told.

She had been formally promised to Raphael since she was sixteen years old, and he appealed to her no more now that she was twenty-two than he had at the very first meeting. It was a strange thing. He was a handsome man, that was not up for debate. But in spite of all that handsome, he left her cold.

Unlike her older brother, he kept himself out of the tabloids. The very picture of respectability and masculine grace in suits, and in the more casual wear he favored when her family met with him for holidays in his homes around the world.

Perhaps it was part of her mercurial nature that she had never felt tempted to do more than accept perfunctory kisses on her cheek from him. That she couldn't find it in her to feel passion for him as some sort of rebellion against what she was being commanded to do. Or perhaps, it was him. Perhaps he was simply too...cold.

Was it so much to want someone with a passion that matched her own?

Though, her passion was theoretical. Both for life and for men. It made her want to break free. Made her want to challenge the life that had been set out before her.

No doubt Cristian would tell her she was being selfish. Of course, Cristian had always acted like he held a personal stake in her engagement. Possibly because he'd arranged it.

It made her wonder what else he stood to gain from her marriage. Probably infinite favors from Prince Raphael himself. Which was likely the reason Cristian loomed so large every time he was over for dinner at her parents' house.

Cristian was the only person who ever made her lose her cool. The only person who inspired her to let loose on her control and rage when he made her angry.

With her parents, when push came to shove, she did as she was told.

In reality, her existence was staid. And she felt like she was in a constant struggle against it.

Or at least, she intended to struggle against it. To pull, to give some sort of indication that she was unhappy. She swallowed hard, forcing herself to turn her attention to the rest of the ballroom, to keep herself from looking back at Death again.

Allegra wandered over to the far side of the ballroom, picking up a plate and availing herself of the various delicacies that were spread out before her. If she could not indulge in men, she would indulge in chocolate. If her mother was here, she would remind Allegra that she had a wedding dress she would need to fit into in only a few months, and that eating chocolate was potentially not conducive to that.

And her mother needed everything to be…conducive to something. Needed her children to fit into the proper mold so that they could fulfill their duties and all of that. So that they could build upon what their father had begun and bring honor to their family name, and just a whole lot of things that Allegra found very daunting to take on.

In a fit of rebellion, Allegra grabbed another cream puff. Her mother was not here. Anyway, they employed a very accomplished seamstress. Surely she could do something with the gown should it not fit her more abundant curves.

Renzo wouldn't stop her. Though, he did not oppose her parents pushing her toward this marriage, he only ever seemed amused by her moments of spirit.

But then, Renzo seemed to take his mantle on easily. It was a strange thing. As a man, his life had to bend where work was concerned. He'd had to take over their father's real estate development firm, but nothing else in his life was dictated to.

As for Allegra…she imagined she could have whatever job she wished as long as it left her on hand to devote her personal life to the husband her parents deemed fit.

Perhaps that was why Renzo was so much more indulgent. He saw the disparity in what they were asked to do, who they were asked to be.

Her parents did not. And neither did Cristian, who had enabled her parents in their attempts to marry her off. Additionally, he was always on hand to play the opposing, humorless figure. Though, she knew his life had its share of hardships, and it almost made her feel guilty for finding so much at fault with him. Endless fault, really.

But still, his personal tragedies—and his involvement in her upcoming marriage—didn't give him a right to be so harsh with her.

She blinked, looking back down at her food. She didn't know why she was thinking of him now. Maybe because were he here, he would lift a sardonic brow at her if he saw her indulging in a plateful of sweets. Likely, using it as evidence to support his thinking that she was only a child. A spoiled one, at that.

She thought he was an ass. So, she supposed they would have to call it even.

The music began to swell, a dramatic waltz wrapping itself around her, enveloping her in the smooth and easy sensuality. She turned and looked at the couples out on the dance floor, holding each other close and moving with effortless grace.

What would it be like to have a man lead you like that? To hold you so close, with such strength? She imagined that her future husband was a very accomplished dancer. He was—after all—a prince. As far as she knew they began taking classical ballroom from the moment they learned how to walk.

Suddenly, a black-gloved hand came into her view. She looked up and her breath fled from her lungs. She parted her lips, preparing to speak, and he lifted his other hand, pressing his index finger to the cold, still mouth of his mask.

He had seen her too. He had noticed her. She had not been alone. That rush of heat, of excitement she had felt when he'd descended the stairs, that impression that he had not been touching the banister, but her skin, had washed over her for a reason. The connection was real.

Excitement, emotion, swelled in her chest even as the

music began to swell, filling the space in the room, and inside of her.

She allowed him to lift her from her chair, and even though they made no skin-to-skin contact, though the leather glove provided a bit of protection between her hand and his, she felt a lightning bolt of heat straight down low between her thighs.

She was being ridiculous. He could be anyone. He could be any age. He could be hideously disfigured beneath that mask. He could, in fact, be Death himself.

But she did not think he was. Because this feeling was too certain. Too deep.

When he pulled her into his hold, when her breasts pressed against the hard wall of his chest and heat sparked through her, she knew that whoever he was, he was the one that she wanted.

A strange thing. To have such an instant, intense attraction that transcended reality on such a visceral level.

He swept her over the dance floor like she weighed nothing, weaving between other couples as though they didn't exist. Didn't matter. She looked up and caught his dark gaze and a shock wave blasted through her. She focused on the crystal chandelier above that cast fractals of light over the people below, and at the rich velvet drapes that hung over the walls, partly concealing murals of frolicking goddesses painted over the plaster surface.

Each brush of her body against his made her tremble. Every brush of that gloved hand on her lower back sent a sweeping wave of longing through her. She ached between her legs, desperate for his touch. This wasn't just a dance. It was a prelude to something much more sensual.

She had never responded to a man like this before. Of course, she had never danced with a man like this before either. Still, she didn't think this had anything to do with the dancing, as arousing as it was. She didn't think it had anything to do with the music, as deeply as it affected her. This was all about him. And it had been from the moment he had walked into the room.

She was dizzy. That had nothing to do with the dancing either.

She slid her hand down from where it was looped around his neck, pressed her palm against his chest, making sure to meet his gaze. It was dark, obsidian and unreadable beneath the mask. Perhaps he was disgusted. Perhaps he could not imagine why she had taken his request to dance as an invitation for more.

He caught her hand, wrapping his fingers around her wrist and pulling it back.

She froze, thinking she had made a terrible error. Then, he turned her hand, slowly rubbing his thumb over the sensitive skin on the inside of her wrist. She shivered, her body taking his touch for exactly what it was. A response. A *yes*.

She swallowed hard, looking back off the dance floor to try to catch sight of her brother. He was nowhere to be seen. Which meant he had likely already taken off with a woman who had caught his attention. Good for her, he wasn't here to babysit.

She had no idea how to do this. Most especially without talking. And her mystery man seemed intent on keeping things silent between them. She didn't mind it. It heightened the electric feelings coursing through her.

She had no idea who he was, and he had no idea of her true identity. That was only a good thing. Her engagement to the prince of Santa Firenze was highly publicized. And though she doubted she would be famous worldwide, in Venice, there would certainly be some awareness of who she was.

But, soon, there was no decision to be made. Because he was moving her off the dance floor, away from the crowd and down an empty corridor. Her heart was thundering hard. And for a moment, she had the big concern that she was perhaps being kidnapped. She had not imagined that kidnapping might feel so close to seduction, or vice versa.

Now she was just thinking crazy things because she could hardly breathe for the fear and excitement that were jockeying for pride of place inside her.

He pressed her into an alcove, the music fading completely into the background. She could hear no one, and nothing. And in that moment, as the mysterious man in black filled her vision, it was as though they were the only two people on earth.

He pressed his thumb against her lips, tracing the edge of her mouth, a sensual shiver racking her frame. Then he let his fingertips drift down her neck, and down farther, to the neckline of her gown. His touch was featherlight over the rounded swells of her breasts, but it resonated inside her, deep and low. All consuming.

That was when she knew for certain she had *not* misinterpreted the situation. When she knew for sure that this was a seduction. And she was perilously close to being seduced.

But would she allow it?

Even as she had the thought, she realized how ridiculous it was. She had already allowed it. From the moment she had taken that offered hand, she had been saying *yes*.

His hand traveled all the way down to her hip, and he began gathering the deep purple fabric of her gown, pulling it up around her thighs. His fingertips brushed between her legs, brief, tantalizing contact in the place where she was beginning to burn for him.

Then, he pressed his palm against her stomach, pushing his hand upward, tugging the neckline of her dress to the side, exposing one of her breasts, then the other. She gasped, barely able to believe what was happening. What she was allowing him to do.

In truth, she wasn't *allowing* anything. She was simply a captive to it. To him. And she didn't mind. She didn't mind at all.

He dragged his thumb over one sensitized nipple, and she gasped. Then he pinched her tender flesh between his thumb and forefinger.

She arched more deeply into his touch, and he lifted both hands, cupping her, squeezing her tight. Then his hands were back on her skirt, drawing it up, exposing her to him. His fingers slipping between her thighs so that he could tease her. Then beneath her underwear, touching her more intimately than anyone ever had before.

She felt lost in him, in this. She had never known pleasure like this. It was like being in the center of a sensual storm. She felt his touch everywhere, teasing her, pushing her toward the brink.

She raised her hands, pressing them up against his chest, parting the buttons on his shirt. She sucked in a harsh breath, her fingers making contact with his skin for the first time as she traced his hard muscles, the heat of his skin shocking, so sexy she thought she might collapse onto the floor. A crumpled bit of Allegra. And she couldn't have that. Because then, he would probably figure out her inexperience, and he would very likely leave her standing there unsatisfied.

He was too perfect for words, a temptation she didn't want to turn away from. She leaned in, kissing his neck. His lips might be covered by the mask, but hers weren't. The touch of her skin against his left behind a smudge of red, and a bit of white from all the paint on her face. She didn't care. She liked it. She wanted to leave him marked by this, because God knew she would be.

She moved her exploration down, to his hard chest. His

muscles and the crisp hair on his skin were completely
new sensations for her. Touching him like this sent an
arrow of desire down low in her stomach.

It didn't take him long to continue on in what she'd
started. He moved his hands down to the closure of his
slacks, and pressed her more firmly against the wall. His
body was flush against hers, his hot, hard arousal seated
firmly against where she was wet and ready for him.

He flexed his hips, his hardness pressing into her softness. A wave of pleasure rolled over her and she let her
head fall back as a small moan escaped her lips.

He moved his hand, lifting her thigh and curving her
leg around his hip, before shifting his stance and thrusting deep inside her. This time, when she cried out it was
in pain.

She had known that losing her virginity would hurt, but
she hadn't realized it would be quite this painful.

Her partner didn't seem to notice that the tenor of her
voice had changed, because he withdrew slowly, before
pressing back. This time, it didn't hurt quite as badly. And
with each subsequent thrust, it hurt less and less, until
gradually the pleasure returned. Until that sharp, tearing
pain transformed into a deep gnawing ache.

It grew, spread outward, pressed deeper, blooming into
hot, frantic pleasure. She began to rock against him, grabbing hold of his shoulders, burying her face in the crook
of his neck as her climax overtook her completely. She
pressed her lips against his skin as her orgasm washed
over her. A never-ending assault that left her spent, breathless.

Then, on a growl, he thrust inside her one last time,
bracing himself against the wall as he found his own release.

For a moment, the world seemed to spin around them.

She was dizzy with pleasure, with desire. And she felt... connected to this man. To this man she didn't know at all.

He withdrew from her body, taking a step back. He began to button his shirt, doing his pants up again, his mask still firmly in place. He was as dark and mysterious as he had been from the first moment she'd laid eyes on him. And, were it not for the smear of red and white on his neck, she would never have known he'd been touched.

But the evidence was there. If the electric sensation coursing through her body and the throbbing ache between her thighs weren't evidence enough, then that would serve.

He looked at her for a moment, then he tugged his gloves more firmly in place, and turned, walking away from her, back toward the ballroom.

Leaving her alone.

Leaving Allegra Valenti, who had never done anything but quietly protest her position in life, who had certainly never made a move toward actual rebellion, standing there, having just lost her virginity to a stranger.

Without protection. Without thought for the future, or...anything at all.

Her excitement morphed into horror, into fear.

As she watched him disappear from view, she didn't know whether to be heartbroken or relieved over the fact that she would never see him again.

# CHAPTER TWO

ALLEGRA WAS CONVINCED that things could not possibly get worse than they already were. It didn't matter how many times she had wished over the past few weeks that her period would come. It refused to come. It did not matter how fervently she prayed that there would only be one pink line on the test that she took at home that morning. There were two.

It did not matter that she was engaged to be married to a prince and that she was supposed to give birth to *his* royal heirs. Because he was not the man she had slept with. No, she had slept with only one man, and she had no idea who he was.

She had gone over a great many options in her mind since making the unsettling discovery that morning. The first being that she could quickly fly to wherever her fiancé was and seduce him.

There were several reasons that wouldn't work, not the least of which being that she couldn't spend her entire life lying to a man about the paternity of his child. Also, Raphael wasn't stupid. He was a prince, and he required an heir. An heir who was his by blood. That meant that he would undoubtedly be doing paternity tests to establish whether or not the child was *actually* his. And, since Allegra knew it wasn't, there was really no point at all in

considering that kind of subterfuge. But she had. For a
moment. Only because the alternative was going to blow
her life wide apart.

Ultimately, she had decided on blowing her life apart.
Because there really was no other option. And so, she was
here at her brother's office in Rome, ready to confess all
to the one person who might not kill her where she stood.

Though, before she actually engaged in confession she
thought she might try a soft introduction.

"Did you enjoy the party?" she asked.

Renzo looked up from his work, one dark brow raised.
"Which party?"

"Right. I forgot. You go to a lot of parties. The one that
you took *me* to."

"It was very good. What little I stayed for."

"You were there for a while." She tapped the top of the
desk with her fingertip, carefully not looking directly at
Renzo.

"Yes," he said, pushing his chair away from his desk
and moving into a standing position. "Why are you questioning me? Is there some kind of unflattering tabloid
story? Photographs?"

"Could there be?" she asked.

"I am *me*, Allegra. It is always a possibility."

"I suppose that's true." It occurred to her that she may
very well end up as a tabloid spectacle too. All these years
of behaving, of fantasizing about *mis*behaving, but never
stepping out of line, and she had potentially created the
biggest scandal of all.

"You have something to ask me. Do it. And you can be
on your way. You can shop. I imagine that's why you're
actually in Rome."

He could imagine it all he wanted, it didn't make it
true. She was here to speak to him, because she had to

find out what he knew about the masked man at the party in Venice.

"You know almost everyone important," she said. She knew in her gut that the man she had been with was important. He had that air of authority about him. That sort of personality that commanded the attention of everyone in the room.

"Almost everyone," he said dryly. "Presidents. Kings. Why do you bring that up?"

"Because I... I just was curious. There was a man at the party."

"You should not be inquiring about men, Allegra," he said, his tone warning. "Especially since I believe you are already engaged."

"Sure. *Technically.* But I'm just curious about this one."

"And that is enough for me to know that if I tell you anything our father may well separate my head from my body."

"You don't care about that," she said. "I know you don't. You don't go to great lengths to please them. In fact, you don't try to please them at all. Stop pretending that you care when you don't."

He let out a long-suffering sigh. "All right. Ask away."

"He arrived late. He was wearing a mask that looked like a skull, dressed all in black."

A smile tugged at the corner of Renzo's lips. And then, he did something that Allegra rarely saw him do: he laughed.

"What?" she asked, fury rioting through her. She was having a crisis and he was laughing at her. "What's so funny about that?"

"I'm very sorry to tell you that I believe your head was turned by Cristian. I know you will loathe that. As I know you loathe him."

Ice slipped down through her, chilling her, making her feel ill. "No," she said. "That was not Cristian."

"Protest all you like, but it was. Perhaps it's for the best that Mother and Father have arranged your marriage? It seems that left to your own devices you have terrible taste."

*"No,"* she said, getting more furious. "There is no way that that was Cristian Acosta. I would have… I would have… Turned to stone."

"Just by looking at him?" Something strange crossed over her brother's face.

"Yes," she said.

Obviously he would find out eventually. They all would. Unless… They didn't. Perhaps, Cristian did not have to know.

Raphael would have to know, there was no way around that. Their engagement was off. And her life would be all the better for it. But, if the man she had been with was truly Cristian, then he would no more believe it than she did.

He saw her as a spoiled, selfish child, and nothing more. If she turned up pregnant, he would never connect the woman he'd had up against the wall with Allegra.

Her stomach turned. Cristian. It didn't seem possible. How could she… How could she have ever…

A question she had asked herself over and over again, even before she had discovered the identity of the man she had been with.

And so she made a decision then. She was not going to tell him. What good would come of it? He would either want nothing to do with her and the baby, or he would want everything to do with them. Frankly, she preferred the former, but feared the latter.

"Never mind," she said. "Clearly I was being silly."

"Clearly," Renzo said, going back to his work.

Allegra's mind was made up. She would break off her engagement, and seeing as she was already going to be disgraced, she would embrace it fully. She would raise her child alone.

She would ask nothing of Cristian.

"Your sister's broken engagement seems to be making headlines." Cristian poured himself a drink and turned to face his friend.

Anger that was somewhat unequal to the situation rioted through his blood. He had put his own reputation on the line, introducing Raphael to the Valentis. Vouching for Allegra as a future spouse.

He and Raphael were not really friends, more acquaintances. A hazard of being nobility, especially in these times when titles and the like were sinking into obscurity and obsolescence. But still, he had been the one to make the introduction. The one to suggest the union.

Out of respect and gratitude for the support the Valenti family had always shown him, more than anything else. He should have known she would ruin it.

It had only been a matter of time before Allegra had blown her life up completely. She had always seemed on the verge of it. A shimmering flame even while she sat, trying to look serene at parties and family meals.

He had always seen it. That restlessness. That dissatisfaction. But he'd hoped she'd find herself safely married to a prince and not...well, headline news.

A woman with her temperament was always in danger of being tabloid fodder, and he'd tried to warn her. She was too headstrong to listen.

He had hoped the promise of Raphael would keep her in line. Had hoped it would keep her secure.

It apparently had not.

"The cancellation of a royal wedding is always going to be a major deal," Renzo said.

"I suppose that's true."

Cristian remembered, clearly, her behavior the one time he had been at dinner when Raphael was in attendance. The one time he had seen the two of them together. She hadn't had a clue what to do with him, and he clearly hadn't the inclination to handle her.

Raphael was a prince, and accustomed to deference. Allegra didn't seem to know how to give it and had remained sulky and silent throughout the meal.

She'd been very young then. He'd hoped she might mature.

*Perhaps it's for the best.*

He knew all too well how marriages made for political gain could end up. And how unhappy a young bride who wished to have some freedom might crumple beneath the weight of expectation.

*But she is not Sylvia. And he isn't you.*

Yes, undoubtedly Allegra could have made good on this marriage. Had she any notion of just how good she had it.

"Thank God the reasoning behind the breakup has not come forward yet. But it will," Renzo said, standing and making his way across the office, helping himself to the alcohol as well.

He frowned. "What's the reason?"

"She's pregnant."

Something about that hit him hard and low. The image of her growing round…of her holding a baby in her arms…he despised it.

Which was ridiculous. She'd been set to marry Raphael in a few months' time, and she would have been pregnant by him soon enough. Why it should feel such an assault now, he didn't know.

He gritted his teeth, fighting against the rising tension in his body. "Not with her prince's child, I take it?"

"No. She refuses to tell our parents, or me, who the father is. I have never even seen her with anyone. I don't even have a guess." He frowned. "I worry about the circumstances behind it, frankly. Unlike me, Allegra has never been particularly wild. I have concerns she was taken advantage of."

It was strange to hear Renzo's assessment of his sister. Cristian had always sensed wildness in her. And he wouldn't be surprised if she had been conducting something of a double life behind the backs of her family members all this time.

The idea made his skin feel too tight for his body. That all the time she'd sat there at the dinner table during evenings he'd spent with her family, pretending to go along with her parents' plans, she was going out. Letting men touch her. Kiss her.

*Have* her.

"Has she not?" he asked, attempting to keep his tone innocuous.

"No. She has no experience with men, as far as I know. As far as I knew," he corrected. "In fact only recently she was asking me quite breathlessly about a man she saw at the masked ball we went to a month or so ago."

Cristian gritted his teeth, a strange tension taking him over. "Was she?"

Flashes of the ball played back in his mind. A beautiful, lush figure. Tight, wet heat. A kind of indulgence he had not had in years.

"Yes. She was chagrined to discover that the man who'd caught her eye was you."

Cristian set his glass down, his pulse thundering in his temples. It was not possible. But he had to ask. He had to know.

"What was she wearing?" His heart was thundering hard now, his blood roaring through his veins.

"A mask the same as all the other women. She had some purple in her hair and a purple dress. A dress our parents absolutely did not approve of."

*Cojeme.*

It could not be. The first woman he had touched in years... And it was Allegra Valenti. And she was... Well, she was pregnant with the Acosta heir.

While the concept of a dukedom was somewhat outmoded, his own was still functioning. With whole swaths of property and farmland left to his management, and hundreds of families dependent on his continuing bloodline.

He was the last, and he'd known he could not let that stand. Now, he didn't have to.

Apart from that, he was part of Allegra Valenti's double life. Part of her sin. And such sin it had been. The kind that haunted his sleep with flashes of memory so erotic and sweet he woke up on the verge of release every night.

"Where is she?" he asked, an edge of desperation in his voice.

Renzo frowned, realization dawning slowly over his friend's face. "I'm not going to like this, am I?"

"No more than I like it," he said his tone hard. "Where is she?"

"Holed up in one of my apartments in Rome."

"I need to speak to her. *Now.*" He had no time for subtlety. If his suspicions were correct, there would be no keeping secrets anyway.

*Damn.* They could not be correct.

Renzo's expression turned suspicious. Dark. "I assume that afterward you will be speaking to me."

"We can only hope not." Then Cristian turned and walked out of his friend's office.

He had to see her and put all of this to rest. It cannot

be. He refused to believe it. But he would have to see her, so that he could know.

He had to prove to himself, once and for all, that Allegra was not his mysterious lover from the masked ball. It could not be her. That little brat could not be the woman who had touched him, who had aroused such heat and fire in his blood.

Impossible.

He refused to believe it was true. And he would prove that it was not.

Allegra was doing her best to avoid the media. But sometimes she would forget. And then she would turn on the TV and be assaulted by the news, or open up her computer and go to the wrong webpage and see yet more headlines.

It was horrible. Seeing her painted as the person she simply wasn't. Bold enough to call off the engagement to the prince at the eleventh hour, without a care for his feelings or for the future of his country.

She wasn't very bold at all. And she really *did* care about leaving everything in the lurch. And if Raphael had feelings, she'd never seen them. Not that that excused her.

When she'd given in to her fantasy and taken a lover at the ball, it hadn't been with the mind that she would abandon her upcoming marriage. It had been with the idea that at least one thing would be her choice. A stolen moment that would always be hers, and hers alone.

Well, now it was everyone's.

The world knew she'd broken off the wedding. Her family knew she was pregnant. It was only a matter of time before speculation began flying about that too.

Strangely though, as ownership of her and her mistakes became the world's, she felt more and more like her life belonged to her. She had decided, firmly, to keep the paternity of the child a secret.

It was her key. Yes, she had let everyone down. Yes, her parents may well cut her off—they seemed to be making a decision on that score still. But apart from all that... her life was suddenly filled with possibilities it hadn't been before.

She had always known she would be a mother. But part and parcel to that had been being a royal wife. As a princess, her life would never truly be hers.

But now for the first time, it just might be. At least she had choices. Even if they weren't infinite. At least she would only have to answer to herself. To her own mistakes.

Even her relationship with her child...it would be her own. And maybe it wasn't the most ideal thing to try to find yourself as a person while you were finding yourself as a mother, but it was still better—more—than she would have had as Raphael's wife.

A knock on her apartment door sent her scrambling out of her seat on the couch. No one had rung in downstairs, requesting permission for entrance. Which meant it must be an employee of her brother's building.

God bless Renzo for allowing her to hole up here. He might be angry with her for her choices, but at least he understood, in some ways.

He had never been very well behaved, after all.

She walked over to the door and opened it, then her heart fell into her feet. "Renzo isn't here, if you're looking for him." She tried to keep her face straight as she stared into the dark, uncompromising gaze of Cristian Acosta.

He couldn't know. He *couldn't*. She refused to believe it.

Though, standing there, looking up at him, and those coal-black eyes, she wondered how she hadn't known it was him the moment he'd walked into that ballroom.

He'd looked like Death come to collect then. And he looked like it now.

His black brows were locked together, as was his hard, square jaw. His lips, usually the softest-looking thing about him, were pressed into a grim line.

He filled the space, and he wasn't even in it yet. So tall, so impossibly broad. He made her feel small. He made her feel weak.

He made her feel like he was looking straight through her.

That brief moment of hope was crushed beneath the weight of that stare. That knowing, intense stare. For just a second, she'd had freedom.

And now, there was Cristian.

"I am not," he said, his tone hard, uncompromising. Like everything else about him.

"Well, did you come to congratulate me on my upcoming marriage? Because if so—"

"Quiet," he said, brushing past her and into the apartment. "I am not here to play games with you. Were you ever going to tell me?"

"About…" Her throat was completely dry and excuses were swirling around her head like foxes chasing their tails.

"The baby," he said.

"I… I don't…"

"I know," he said, his lip curling slightly. "I know that you were the one. And I know you found out that it was me, so do not stand there looking like a wounded innocent."

She frowned. "I am *not* an innocent. As you have no doubt deduced."

"There is no star in the East, so you must not be."

She crossed her arms, as if it might put a barrier between them. "Nice of you to check for divine symbols before you came."

"So you admit that you *knew*. You admit that you knew that I am the father of your child."

"I admit no such thing." She crossed her arms, wishing that she could fold in on herself. Wishing that she could disappear completely.

"And yet, you said that I should know that you aren't an innocent. How else would I know if I weren't the one to take your innocence?"

"Oh, I don't know. The simple fact that I'm pregnant? Honestly, Cristian, it could be anyone's. I'm a known whore."

"Enough," he said, his tone firm. "What is the point of this fiction, Allegra?"

"The point of this fiction is that I don't want to deal with you. I don't want to deal with this. I... I would never... I would *never* have touched you if I'd have known that it was you."

"But it was." There was a dark light in his eyes, but it looked nothing like triumph. It was a grim sort of determination. He was no happier about this than she was. She wasn't sure how she felt about that.

"I don't want you," she spat, feeling desperate. "I don't. I had no idea that it was you."

"Don't flatter yourself by believing even for one moment *I* thought it was *you*, Allegra. You are nothing more than a spoiled child. One who threw away a future that would have been infinitely preferable to this one. You have never understood what you had. You have never understood all your parents have done for you."

"If I don't, then Renzo doesn't either. And yet, you seem to be able to continue in association with him without lecturing him every thirty seconds."

"Renzo has taken over the running of your father's company. He has not shirked his duties."

"Or, you have a double standard."

"If I have a double standard, then it is not a different double standard than that held by the rest of the world."

She flung her hands up into the air. "Congratulations then, you're as infinitely terrible as the majority of the population."

Silence settled between them. It was not an empty silence. It was full. Of anger, of something else that she did not want to identify.

"If there is one thing I have learned, Allegra," he said, his superior tone maddening, "It's that you cannot outrun consequences. It doesn't matter who your father is. It does not matter how much money you have. Consequences will catch up to us all."

"Especially when you don't use a condom," she shot back.

Perhaps she wasn't blameless in the lack of contraception, but he was the man. Surely he should have been responsible for that. She had been a virgin, besides.

"You didn't say anything."

"You made it clear you didn't want me to speak!"

"You didn't protest," he said.

She growled. "You don't have to do this. I was prepared to deal with this by myself."

His dark eyes narrowed. "What is your definition of *dealing* with it?"

"I was going to have this baby and raise it as a single mother. It isn't as though I don't have assets. My parents are upset, but they're hardly going to cut me off." She was bluffing. Her parents were infuriated and she had no idea what they would do at this point.

"You think?"

"Well, even if they do, Renzo won't." Honestly, she

wasn't entirely certain about her parents. They had not spoken to her since she had told them the news.

But her parents had been so deeply enmeshed in every aspect of her life for so long, she couldn't really imagine them fully disowning her. She had no idea what her mother would do with her time. But then, maybe that had more to do with the impending royal wedding than an actual desire to spend any time with Allegra. Allegra didn't want to think about that.

"Frankly, I don't care whether or not your parents are planning to disown you, or whether or not your brother will support the child and you. You are not doing this alone."

"No one will believe that we slept together. Nobody."

He chuckled, a dark sound that wound its way through her body, wrapping itself around her veins, heating her blood. He had never affected her like this before. Usually, when Cristian heated her blood it was because he made her angry. This was something else. A shared memory of the two of them that she didn't want.

"We did not *sleep together*," he said, his voice filled with grim humor. "We had sex. Against a wall."

Heat stung her face. "No one will believe we did that either."

"Why? Because of my impeccable reputation?"

"For a start."

"But no one has to know how it happened. Obviously, when we present this to the world it will be in a much different light. You will, of course, tell your parents that you have fallen in love with me, and it was your great passion and deep feelings for me that inspired you to compromise your engagement."

She sputtered. "They will be more inclined to believe that you impregnated me in a public hallway without knowing my identity."

"Is that so?"

"*No one* will believe that I love you. Everyone knows how we feel about each other."

"That's fine. It isn't my reputation that will suffer as a result. You were the one who was engaged. You are the woman. Therefore, all of the judgment will be heaped on top of you."

She snorted. "It's already being heaped upon me. In case you hadn't checked out a headline recently."

"It may surprise you to hear this, but my life does not revolve around reading news stories concerning your exploits.

"Why should I read the tabloids? I went to Renzo instead and he knew much more than any of the so-called breaking news."

She recoiled. "Does that mean that... Does Renzo *know*?"

"Renzo is not an idiot. I assume that once I began questioning him about what costume you had worn to the ball, and then stormed out after the revelation of your pregnancy—combining that with your inquiries about me earlier—he was able to do a bit of simple math."

"But you're still alive," she said, confident that if her brother truly knew that she had made love to Cristian, Cristian would, in fact, be dead.

"Of course. I'm sure it only makes sense to him that I had no idea it was you. He knows that under normal circumstances I would never consider touching you."

Rage and wounded feminine pride poured through Allegra like a toxic elixir. "Well, he must be very proud that your standards are so high. I'm so sorry that my identity was a disappointment to you. However, we both know that you quite enjoyed what happened. In fact, you enjoyed it so much that it was extremely brief."

His top lip curled. "You enjoyed it no less for the brief nature of it."

"So confident?"

"I have a very strong memory of how intensely you came around me, Allegra," he said, his voice rough. "You cannot fake that."

"Women," she said, her voice trembling, "can fake things."

"Women can only fake things if their partner is stupid, or inexperienced. I am neither." He took a step toward her. "I felt you. I felt you trembling. I felt the waves as they washed through you. I felt your pleasure as keenly as I felt my own. Do not pretend it was somehow less than satisfying now that you know my identity."

"It's so important for you to have your male ego stroked, and yet you can barely stand the sight of me. That's sort of twisted, Cristian."

He laughed, dark, merciless. "I never claimed to be anything else."

"You don't want me. I doubt you want the baby."

"Oh," he said, "that's where you're wrong. I need the baby."

"If you need him for some kind of ritual sacrifice then you're definitely out of luck."

"No, thank you. My life has quite enough death in it without adding any more, thank you. That was very poor humor."

She looked away. "I'm sorry."

"Don't apologize to me now. You don't mean it."

"Why do you need the baby?"

"Because. For as humbly as I present myself, I am in fact an aristocrat. A duke."

"I did know. Your arrogance announces it before you walk into a room."

"Then you must surely understand that I require an

heir. A legitimate heir. My child cannot be born a bastard, Allegra. Neither can I afford to miss this opportunity."

"Our...baby is an opportunity?"

"Certainly it is an opportunity for my bloodline. I am a widower, and thanks to those circumstances I have failed to produce an heir. As I am now in my thirties, it becomes yet more and more important. Of course, my own father produced his heir quite by accident. But in spite of the fact that my mother was nothing more than a washed-up model, he still did the right thing by her, by me and by the dukedom dependent upon the bloodline continuing. I can do no less. Don't you agree?"

"What exactly are you proposing?"

"Exactly that. I am proposing."

"What?" Her heart was thundering so hard, her blood pouring through her ears. She felt like she was underwater. Could hardly breathe, could scarcely hear anything.

"Allegra Valenti, you are having my baby. And you will be my wife."

# CHAPTER THREE

CRISTIAN STARED AT the recalcitrant woman sitting across from him on his private plane. He could not remember a woman ever looking quite so angry when in the presence of such luxury. At least, as far back as he could remember. It had been quite some time since he'd had a woman on his plane in that sense of the word.

Quite some time since he'd had a lover.

Not that Allegra was his lover. She absolutely was *not*. A quick screw against the wall didn't make her anything. It simply made him weak.

Three years of celibacy. It was to be expected, he supposed. And yet, he had not imagined that he would be punished quite so spectacularly for his loss of control. He felt as though he had been punished enough.

Clearly, there was a particularly capricious deity somewhere that disagreed.

And such a punishment was Allegra Valenti.

She was looking particularly pretty and sulky, nearly curling in on herself as she leaned against the window, as though she would rather be thrown through it and hurled down to the earth than spend one more moment in his presence.

"Have you anything to say, Allegra?"

"Why? I believe I shouted it all at you in the apartment. And again when we got into the car. I could shout the same things at you, but I fear it would be repetitive."

"Oh, please do. I never tire of your excuses. All of which are incredibly selfish."

"It isn't selfish to think *perhaps* it isn't the best idea for two people who can't stand the sight of each other to get married."

"Why not? Plenty of people do it. You only have to survive it until death separates us."

"How easy is it to get a hold of arsenic in Spain?"

"Such a delight, Allegra. How is it that you and I never acted on our feelings for each other before?"

"You mean the arsenic feelings?"

He laughed. "I meant our attraction, *mi tesoro*."

"We don't have an attraction, *Cristian*," she said, sounding very much like a disgusted teenager. "In fact, the two of us had to be completely disguised before anything like heat flared between us at all. I would say that we don't have to worry about anything."

Referencing that night sent a kick of heat through him. He had done nothing but dream about it ever since it had happened. The fact that it was Allegra Valenti he had lost his mind with twisted it into a nightmare. But it was a nightmare that was no less erotic than it had been before.

He hadn't been with a woman since Sylvia's death. Had not even been tempted. And then, he had descended the stairs of the ballroom to see a wild, purple creature, barely wrapped in that sensuous dress, her curves golden and generous. Her dark hair curling luxuriously around temptingly exposed shoulders.

He had known only one thing in that moment. *Want*. He had wanted her with a deep, feral desire that had transcended anything else. It had transcended reason. It had transcended decency. He had wanted nothing to spoil the moment. And so, when he had approached her, he had prevented her from speaking. He had not said a single word to her. He had not wanted to lose whatever spell had been cast over them.

He should have known that it was witchcraft. And that he would burn for it.

One indulgence in a lifetime of obedience and he had destroyed everything.

"I fear you are wrong on that score," he said, schooling his tone into a bored, steady rhythm. "Chemistry like this is undeniable."

She waved a hand. "Look at me. Denying it."

"Your denial is empty as you carry my child in your womb."

"Only because I didn't know it was you that I was... with that night at the ball," she shot back.

"So you say."

"A marriage between us will not work," she said, her words brittle.

"Oh, I have no doubt that it won't. But you will marry me before the child is born, and you will stay married to me for what appears to be a suitable amount of time. Afterward, divorce me. As quickly and painlessly as you would like."

"There will never be anything painless about a divorce where my parents are concerned."

"I imagine not. They are very Catholic, are they not?"

She frowned. "I shall be married to you until the end of time in their eyes."

"And yet, I find that my need for an heir transcends my concerns for your sense of family."

"There is nothing simple about this, that's my point. Anyway, you're acting as though I can just take a couple of years out of my life to molder away in some Spanish castle."

"It's more of a villa."

"And you're only a duke. I was supposed to marry a prince."

"It was not the prince who had you up against a wall, Allegra. I doubt you're regretful of the fact that you can no longer marry Prince Raphael."

"That's almost like admitting you're wrong, isn't it?" she asked, her tone baiting. "Seeing as you essentially arranged our engagement."

"I was not wrong about it being advantageous. Chemistry, on the other hand, is harder to predict. You clearly have no great passion with him."

Her cheeks colored. "What makes you think that?"

He lifted a shoulder. "You didn't think for one moment the child could be his. Otherwise, you would not have broken off your engagement. What other conclusion can I draw but one which suggests you are not actively sleeping with him?"

She looked at him, her expression unreadable. "Maybe it isn't yours. Maybe I make love to all manner of strange men in corridors at parties. Maybe the only thing I'm certain about is that it isn't Raphael's because he's such a gentleman that he wouldn't touch me."

"Still trying that story out?"

"Perhaps it's the truth. Perhaps, I am the very whore of Babylon." She lifted her chin and shook her head, her dark hair shimmering in the light. "You don't know me, Cristian. Not really. At least, you don't know the woman I have grown into. You have this idea that I'm a child, but I *am* in my twenties."

He laughed, suddenly feeling quite old. "Ancient."

"I only mean that I am a woman. Whatever you might think."

"I am under no illusions about your femininity, Allegra."

He was gratified to see her cheeks turn a deeper shade

of pink, however, there was a cost to the victory. It made his stomach tighten with hunger. Made his body ache with need.

For *Allegra*.

It was unacceptable.

"Well, there are a great many men who have no illusion about it," she sniffed. "They know about it. Personally."

He didn't believe her. And yet, the thought of Allegra with other men angered him. He could only attribute the possessiveness to the fact that she was having his baby. Perhaps combined with the fact that she was the first woman he had been with in quite some time.

"Or perhaps," Cristian said, watching her face closely, "you are so certain about it because you were a virgin."

He relived the moment that he had pushed inside her body. She had been tight, there was no doubt about that. He had attributed the cry she'd made at the time to pleasure. Now, he wondered.

The realization was…intoxicating. He should be disgusted with himself. But he was…triumphant. He wondered about himself. At whether or not he was still under some kind of black magic spell.

The color in her face deepened. "That's ridiculous."

"Closer to the truth, I think."

"Who would lose their virginity that way?" She sounded close to hysterical.

"Perhaps a woman who is being married off to a man she doesn't love?"

She said nothing. Satisfaction surged through him, and he gritted his teeth to hold back a growl of triumph. "The child is mine then. For certain."

"I didn't say that."

"You didn't have to." He kept his eyes trained on her, trying to ignore the riot of heat that was coursing through him. "You will give me my heir, my legitimate heir, and preserve the reputation of the child, and then you can move on as though none of this happened."

"I haven't agreed to anything yet! And are you suggesting I leave our child with you?"

"The Acosta heir should be raised in Spain, I should think."

"That's ridiculous," she said, crossing her arms beneath her breasts. Helplessly, he found his gaze drawn to the soft swells. "I'm not leaving my child. Regardless of our arrangements."

"Perhaps I can install you in the servants' quarters once our divorce is finalized."

"You wouldn't dare."

"You have ample evidence that I dare quite a few things, and yet, still you challenge me?"

She turned away from him, all shimmering indignity. It wasn't that he had never noticed she was beautiful. That much was obvious. She had been beautiful ever since she had been a sullen teenager. He had the feeling that her family missed her moods. Missed the subtle pout in her face whenever her upcoming marriage was mentioned. Or the storm that flashed in her eyes whenever her future was discussed.

Even as he had disapproved of her attitude, he had found her pretty. But that was different than the way he saw her now. Now, he could look at her and see nothing other than the temptress that had greeted him in the ballroom. Who had touched him as though he was some sort of new miracle to her.

*You were. She was a virgin.*

He gritted his teeth, leaning back against his own seat. How was it that he felt like the villain in this situation?

"When we get to Spain I will arrange for you to get an engagement ring. And we will begin arrangements for the wedding."

"I didn't agree to this. You seem to be missing that."

"I'm not waiting for your agreement. I do not require it."

"Yes, you do. My former fiancé was a prince, and not even *he* could force me into marriage. You certainly aren't going to."

"Let us discuss your choices. The choices you seem to feel you have in abundance. You could go back to Italy, an unwed mother who would have to enter into a custody battle with me. And I do believe that your mother and father would likely take my side." He watched as she paled. He nearly felt like a bastard. Nearly. "If you want access to your child, if you want anything other than a life of disgrace where you will certainly be ostracized by your parents as they make room for their grandchild, the grandchild you rejected because you refused to marry the father, then by all means. We can land the plane early and I can allow you to disembark. Otherwise, I suggest that you come to terms with the fact that you have simply traded one arranged marriage for another. But I, at least, will not require the use of your body again."

She said nothing. Instead, she stared straight ahead, blinking furiously, as though she was trying to keep herself from crying. And again, he felt like the villain. He was not being villainous. He was merely being practical.

He imagined that if he told Allegra that, she would not find it to be the same.

"Nothing to say?" he asked.

"As you have made it perfectly clear there is nothing to say. Except that I'll marry you."

# CHAPTER FOUR

ALMOST AS SOON as they touched down in Spain, they were whisked away from the airport and to a luxurious car that spirited them up a winding road leading to the hills that overlooked Barcelona.

Cristian was right, it was much more villa than palace, and there was absolutely nothing offensive or moldy about it. Allegra found that she was wholly irritated by the fact that the setting did not match its owner.

In fact, the entire place was airy and bright, with large windows that overlooked the sea, letting sun wash light into the room.

It was very different from her parents' home in Italy. It possessed none of the old money trappings, and she found herself confused by that. She knew Cristian's family was as old as her own, and titled on top of it. But here there was a lack of dark, encroaching wood paneling, thread-bare rugs that had survived several inquisitions and art-work depicting either scenes from the Bible or portraits of long-dead relatives.

Everything was white. Everything was crisp. It was borderline modern. Which, considering what a relic Cristian was, seemed laughable.

"This is not your family home," she said.

He laughed. "I said that I was not taking you to a *castillo*. I did not say we didn't possess one."

"What was all that about your son needing to be on your hallowed family grounds, and all of that?"

"I'm Spanish. Sometimes we exaggerate for dramatic effect. Mostly, I require my child be born in Spain. And I require them to be born during my marriage. Whether or not it's here or in my family's ancient ruin is beside the point."

"You have a ruin?" she asked. "That sounds…well, archeologically significant if nothing else."

He shrugged. "I'm not sure if it's a ruin, exactly. More a large plot of land centered around an ancient castle I have no desire to inhabit. I keep a full staff on to take care of the castle and the grounds. I also have a steward for the land who helps manage the farms and tenants. But my mother has long since fled, and—as you know—my father is long since dead."

He spoke of his parents with such studied neutrality that she knew it wasn't accidental. It was hiding the truth, whatever that was.

"My parents are wedded to the old halls of our family estate. They would never dream of leaving. In fact, if my parents died and Renzo left it to rot, I can assure you my father would haunt him from beyond the grave and rattle his chains over the unpolished silver."

Cristian studied her closely, a strange light in his eyes. "Do you imagine your father will be in chains in the afterlife?"

"I was being dramatic. I'm Italian. We are also capable of exaggerating for dramatic effect, if you didn't realize."

He looked up, somewhere past her, the sunlight shining in his eyes, revealing the deep, rich coffee color of his eyes, revealing that they weren't pure black. That there was humanity behind them. "My father is most certainly in chains. If there is justice in the next life, that is."

"I certainly hope there is. There is rarely justice in this one."

He looked around the room. "Do you find this situation unjust?"

"How could I find it anything else?"

He lifted a hand. "You are in a multimillion-dollar home in one of the most beautiful parts of Spain. You have a man with a title—and several billion dollars—willing to marry you and give your child legitimacy. I would say many people would not feel quite so persecuted."

She arched a brow, not to be undone. She would *never* be undone by Cristian again. "Those who would not feel persecuted by the situation couldn't possibly know you as well as I do."

He took a step toward her, his eyes glittering like black diamonds. "Ah yes, and you do know me, don't you? *Intimately.*"

She despised the heat that washed over her face, and the color that no doubt accompanied it. She despised that he could affect her so. "I don't think that counts. As far as I knew, you were Death."

"Very romantic. Conquering Death by taming him. However—" he rubbed his hand over his chin, the sound of his whiskers whispering over his skin strangely arousing "—I was not tamed."

"I'm actually fine with that. Were you ever to be tamed, Cristian, I should hope that it isn't by me. I don't wish to be stuck with you as a child might be stuck with a dog that followed them home."

She knew, the moment those words left her hot mouth, that she had made a mistake. She knew it, even as he advanced on her, but she found herself frozen, unable to move. Then, as he drew closer, she took a step backward, then another step. Her back came into contact with the wall behind her, and she was thrown back into a flash of memory. From that night. From when Cristian had put his hands all over her, from when he had made her lose her mind, and her purity, in that one brilliant blaze of shameful glory in a quiet palace corridor.

"I am not a dog," he said, his voice low. He was so close she could feel the heat radiating from his body, but he didn't touch her. Shamefully, wantonly, she felt her body begin to soften for him. Felt a dull ache begin to grow beneath her thighs, beating a tattoo in time with her heartbeat.

"I think it much more likely, Allegra, that I should tame you. I think it is you who could be brought to heel." He tilted his head to the side, studying her closely. "Yes. Even now, you want me. You can say you didn't know who I was, you can talk of despising me all you like. But you want me. As much now as you wanted me then. You want me now, even knowing who I am." He pushed away from her, and she let out a breath, feeling nearly dizzy with the effort that had been put into holding it before. "Interesting."

"There is nothing interesting about this," she said, holding her jaw tight as she spoke. "*Disgusting* is more like it."

She and Cristian had always fought. Always. But this had a new edge to it. So sharp she feared it might cut her straight through.

"So disgusting that you wish to be filled with me even now. What does that say about you?"

She gritted her teeth against the rising heat and humiliation inside of her. "I do not understand the point of you baiting me, Cristian. I will agree to the marriage, but you will not touch me. And you will not wed me in a church. Even I have my limits."

"Pity. I find that I don't."

"The state of your eternal soul is your affair. I would

like mine to remain as unscathed as possible." She didn't want to lie in front of her parents, but she would. Lying in a cathedral was a step too far.

"I'll do my best. Though, it's entirely possible you will leave your association with me *terribly* scathed."

She huffed out a breath and walked across the room, folding her arms across her chest and holding on to her elbows tightly. "At least with post-baby weight."

"Yes," he said gravely. "That is entirely possible."

"We're going to have to tell my family."

"Your parents are quite fond of me."

"I think they were more fond of the prince I was going to marry. You're a duke. It's a bit of a downgrade."

He shrugged. "Spain is a much larger country than Santa Firenze. I would say if anything you broke even."

And in spite of herself, she laughed. Really, there was nothing funny about the situation, and his comment was so dark she could scarcely find humor in it. But she found herself too filled with tension to do anything else. If she didn't allow herself the release she would shatter completely.

"If you are intent on withholding your body from me, you must know that I will seek pleasure with other women," he said. He sounded so bored with it all, and she felt like she was on fire.

That brought to mind an entirely different vision. A vision of Cristian with another woman. A blonde, someone pale and very different from herself. Would he press her against the wall? Would he unleash his passion upon her?

There was no doubt that in that corridor, with her, he had been passionate. Passionate enough to forget a condom when he was, by his own admission, experienced. Anyway, he had been married, so she'd known he had experience.

But now, she was thinking of him with *other* women.

More women. It filled her mouth with bile. It shouldn't. She should be thrilled. Happy that he would seek his release elsewhere, rather than foisting his demands on her. However, she did not feel happy about it.

"It makes no difference to me," she said, sniffing with indignation. "I don't care at all what you do. Or *who* you do it with."

"You do not look so neutral." And he sounded amused by her lack of neutrality.

"If it serves your ego to believe that, Cristian, you're welcome to your fiction. However, I don't care what you do with other women. As long as I'm not involved."

He lifted a shoulder. "I have never seen sex as a group activity, but my mind could be changed, Allegra." He leaned in, his voice getting deeper, huskier. "Last time all we had was a few moments against a wall. Just think of all that a man like me could accomplish with a large, soft mattress. I could have you beneath me…over me… in front of me."

She stiffened, her face so hot she was certain she was going to burst into flame at any moment. It was enraging and humiliating. Enraging because he was trying to get a reaction out of her. And humiliating for the same reason. He didn't want her. He wanted to one-up her. Wanted to enrage her, as he always had.

She shouldn't care. She shouldn't care at all.

"Absolutely not," she sniffed. "I will not be a carnal accessory that you drape over your body like a mink."

He laughed. He *laughed*. "Evocative."

"The only real issue I see is in people believing that I would choose you for a wife, Allegra," he continued.

"Why? I am from a noble family. I was poised to become a princess."

"And yet, all the world knows of your failing now. That

you either fell out of favor with the prince, or you were unfaithful to him."

"They will lump you into that as well," she said. "I was not unfaithful to Raphael *by myself.* That would be a trick."

"And a very enticing visual."

Heat stung her cheeks. "Stop. None of this is fair."

"The world is rarely so fair to women, as I'm sure you're well aware."

She knew that he was right. "Well, if I'm going to visit such shame upon your family name, perhaps you *should* consider getting another woman with your holy Acosta child. It would cause you less trouble in the end. Clearly, all of your parts are in working order. It should not be so difficult for you to conceive."

His face turned intense. Feral. "Are you suggesting that I could so easily replace a child of mine? That all I need to do is spread my seed to another woman and it will make no difference. Never. My child shall want for nothing. And I will not leave a child of mine illegitimate. I will not deny him his birthright. It is non-negotiable."

She looked down at her fingers, began peeling the edge of her fingernail polish. What was the point in having a perfect manicure? What was the point of presenting herself as perfect to the world when, in reality, nothing about her was perfect at all. She was beginning to fall apart at the seams. And at the edges of her nail polish.

It terrified her. If that happened, how would she hide?

"I didn't realize having a child was so important to you," she said.

"I married young in the hopes that I would have produced a child already, Allegra. I know you aren't ignorant to my history. Unfortunately, Sylvia's health made it impossible for her to carry a child. And, when she passed away, I was left with no wife *and* no heir."

"And I'm sorry," she said, at least feeling sorry for him in the moment. It was difficult to be awful to him, or even to see him as awful, when he was talking about his loss. "But you know you can't just replace her with me. You know you can't just… This isn't a fix for the past."

"Of course not," he said, his tone filled with disdain. "You are nothing like her."

His disdain touched some deep, needy part of her that craved approval she would never have, and made it feel like it was on the verge of shattering.

"You must have loved her very much," she said. At least his pain helped with her hurt feelings. The fact that he was being so dismissive of her being linked to his grief was…something at least.

"She was my wife," he said. Flat. Simple.

Allegra noticed that it wasn't precisely an answer to her comment. Much like the tone he'd used when he'd spoken of his parents. She didn't think it was accidental.

"I didn't realize being a *father* was so important to you."

He lifted a shoulder. "Being a father is *essential* to me. I must carry on my bloodline. I must ensure that my title continues. That our holdings, our responsibilities are carried through to future generations. If you think that I intend to spend my days playing nursemaid, however, you are mistaken."

"Excuse me?"

"I'm sorry, did you imagine that I wanted this child out of some sense of sentimentality? It is duty. Pure and simple."

"But you just said that you could not replace this child with another so easily."

"I have *honor*, Allegra. I will not rob my oldest son or daughter of their birthright. I will not relegate them to a life of illegitimacy because I could not come to an agreement with their mother. However, while I am not a man without honor, I am a rather cold bastard. A child would only freeze in my arms."

"Why would you say something like that?" she asked.

He arched a brow. "It is the truth. I was a terrible husband, Allegra. Incapable of giving to Sylvia what she needed, what she craved. Why should it be different with a child?"

"Why do you think you were…incapable? I don't understand. She always seemed very happy with you, when I saw the two of you together. And you with her."

"She was desperately unhappy," he said, his tone grim. "And I could not make her less so."

"Did you try?"

His eyes were hard, black as midnight. "Of course I tried. But it was not enough. I'm not the sort of man suited to soft things."

"Babies are very soft," she pointed out.

"I'm aware of that."

"Who do you propose will be raising our baby? You intend to kick me out of your home as soon as our association is finished, and you have talked about having the child stay here."

"I shall employ staff. Well-trained, qualified."

A thread of anxiety began to unravel inside of her, becoming tangled up with anger, resentment, fear. She had no idea how to be a mother, but of course, she had always imagined she would be one. As she'd been set on marrying a prince, producing an heir had always been one of the most important things in that bargain. She hadn't imagined being pregnant quite this soon, but, she was. And, while she didn't feel overly…sane at the moment, she knew for a fact that she wanted her baby.

"Who is more qualified to care for a child than its

mother?" she asked, feeling a deep, primitive surge within her as she voiced the question.

A *mother*. She was this baby's mother, and she would do all she could to give him or her everything. While everything else might be uncertain, that was not.

"Someone with a degree in early childhood development?"

She laughed. Not because it was funny, but because she was shocked. Because there was genuinely no other response when you were staring down your older brother's best friend—who probably hated you—while carrying his child. "You think that somebody who went to school to take care of children would be better suited to caring for *our* child then we would be?"

"Than myself, certainly. I cannot speak for you. However, as you were poised to take on the life of a princess, I can't imagine that you thought your day would be filled with changing diapers and running back and forth between sporting events and playgroups."

She shook her head. "You have no idea who I am, Cristian. You have built up an entire idea in your mind that I'm some kind of spoiled little brat. But you truly don't know me at all."

"And where would I have come up with the idea that you were a spoiled brat? Perhaps, through our interactions."

"Which interactions?" she asked, tossing her hair back, treating him to her sharpest look.

"Well, there was that time at Christmas when you told me in no uncertain terms that I could go to hell."

"You said my outfit made me look like a desperate shepherdess who wanted to find a stable boy to flip up her skirts!"

His lips curved into a half smile. "So I did. And so you did."

She hadn't thought he would remember. She had imagined she was nothing to him. That their every argument, every sniping match, faded away in his mind as soon as it was finished.

"And then that night you dragged me down the hall to lecture me about being sulky to Raphael at a summer party my parents had thrown."

"You were. He was supposed to be your fiancé. The man you were to spend your life with and you acted like he was a piece of food you didn't want on your plate."

"And you couldn't have that because it might have reflected poorly on you, is that it?"

"Naturally," he said, his tone hard, his dark eyes glittering.

"You're *awful*. You're awful to me, and you are dismissive of my feelings. You think that because my parents arranged for me to marry a prince that I should get on my knees and thank them."

"No," he said, his voice turning dark, thunderous. "I think you should get on your knees and thank your parents for being the caring people they are. For having strong emotions about what you might become one day. For believing that you could stand up to the pressure of being a princess. It says nothing but good things about who they think you are that they imagined you could handle the pressure of being married to Prince Raphael. They believe in you. Both you and Renzo. Even if you cannot see it, that is an asset that a great many people are not afforded."

She had to wonder if he meant himself. She knew that his father had been older when he was born, and that his mother was mostly absent. She also knew that he'd spent holidays from the time he was a boy with her family, which most certainly seemed to indicate that his family did nothing around those times.

"I hear what you're saying," she said, "but the only

problem is, they are much more supportive of their idea of me than who I actually am."

"Are you saying you would not have gone through with your marriage to Raphael no matter what?"

She shook her head. "No. I would have married him. I would have done it, because I was asked. It is interesting that you imagine my parents attributed my ability to be a princess to my strength. Because I'm not sure that I'm strong. I think I might simply be obedient." She took a deep breath, and looked out at the ocean below. "Show me to my room, please. I'm exhausted, and I can't argue with you anymore."

There was no argument to be had, anyway. She had made this deal with the devil. She had agreed to marry him. For the sake of their child. That was her life. But, at least, unlike her marriage to Prince Raphael, this had an escape route. She would simply keep her eyes on that, and think of nothing else.

# CHAPTER FIVE

"WHAT EXACTLY IS going on, Cristian? I had anticipated I might hear from you sooner. Instead, I have heard nothing since the day you stormed out of my office, and now, I hear through the grapevine that you have spirited my sister off to Spain."

He and Allegra had been in Spain for only five hours, but word had apparently traveled quickly to her enraged older brother.

"You are not a stupid man, Renzo," Cristian said, turning around to face the window in his home office. "I imagine you can piece together exactly what's happening."

"Are you telling me that you are the father of my sister's baby?"

"It would appear so," he said, through gritted teeth.

"Then it is a good thing that you have gone off to Spain, or I would personally be at your place of residence now, ready to kill you myself."

"And then your nephew would find himself without a father, and who would that benefit?"

"How *dare* you?" He could hear barely leashed violence in his friend's tone. "How dare you lay a hand on her? She is not what you think she is. She is far too innocent, and far too idealistic for her own good."

Cristian rubbed his hand across his forehead. "Whether or not you believe it, I didn't mean to defile your sister. It was an unfortunate case of mistaken identity. Or rather, two people who didn't care to know the identity of the other."

Renzo's crack of laughter carried no humor at all. "And you expect me to believe that no part of you had any suspicion it was Allegra?"

His friend's question was so pointed it burrowed beneath his skin with sharp precision, cutting him deep. "I have no interest in *girls*. Particularly girls who are spoiled brats that are also engaged."

There was a pause, and Cristian had a feeling Renzo was debating whether or not to hire a hit man. "What are you going to do?"

"Obviously I intend to marry her. I am holding a ring in my hand as we speak." He reached down, picking up the velvet box from the surface of his desk, and opening the lid. He'd had the most ostentatious ring in his family collection couriered to him from the *castillo* earlier today.

He intended to put it on her finger tonight during a dinner that his staff had prepared. She was angry with him, that was understandable. He was not good at catching flies with honey. Vinegar was more his talent. However, he could see that would have to change. He did not have to be a tyrant where Allegra was concerned. She was the mother of his child, and he saw no reason why they could not live together somewhat peaceably.

"And she has agreed?" Renzo asked.

"Yes," he said.

"Somehow, I cannot imagine Allegra consenting to marry you. She hates you."

"Oh, make no mistake, her hatred of me is still intact. However, she is not stupid. And I am a duke. I cannot have my child born a bastard, no matter who is carrying the baby. I understand this may damage our friendship, but it is something that must be done."

"It doesn't damage our friendship half so much as you getting my sister pregnant and then throwing her to the wolves. However, the life my parents have envisioned for her is not the life that I wanted her to have. She never wanted to marry Prince Raphael, and so I didn't want her to either. Simply because she is a woman she is expected to put aside all of her aspirations in order to make an advantageous marriage. As though this is the eighteenth century."

"It is not so different from you. You are expected to carry on your father's legacy. You must marry, eventually. Have a child so that your money and your company will have hands to pass to."

"And yet, my parents are not overly concerned with who I marry. I could do it at any point, with any bimbo I choose."

"But you won't."

Renzo chuckled. "You underestimate my shamelessness. In fact, I intend to marry the most unsuitable woman I can find when the time comes. And I intend to tarry another twenty years or so with that."

Cristian had never understood how Renzo could be so cavalier about following his parents' wishes. His friend had no idea how fortunate he was.

"When next we speak, I will be formally engaged to your sister, after which point I will speak to your parents myself."

"Why did you take her to Spain?" Renzo asked.

"In part, so you wouldn't be able to kill me without taking a flight. But also because I was not above attempting to force her hand. She has been slightly more reasonable than I anticipated. But it wasn't until I had her loaded onto my private plane that she actually agreed to the union."

"We cannot speak of this or I *will* kill you with my bare hands. And lose no sleep over it."

"Then we will not speak of it. Now, if you'll excuse me, I have an engagement to get to."

"I am so glad you are here," Maria, who had just introduced herself to Allegra as Cristian's household manager, was gushing as she draped a garment bag over the bed. "He has been too sad these last few years. Too serious."

Allegra imagined the housekeeper was meaning since his wife had passed away.

"It will be good to have a new woman in the house." Maria continued on. "It is not good for a man to be alone."

Allegra imagined Cristian almost preferred being alone. At least, he would prefer being alone to being with her. But she would not say that.

"I'm glad that he doesn't have to be anymore," she said softly, turning her attention to the garment bag.

"Your dress for tonight," Maria said, as if reading her mind.

"I'm not sure that I need a special dress for dinner."

"Of course you do. Cristian insisted that you have something special to wear, and I did my very best. You would not reject my very best," Maria said, treating Allegra to an incredibly steely gaze.

Allegra shook her head. "Of course not."

Maria looked triumphant. "Good. Then I will leave you to get ready."

Maria's best was a little bit over the top in Allegra's estimation. Though, the dress was beautiful. A deep red lace that complemented Allegra's skin tone and figure to perfection. It was snug fitting with long sleeves that showed off hints of golden skin beneath. The neckline was shaped like a heart, conforming to her bustline in a very dramatic fashion.

She turned to the side, examining her waistline. She wondered how long it would be before her pregnancy started to become obvious. Already, she was nearly eight weeks along. But there was no outward sign of the changes taking place within her. A funny thing. The small, little creature in her womb had disrupted absolutely everything, and it didn't even have the decency to show itself.

She looked at her reflection, and wondered if it appeared that she was trying too hard. But once she had the dress on, she felt obligated to fix her hair as well. And then, she found makeup in the bathroom, just her shade, and she imagined likely provided by his household staff in advance. Well, she had not been able to imagine wearing this dress while barefaced. So, she had added some golden eye shadow, liquid liner and a crimson lipstick.

Of course Cristian would think it was for him. And attribute her behavior to her uncontrollable attraction to him, that she simply didn't have.

She took a deep breath and opened the bedroom door, steeling herself as she stepped out into the hallway, and made her way toward the staircase.

She took each step slowly, the snug fit of the dress, that ended just at her knees, restricting her movements.

When her stiletto-clad foot touched the bottom floor, she looked up and saw Cristian. Her heart turned over in her chest, her stomach squeezing tight, and a pulse began to beat at the apex of her thighs, steadfastly calling her previous assessment that she was not attracted to him a bold lie.

Things were different now. It was impossible for them to be the same. Not when she knew what he could make her body feel. So strange, because of course, she didn't have any memory of how he looked. Except for his bare chest, she had not seen him naked. And she had never seen his face. She didn't know what Cristian looked like in the throes of pleasure, because he had been concealed during the act. She did not know what his kiss tasted like, because his mouth had been covered. And still, her every interaction with him felt colored by the fact that her body had been joined to his.

Fair enough, she imagined, because her entire life had changed because her body had been joined to his.

"I half expected you to show up looking like an indignant creature."

She frowned. "I do not look like an indignant *anything*. I am neither a creature nor a child. I am a woman, and I know how to dress like one, particularly when I receive a dinner invitation."

"Consider me pleasantly surprised." He reached out, extending his hand, and the moment threw her back violently to that night in the ballroom. When he had extended a leather-covered hand in her direction, the moment she had consented to being led down into the underworld. "Shall we?"

She felt as though he was asking a different question entirely. As though he was asking for her very soul, and not just her hand.

Her arms felt like lead at her sides, and she could not bring herself to accept the offer. Not again. Not with visions of that night swirling around in her head, making her feel dizzy, faint. Slowly, he dropped his hand back to his side. "Or, you could just follow me."

He turned, blazing the trail to the terrace, where a table had been set for two. It was a gorgeous setting, no less lush and perfectly suited to her than her dress had been. Her favorite foods were set out on the table. Pasta, thin slices of beef, green salad drenched in vinaigrette dressing, covered in cheese.

"How did you know?"

"I have spent a great deal of time eating dinner at your family home, Allegra. I have observed things."

Something about his words made her feel like he had

reached inside her and grabbed hold of her heart, squeezing it tight. She gritted her teeth, pushing against the sensation. "I don't believe you were paying close enough attention to me to figure out what I like to eat."

"Or, perhaps I called your brother and asked. It's up to you. Figure out which one makes the most sense." He took a step forward, grabbing hold of the back of the chair and pulling it out from the table. "Have a seat."

He made her feel guilty. Made her feel as though, somehow, she was the one who was out of line, when in fact he was the one who had loaded her up onto a plane and coerced her into saying yes to this engagement, complete with custody threats. She should not be feeling guilty simply because she didn't respond warmly to his apology dinner. Or, whatever it was.

"It looks delicious," she said, but, she nearly choked on the words.

"I have no doubt it is. My staff does very good work."

"Italian food as well as Spanish, I see."

"I had someone brought in specially to make the food in a manner you would enjoy."

He said those words dismissively, almost icily. And yet, she couldn't help but be almost touched by them. It seemed as though he was actually trying to make her feel welcome here. Though, she had much the sense that she was a prisoner being offered her last meal. She was caught between those two sensations. Of feeling warm, cared for, and feeling as though she was trapped.

"Don't you think that perhaps we should delay our marriage a little bit?"

"Not long. I don't have any desire to see tabloid pictures of you walking down the aisle looking as though you are about to burst. Those will be photographs our child will have access to later. And while I imagine someday they will be able to do the math on their conception, I would rather it were not so plain. In the age of the internet, there are no secrets to be kept."

"I'm not suggesting we get married directly before my induction. But maybe until I'm past the most unstable part of the pregnancy?"

"And when will that be?" he asked, not waiting to start eating the meal set out before him.

"In about a month."

"Well, it will take at least that much time to gather all of our plans. The wedding of nobility will never be a small affair, even if we do limit the guest list. There will be interest, and I have no desire to sweep this marriage beneath the rug. Again, for the sake of our child."

Allegra had not imagined that he wanted to have a full-on wedding ceremony. Instead, she had been sort of picturing a courthouse situation. But then, she imagined Spanish dukes didn't do courthouse weddings.

"Oh," she said, sounding every bit as confused as she felt. "It's only that… I mean, you have been married before."

"Precisely," he said, taking a sip of wine. "I have been married before, and those photographs will be available for our son or daughter to see. I do not wish for that child to think that I married his or her mother in haste, and with less honor than I gave to my first wife."

"But that's exactly what's happening."

"Appearances," he bit out, "are essential when you live life in the public eye. Appearances are often more essential than reality."

Allegra knew well enough how true that was. It was why her parents were constantly rolling their eyes at Renzo's antics. He was a playboy of the highest degree, but because he was a man his acumen in business canceled out his behavior. She had been warned, from a very early age, that the public would not be so forgiving of her.

The discussion was never so much about what she actually did, so much as about what became public.

"I do understand. It's just that… I suppose, we could make the argument that we were so very much in love we had to rush to get married?"

He laughed, a bitter, hollow sound. "A fact that would be much easier to create, were we not planning on divorcing within two years."

"Marry in haste, divorce just as quickly?"

"While that makes its own sort of sense, I insist that we do this right."

She let out a heavy sigh, and the two of them continued eating in silence. She never knew what to say to him. She never had. Whenever he would come over for dinner in the years past, she would simply sit and listen as he and Renzo bounced stories off each other, their interplay effortless, and delightful to her father and mother.

Delightful in a way that Allegra never seemed to be. She was always afraid of saying the wrong thing, and when she did speak, she inevitably did. Either she didn't have the answer people were looking for, or she ended up in a fight. That was how it always went with Cristian. Tongue-tied, or angry. There was very little in between.

True to his word, the food was excellent, and Allegra ate more than she should. In spite of the fact that she still had a wedding dress to fit into. She wondered if she would be expected to wear the same wedding dress. That was a terrible thought.

On the heels of that thought came the realization that she would indeed be too big for that dress by the time her wedding date to Cristian rolled around. She was pregnant—she wasn't going to go on any prewedding crash diets.

Her mother was going to be apoplectic.

She was still brooding about this when she finished

her dinner. And then, Cristian moved from his position in his chair, rising to a standing position and reaching into his coat pocket. He made for a striking figure, standing there in front of her, backlit by the sea and the sinking sun. He was wearing a sharp, black suit, as he often did, and yet, something about now made it different. Maybe the fact that they had been lovers, even if using that word was stretching the truth a bit.

Sex against a wall was hardly making love. And being with a man once—when he didn't even know who you were—was hardly the same as being his lover.

When he fished his hand back out of his pocket, he was holding a velvet ring box between his thumb and forefinger. Her heart stalled out. "Cristian…"

But before she could protest, he was sinking down to one knee in front of her on the terrace, opening the lid on the box and revealing an intricate, glittering ring, an emerald blazing at the center of a finely etched setting.

"We must make it official," he said, his voice low, grave. "If we are to have a real wedding, then we will have a real engagement."

He reached inside the box and took the ring out, holding it up so that it caught the light. It glittered there, like a promise. The fire dancing inside of it so small and tentative that she knew the slightest breeze could snuff it out.

And then, he lowered it, and extinguished the light, along with the metaphor that was overwrought at best.

He took hold of her hand, slipping her ring onto the fourth finger. "You will be mine," he said, his tone firm, his words sure. "You will be my wife."

Through all of it, she had been unable to speak. Unable to say anything.

"Say yes, *querida*."

Her mouth was dry, her throat tight, and she couldn't speak. So, she nodded instead.

This was her second engagement. But it was the first time a man had ever gotten on one knee in front of her. It was the first time a man had ever proposed to her. Though, she supposed that Cristian hadn't exactly proposed. He had told her that she would be his, and she had nodded her agreement.

She imagined that was a brilliant summation of Cristian's existence. What he wanted, he commanded. And he received.

She was angry with herself for not being an exception.

When he reached out his gloved hand, she had acquiesced. When he had demanded silence, she had given in. Now, out on this balcony overlooking the sea, he had asked for her hand, and again, she had allowed him his way.

He smiled. The curve of his lips was slow, lazy and something quite unlike anything she had ever experienced before. He had never looked at her like this, not once. His smiles had always been directed at her family, and any that had been tossed her way had been sardonic at best. There was something sensual in this, something hot. Something that seemed meant for the masked woman she had been in that Venetian ballroom, and not for his friend's younger sister who he could barely stand.

"There," he said, his tone triumphant. "Should we have any reporters following us, they will have seen that this is authentic."

He moved back to his seat, taking his position in front of his plate.

"What?"

"You are headline news," he said, his tone conversational, casual. "If we had been followed to my home, I would not be surprised. There is likely someone hidden in an alcove just outside the property using a telephoto lens to try and figure out what the two of us are doing together, given your scandal. Now, they know."

"So…this was all for show?"

Something about that realization enraged her, insulted her. Yes, she knew that there was nothing between herself and Cristian, but he was proposing that the two of them get married, and stay married for the next two years. He had gotten her pregnant with his child, and for a moment… For just a moment… He had made her feel something. He had made her feel as though he was looking at her. As though he saw her. And then, it had turned out that it was all a ruse.

Before she could fully think her actions through, before she could stop herself, she found herself rising out of her chair, crossing the short space between them. She leaned in, her heart pounding heavily, her hands shaking. Her stomach was tied up in knots so tight she could barely breathe. "If you intend to put on a show, Cristian, you're going to have to do better than that. You missed the most essential thing in a proposal."

He tilted his head back, looking up at her. "I do not think I did," he said, reaching out and taking hold of her hand, brushing his thumb over the gem on her finger. "Are you not wearing my ring?"

"It isn't about a ring," she said, reaching up, bracketing his face with her hands, his skin hot beneath her palms. "It's this."

And then, she leaned forward, and pressed her lips to his.

# CHAPTER SIX

CRISTIAN FELT LIKE he had been lit on fire inside. And that it was slowly burning its way outward. Allegra's lips were soft, her kiss unpracticed. And it was undoing him completely.

They had not kissed before. He had been inside her body, had felt the press of her mouth against his neck, his chest—all before he had known it was her. That day they had made love up against the wall, he had skimmed his hands over her bare curves.

But he had never tasted her lips.

She was innocence and sin, and he knew for certain this was how a man was drawn through the gates of hell. With the kiss of a temptress masquerading as an angel, unpracticed carnality disguising the depth of debauchery that was hidden beneath the surface.

He knew that. But even knowing it he did not pull away.

Allegra angled her head, parting her lips and brushing the tip of her tongue against the seam of his mouth. He opened, allowing her entry, growling as she breached him, tasted him, tested him.

He grabbed hold of her hips, steadying her as she pushed her fingers through his hair, clinging to his head as she kissed him with a desperation that transcended skill. Had a woman ever kissed him like this? If she had, he couldn't remember. He couldn't remember anyone. Anything.

Just like that, a kick of guilt hit him square in the ribs.

His wife. He had forgotten his wife. Yes, she had been dead for three years, but that was no excuse. She was the woman he had made vows to. The woman he had failed. The last woman, before Allegra, that he had kissed.

*But Allegra will be your wife. She is the mother of your child.*

And if he wasn't careful he would break her, the same as he did everything else.

He wrenched his mouth away from hers, pushing her back. "Enough," he said. "That should be sufficient enough to convince anyone."

She looked dazed, her lips swollen, her hair tumbled. She looked a bit too much like the wanton creature he'd had the night of the masquerade. And a bit too familiar. Pushing against his conscience, against his steadfast assertion that he certainly had no idea who she was that night.

But of course he hadn't. Had he known, he never would have touched Allegra. He gritted his teeth, fighting with the beast inside him, fighting to keep his focus trained on a point behind her, and not on her kiss-swollen mouth.

She was breathing hard, her petite shoulders moving up and down with each and every intake of air. He was determined to ignore that as well.

"Did he ever kiss you?" He should not have asked that question. He should have stood up from the table and gone back into the house. He should put as much distance between the two of them as possible.

"Did he…" She blinked rapidly. "Raphael. Did Raphael ever kiss me?"

"Yes. Unless you have another fiancé that you neglected to tell me about."

"Of course he did," she said, her tone defensive.

"How?"

He was warming his hands on hellfire, with every word he spoke. But knowing it didn't change his desire to do exactly that. Hell, he had broken off their kiss. He deserved something for that.

"What do you mean *how*?" She sounded intensely irritated, and confused. No different from the way Allegra typically sounded when she spoke to him.

"Did he kiss you on the mouth, as we just did? Did he slide his tongue against yours? Taste you deeply? Savor you as though you were a dessert?" Every suggestion he spoke stoked the fire of his arousal even hotter. "Or did he kiss you on the top of your head like you were his puppy?"

A dusky-rose color spread over her high cheekbones. "That is none of your business."

"Like you were a puppy, then." He watched as fury lit her dark eyes. This, at least, was a familiar sight. Allegra, enraged at him. "Have you ever been properly kissed, Allegra?"

Her dark eyes went round, her lips tightened into a flat line. "Of course I have."

"Before the kiss we just shared?"

"You're awful." She turned to leave, and he rose from his seat, following slowly after her.

"Try not to destroy the illusion," he said.

"What illusion?" she asked without turning around.

"That the two of us are blissfully happy about our new engagement. And that I am following you into the house so that I can ravish you on the nearest piece of furniture."

Her shoulders stiffened, but she didn't turn again. Instead, she continued on into the house, and he went behind her, closing the door and pressing a button that lowered all the curtains.

"Now you're welcome to unleash a volley of weapons upon me. It is private."

"I'm too tired to attack you with weaponry. Verbal or otherwise. I want to go to bed. Alone."

"You speak as if there was another option. It may surprise you to hear this, Allegra, but I am not going to play the part of wicked seducer." His body throbbed in response to those words, calling him a liar. "I have every desire to ensure that you exit our marriage as unscathed as possible. If you choose, you could leave the child in my care. If you want to move on from this as though it never happened, you would receive no judgment from me."

She shook her head. "That is not what I want. I'm not going to leave my child. I'm not going to act like I had no stake in this mistake. I did. This is my consequence, and I'm happy to take it. I want a child, Cristian. Maybe not yours, and maybe not now, but I have always wanted one. As for the pieces of this that are less than ideal, I will simply accept them."

"Then, from now on I expect that you will not act as though you are a prisoner. You were given a choice."

She tilted her chin up. "I will act however I choose. I have gone past the point of pretending to be perfect. I have ruined every plan my parents ever had for me. I have ruined myself. I think the payoff is that I no longer have to behave. Good night."

She turned and walked up the stairs, leaving him angry, hard and aching, and with absolutely no relief in sight.

Allegra did her best to avoid Cristian over the next few days, and he seemed completely all right with that.

Instead, she rattled around the house attempting to amuse herself. She had a few charities that she was involved in that she checked on, but otherwise, she was at loose ends. That was the problem with spending your whole life training to become a princess. You ended up with a lot of skills that didn't apply otherwise.

Suddenly, she felt hollowed out, useless. She had spent her entire life leading up to the moment when she would become Raphael's wife. And now, she wouldn't be. In two years, she would be Cristian's ex-wife, and then beyond that what was she supposed to do?

Unless her parents spent money supporting her, she didn't know how she was going to live. She didn't have job skills. She didn't have any goals that existed outside of doing exactly what her parents had told her she should. And that was… It was pathetic really. If she had a daughter, what kind of example would that be?

Even if she had a son, it was a pretty awful precedent.

She looked over at the table by the bed and saw that her phone was lit up. Her mother was calling. That meant word had gotten back to her. Allegra had been avoiding the news—and her phone—in addition to Cristian.

Sadly, she could not avoid her mother. That was like attempting to avoid the hand of God.

She reached out, grabbed her phone and swiped her thumb across the screen. "Hello?"

"Allegra, I'm shocked that you have made no effort to get in touch with me."

Allegra let out a weary sigh. "I'm sorry. Everything has moved very quickly."

"When you made your little announcement about needing to break off the engagement with Raphael because of your pregnancy, you might have mentioned that Cristian was the father."

"I wasn't sure yet what Cristian would want to do. I was afraid to tell him."

"You should not have been more afraid to tell him than you were to tell your father," her mother said, her tone icy. "However, it is clear that you have now spoken to him."

"Yes," she said, "I have."

"And it appears he has agreed to marry you, which means that your father will not have to castrate him. Which is good, as he has always been fond of Cristian."

A strange relief rushed through Allegra. Her mother sounded…well, not angry. "I imagine Cristian is grateful."

"It was wrong of you to betray Raphael."

Allegra let out a long, slow breath. "Was it wrong of me to betray him? Or was it wrong of me to get myself into a predicament where I couldn't simply go ahead and marry him anyway?"

"Obviously the latter," her mother responded, and Allegra could just picture her waving her hand dismissively. "I imagine that Raphael has not spent the past several years being celibate. Therefore, I imagine he did not expect the same of you. *I* certainly didn't. You are a Valenti," she said that as if it explained everything. "But a Valenti has to be careful to control the situation. And you did not."

Allegra's face heated. She felt like she was a child again, being scolded for being too noisy. For not being mindful of their surroundings. For not being aware that there were photographers nearby, and that she needed to sit up straighter, keep her voice down and not take such large bites of food.

"No, I did not."

"However, I'm very grateful that you did not manage to get yourself with the child of some no-account artist or something equally horrifying, like a footballer."

"You're happy that it's Cristian?"

"I would not say *happy*, as we now have damage control to see to. But, if you must have an indiscretion, then I suppose having one with a Spanish duke is the lesser of evils."

"I suppose."

"Of course," her mother continued, "Raphael was a prince."

"And Spain is a larger country than Santa Firenze," Allegra said, echoing something that Cristian had said earlier.

There was silence on the line for a moment. Then her mother sighed. "I suppose that is true. When is the wedding?"

"Cristian would like to have it a month from now."

"That does not give us much time to plan."

Allegra sat down on the bed. "No, but the alternative is me walking down the aisle looking like I'm smuggling a beach ball under my gown."

"We can't have that," her mother said, sounding horrified.

"Indeed not. One month."

"In Spain, I assume?"

"Of course." Because Cristian had insisted, and Allegra didn't care. Actually, Allegra was starting to feel pleased that she wasn't back home in Italy. Contending with her mother over the phone was much easier than contending with her in person.

"We will be in touch. I shall contact the designer from your first dress about having a second done. Something with a bit more Spanish flair?"

"Something perhaps not fitted at the waist. Beyond that, I don't really care."

Her mother missed the sardonic note to her voice. "Perfect. We shall speak soon. And… Allegra, this wedding had better go forward. If it does not your father and I may be forced to cut you off until you've learned your lesson."

And with that, her mother hung up.

Allegra scrubbed her eyes with her fists, feeling gritty and tired, in spite of having done nothing all day. She wondered if it was pregnancy symptoms, or if it was just the effects of being in a strange situation, in very strange circumstances. And dealing with her mother. Who was challenging when she felt well, forget feeling terrible.

Either way, she wanted some food.

She looked in the mirror briefly, before continuing out the door. It didn't matter that her hair was a mess, or that she was wearing just an oversize button-up shirt and a pair of stretch pants. She had no one to impress. Least of all Cristian.

He had pushed her away after the kiss, after all. Nothing could have signaled his disinterest louder.

And then he had asked if she had been kissed by Raphael, and she had wanted to defend herself. But, the truth was, Raphael had never kissed her. Unless you counted solicitous kisses on the cheek and hand. But they had been…brotherly, if anything. No, not even brotherly. That implied some sort of affection. These had been dutiful. And that had been the end of it.

She supposed she really did need to look at a headline or two. Just to see if there was an indication of how Raphael was doing. She did not like the thought that she might have hurt him. Of course, that would imply she had some sort of hold over his emotions, and she had seen no evidence of that.

"It appears that Raphael has replaced you already."

Allegra turned around to see Cristian standing in the doorway. He looked… Well, he made her throat dry. He was dressed in nothing but jeans settled low on his hips and a tight black T-shirt. Much more casual than she was accustomed to seeing him. And she found that, on him, casual worked. She felt slightly scrubby by comparison.

"He *what*?"

"It is the companion headline to our own engagement. You will be pleased to know that we were in fact being stalked by the paparazzi, as I suspected. And your kiss made for quite the definitive exclamation mark on the whole thing."

He reached out, handing her the newspaper he was holding. She looked down, and her face heated. There, in bold print, was a photograph of her kissing Cristian. Her fingers were threaded through his hair, and she was leaning in, while he looked to be holding her steady, his hands resting on her hips. Even in the photograph, the giant engagement ring he'd presented her with was visible. The perfect engagement photo. Even if it was a lie.

Then her eye drifted to the photo next to it. In the picture was a blonde woman, wearing a baggy university sweatshirt, and looking angry. Next to her was Prince Raphael, wearing large dark sunglasses and a suit. He had his arm around her and appeared to be ushering her onto his private plane.

"She is an American," Cristian said.

"No," Allegra responded. "That can't be."

"Yes. An American student. From Colorado. Bailey. *Princess* Bailey, as she would be known if they were to marry." Cristian sounded amused, which was irritating because he was never amused.

"Now you truly are lying. That does not sound like a princess, that sounds like a beagle."

He laughed, a dark, sensual sound. "Are you jealous?" He sounded even *more* amused at that.

She couldn't pretend it wasn't strange that Raphael was engaged already. And to someone who was so different than she was. But then, while Cristian had a title and similar coloring to Raphael, that was the extent of their similarities.

Raphael was circumspect at least. Cristian was… *Cristian*.

"I'm not jealous," she sniffed. "Just surprised. My reputation, my family connections, were so important to him."

She looked back at the photograph of him with the rather enraged-looking woman. "She's nothing like that."

"She is not. And, as little as I know Raphael, your pedigree did seem important."

"Now you're making *me* sound like a beagle."

"It is only the truth. I came up with the idea to introduce your father to Raphael after he was telling me about the challenges he was having finding a wife. I made the introductions and the rest was set."

"Which is why you've been all over me about my behavior ever since then. Except…wow, the bitter irony. It's your fault the engagement was broken. All your looming and sardonic comments were for nothing, because at the end of all things, you were the one who destroyed what you set up. I'd laugh, except it's hard to be too smug in my current position."

"I should say so," he said, his tone dry. "Though I must point out, were I not the one compromising your engagement, you likely would have found another man."

"Who might have practiced safe sex."

The look he treated her to nearly burned her from the inside out. "What are you doing down here? You've been hiding up in your room for days."

"I'm hungry. And it isn't feeding hours at the zoo yet. So, I thought I would see what I could get for myself."

"Do you feel as though you are in captivity?"

She let out a long slow breath, and walked past him, making her way to the fridge. "I am being kept in a house in a city and a country that I don't know my way around. How else am I supposed to feel?"

"I told you that you might want to take your dramatics down a couple of notches."

She huffed. "And I told you I reserve the right to my dramatics."

"Another impasse we find ourselves at."

She paused in her hunt through the fridge and looked at him, arching a brow. "Indeed."

"I do not wish for you to feel as though you're captive."

"If you were waiting for those words to magically make me feel differently, you will have to wait longer."

"I was not. I would like to take you to the beach."

"The one just outside."

"No. I have a beach house. In a more private location, one that you might enjoy."

She tamped down the surge of giddiness that rioted through her. She did love the beach. She always had. But she didn't like crowds. It was almost like he knew. "I love the beach," she said.

"I know."

His words settled between them, significant and far larger inside her than they should be, making it hard for her to breathe.

"We will have to fly," he said. "I hope you don't mind."

"Well, we did just fly to Spain a little less than a week ago."

"You are officially jet set. Consider it a consolation prize as you have lost your formerly pending princess status."

She swallowed hard, trying to ignore the tightness in her throat, in her chest. Trying to ignore the fact that this felt heavy, and significant, when it absolutely should not.

"Well, as consolation prizes go, I suppose it's a pretty good one."

"Excellent. I will call ahead and make arrangements, and we will leave tonight."

"Aren't you going to tell me where we're going?"

"I would rather surprise you."

# CHAPTER SEVEN

CRISTIAN WATCHED ALLEGRA'S face as they walked into the large, oceanfront home on the island of Kauai. It was not as large as his home in Spain, but it was private. Shrouded by palm and banyan trees at the front, and facing white sands and velvet-blue water in the back.

It was his own personal, private paradise. Which felt slightly over the top, even to him, considering that he owned a piece of paradise already in his native Spain.

This belonged only to him. Not to his blood. Not to his family. He supposed the appeal lay there.

The paparazzi would not find them here. And it would, perhaps, benefit both him and Allegra to be on neutral, private ground, if only for a while.

There was no point in making her miserable. That wasn't his goal. They were going to have to deal with each other, come to some consensus on how to raise their child. They didn't need to be embroiled in a constant battle.

"What do you think?" he asked, growing impatient waiting for her to voice her response.

"It's beautiful. Of course it is."

"But do you like it?"

"I've always wanted to go to Hawaii. And I do like it."

A surge of triumph poured through his veins. He had known that she liked the idea of going somewhere tropical. He also knew that she had not been. She did not possess the independence of her older brother, and did not travel quite as freely. She had gone on strange family vacations with her former fiancé. To the East Coast of the United States, and to the Amalfi coast. But no one had ever taken her to the kind of tropical island he had heard her wax poetic about at the dinner table one night when she'd been in high school.

Now someone had. *He* had.

"Good," he said.

"How long have you had a house here? I don't remember you ever mentioning it."

"I bought it quite some time ago. Five or six years at least. And I have done my very best to keep it a secret. As you saw, the paparazzi are all too willing to try and get a window into my life using any means necessary. This, I have managed to keep to myself. I don't have to worry about photographers or indeed anyone invading my privacy."

"Why are the paparazzi so fascinated with you? I've never heard of you setting a single foot out of line, Cristian. I understand why they chase Renzo. He seems to court controversy. You don't."

"I am titled. I am part of an old family. Also, my mother does engage in rather scandalous behavior. I suppose just by being her son I am a bit interesting. And the fact that I cause very little scandal considering who I'm related to is also notable."

He watched her face closely to see what her response was to this. She must have some awareness of his mother's exploits. He rarely spoke to the woman, but she was his mother. And while he found her behavior reckless at best, he could scarcely blame her. Life at the *castillo* had been oppressive. When his father had been alive everyone had lived quietly. Doing their very best not to trigger the hammer of his father's anger. To keep themselves from being crushed beneath the weight of it.

He had only gotten worse after Cristian was born. That was how the story had always been told. By household staff, by his mother. Fueled by jealous suspicions that his accidental heir might not truly be his.

He had been obsessed by the thought, but had never ordered a test for fear of scandal. And so he had simply spent his wrath upon the child he suspected might be a betrayal to the bloodline.

Once the duke died it was only understandable that his widow would seek liberation. And she had. Away from Spain. Away from her son. And she had never once looked back.

It had been nearly a decade since he'd spoken to his mother, his calls finally going unanswered, whatever guilt she felt over her initial abandonment easing enough that she no longer felt obligated to pretend she missed her only child.

It didn't matter to him at all. Any distance he could find from that time of his life suited him fine.

"I suppose that makes sense," Allegra said, her tone carefully neutral.

"No additional commentary on my mother's behavior?"

"Why would I comment on it? I don't know her."

"Because people who live life in the public eye are always inviting comment. Every time they breathe, are they not?"

"I've never felt like that was fair," she said.

"You are in the minority."

"Then I am. But my life has always been dictated by the fact that people cared what I did. People that I will never meet. My mother has always been consumed with appearances. It was funny, I had a conversation with her about you. About you being the father of my child. She was not upset to find out that I had slept with you, Cristian. She was only upset that I had caused a scandal."

His brain was completely hung up on the part about them sleeping together. Because truly, they never had. They'd found release up against the wall, a release that had been long in coming for him. But they had never slept together. They'd never had the luxury of lying next to each other, skin to skin, their legs tangled together as he smoothed his hands over her abundant curves.

His body hardened at the illicit fantasy. A fantasy he would not carry out.

"I suppose that is common," he said, in lieu of taking her into his arms and pressing his lips against hers. "To live life as though all that exists is done in the light. While we all obsess about things done in the dark."

Color mounted in her cheeks, and he knew that she, like himself, was thinking of things the two of *them* had done in the dark.

"I suppose. I'm very tired. Perhaps we can talk again at dinner?"

"You're so desperate to get rid of me." It was not a question. He could see that she needed distance from him. And he desperately needed it from her. Still, he didn't feel inclined to press for that distance. Instead he wanted to keep her close. Wanted to keep baiting the beast inside him. Just so he could jump against the bars of his cage.

"Why would I want to get rid of you?"

"So that you don't kiss me again."

He did not know what was possessing him to push her. To push himself. To test limits between them that he knew from experience were quite easily broken.

He had never been a man who allowed himself to be ruled by passions. He'd had a few lovers before his marriage, but no great affairs. And then, he had chosen Sylvia to be his wife based on their mutual compatibility.

He had also cared for her. A great deal. But she had not made him feel like he was fighting a war with himself.

"I don't think there's any danger of that," she said, her tone flat.

"Perhaps if I were wearing a mask?"

"Then I wouldn't be able to kiss your mouth."

"I could offer up other suggestions."

She drew back, her eyes round, glittering. He knew, as well as she did, that while she was angry, that was not the only emotion she felt. He was tempting her. Just as he was tempting himself.

"Just a nap," she said, "thanks. I'm a little bit too tired to be kissing adventurous places on your body."

"Perhaps when you're feeling a bit more rested?"

"No." She turned away from him, heading toward the stairs. Then she stopped, and whirled back around to face him. "And you don't even want me to. You just want to push me. I don't understand why. Why can't we have a few companionable moments? Why do you have to be a constant ogre?"

Then, the beast didn't just rattle the cage. He broke through it completely. Cristian crossed the space between them, backing her up against the wall, his hands bracketing either side of her face. "Is that what you think? You think I don't want you? You think that I'm simply playing a game? Tell me, Allegra, have I ever struck you as the sort of man who plays games?"

His actions seemed to have struck her mute. She shook her head, wide, dark eyes never leaving his.

"Then why, *querida*, do you think I am playing a game with you? I don't say things I don't mean. I don't make empty promises."

"And yet you promised me that our marriage would remain chaste. So I'm forced to believe that either you're a liar, or you're playing a game."

"What is logical and preferable, and what I want are two different things."

"And what do you want?" she asked, her voice husky.

The air changed between them, got thicker, filled with all of the tension that was pulsing between them like a living thing.

"Right now?" He leaned in close, her scent rising up, filling him, enticing him. "Right now, I wish to push your dress up and bury myself inside of your tight body. I can remember, so clearly what that was like. There is no man on earth who wouldn't jump at the chance to have you again. Myself included. I consider myself a man with superior control. A man who is not controlled by baser urges. And yet, with you, I feel I am entirely comprised of baser urges."

"You don't like me," she said, her words helpless.

"Perhaps that is why. Perhaps it's exciting."

"That's sick."

"Maybe. But you like it too." He raised his hand and skimmed his thumb across the pounding pulse at the base of her neck.

"I just want a nap." She ducked beneath his arms, beating a hasty retreat for the stairs, taking them two at a time on her way to her room.

His body relaxed slowly as she moved farther and farther away. He swore, turning away from the stairs and walking outside, staring at the ocean. Normally, he found the view calming. That was not the case now.

He had to get a handle on himself. There was no point in playing these games. No point in feeding the attraction that he felt for her.

Perhaps he did need to go out and find another woman. After this stay here, he would do just that.

One thing was certain, he would not lose his control again.

* * *

Allegra felt much like she was getting ready to approach a panther in its lair. But then, why wouldn't she? The last time she had been face-to-face with Cristian he had looked very much like he might want to eat her.

Again, much to her chagrin, she was not as disgusted by that as she would like to be. In fact, she felt… She was more than intrigued. She was…enticed. Attracted. Aroused.

She gritted her teeth as she walked through the house keeping an eye out for said panther as she went. She looked out the large windows that provided a view of the ocean and saw flames.

She walked through the door that led out to the sand, only to see Cristian sitting by a bonfire. The orange light illuminated the planes of his face, throwing the hollows of his cheekbones, the square line of his jaw, into sharper relief.

"What are you doing?"

"I thought you might appreciate a dinner by the water."

He stood, and she noticed the table set behind him. "I do," she said, taking a step forward, feeling a little bit shocked. She didn't know how to reconcile these moments where he seemed like he might know her, with the other moments. The ones that were filled with intensity, anger. Desire. Anger at the desire.

"It isn't seafood. I remember that you don't like fish."

His words hit her with the force of a blow. "I don't. You're right. I mean, thank you. For remembering."

"I have a good memory," he said, as if he could make the actions weightless with that careless statement.

She nodded, moving toward the table. "Of course you do."

"I do not wish to make you miserable," he said.

"Well, if my happiness were entirely dictated by being well-fed you would have me set for life."

"Can it not be so simple?"

She took a seat, marveling at the very nicely cooked chicken and vegetables. "Sadly, not. Otherwise, I really would have chosen to marry Raphael. I'm not sure you can top a palace chef."

"I cooked this myself. So, you're right there. The quality may be suspect."

"You...*you* made this?" It was difficult to imagine Cristian cooking.

"I value my solitude, so I don't like to have staff around all the time. And I have spent the past few years as a single man."

"Of course."

"Do not look like that every time Sylvia comes up."

She looked up. "Like what?"

"Like you're on the verge of weeping."

"It's just... It was very sad. She always seemed... She seemed lovely." Allegra had met his late wife on only a few occasions, but the beautiful blonde had appeared to be sweet. An interesting match for a strong and rather gruff man like Cristian, but they had been married for a couple of years and had always seemed happy enough.

"She was. Effortlessly. A sweet woman who, when things were well, added a sense of tranquility to her surroundings."

There was a strange note to his voice when he said those words, and Allegra could not guess at why.

"How long was she sick?"

His expression changed. "She was not sick in quite the way you might think. Sylvia struggled with mental illness."

"Oh. I didn't know."

"Her parents did not wish to disclose the issues. I have always respected their wishes."

"But I assumed… I assumed that it was a physical illness. I thought that was how she…"

"It is," he said, his tone hard.

His words settled over her, a slow horror creeping over her skin. "She didn't…"

He nodded slowly. "She killed herself, Allegra. And I do understand why her parents didn't want that to become public knowledge. So there was much vague noise made about illness and her fragility. Still…sometimes I question covering up the truth. Her truth. As though it was some flaw in her. I never blamed her. I fear they do."

"I'm sorry."

"Everyone is. I most of all."

"I shouldn't have brought it up," she said.

"I'm the one who brought it up. I'm more comfortable with it than most other people are. As comfortable as one can be with loss. She was my wife. I will not pretend she didn't exist."

"Of course. And I won't either."

"It is as you say, though," he said. "When you live life in the public eye everyone will have an opinion. Likely, comparisons will be made between yourself and Sylvia."

"That's okay."

"Is it?"

"I don't know. It doesn't bother me now. Maybe it would be different if I…if we…if I felt like I was competing with her for your…feelings."

"I see. And, as you are not, you have no concerns about the comparison?"

"It seems a little bit small and petty to be envious of a dead woman."

"Still, some would be."

"I'm not one of them. I don't know what happened to

make you hold me in such low esteem, Cristian, but I'm not a terrible person."

"You always seemed unhappy. In your home, which to me is the most shining example of a functional family, you never seemed very pleased with your position."

"That's why you don't like me? Because you don't think I'm grateful enough for what I have?"

He nodded. "Exactly that."

"Appearances. It all comes down to appearances. No, my parents aren't evil, but they care a lot more about me having a life that looks a certain way, than me having a life worth living. It's never been about what *I* wanted."

He frowned. "Everything they do is to try and ensure that you have a stable future. I understand that you have a romantic idea that you want more freedom, but believe me when I tell you that you only have good options in your life."

"You would say that. You have freedom."

"And more than my share of tragedy. The ability to do whatever you want doesn't guarantee any kind of happiness. The fact that you have a family that cares, that loves you, is a bigger gift than I think you realize."

She gritted her teeth. "Maybe. But I do think the fact that I did…what I did with you at the ball proves that I could never have lived that life. And I wasn't brave enough to take the step forward, to say that it wasn't what I wanted. I had to go about it in the wrong way. I should have taken a stand. That's the only thing I regret. The only place I really see a maturity. Going along with it while I resented it all."

"Was Raphael so bad?" he asked.

"No. He wasn't. But he was…exacting. He definitely had an idea of what he wanted. He expected me to fall into line with that. He was also more impenetrable than you are, if such a thing is possible."

"He is marrying her, by the way. There was a press conference."

Allegra smiled slightly. "I'm happy for them. If he can thaw himself out for her, then she's welcome to him."

"You had issues with his distance?" Cristian asked, lifting a brow.

"Yes," she said sardonically. "I found him impossible to read. And entirely too full of himself."

"And you exchange him for me?"

"Out of the frying pan and into the bonfire," she said, her tone dry. "I have never quite seen myself fulfilling the position that my parents wish I would. Obviously, I'm not the woman that you wish I'd be either. I wanted to try. I wanted to do the best that I could. But I made a mistake because I don't think I was ever intended to be a princess. It was definitely self-sabotage on my part."

"I do make a fairly effective sabotage, if I say so myself."

She wasn't sure whether or not she should apologize, or whether she should say she didn't exactly mean it that way. "I didn't know it was you."

"Did you truly not?"

Her stomach twisted. "Of course I didn't. What do you think? I was harboring some sort of secret crush on you?" As soon as she said that images of him sitting at her family dinner table over the years flashed through her mind. Him as a young man, as a grieving widower and again looking more like himself.

And then she saw those images cut together with a memory of him in his mask, descending the stairs, and that sensation that had overtaken her that had been a lot like discomfort. A lot like the kind of unsettled adrenaline that often filtered through her body when she found out that Cristian would be at dinner that night.

"I suppose it's possible," he said.

She shook her head. "I didn't know."

She hadn't. Of course she hadn't. To imagine that something in her subconscious had picked up on it was simply ridiculous. And attributing far too much intelligence to her passive mind. Or rather, stupidity. Because if she would have known it was Cristian, of course she never would have...

That train of thought trailed off as she looked at his face, half of it shrouded in shadow, the other blazing in the firelight.

Whatever she had thought, whatever she had felt, it was much more difficult to grasp it now. Because she simply couldn't divorce what she felt for Cristian now from what she had felt then. Now that she had been with him. Now that she had kissed him. Ever since he had pressed her up against the wall for the first time, then again in this house earlier.

"It doesn't matter what you think of me," she continued, more for herself than for him. "And it's somewhat ironic that you were my path to freedom. Seeing as you don't think I deserve freedom."

"It isn't that I don't think you deserve freedom, Allegra. It's simply that I think freedom might be a different thing than what you mean. Do you imagine it's the ability to do whatever you want?"

"I suppose I imagine it's the ability to marry a man that I love. You act as though I want the entire world. As though I'm selfish for wanting to be able to choose the person that I spend the rest of my life with."

"I think you misunderstand the way the world works. You could have married a perfectly decent man and been in a position to do some good in the world. He would have treated you well, and you likely could have come to love him. Instead, you threw your virginity away with a stranger in a darkened corridor, got yourself pregnant with his baby... And now, here you are."

"You present yourself as the worst choice now? I thought you were an upgrade. Due to Spain's size."

"I grant you," he said, his tone dark, "Spain's size is rather impressive. However, you would have been much better off with your prince, Allegra."

"Why do you think that?"

"Prince Raphael seems to be a nice man. I am not a nice man."

"Well, I could've been the first person to tell you that."

"But you don't know the half of it."

"I'll never have to know the whole of it either. Especially not since we'll only be married for a couple of years. It won't matter. We're never going to... We're never going to touch again."

For some reason, those words sent her stomach plummeting down into her toes. Disappointment. That's what it felt like. But it couldn't be that. There was no way on earth she could possibly be disappointed at the thought of never touching Cristian again.

"Good for you. Though, it was certainly enough time for Sylvia to destruct."

"Sylvia was ill. You said so yourself."

"Yes. I'm sure that being married to me didn't put her under any undue stress."

"Do you really think that? Do you think that you somehow..."

He reached across the table, pressing his hand down firmly over hers, his dark eyes blazing with black fire. "We will not have this discussion." His hold on her was firm, hot. She wanted desperately to pull away, to put distance between them. And at the same time, she wanted him to hold on to her forever. Wanted to be caught in this intensity for as long as it could possibly go on, even if it singed her from the inside out.

"You should go back inside," he continued. "Get away from me."

"We were fighting."

"You think it matters?"

"It should," she said, her voice sounding thin, strained.

"Of course it should matter. But it hasn't so far, has it? It didn't even matter when you didn't know who I was. It exists. With another man's engagement ring on your finger, with a mask over your face and when the mask is ripped from mine. It exists. This thing between us. So go back inside. Go back inside and perhaps I won't touch you again."

She thought about it. She thought of extricating herself from his hold and fleeing for her life. For her sanity. Instead, she sat, unmoving, her hand still beneath his.

"And what happens if I stay?"

# CHAPTER EIGHT

HE SHOULD TURN her away. That much was obvious. He wasn't going to, and that was equally obvious.

Cristian wondered—in the moment before he sprang into action—when he had lost this war. Was it when he'd brought her out to the beach? When he'd brought her here in the first place?

Or was it on that night in Venice, when he'd approached a beautiful stranger with glossy, dark curls that cascaded over honey-gold shoulders in a teasing manner that reminded him of sunshine and warmth. Heat and a kind of restless energy that had only ever made him think of one woman.

It didn't matter when, only that he had. And now that he was facing it, he had no desire to go back and undo it.

He tightened his hold on her, pulling her forward. Her eyes widened, and she gasped. Her lips were shaped in a soft, perfect O, and he couldn't help but think of that moment in the ballroom when he'd taken her hand.

And then, he leaned in, prepared to take what he had been unable to claim when the iron mask had covered his face. When they had both been concealed, from each other, and from the world.

*Could she ever really hide from you?*

He looked into her dark, glittering eyes. Eyes he had seen on fire for him weeks ago.

He turned his attention back to her mouth, wrenching his thoughts away from that particular path. There was no point in dwelling on any of it. No point in second-guessing his decisions. Both those that had occurred more than a month ago, and the one he had made here and now.

He stood from the chair, tugging her up to her feet, and bringing her against his body. She clung to his forearms for balance and he wrapped his arms around her waist, closing the distance between them and capturing her lips with his.

It was there in her kiss. Warmth. Sunshine. And all that shimmering, reckless heat he'd taken a dislike to from the moment he'd first met her. That spark inside her that found itself burrowing beneath his skin and crackling along his veins.

He traced the line of her lips with the tip of his tongue before taking it deep again, claiming her with everything he had in him. She was his. Only his. No other man had ever touched her before, and that was a novel experience. He'd never been a woman's first, and there was something intensely wrong and exciting about the fact that he had been Allegra's.

He was not a man who had ever thought he would be aroused by taking a woman's virginity, but he could not deny the fact that in this instance he was. It called to something purely primitive inside of him, something he'd not been aware he possessed.

Or perhaps, that was simply Allegra.

She had always done things to him. Had always turned the tides inside him, had always elicited responses that no one else ever had.

Perhaps that was why he gloried in being her first. Because, at least then he could be certain that this unique response wasn't just inside of him. That he did the same to her.

He had purposed in himself that he would not do this. He had purposed to stand strong. But the dark, raging creature inside him was in control now. And he had no inclination to try to wrench it back.

Instead, he held on to her even more tightly, gripping her chin, holding her steady as he continued to allow the fire between them to consume them both.

He released his hold on her waist, grabbing hold of her hair. She whimpered, leaning in to him even more deeply, either because she was desperate for him or because he was pulling too hard. He didn't know. He wasn't certain he cared.

He didn't know who he was with Allegra. Which was a strange thing, because of all the women he could have chosen to be with, he knew this one. Had known her since she was a schoolgirl. Why she should make both herself and him feel like strangers was a mystery to him.

Suddenly, he was desperate. Desperate to see everything he had not seen on the first night they were together.

They had coupled quickly in a corridor. Neither of them had undressed. He hadn't had the chance to get a full view of her beautiful curves. Hadn't been able to press her bare body against his.

He could wait no longer. He reached around, gripping the zipper tab on her dress and pulling it down, letting it fall to her feet.

That left her in nothing more than a lacy bra and a matching pair of panties. He stood back for a moment admiring her perfect, golden curves. She was the sort of fantasy men started wars over. Evidenced by the war raging inside his body. The knowledge that he should leave her alone. That he shouldn't destroy her with his touch any more than he already had. Wasn't her pregnancy—the fact that she now had to spend two years of her life bound to him in marriage, and the rest of her life bound to him because they shared a child—enough of a reminder that he altered everything he touched in irreparable ways?

But he already knew that the darkness in him was going to win tonight. That destructive, terrible thing that told him he could possess, even if he couldn't tend. The insidious voice that had convinced him that marrying Sylvia would be fine. He needed only to marry her, and the rest would sort itself out.

But no, he had destroyed her. As he'd done his parents. She had needed more and more, and he had been less and less able to meet the needs. Because she had wanted access to parts of him that were dead.

And now Allegra. Allegra, who had agreed to marry him. Allegra, who was pregnant with his child.

But why stop now? After all, the damage was already done, wasn't it? How much worse could he possibly make it?

He almost laughed. That was a dangerous question. Because he had seen the worst. He had lived through the worst. Worse, he had brought it on other people.

But right now, out here on the beach, with no photographers, no witnesses but the stars above, he simply couldn't find it in him to be noble.

"Take the rest off," he commanded, his voice rough. If he touched her, he wouldn't be able to go slowly enough to take them off without tearing them. Or perhaps, he wouldn't take them off at all. Perhaps, he would just sweep her panties to the side and plunge inside her, whether she was ready or not.

He gritted his teeth, battling against that fantasy. Slowly, Allegra began to remove her bra, revealing the perfect curve of her breasts, her tightened nipples, signaling her arousal. Then, she pushed her panties down and his focus went to the perfect, dark triangle at the apex of her thighs.

How he wanted her. Wanted to bury his face between her legs, bury himself inside her, lose himself completely.

"You're looking at me like you want to eat me," she said.

He couldn't tell. Couldn't tell if it was an innocent comment, or if she was well aware of the double meaning.

"Because I do," he growled, leaning forward and pressing his lips to the curve of her neck, sucking on her skin. She gasped, and he gloried in the sound. Then, he moved down, tasting the sweet curve of her breast before sliding his tongue over her nipple. He sucked the tightened bud deeply into his mouth, then scraped his teeth over it before moving to the next.

She threaded her fingers through his hair, held his head against her as he repeated the motion again, and again.

He gripped her hips, steadying her as he traced a line down the center of her soft stomach with the tip of his tongue. His lips hovered above where he ached to taste her most, and he felt her trying to move away from him. He tightened his hold, preventing her from escaping.

"Mine," he said on a growl as he leaned in, his tongue gliding through her slick folds.

"Cristian," she breathed his name, for once a prayer on her lips instead of a curse.

He tasted her even more deeply, glorying in the way she trembled beneath his touch. In the way she sobbed his name, broken, helpless. Reveled in every piece of this that he should deny. Her scent, her sound, the very fact that she was Allegra and there was no denying it.

That realization was a deep tug of longing inside of him that never seemed to end. A bottomless well of need. For her. *Allegra.* As though it had existed inside him for as long as he'd drawn breath. Not acknowledged. Not satisfied. Until now.

She clung to his shoulders as he pushed her, further,

faster, harder. He could feel her beginning to unravel, could feel all of her control spinning into nothing as he slid his tongue over that sensitive bundle of nerves. And then, on a hoarse cry, she gave it all up completely, gave it to him, her pleasure, her release, and he let it wash over him in a wave. His reward more than hers.

Then he slid his hands down her smooth thighs, to her knees, tugging lightly until they buckled, drawing her down onto the ground, her legs wrapped around his waist, her damp core brushing against the head of his arousal.

And he knew then that he was a selfish bastard. While she still shook and moaned from her release, he pushed inside her, the tight clasp of her body around his almost enough to send him over the edge. But he wasn't ready to go. Not yet. He moved his hands to the rounded curve of her ass, holding her tightly as he thrust up inside her, pulling her down more firmly onto him with his every movement.

She arched back, and he leaned forward, accepting the offering of those beautiful breasts as his due, sliding his tongue over her sensitized flesh. She wrapped her arms around him, held tightly to him as he worked to drive them both completely mad.

How had he never seen it before? That this was what lurked beneath the surface of his every word exchanged with Allegra? That this was why he felt like his skin was on fire every time she was near him. It made sense now. A great many things made sense when he was buried as deep as he could possibly be inside of this woman. They made sense, but they didn't work. They weren't sustainable. They weren't right. And at the moment, he didn't care.

He was lost in this. In her. In Allegra. No other woman had tempted him since the death of his wife, and in truth, he didn't recall any woman ever *tempting* him before that. Either he wanted a woman, or he didn't. But Allegra fell in some strange category that was all her own. He wanted her. He wanted her with everything he had inside him, just as much as he wanted to turn away from it. He needed her, like someone needed breath. Or, more accurately a fix from a drug. It would offer nothing but a temporary high that would lead to chains, withdrawal and suffering after. But it didn't lessen the addiction to know that.

In the moment, he felt it was worth all the pain after. For this high. This moment. When his orgasm broke over him, it was roaring, howling blackness, a perfect punch of pleasure and pain that wiped out everything else that surrounded it. Leveling every other thought, every other emotion, every other sensation and rendering it dust.

When he came back to himself, he realized that she had reached her own peak, her nails digging into his skin as she cried out her pleasure, her internal muscles pulsing around him, forcing another wave of pleasure to wash over him.

It took a while for him to realize that the sound of crashing surf wasn't in his head. That it was the waves on the shore. That he was on his knees in the sand in front of his house, and Allegra was straddling him. He traced a line of her delicate spine, slid his hands through her hair, keeping her from looking away, even as she attempted to avoid his gaze. "Don't," he commanded.

"Don't what?" she asked, her voice soft.

"Don't hide from me." She lifted her gaze, meeting his own. He slid his thumb over the edge of her top lip. "You don't have your mask tonight."

"It was easier when I did," she said. "Easier when you abandoned me afterward."

"Why is this so difficult?"

"Because. I…" She swallowed hard, moving away from him, the cold air hitting him like a shock when she removed her body from his. "I need to go inside."

She stood up, completely naked, and walked back into the house.

He watched her, her silhouette thrown into sharp relief by the glow from the house. He was entranced by her curves, even now.

He knew that he should allow her to have space. That's what a decent man would do.

But Cristian Acosta was past the point of pretending he had ever been decent. And tonight, he had claimed Allegra. Which meant there was no turning back now.

Allegra was desperate for some privacy. For a shower. For a moment alone. That had been nothing like the sex in the hall.

Yes, it had been the same man, but it had been an entirely different experience. Knowing it was him, seeing his face the entire time, seeing his eyes...

She felt completely exposed. Because as intimate as it had been to witness him in that position, the most confronting part about it was knowing that he had seen her. That all of her vulnerabilities had been on show for him. Every deep, tender feeling that she didn't want to examine.

She walked as quickly as she could up the stairs, trying to ignore the fact that she was naked. She went into the bedroom that she had claimed as her own earlier and through into the bathroom, turning on the shower. It was a glorious shower, with two showerheads, beautiful marble inside and a large window that she could just barely tell overlooked the ocean, thanks to the wash of pale moonlight glittering over the waves.

But she couldn't really enjoy it now. Because she was simply desperate to get beneath the hot spray and wash some of her humiliation off her skin. To rinse some of the rawness down the drain.

She needed to be able to breathe. Needed to be able

to think. And as long as she was anywhere near Cristian she wouldn't be able to do either. There was something about him. Something that made her act completely out of character. Something that made her crazy. She didn't want to know what it was. Didn't want to know any of it.

Perhaps, the most confronting thing of all was finally being faced with just how very *Cristian* her mystery lover had been. The man at the masked ball could no longer be a separate entity in her mind. Not now that she had felt him inside her again. Not now that she had watched his face as he'd reached his peak. Not now that she was trembling all over and tingling with the aftereffects of not one, but two orgasms.

She squeezed her eyes shut tight, willing herself to cry, because at least that would do something to alleviate the pressure in her chest. Sadly, her eyes remained stubbornly dry. Even as the warm water cascaded over her skin.

"Allegra?"

The door to the bathroom opened, and in walked Cristian. Completely naked, and clearly unconcerned about his state of undress. She could not be so casual.

She couldn't stop herself from staring. From studying him. He was the only naked man she had ever seen in person, and she found it captivating.

He was beautiful. His broad, muscular chest, his well-defined abs, lean hips with hard cuts in the side pointing down to the most masculine part of him.

She was seeing Cristian naked. Cristian Acosta. A man she had known almost half her life. Though, always in clothes. Always. She knew him naked now. Knew him inside of her.

The thought made her want to hide again. But she couldn't hide, because he was here.

"Are you all right?" he asked, standing outside the glass

shower, with, what she assumed, was as clear a view of her as she had of him.

"I just thought…"

"Thought you would wash me off your skin?" There was an edge to his tone that cut her deep.

"No, that isn't it. I just needed a minute."

"Then I shall take it with you." He opened the shower door and got inside.

"I don't think you quite understand. I needed a minute to myself," she said, taking a step away from him.

"Why is that?"

"Because, you're the only man I've ever had sex with. This is only the second time I've ever had sex. I feel… I feel a little bit disoriented."

"You're the only woman I've had sex with since Sylvia died. If anyone needs a minute it's me."

His words were strangely flat in the echoey room. "You… I… I am?"

"I have not been with another woman since she passed away. That night at the ballroom…"

She wasn't sure how she felt about that. She supposed, if she had found out that Cristian went around having one-night stands with mysterious women all the time it would be its own kind of pain. But having to wonder if she was simply a result of him reaching the end of his celibacy rope wasn't exactly pleasant.

"What happened? You simply lost your control?" She couldn't keep the emotion out of her voice. That was just another reason she had wanted time alone.

"You say that as though it's a simple thing. I suppose it is for some. To lose control. Something that happens periodically. But I do not. I don't lose control, Allegra. Ever." He took a step toward her, wrapped his arm around her waist and pulled her up against him. His skin was slick, hot, and she felt herself responding to him immediately.

"And around you... I question whether or not I ever had any to lose. If I have been lying to myself all this time. It is something else entirely."

He moved his hand down the curve of her waist, to her hip, his large palm resting there, the weight comforting and disconcerting all at once.

"It *is* that simple. I know that you think you're some sort of god, but you are just a man." As she spoke the word, she extended her hand, brushed her fingertips over his hard chest, shivering as she felt that unique, male combination of hot skin and crisp hair.

She shouldn't be touching him, not when she was trying to make a case for alone time. For needing space. But she found herself brushing her fingertips over his skin again. Suddenly, what he was saying about control made a little bit more sense. When it came to the two of them, she had to wonder if control even existed. Their behavior had transcended *typical* for both of them.

She didn't even feel regretful about it. Couldn't bring herself to. Here she was, ready to enter into a temporary marriage, pregnant with this man's baby, this man that she could barely look in the eye, and she couldn't even regret being with him.

"The fact that you find it so simple only reveals your inexperience," he said, his voice husky. "You don't know how uncommon this is. You don't know what we are playing with."

"Is it special?" She despised that needy note in her voice, hated just how transparent it was.

"It is unlike anything I've ever experienced. But these things... These crazy, dark things, that grab hold of you inside and make you behave more like an animal," he said as he traced the line of her jaw with his fingertip, "they are rarely good. They might feel good for a moment, but they can only end in destruction."

"You think we're going to destroy each other?"

"I think we already have."

Her heart thundered in her ears, echoing through her body. "Then I guess there's nothing more to be afraid of, is there?"

He painted a compelling picture, one that suggested the damage had already been done. That the fact she was pregnant, the fact that they now had to enter into this farcical arrangement, was truly as bad as things could be. And if that was the case, why shouldn't they continue on in the only part of this that seemed to bring them any pleasure? Why shouldn't they indulge themselves?

That made her tremble. The idea of letting herself loose, giving in to everything that she desired was both intoxicating and terrifying.

Really, her entire life was that way. The door had always been unlocked. No one had ever truly been able to force her to do anything, and yet, she had always gone along in a lockstep for fear of pushing her parents away. For fear of putting a foot wrong. Even now, with Cristian, she had pulled away because she was so terrified that she might do something to reveal herself.

She wouldn't even confess to *herself* what she might reveal.

She was such a terrified little creature. She was defined by it. By her need to always be in line, her need to always please, her need to never shock or appall.

But who cared if she did? That was the real question. She had ruined everything, Cristian was right. There was truly nowhere to go from here.

"If we're already at rock bottom I suppose we might as well just see what else is down here," she mused.

"If you can bring yourself to roll around down here with me," he responded, holding her chin tight between his thumb and forefinger, his dark, fathomless eyes burning into hers.

"What's happened to us?" she asked.

"Nothing more than a little bit of destruction," he said.

"Why do I feel like I might have it all a little bit more together now that I've been destroyed?"

He chuckled, leaning in, pressing a kiss to the corner of her mouth. "That's sex. It lies to you. It feels very good. And you find it's very easy to justify a whole host of things to convince yourself that it's okay to have it again."

"Is that what we're doing?"

"I would say so."

"I'm okay with that," she said, and she found that it was true.

"So am I."

She turned her face then, melting into his embrace, melting into his kiss. She felt him growing hard beneath her, and arousal began to bloom in her stomach. She wanted him. For however long she could have him, whatever the reasons were. She wasn't going to worry so much anymore. Not about the future, not about what he might think. For the first time, she was simply going to feel.

The dream was always the same. He looked up to see the cold, stone walls of the *castillo*. He felt so small lying there. And he knew that soon, he would come. In a cloud of rage and alcohol, he would come bringing pain. Last time so much that doctors had to be called in. Clever lies created to come up with reasons a five-year-old boy could be so badly wounded in the middle of the night. Falling down the stairs.

Yes, that was how he had broken his bones. That was why he needed stitches on his head. Lies. That was all they were. And soon, he would come for him again, and

Cristian would have another of his accidents. Nothing was safe. Nothing ever was. Not even his bedroom.

And then, just as always, just as suddenly, the walls of the *castillo* morphed into the walls of his home in Barcelona. And he was standing outside his bedroom door, knowing that yet again, all he would find inside was terror.

He knew that Sylvia was in there. That she was already gone, and that there was nothing he could do to stop it. But even though in this scenario he knew that she was on the other side of the door, even though he knew what he would find, it didn't erase the pain. And he still had to open the door. He pressed his hand against the smooth, cool surface and began to push it open.

"Cristian," a voice pierced the darkness. "Cristian, wake up."

He sat up, heaving a great breath, relieved to be staring out at the darkness, which was a much friendlier sight than what he saw in his dreams.

"Cristian," Allegra said, reality finally piercing the haze of his sleep. "Are you all right?"

"I was sleeping," he said, deciding he would allow her to lead the conversation. Obviously she had woken him for a reason, but he would not supply the reason before her.

"You were… You shouted. It woke me up."

"I'm sorry," he said, gritting his teeth. He had a feeling she was lying about what had happened. He touched his cheek, pulled his hand away and found his fingertips wet. Yes, she was lying to preserve his pride. The realization did something strange to his stomach. Made it feel tight. Made it difficult for him to breathe.

"I just… I didn't want you to be…upset. I thought I should wake you up. Should I not have woken you?"

"It's fine," he said, looking at the clock to find that it

was five in the morning. He swung his legs over the side of the bed, ignoring the tight, sick feeling in his throat.

"I didn't know you had nightmares," she said, her voice soft, her touch gentle on his shoulder.

"Everyone does occasionally." He did all the time. Only worse in the past three years. So much worse since Sylvia had died, adding fuel to the fire, twisting the already hideous vision from his self-conscious into a montage of his life's most difficult events.

"Of course they do."

"I'm going to get up. Jet lag. Plus, it's almost time enough."

"I will too."

"No," he said, his tone a bit harsher than he intended. "No," he repeated. "There's no need for you to get up. You should go back to sleep. I'm sorry that I disturbed you."

Even in the dim light he could make out the concern on her delicate face. "No," she said, "I'm sorry that you were having... That you had that dream."

He gritted his teeth. "It is nothing."

"I'm sorry, Cristian," she said, her voice soft but firm, "it didn't sound like nothing."

"It was a dream. Pieces of memory and things entirely made up twisted together so that they seem strange and unsettling. But it was just a dream."

"It seemed like more than that."

"It wasn't. I don't know if you're trying to find some sort of softness in me, or perhaps find something that we can connect on? Something human about me, but I can only disappoint you by telling you there is very little about me that is human. I am not a soft man. I am not a kind man, and you know this, you have known me for a very long time. Do not start spinning fantasies about me now. This," he said, sweeping his hand along her bare body, "could be a good thing between us. We must be together anyway, why not enjoy it? But you must not get your heart involved."

"We're at rock bottom already," she said, her voice a hushed whisper, "remember? It doesn't get harder than this."

She looked so unbearably young in that moment. And he felt unbearably old. "Yes," he said, "I did say that. But as we discussed, a man can find a great many excuses to justify finding physical satisfaction."

"No," she said, shaking her head. "We're in this together."

"If you say so." He despised the way her expression changed. The fact that his dismissive statement had hurt her. But, still, he wouldn't take it back. This was dangerous ground. Dangerous for her.

"We both said so," she said, insisting.

Allegra. Stubborn to the end. At least, with him. So much fire, so much spirit. So much of it crackling beneath the surface of her skin. It was strange, because he had always thought of her as being defiant, and yet, when he truly let himself remember all those moments he had been angry with her, her responses had been very small. Very contained. It was only he that had sensed them. Had felt her anger simmering beneath the surface. Felt her discomfort when her parents would mention her impending marriage, had sensed her anxiety with it, her rejection of it as loud as a shout.

He wondered then if anyone else had even seen it?

"Stay in bed," he said, insisting.

He got up, realizing that he had no clothes in her bedroom, because he had joined her in the shower naked, and then they had stayed naked through the entire night. But it was no matter to him. He walked out of the bedroom then, leaving Allegra alone. Part of him felt guilty for his treatment of her, but most of him realized it was the only thing to do. He had committed a great many sins in his life, and he had committed his greatest against Allegra. He would not compound his sins further. Not for his sake. He was already lost. No, he was going to act entirely out of concern for her.

If there was one thing he had to ensure, it was that she didn't begin to believe that she cared for him.

The greatest cruelty of all would be allowing Allegra to love him.

# CHAPTER NINE

THE NEXT FEW days in paradise felt much more like days serving a prison sentence with a taciturn warden.

In a cell with a gorgeous view. And the taciturn warden turned into a passionate lover at night. But basically otherwise the same.

He'd been different since the dream. And he never spent the night with her after they made love. Instead, he left her boneless and sated then walked out of the room. He didn't go back to his bed, though. She'd checked. She was starting to wonder if the man slept at all.

He was shutting her out. That much was clear. And it hurt. It shouldn't hurt. She knew what their situation was. They were having a child. One he didn't even want a hands-on part in raising. She was to be his temporary wife to appease both her parents and the media, and beyond that what they did in the bedroom had nothing to do with anything.

It certainly had nothing to do with feelings.

But from the moment she'd met Cristian feeling had bloomed inside of her. Annoyance, for no reason at all. Simply because the sardonic lift of a brow or the glitter in his eyes felt like it was mocking her.

Because his jaw was too square, his lips too captivating.

Then later, the wedding ring on his finger far too

bright. So golden and bold she could sometimes stare at nothing else when he sat at her parents' dinner table. A reminder, even when his wife wasn't there, that he belonged to someone. And that his wife belonged to him.

A realization that burrowed beneath her skin and itched and chafed and left her feeling scraped raw by the end of the evening.

He was always like that for her.

The idea she was suddenly supposed to try to feel nothing for him now they were sleeping together, now that they were having a child and planning to marry each other, was ridiculous.

He was right. People would come up with all kinds of excuses to continue existing in that hazy realm of pleasure they'd found together.

But excuses wore thin. And the reality began to show through the threadbare little lies, revealing the whole inconvenient truth beneath.

She blinked furiously, not wanting to think about it at all. It was like tugging the already fragile threads, showing more and more of the truth to herself and she despised it.

*Why do you think you've always felt such big things for him? Why do you suppose that wedding ring was a physical pain to witness?*

She wiped at a tear that tracked down her cheek and took in a shuddering breath. It didn't matter. It didn't matter at all. Whatever she might feel, Cristian didn't.

She laughed, a shaky, watery sound. He'd had to be tricked into an attraction to her. Had he known it was her the night of the ball…well, the night would never have happened.

But if she had known…if he'd been without a mask and he'd extended that hand to her, and she'd looked up and seen his gorgeous, familiar face looking down at her…she would have taken his hand. She would have gone down the corridor with him.

She would have given her virginity to Cristian knowing for a fact it was him, if instead of raising a brow and looking bored he'd put out his hand and asked her to go with him.

It was what she'd been waiting for. Always.

Pathetic. She was pathetic. And she was always waiting. Waiting for her parents to magically see that the marriage to Raphael wasn't what she wanted. Waiting for Cristian to see that she wasn't a child. Waiting and waiting and waiting and for what?

To feel constantly maligned when she'd never spoken out? What a great plan.

She *had* no plan. That much was clear. Not beyond sitting still and wishing someone would see the truth that burned within her like an ember. An ember she could feel, but they couldn't see.

What good was it? It would just burn her alive.

Of course, that didn't help her figure out what to do with Cristian now.

"We have to go."

She turned around in her seat to see Cristian walking out of the house and toward the beach, his expression dark.

"What?" she asked. For a blinding, almost joyous moment, she imagined that he meant they had to go because he needed to have her now.

"We have to get on a plane. We need to get back to Spain." She realized then that he looked different. Haunted.

"What happened, Cristian?"

"There was a fire at the *castillo*."

"Your family home?"

"Yes," he said, his expression unreadable.

"What about the…the farmland? The rental properties with your tenants and everything?"

He shook his head. "Everyone is fine. The only thing affected was the *castillo* itself."

She wrapped her arms around herself. "What happened?" she asked.

"Wiring, as far as they know. It's an old building, and electricity was added after the construction. Some of the wires, I believe, were original to the early 1900s. That proved an issue. I have to go and make sure that everything is being handled. I will leave you at the villa before I make my way there."

She frowned. "No, I'm going with you."

"There is no reason for you to accompany me."

"Except that I want to."

His expression turned ferocious. "You are so desperate to come and gawk at what has now become a ruin, as you called it when we first discussed it?"

"I'm so desperate to support you, Cristian. Forgive me for attempting to be a good…" She almost said wife. But she knew that was wrong. She could say fiancée, but that seemed wrong too.

"This is not a discussion, Allegra."

"Of course it isn't, Cristian. It never is with you. You speak, and you expect others to fall in line. And that has been the way that I lived my life. Obeying."

"That's funny, that does not seem to be my memory of you."

"Yes," she said, "and why is that? You seem to have this entire idea of who I am. Of the fact that I am constantly kicking against the goads, and yet, I cannot recall a single time I've ever actually done it. I fought with you, I never opposed my parents. I didn't reject Raphael. So why is it you think I'm some sort of recalcitrant child?"

"I can feel it," he said, "it burns inside you."

His words struck her hard, fanned that flame inside of her that was there. That he knew was there. He saw it. Even when no one else did.

"Cristian…"

"Gather your things. We're heading to the airport. And you are being dropped off at the villa." Then he turned and walked back into the house, leaving her by herself.

She knew there would be no pushing him, at least, not now. But she wasn't going to sit in silence anymore either. On that she was determined. She would figure out some way to handle Cristian. He wouldn't like it, but right now, pleasing him wasn't really her number one concern.

She simply wanted to be there for him. And if that meant being defiant, if it meant being open about certain feelings, then she was going to do it.

She was not going to sit in silence anymore.

Half of the *castillo* was gone, the centuries-old building, and home to more than one ghost, was reduced to a pile of rubble on one side. Of course, the building was old, and large enough that the half that was intact was still structurally sound. But there was no power in the place.

Cristian walked through the front door, looking to the left and seeing piles of stones that were still smoldering, and then to the right, where a staircase still curved around and up to a tower.

It was such a strange thing, to see his childhood home, this house of horrors, brought down in such a way.

He walked up the staircase slowly, brushing his fingertips over the stone walls that still haunted his dreams. He wondered if his father's ghost had burned along with it. He supposed that was a very ambitious wish.

He kept on going until he made his way to his childhood room. Of course, it was one of the things that had survived. He found that perverse in more ways than one. That these very stairs, these walls, this room, had not had the decency to go up in smoke.

This floor where his small body had been broken, those stones he could still remember digging into his ribs, his spine.

Of course all of it still stood.

He crossed the empty space, going to stand in front of the small bed in the corner. Strange that it still had a place here. But then, he imagined no one had had any use for this room once he'd gone. His mother hadn't lived here since then either.

He sat down on the edge, the mattress creaking beneath his weight. He let out a breath and looked up, looked at the gray stone walls and the wooden slats that ran across the ceiling. It was just like his dream.

He sat there and waited. Waited to feel a sinister presence. Waited to feel some kind of terror. There was nothing. He supposed that was the greatest insult of all. That there was nothing here. No answer. Nothing to rage at.

There was only him.

He stood, letting out a hard breath and pushing his shirtsleeves up to his elbows. He was going to start digging through the rubble. Seeing what the fireproof boxes had protected. How much of the jewelry and various important papers had survived.

That was all he would find here. Relics. He sure as hell wouldn't find answers.

Cristian spent hours sorting out what was trash, and what wasn't. By the time he was finished, he was exhausted. He certainly could have afforded to bring in a cleanup crew. He could have had any number of people take care of it. But the *castillo* was his responsibility. It was a part of him. A part of his title.

And this, this strange sort of exhumation of the corpses

of family treasure and history found in the midst of this rubble, felt essential to him.

He stood, wiping his forehead with the back of his arm, trying to keep the sweat from rolling down into his eyes.

He was covered in ash and soot, his clothing completely ruined. He reached up, beginning to unbutton his shirt. He might as well leave it here with the rest of the unsalvageable items.

"Cristian."

He turned at the sound of his name and saw Allegra standing there, looking wide-eyed and far too delicious for his own good with her dark hair cascading around her shoulders, her slender figure showcased by a simple black dress.

"What are you doing here?" he asked, continuing to undo the buttons of his shirt before casting it down onto the ground.

"What are you doing?"

"Looking for buried treasure. What are you doing here?" he repeated.

"I decided to try and make myself the nuisance that you are so convinced that I am."

"Why exactly did you decide to do that?"

"Because I'm a contrary beast," she said, taking a step toward him. The breeze rippled across the dress, and he looked down, his breath catching in his throat when he noticed a slight, rounded bump where her stomach had once been flat. Evidence of the child she carried. His child.

His child, here in this abomination of a place.

"I told you not to come here," he said, his tone hard.

"And I didn't listen. Because I am not your servant, I am not a child and I am not a pet. Which means I will do as I please."

"Yes, you often do. And look at what a spectacular position it has put you in so far."

She growled, crossing the space between them and frowning when she looked down at his hands. "You're hurt," she said, reaching down and taking hold of him, brushing her thumb near his cracked, bleeding knuckles.

"I'm fine." He pulled away from her, the tenderness she demonstrated toward him strangling him.

"Cristian. You're being ridiculous."

He laughed. "I don't know that anyone has ever called me ridiculous before."

"Obviously somebody should have. Maybe you wouldn't be quite so nonfunctional if they had."

"Has anyone ever told you that you are quite ridiculous, Allegra? Because from where I'm standing it seems you could benefit from it as well."

"Only you." She crossed her arms, tilting her chin upward. "Only ever you."

"That's right. It has only ever been me. And don't forget it." He watched as the erotic truth of his words washed over her, coloring her cheeks a delicate rose.

His stomach tightened, arousal tearing at him like a wild animal. He gritted his teeth and walked past her, heading into the unruined portion of the *castillo*.

# CHAPTER TEN

ALLEGRA TOOK A deep breath and went after Cristian. She was careful walking through the piles of stone, broken wood and burned-out furniture, making her way into the portion of the structure that stood intact.

"Cristian," she said.

He turned, his expression fierce, and her heart stopped completely. He had ash and soot smeared over his face, over his bare chest. He looked… Well, he looked completely uncivilized. Stripped down like this, sweat on his brow, his knuckles bloody from the work he'd been doing, from digging through hard, sharp rubble, he looked like a man who'd been out all day fighting for his life.

"What are you doing?" she asked, softening her tone. "You could have a whole crew out here at least helping you do this. Why are you here by yourself? Where is your staff? Why didn't you want me to come?"

"This is mine," he said, his tone hard as the rock he'd just been digging in. "It is my legacy, and it is yet more fitting now that it's been reduced to ash. It is no one else's to sort through."

"Why?" she asked. "It's a house…it…it…"

"It's more than that. We're a titled family, aristocracy, and this—keeping this—has always been one of the most important things. And it has crumbled beneath my watch. For centuries it stood. And now…here it is, reduced."

"It isn't your fault," she said.

"I don't even care if it is. This is nothing but centuries of corruption left to stand for far too long. I only wish it had all burned."

And yet he'd come right away. Had spent the day digging through it all with his bare hands. So regardless of what he said, she knew it wasn't completely true.

"Why is it corrupt?" she asked.

"Do you even have to ask that question? You've heard about my father. A drunk. Debauched. He only married my mother because he got her with child. I think it was a miracle he hadn't had about a hundred bastard children by then." He laughed. "I suppose I'm much more like him than I like to think."

"How?"

"The woman pregnant with my illegitimate child has to ask?"

Shame lashed her, and rage, all at the same time. "You said yourself you hadn't been with any women since your wife. I hardly think that makes you a legendary womanizer. Three years of celibacy and an unintended pregnancy hardly make you…make you him."

"It's all in me," he said, his tone hard. "I've yet to see much evidence to the contrary."

"What? What is all your dark muttering actually about? You talk about debauchery and illegitimate children and all of that, but we've managed to work all of this out so far. I don't know what you think you do that's like him. Or what you're so afraid of."

"Because I've hidden it from you," he said. "Be grateful."

Then he turned and made his way up the curving staircase, leaving her alone in the quiet, empty chamber. There was no sound beyond his heavy footfalls, growing fainter as he moved farther away.

Coming here had seemed like a good idea when she'd first thought of it, now she was doubting it.

*No. You're doing it again. You're shrinking. You can't do it. You won't be silent. Not this time.*

She took a breath. She had come here because she was determined to break down that wall he'd thrown up between them, not just in Hawaii, but in the years before, because she knew that's what this was. What it had always been.

She was starting to get all the way down to the truth, and she wouldn't stop now. But that meant that she couldn't protect herself. It meant that she was going to have to reveal herself to him. And that…well, that was terrifying.

But she was starting to realize a few things. She didn't want a temporary marriage. She didn't want a taste of a life with him. Didn't want her child growing up in separate homes, reading about his father going out with other women.

She wanted their lives to be one. She wanted to be with him always.

Because she loved him. She loved him so much it hurt.

She couldn't say when that had happened. It wasn't recent. She'd only just discovered it, but she had the feeling it had always been there. A part of her from the moment she'd first set eyes on him. A part of her as she'd felt enraged by his mocking gaze, because it had nothing to do with the sort of feelings she had for him.

A part of her as she'd stared at his wedding ring, sick over the fact he belonged to another woman.

And most certainly a part of her as she'd watched him descend the staircase that night at the masked ball.

Her heart had known. Her body had known. It was her brain that hadn't wanted to know.

But she knew now, all of her.

And tonight, she wasn't going to hide it. She was going to show him.

The *castillo* was still without power, so when darkness fell, Cristian lit the candles that were situated in Gothic candelabras, casting the entire room in a golden glow. He supposed, post-fire, he should be a bit more reluctant to introduce yet more flame, but in some ways he felt like he was daring the universe to burn the rest of it down.

He looked around the sitting area, at the wide, low chaise longue in the corner, then over at the bar that was situated across the room. He wondered if this was his father's personal stash of alcohol. If so, it hadn't been touched in a long time.

Either way it hadn't, really. No one but staff had been to the *castillo* in years. His mother had fled as soon as possible, and he had done the same. Why wouldn't they? This had been the site of their terror. Of their pain.

Interesting to be in it now, testing its power, its weight.

And, in a moment, tasting its alcohol.

He moved across the room to the bar, taking a look at the various different poisons on offer. He settled on a very old bottle of whiskey that he imagined was of a superior quality. He drank his first glass like it was nothing more than water, relishing the burn as it slid all the way down into his gut. Then, he poured another.

The door to the bedroom opened and he looked up, just in time to see a petite figure slipping in.

His hands suddenly felt unsteady and he set the glass back down on the bar.

It was Allegra.

Her shoulders were bare, her figure constricted by the

incredibly tight bodice of the dress she was wearing, her breasts spilling up over the top of the midnight-colored fabric. The skirt billowed out around her, covering her shapely legs, much to his dissatisfaction.

Her dark hair was loose and curling, teasing him with glimpses of her skin every time she moved.

But it was her face that truly held him captive. She was wearing a gold mask, reminiscent of the one she had worn that night in Venice. Her mouth painted the same lush color as the gown, giving him the impression that were he to kiss those lips, they would leave him intoxicated as though he'd taken in a whole bottle of wine.

"What are you doing?"

She lifted one bare shoulder. "I suppose if you have to ask, I'm not doing it right."

She put one arm behind her back, and the bodice of her dress loosened, then slipped and fell around her hips. She stepped out of the billowing fabric like a nymph stepping out of the water. She was completely naked underneath, her body slightly dusky in the dimness.

Then she took a step forward, and another, until the golden glow touched her skin, illuminating her, bathing her in light.

It curved around her soft body, wrapping itself around her stomach, the swell of her breasts. Exaggerating each dip and hollow as she moved toward him.

"Do you still want me to go?" she asked.

He ground his teeth together, so hard he was sure he was in danger of cracking them. "No," he said.

Her Bordeaux-colored lips turned up slightly. "Well, that's good."

"Come here," he said, feeling like his control was slipping away from him. As though he had lost his hold on absolutely everything.

"Not quite yet," she said, her words slightly unsteady. "I need you… I need you to take off your mask, Cristian."

"You're the one who's wearing a mask, Allegra."

"Yes, but I'm naked. For you." She spread her arms wide. "And that's the hardest thing for me. To let you know just how much I want you. To stand before you like this, knowing that you might reject me."

"Never."

"How am I to know that? You're as hidden from me as the first day we were together." She closed the distance between them, reaching out, tracing his face with her fingertips. Starting at the edge of his brow, drifting slowly down his cheek, to the corner of his lips. "I want to see you. *Really* see you."

He reached up, wrapping his fingers around her wrist, holding her hand still. "You don't want to see me without my mask, Allegra."

"That isn't for you to decide. It's one thing for everyone to ignore my wishes when I'm sitting there bottling them up. When I am not making it clear that I know my mind, that I know what I want. But you don't get to decide now. I want you. I want all of you."

"What if everything underneath the mask is ugly? What if all you find is a monster?"

She stared at him, those dark eyes fathomless. "Then I guess I get the monster."

That made something wounded howl inside of him, its pain echoing through his tattered, empty soul. "You can't mean that."

"Stop it," she said, her tone fierce. "Stop telling me what I want, stop telling me what I mean. Stop telling me who I am. I'll tell you who I am. I am Allegra Valenti, and I want you. All of you. I want you to stop being so controlled all the time. If I test you, then I expect you to prove it, Cristian. Push me." She tightened her hold on his face, curving her fingers around to the back of his neck, her nails digging into his skin. "Push us both, dammit."

He sucked in a sharp breath, doing his best to keep his hold on what was left of his control. He could hear what she was demanding, he understood, but he knew that she didn't. He was everything dark, everything wrong, he brought out the worst in everyone and everything that touched him. And if he let that black nightmare spill out onto her, then he would ruin her as well.

It seemed impossible here, though. A strange thing, since his demons shouted all the louder in the *castillo*. But with the golden light of the candles glowing on her skin, it seemed like there was no way darkness could ever touch her.

A neat trick of the flame, to be sure. But one he was ready to believe.

"Take me," she said, her voice a husky whisper, laden with desire, with an intensity that matched his own.

She fit him that way, she always had. It was why he had rejected her from the first, why he had decided she was a problem. Why he had rejected the feelings that burned inside him every time she was near. Far better to marry a woman who he found pleasant, attractive, but not overwhelming.

Allegra could never be anything but. Not for him.

But with that urgent demand on her lips, he could do nothing but comply. He reached up, grabbing hold of her hips, his blunt fingertips digging into soft flesh. He was so hard for her he ached. He wanted to be inside of her now, buried so deep he wouldn't be able to tell where he ended and she began. Surrounded completely by her. By her softness, by her scent.

She said she wanted him. She said she wanted all of him. Well, after tonight, she would either run away from him, or she would be bound to him forever. Either way, she would realize her mistake. Either way, it would be too late.

If he was a good man, he would stop now.

But no matter how many layers of stability he had attempted to wrap himself in, no matter how decent a man he fashioned himself to be, the truth was, there was nothing but darkness beneath it all. And if she wanted him laid bare, then darkness was what she would get.

He pressed his forehead to hers, holding her body at a slight distance from his. "You want me unmasked, Allegra?" he asked, his voice sounding frayed, unraveled. "You want all of me?"

"Yes," she said, the word tremulous.

"You want me to hold you down and spend all of my darkness into you?"

He wanted her to say yes, as badly as she needed to say no. He had destroyed everyone he'd ever cared for, from the moment of his birth. He had always imagined that destructive power as a shadow where his soul should be. One that reached out and wrapped inky fingers around those who touched him and dragged them into the abyss.

It had been so with his father. His mother. His wife.

It would be no different with Allegra, and still he asked her for this.

She looked up at him, her dark eyes luminous. "If that's what you have for me. That's what I was made to take."

Her words reached down deep, filled those empty spaces inside him. He had no right to such comfort. Had no right to find such healing power in those words. Not when he could give her nothing in return.

"Stand there," he said, releasing his hold on her and moving away from her. He began to work at the buttons on his shirt, casting it onto the ground, then moved his hands to his pants. He kept his eyes on her as he slowly worked his belt through the loops before moving to the closure on his slacks. He undid them, drawing the zipper down slowly. And she watched his every movement with wide eyes. There was something perversely intoxicating about seeing the way she watched him. Seeing the way she anticipated a glimpse at the most masculine part of him. That member that was hard and aching only for her. She was as desperate for it as he was for her. She wanted him, even though she shouldn't. Even though he would be the ruin of her.

He gritted his teeth against the rising pleasure that was threatening to choke him. How he wanted to ruin her. To kiss her until that dark lipstick was smeared all over her face, all over his. To sift his fingers through her hair until it was a tangle. To hold tightly to her hips until he left marks from his touch. To pound into her until she cried out, until her voice was husky from sounding her pleasure.

He pushed his pants and underwear down his hips, kicking them both to the side. She licked her lips slowly, and he knew for a fact that there was one place he wanted her to leave lipstick behind more than any other.

"Get on your knees for me," he said, his tone hard and firm in the empty stillness of the room.

She didn't hesitate. If she was confused, it only flashed through her eyes for a moment. Then, there was nothing but obedience.

What a sight she was. Such a beauty kneeling on the stone floor in front of him. An offering he didn't deserve.

"You are quite obedient now, aren't you, Allegra?" he asked.

"I told you. I want it all. I want everything. I want you. I want to give this to you."

"You should never offer gifts to a man like me. I will take until you have nothing left."

"Then you will," she said.

He gritted his teeth. He wanted to push her. Wanted to

push her to a point where she resisted. Wanted to see that spark, that challenge.

He moved closer to her, taking hold of her hair, holding her head steady. He looked down at her, the golden mask glittering on her face, her lips parted in anticipation. "Take me into your mouth," he commanded.

She kept her eyes on him as she leaned forward, as she touched the tip of her tongue to the head of his arousal. Fire streaked through him, as potent as the flame that had burned the *castillo* to the ground, threatening to raze him to the earth as well.

He held on to her tightly, under the guise of controlling her movements, but the moment she took him into her mouth all the way, the moment he was enveloped by her wet heat, the soft suction pushing him to the brink, he knew she was the one in command.

He was nothing but a captive, the most vulnerable part of himself a slave to the sensations she was lavishing upon him.

She raised her hands, soft palms pressed against his thighs as she continued to torment him with her wicked mouth. Her tongue slid over the length of him, dark eyes crashing into his as she traced his shape before moving her hand to cup him gently.

Allegra. *Allegra* touching him like this, tasting him like this. It was enough to bring him to his knees. Enough to send him over the edge completely. He held more tightly to her hair, using her to anchor him to the earth, to keep himself from losing it altogether. He was close. So close. And he didn't want it to end like this.

He wrenched her away from him, a harsh groan on his lips as the pleasure was lost to him. "Enough," he said. "That is not how I want things to end."

"I wouldn't mind," she said. The minx.

"I need to be inside you," he said. "Very deep inside your tight, wet body, while you beg me to take you."

She gasped, and he pulled her to her feet, using the hold he had on her hair. She purred as he pulled her against him, her hands pressed to his chest. He knew that she would be able to feel his heart thundering beneath her touch.

That she would be able to sense just how much she affected him.

But that was fine with him. If she wanted him unleashed, then that was what she would have.

He bent his head then, claiming her lips with his own as he maneuvered them both over to the couch. Then, he slipped his hand down, gathering her hair into his fist before sliding it down the length of her dark curls slowly, until he reached the very end. Then he twisted his wrist, wrapping her glossy curls around his fist, tugging back.

She whimpered, the sound one of pleasure, and pain.

"You're at my mercy," he said, holding tightly to her hair and reaching around with his other hand, tracing her delicate throat with his fingertips.

"Cristian…"

He leaned in closer, whispering in her ear. "Are you going to let me have control?"

She tried to nod and he held her fast.

"Good," he said. "You said you wanted this, Allegra. That you wanted me. All of me. I only hope you don't regret it."

He said that, even while he hoped she would. Because the kindest thing for her would be if she ran away, far away after this, and never looked back at him.

He turned her away from him, so that she was facing the chaise, then curved his hand around her, pressing it to her stomach before guiding her down onto the velvet-covered surface.

She gasped as he pressed his hardened length against the curve of her ass. But she didn't protest when he positioned her so that she was on the chaise, leaning over the side, her breasts pressed against the arm. She was on her knees, open to him from where he was kneeling behind her.

"I'm going to have you now," he said, his voice rough. "I want you so bad I ache with the need to take you."

"Yes," she whispered.

He placed his hand on the curve of her hip, his fingertips brushing the tender place at the apex of her thighs. Then he gripped his hardened length, positioning himself at her slick entrance before testing her readiness. He flexed his hips, teasing her, delighting in the kittenish sounds she made as he tortured them both with near penetration.

He could stay like this forever. Poised on the brink, caught between heaven and absolute hell. Needing her like this, feeling so close to the edge was like a stay in the pit of fire, being inside her would be salvation. Though not for her.

He had a feeling that this, this edge, was her last chance to cling to her soul. While joining with her might save him, it would only ruin her.

He cursed himself as he pushed his way into her tight body, gritted his teeth as he gloried in the feel of her. The hot, wet clasp of her taking him in, holding him tight.

He swore as he rocked his hips, deepening his thrusts. Swore again as she gasped at the invasion.

He started slowly at first, gently, until he could no longer control himself. Then he began to up his pace, pushing them both toward the release they so desperately craved.

"You like that," he growled, "you like me inside you."

"Yes," she moaned, lowering her head, arching her spine slightly.

He pressed his hand against the center of her shoulder blades, then let his fingers trace downward over the line of her spine, dipping it between the elegant crease of her buttocks. She gasped, shuddering beneath his touch. He teased her where they were joined, torturing them both with the slick pressure.

"I can't," she said, her words a gasp. "I can't."

"You will," he whispered. "Go ahead. Come for me, *querida*."

He pressed more firmly into her, moving his hand around to the front to sweep his fingertips across where he knew she was aching for his touch. And then, he felt her shudder around him, felt her give herself up to her release.

She was breathing hard, and he could tell that she was exhausted.

But he wasn't finished. She had asked for all of it, and he was going to give her all of it.

One hand firmly placed on her hip, he used the other to grab hold of her arms, her body still braced over the arm of the couch. He moved her hands behind her back, wrapping his fingers around her wrists like an iron manacle, holding her as he continued to thrust into her, hard, ruthless.

"I can't," she said again, the desperate note in her voice pleading with him to stop. But she didn't say it. She didn't tell him no. And so, he continued on.

He wanted to stay inside her forever, to keep himself like this for all time. On the knife's edge, thrusting into her until neither of them could breathe. Claiming her, taking her, until she was his. Only his.

But his orgasm began to burn inside of him before igniting. Racing through his veins, wrapping its fingers around his throat and strangling him as it stole the very last vestiges of his control. He held more tightly to her, increasing the pace, the only sound in the room his skin slapping against hers, and the harsh, broken sound they both made as he drove them both to the peak of pleasure.

Her release sounded wrenched from her, her groan like broken shards of glass in her throat. And when his own climax overtook him, he shook with it as he spilled himself inside of her, marking her, claiming her.

And then, he collapsed over her, bracing himself on the arm of the chaise, still buried deep inside her. Their breathing was labored, echoing in the room, like a whispered prayer meant only for the two of them.

"I would have you like that always," he said, his voice sounding rusty. "With nothing between us."

"Undressed?"

Her question was so innocent it felt like a dagger plunged straight into his chest. "Without a condom," he said, his tone a bit brisker than he intended.

He withdrew from her body, moving to a standing position. He looked around the room. At the erotic carnage they'd left behind. Clothes littering the floor, announcing their haste, their impatience.

"Does it feel different?" she asked.

"Yes," he responded.

"Oh. I wouldn't know."

Guilt turned even more ferocious, snapping at him now. Of course she wouldn't know. She had only ever been with him, and he had been careless with her.

He studied her. Her kiss-swollen lips, her wide, sincere eyes, and that weight in his stomach grew graver, heavier.

It was not guilt.

He realized then that he had mistaken satisfaction for guilt. It was an intense feeling, one he was unaccustomed to. Yes, the worst part was the absence of guilt. He felt none. He only felt triumphant. That he was the only man to have ever been in her body. That he had laid claim to her in such a profound and undeniable way.

He looked at her, at the red marks around her wrists, showing where he had held her, at the lipstick stains on his body, where she had marked him.

He was a bastard. And he couldn't even regret it.

"Why didn't you want me to come here?"

she looked at him, the red marks around her wrists showing where she had needed it. The feel of it came up his body, since she had watched her

He was a beast. And he wasn't, even hated it.

Why didn't you want me to come here?

# CHAPTER ELEVEN

HE WASN'T SURE he liked where the conversation was headed. Wasn't sure he wanted this to move on from sex. The sex had been challenging, nothing simple about it, but at least it hadn't required verbal honesty.

"It's beautiful," she said, rolling over onto her back and stretching her arms over her head. With the gold mask still in place, the candlelight shining over her curves, the slight arch in her back thrusting her breasts into greater prominence, he felt like he was looking at a beautiful work of art. Art he certainly had no right to possess.

"Take off the mask if we're going to talk," he said. "You can hardly demand I remove mine when you keep yours so firmly in place."

She reached up and easily flicked the lovely golden piece from her face. Making a mockery of the request. Because the mask she had asked him to remove was one much more firmly affixed, he knew. And here she was, lying in front of him, both naked and fully exposed, and clearly unconcerned about it. Yet more he didn't deserve.

"Why didn't you want me to come?" she repeated.

"This is not a happy place for me," he said.

He questioned the wisdom of telling her all this. He didn't talk to anyone about it. He had never told Sylvia about his childhood. And when she had asked him about the slight bit of scarring that remained on his body, he had always deflected. It wasn't terribly obvious, not overly grotesque, and certainly not something you would notice unless you had spent years being intimate with someone, as a wife did. But he had never told her the truth.

So, he was a bit confused as to why he was prepared to confess all to Allegra.

But then, she had asked to see all of him. She had asked for his mask to be removed. So in this space, in this moment, in his home that was now a pile of rubble, why not? Perhaps it would finally exorcise the demons. Perhaps it would finally steal the power from this place.

"I figured as much," she said, her tone muted. "But why? Most people would be happy to grow up in a castle."

"You know as well as I do that money does not make for a perfect upbringing. You certainly feel maligned enough, in spite of the beauty of your surroundings."

"I know," she said, sounding subdued.

"My father was the life of the party," he said. "Always with a new woman. Always with a joke. But the man did like to drink. And when he drank he got careless. In one instance, he got his mistress with child. Of course, he wasn't as upset about that as he might have been. He was older, and it was most certainly time for him to begin settling down. So, he married her."

"That was your mother?"

"Yes. But, once I was born, things changed."

"What?"

"According to her, it was as though a demon possessed him. There was something about me that angered him. He became violent with her."

"No… Cristian that's awful."

"It is. But my father was a terrible man. A son of hell, if ever there was one. And whatever possessed him only sent him after her, for a while. But then, that changed.

It was me," he said. "I was the thing that infuriated him most of all. I'd changed his life, changed his mistress's body. He despised me. Whatever the reasons. And yet, he needed me. Because I was to be the heir of his title, the heir to his fortune. And so, even though he hated me, there was nothing to be done. Still, he drank."

"Cristian," she said, "what happened here?"

"Here specifically?" He looked around the room, his gaze landing on the bar. "Over there, the bar didn't used to be there. But there was a large piece of furniture, made of marble, I think. He threw me against that. I don't think he broke anything that time. Bruised ribs? It's difficult to remember."

She gasped, covering her mouth with her hand. She looked around the room, and he knew that she was looking for her clothes. Because, for whatever reason, this was not a discussion she felt she could have naked. She needed protection. From him. From his truth. He didn't blame her. He would probably rot in hell for telling her any of this.

"That evening my transgression was being in the way. But, on countless nights, it was just that he was so full of rage he needed someone to expend it on. So, he would get drunk. And then he would come to my room. Sometimes he would beat me with his fists. More than once, he threw me down the stairs."

She let out a strangled cry. "Was he trying to kill you?"

"Of course not. How then would I carry on his title?" He let out a cynical laugh. "A broken heir is fine. A dead one is a little bit harder to work with."

"I can't… I can't…" She put her hand to her chest, looking down, breathing hard.

"It's terrible. Terrible to imagine that someone could do that to such a small child. I know." He met her gaze. "The best thing my old man ever did for me was drink himself into a stupor and throw himself down the stairs.

Quite by accident. But that is what killed him. Here. When I was ten."

"Cristian…"

"My mother can't even look at me. I think she blames herself for staying in the situation until my father died. Or, perhaps she blames me."

"How could she blame you? You were only a child."

"It wasn't until after I was born that things changed."

"But that doesn't… It doesn't excuse anything."

"It also doesn't mean they didn't change." He was matter-of-fact about it. At this point, he had learned to be. But here in the *castillo* it was a bit difficult to be matter-of-fact. When the walls felt like they were closing in around him, when the past seemed to be bleeding in with the present. Suddenly, he wanted to get out of here. Needed to go and make sure that half the place was still crumbled. That he was indeed living now, and not in some tortured version of the past.

He wrenched open the door, and stalked out into the corridor, making his way down the curved staircase, not caring that he wasn't dressed. What did it matter? There was no one here to see. And anyway, he could not possibly feel more stripped than he already did.

He moved down to the front room, to the half of the *castillo* that lay in ruin. He stood and looked out at the scene beyond, at the ink-dark mountains just barely visible in the distance, and the midnight blue sky, dotted with stars.

And then, he heard movement behind him.

"You truly don't like to leave me alone, do you?" he asked, turning to face Allegra.

"You don't like to leave me alone either," she said, taking a step toward him. He turned away from her again, back out toward the scenery.

"It's almost funny. This half of the castle is just kind of

open to the elements now. It might become a new trend."
He tried to force a laugh. "A new way to make the most
of the view."

*"Cristian."*

"Careful. You sound perilously close to scolding me."

"You're avoiding me. You're avoiding what you just
told me."

"There is no point turning it over. No point discussing the past. I cannot say that I came out of it unscathed,
because that would be untrue, and you and I both know
it. You do not come away from that without a mark. And
that has nothing to do with the physical."

She said nothing for a moment. "I'm surprised that
you... I mean..."

"You're surprised I can admit that having my bones
broken by my father might have screwed me up psychologically? How emotionally stunted do you think I am?"

"Just enough," she said.

"It doesn't matter," he said. "It's in the past. There's
nothing more to say about it."

"That's why you were upset when you felt like I didn't
respect my parents. When you felt like I didn't understand
what an amazing thing it is to have both of them."

He pushed his hands through his hair, taking a deep
breath of the night air. It smelled like smoke, and the
ocean, and if he closed his eyes, a little bit like Allegra.
"That was unfair of me. My trials don't negate yours. Just
because my life was difficult growing up doesn't mean
yours didn't have challenges."

"Nobody...broke me."

"But you were afraid, weren't you?"

As soon as he spoke the words, he realized they were
true.

"Yes. But it wasn't really fair. It was never anything
I tested."

"Fear doesn't come from nothing, Allegra. Someone did something to you."

She shifted, and came to stand beside him. "It was only that my parents used to get very upset at me. I was not like Renzo. Renzo is charming. He always has been. He has that way about him. People are drawn to him like he's a magnet. Not just women, but everyone. He knows just how to act in every situation, and that has never been me. It was hard for me to learn. To learn how to sit still. To learn to be quiet. To learn that a Christmas ball at my parents' house was not the time to go out and play in the snow, roll around and come back in soaking wet and with red cheeks. They never yelled. They never hit. But I feared their silence most of all. I still do."

"What is the worst that would come from their silence, Allegra, if you were able to live the life that you wanted?" It was at odds with what he had always thought. He had imagined, that because she had parents who treasured her as hers clearly did, that any act against them would be treason. But, looking at Allegra now, hearing her voice her fears, he could no longer see her parents on the same pedestal as he had before.

He didn't believe they were cruel people, nor did he believe that they intended to hurt their daughter in any way. However, it was clear that she was wounded. That she had been prepared to enter into a marriage with a man she didn't love, for fear of losing the relationship she had with her family.

And he could see that it terrified her.

"I wouldn't know who I am," she said. "Without the Valenti name. Without my family home, without their Christmas parties, even if I do find them boring, I… I wouldn't know who I was."

"You have just stated very forcefully to me a few moments ago that you know who you are. That no one else can tell you what you want."

"I guess that's how I feel now. But when I... When I met you at the ball," she said, smiling slightly at the humor in the words. Implying that was the first time they had met. Implying that all they did was meet. "When I met you then, I sort of had this moment where I thought maybe I could just burn it all down. Throw caution to the wind. At least for a moment. To get a glimpse of who I was. Of what I wanted. To see if maybe it was worth chasing."

He wanted to know more. How it had felt to finally break away. To feel something big enough, strong enough, that it canceled out her fear. What was as large as that? He had no idea. "And how did you feel after?"

"Terrified. I knew that I couldn't marry him. The moment you left me alone in that hall, I knew I couldn't marry him. And while the pregnancy certainly made it easier to break it off, I don't think I would have gone through with it. But it was sort of convenient. To have it smashed into pieces so tiny there would be no repairing it. To know that I had gone too far and that the choice was now taken for my hands. I'm not brave. I had to stumble into my freedom. But now that I have it... I feel like maybe there's more middle ground than I thought. That I can demand what I want, let everyone know who I am, and while I might not have wholesale approval, I may not have complete rejection either."

"I'm pleased for you," he said, feeling something twisting in his chest that didn't feel much like pleasure.

"I think we can make this work," she said, taking a step forward. And that thing in his chest twisted all the tighter.

"We are making this work," he said. "Our child will be legitimate."

"Right. Because of our temporary marriage. But... *Why* does it have to be temporary?"

That simple question could have brought down the rest of the *castillo*. It most certainly sent something crumbling down inside of him. "I told you," he said. "I cannot be the husband that you want."

"You're assuming what I want again. You know that you can be a husband. A faithful husband. As you were to Sylvia for years."

"Living with me stifled her. She needed. And it wasn't her fault she needed. It was my fault for marrying a woman who so clearly needed what I was not willing to give."

"We all carry our own baggage," she said, "you should know that most of all. Whatever our backgrounds, we have things we have to sort through. Perhaps it was her own issues that suffocated her."

He could not deny that she had a point, however, he could also not deny the fact that the environment of living with him had clearly been one that wasn't ideal for Sylvia. That he had not been able to be the man she needed. That perhaps a more sensitive man, a more attentive man, could have broken through the walls of silence that she'd erected around herself. Perhaps could have intervened in the depression before it was too late.

"All I'm saying," Allegra said, "is that there's little point in planning a divorce, Cristian. Clearly, we are compatible sexually." She attempted to say the words in a blasé manner but her cheeks turned a charming shade of pink. He found that little show of innocence far more arousing than he should. But then, he found everything about Allegra far more arousing than he should.

"Yes," he said, his voice getting rough. "We are."

"And sometimes we even get along," she said. "These days. So what's the point of the two of us planning to create a scandal? I was already going to marry a prince, and I planned on staying married to him."

"What you're asking for isn't that simple. A marriage

implies that we will share a life. That we will have more children." The idea filled him with terror. He already wanted to keep his child as far away from him as possible. Not because he imagined he might be the sort of man his father was, but because he hated the idea of poisoning an innocent life. And that's what he was, he was poison. From the moment of his birth, from the moment Sylvia had said her vows to him.

And here he was, drawing Allegra into that same web.

He knew he would hurt her either way. Whether he promised to remain her husband, or whether he cast her out. That was the impossible nature of the situation.

"We don't have to have more children," she said.

"How about we open this up for further negotiation when two years passes," he said.

"So we'll spend the next two years with the sword of Damocles hanging over our heads?"

"I suppose it will be up to you at the end of those two years to decide whether divorce is the sword falling upon you or whether the real cut will come from staying married to me. And then, perhaps you choose the one that seems less fatal?" He knew which it would be. She would tire of him. Of what it was to be with him. He didn't know how to give. Not really. In the time since he and Allegra had begun sleeping together, he had discovered that she was a well of endless generosity. Even the attitude that he had found so distasteful in her ultimately came from her desire to please.

She wanted to please her parents, at the expense of herself. And if she seemed like she was tugging against the ropes that bound her, it was only because she didn't want to take that final step to free herself. She would give, and give, to avoid hurting people. He knew that about her, and he knew that he was in a perfect position to twist that nature of hers, to play on her fears and to keep her captive.

That was why he should end things now. It was why he should tell her that things could go nowhere between them. That they would stay married only long enough to give their child a name, to make it look real, and then go their separate ways.

But he could not. Because therein lay his flaw. That he was a black hole of selfishness, who wanted to take everything she would give, but knew how to give nothing back in return.

He had locked himself down so tight through all those years, all those years of beatings, of pain, of abandonment, and he had no idea how to open himself back up. Nor did he want to. Now he knew what pain lay on the other side.

"That sounds fair," she said, her voice soft, and he knew that she didn't think it was anything close to fair.

"Good. Then we will revisit the issue when necessary. Tomorrow we will go back to Barcelona," he said, taking one last look at the ruin. "I will send in a crew to salvage the rest."

Whatever he had been hoping to find here tonight, he had not. He had spent the day digging through rubble, and had come no closer to even having an inkling as to what he'd hoped to find.

Only Allegra's arms had contained any satisfaction. Only Allegra had provided him with any warmth at all. He was done here.

"Okay," she said, moving forward, putting her hand on his bare back. The two of them were still naked, standing out in the open, the moonlight shining down on them. He turned, wrapping his arm around her waist, gripping her chin between his thumb and forefinger and tilting her face up. He leaned down, pressing a fierce kiss to her lips.

"I only hope you do not regret me," he said, even as he knew that she would.

"I can't regret you, Cristian. You saved me from my marriage to Raphael."

"And condemned you to one with me."

"What you see as condemnation," she said, lifting her hands and bracketing his face, "I see as being very close to heaven."

Her words washed over him like a balm, healing, soothing. Dammit all, he didn't deserve it. He could give nothing in return. He could do nothing but take this, hold it close, until it ultimately withered and died.

And so he did. Kissing her deeper in the moonlight, offering her nothing but the pleasure of his body. The only thing that he could use to speak now.

Because here in this ruin, where there were no answers, he lost himself in Allegra's body. On the cold stone floor, he took everything she could give, and gave nothing back.

# CHAPTER TWELVE

THE WEDDING WAS drawing closer, and Allegra couldn't say whether she and Cristian were in a better place or not. They had both been dancing around the things that had been said at the *castillo*, the things she had nearly confessed, the things she had asked for. She was dancing around them internally too. Pretending that she didn't need more, pretending that everything would be fine.

It was a glorious avoidance, though.

Every night, he took her into his arms, and every night, he made even more passionate love to her than he had the night before.

If there was one place they connected, it was in the bedroom. An echo of that wordless, anonymous joining that had found them bonding in the first place.

But, during the day, they hardly spoke. Today was her dress fitting. Her mother was coming, which made Allegra unaccountably nervous. Along with the seamstress, which made her even more nervous. Possibly because the evidence of her pregnancy was starting to become a bit more undeniable, and because she knew that whatever her mother had guessed in terms of her measurements would be an underestimation. And so now, Allegra would have to be poked and prodded, and scolded for her roundness.

When the door to her bedroom burst open, and the

seamstress and her mother arrived, Allegra steeled herself for the onslaught of words that were sure to follow.

And she wasn't wrong. She found herself immediately stripped down, and put up on a pedestal, while she was fitted into a strapless bra and some kind of crinoline that was supposed to hold the skirt out.

"There is no reason you can't look like a princess on your wedding day, even if you aren't marrying a prince," her mother said, speaking in rapid-fire Italian.

"I suppose not," Allegra said, shifting uncomfortably as the seamstress began to pin yards of satin into slightly different positions, tightening and loosening where applicable. She could hear seams ripping, and she grimaced.

"You have put on a little bit of weight," her mother remarked, to the tune of the seams tearing as the seamstress worked to let the dress out.

"Well, Mother, I am with child, as they say. That is to be expected."

"Indeed," her mother responded. "Cristian is the father of the baby, isn't he? Or has he simply agreed to do this as a way of protecting your honor?"

Allegra nearly fell off the stool, a crack of laughter escaping her lips. "Trust me, Mother, Cristian has no stake in protecting my honor. He has thoroughly done away with it over the past few months."

Her mother arched her dark brow. "That was a bit too informative, Allegra."

"Don't ask nosy questions if you don't want informative answers."

The other woman made a scoffing sound. "You're in rare form today."

"I've been in rare form for a while now. Hence pregnancy."

"Cristian is a fine choice," her mother continued while the seamstress kept on tugging.

"He is," Allegra answered. "I only regret that I wasn't more straightforward in the way I handled things."

In so many ways. Not just in her engagement to Raphael, but in the way she'd dealt with her feelings for Cristian in the first place. Because they had been there, always, and she had been too afraid to do anything. She might have ended up married to another man, while only ever wanting Cristian. That was a terrifying thought.

"It doesn't matter. Raphael clearly had some sort of bit on the side. *Princess Bailey*, have you ever heard of anything more ridiculous?"

"I did say something to the effect that she sounded more like a beagle than a princess," Allegra said ruefully. "But she is beautiful."

"I suppose. And pregnant, the tabloids say."

"So am I," Allegra said, somewhat pointedly.

"It seems if the two of you were so eager to get started producing children you could have done it with each other," her mother said.

"It's not that simple. If she makes Raphael happy, then I suppose my transgression is all the better. Both of us will get what we want." She smiled. "I don't think we can pretend that we ever wanted each other. He never so much as kissed me."

"Again, a bit informative."

There was a knock on the door, and Cristian's rich voice filtered through. "May I come in?"

"No," her mother said. "You may not. Allegra is in her wedding dress, and it would be fatally unlucky for you to see her."

Allegra laughed. "Not dramatic, are you, Mother?"

"You need all the luck you can get. If anything goes wrong with this wedding, I won't simply disown you. I'll kill you."

Allegra rolled her eyes and gathered her skirts, getting down off the stool while the seamstress helped her out of the gown. Then she hurriedly put her sweatpants back on, which was a kind of inglorious transformation.

"Now you may come in," her mother said.

Her heart stuttered when Cristian walked in. He was looking perfect in a black T-shirt and a pair of dark jeans. In a suit, casual clothes—or her very favorite, naked—Cristian always affected her.

She had a feeling he always would.

"Hello, Señora Valenti," Cristian said, addressing her mother as he always did.

"Cristian," she said. "I haven't seen you since you impregnated my only daughter and started a scandal."

"We've been busy," he responded.

Of course her mother didn't ruffle him.

"Yes, clearly," she said. "Not seeing to the fine details of the wedding, so I assume losing yourselves in debauchery?"

"Mother, you were just scolding me for being informative," Allegra muttered.

"It's true. But I can't unlearn what you told me. I'm forced to assume you've both been lost in depravity since last I saw you."

"The depravity is consuming," Cristian said. "There's barely time for anything else."

"Indeed." Her mother's focus shifted suddenly. "Cristian, I was very sorry to hear about the *castillo*. It would have been the perfect place for the two of you to get married."

"I doubt we would have married there either way," Allegra said, horrified by the thought of forcing Cristian to marry her at the site of his childhood torture.

It was too brutal.

And, she feared, too apt.

"Why not? If you have a castle at your disposal..."

"Sadly," Cristian said, "we don't. At least, not a whole castle. It's more of a...ruin."

"Half a ruin."

"May I borrow Allegra for a moment?" Cristian asked, directing the question at her mother.

"For debauchery?" she asked.

"Nothing so exciting as debauchery."

It surprised Allegra how charming he could be with other people. It shouldn't. She'd seen it play out many times over the years. But she'd forgotten. These past weeks with him had been nothing short of intense. He was kind to her at times, other times closed off. But he was never...easy. Not like this.

"Of course," her mother said. "We're finished with the fitting anyway. But do return her before dinner. I traveled quite a while and won't like to miss a meal. And Allegra shouldn't in her condition."

He nodded, lacing his fingers through Allegra's and leading her out of the room. Her heart thundered hard, echoing in her head as he led her down the hall and toward his room. Holding hands was...not something they normally did. He was all about big, passionate embraces and consuming kisses. But this simple act of intimacy did something to her she couldn't explain.

He swept her into his room then, something that didn't happen often. They slept together at night, but always in Allegra's room. Cristian definitely seemed to keep his own space to himself. And this, combined with the hand-holding, was doing dangerous things to her already tender heart.

"What's going on?"

"I have something for you," he said, moving away from the door and crossing to his desk.

"You mean, something other than the upcoming wedding, all of the accommodations for my mother, and the baby?" At a mention of the baby a strange look crossed his face. He really wasn't comfortable talking about their child. Not beyond the practicalities, anyway.

She had been comfortable with that for a while now, if only because she wasn't exactly sanguine about the situation. It still seemed surreal. But she was nearly three months pregnant now, and it really was time to start facing the fact that they were going to have an actual baby.

Still, she wasn't going to push him. Not now. Not when he had something for her.

"This was found in the rubble of the *castillo*," he said, picking a flat, black velvet box up from the desk. "It is part of the family jewelry. A part of the collection that your ring came from."

He opened the box to reveal an ornate necklace with white-and-champagne-colored diamonds glittering in a beautiful platinum setting.

"It's beautiful, Cristian," she said, taking a step forward.

She realized fully then that these pieces were from a family collection. Cristian had an old and titled family, so of course the ring and the necklace had all belonged to someone else. She had to wonder if they had belonged to his mother. If they had belonged to his wife.

It wasn't fair to be upset if they had. If he had given them to Sylvia, it only made sense. And it was right. The other woman was dead, she had no call to be jealous of her.

Except, she was the woman that Cristian had chosen. Allegra was the woman that Cristian was stuck with.

She gritted her teeth.

"What's wrong?" His dark eyes were far too sharp, far too keen.

She lifted her shoulder, trying to look casual. "Nothing."

"Except that you look upset. Which is not the reaction I expected when presenting you with a piece of priceless jewelry. But I should know by now that I can't exactly predict you, Allegra."

"If you could predict me you would not like me half as much."

"That statement is impossible to prove. Perhaps, you might experiment with being predictable, and see if that is in fact the case."

"I'm not quite sure what you would find predictable. So, I think I'll skip it. I'll remain Allegra."

"And I'll remain bemused. Why are you unhappy?"

"I'm not unhappy," she said, reaching out. "Give me my necklace."

"No," he said, snapping the lid shut. "Not until you tell me why you're unhappy."

"I'm ecstatic. Except for the part where you won't give me my present. That's annoying."

He took a step toward her, slowly opening the jewelry box again. "I will give it to you. But you're not going to snatch it out of the box like a grasping Dickensian urchin. You're going to allow me to present it to you. As a man should present a gift to his fiancée."

He moved so that he was standing behind her, his chest pressed against her back, the heat from his body firing her blood. Even though she was angry at him. It would always be that way, she knew that it would. What a terrible thing that she wanted Cristian in such a way that nothing seemed to cool her desire for him.

He lifted the necklace from the box, and began to settle it over her breastbone, the platinum and gemstones heavy, and all at once it felt difficult to breathe.

"How many other women have you presented this necklace to? For that matter, who else has worn my ring?"

He paused. "No one," he said, continuing his movements as soon as he gave her the answer, clasping the necklace, and letting it rest heavily on her.

"No one?"

"I have been married before, Allegra, you know that. We spent a great deal of time discussing my late wife. If you're going to decide that you have an issue with the fact that you're not the first woman to share my name and my title, then you're going to have a very frustrating tantrum. I cannot change the past." He paused. "I would. Make no mistake I would. But I cannot."

"You wouldn't have married her?"

"For her sake. Not mine. But she never wore the jewelry. If that bothers you so much."

"Why didn't you give it to her? Why are you giving it to me?" She hoped, desperately, tragically, that it meant something that he was giving it to her. That she was the only woman he had offered this piece of his family history to.

"Sylvia liked modern things. She had no desire to have a piece of jewelry that was so outmoded. But these remind me of you. Of your mask. Let's face it, our entire relationship is somewhat old-fashioned."

"If you forget the part where we had sex as strangers."

"You don't think people did that back when these pieces were forged? I guarantee you they did. It's just that when pregnancy occurred, they had to make it right. Which is exactly what we're doing now."

Yes, this was the way that he mentioned the pregnancy. When he was reminding her that it was the reason they were together.

"Yes, I suppose that's true."

"It suits you," he said, meaning the necklace.

"Thank you," she said, reaching up and touching the center stone. "Really, thank you."

"My mother never wore them either. My father didn't

give them to her. He didn't see her as deserving of them. That's another reason I want you to have them," he continued. "Because my father got my mother pregnant, but he considered her a whore. Never worthy of the title. He behaved as though he had to marry her because of her sins, since that had nothing to do with him. And I was an extension of that. She was not the sort of woman he would have chosen, you see."

"Neither am I," she said, her throat suddenly tight.

"No, you are not the woman I would've chosen. But that is not a reflection on you," he said.

"It reflects on you," she said. "And I imagine, given your vaguely self-loathing narrative that's supposed to make me feel better?"

He turned her so that she was facing him. "Yes," he said, his dark eyes fathomless.

"Well, it doesn't. I don't feel any better knowing that you wouldn't have chosen me, just because you think your choice would be suspect. No woman wants to marry a man who didn't choose her."

"You don't have to stay married to me, Allegra. We had this discussion already. From the beginning. You're the one who seems to think that we should try and make something permanent out of this. And I think you're going to find in the end that it isn't a good idea."

"Yes, because of dark mutterings. I know."

"I've made it very clear what I came from. What I've been through. I'm not the kind of man who can give you what you want."

"You know what I want?"

"I imagine you would like a man who can...feel things."

"You feel things," she said, taking a step forward, pressing her palm against his chest, feeling his heart beating beneath her palm.

"It's like there's a wall inside of me. Holding everything back. I can't seem to break through it. And, even if I could, I'm not sure I would want to. That kind of uncontrolled emotion produces ugly things. Dangerous things. The only moment that I have ever let go was with you."

His dark gaze clashed with hers, and she felt the impact low and hard in her stomach. "And you still wouldn't have chosen me?"

"It's the very reason why," he said, his voice hard.

The words sent something shooting down her spine, like an electric shock. And from that, came a sense that something was blooming in her stomach. Hope. Why anything he had said just now should make her feel hopeful, she couldn't be sure. Except... Except that she frightened him. This man who might as well be made out of stone. This man who was so very like the *castillo* he hated so much.

Imperious, but vulnerable. Hollowed out by flame and reduced to rubble inside, while the undamaged parts of him did their very best to stand proud and firm.

He would not have chosen her because she challenged him. Because that terrified him. He said that the wall could never fall, but she knew that it could. She knew that she was perilously close to testing it, to cracking it. Destroying it. And that was why he would have rejected her.

"Did you know it was me?" she asked.

"No," he said, his tone fierce.

"I don't believe you."

"You said you had no idea it was me. That if you'd had any inkling I was the one who had extended his hand to you that night you would have turned away."

"I'm a liar. But I didn't lie half as cleverly to you as I did to myself. I believed it. I believed that I didn't know who it was. But of course it was you. You descended the stairs that night and my world stopped turning. Cristian, it could only have ever been you."

"Why?" he asked, his voice frayed, shredded.

"Because you're the only one who ever made me feel that way. Why do you think you irritated me so much? Because you made me feel things. Things I wasn't ready to feel. I was a girl, and you were older. And then, you were married. You can't imagine the indignity of that," she said, laughing. "Hating you and wanting you, knowing that someone else had you. It was a teenage fantasy in many ways. To be so tortured. There are gothic literary heroines who are more well-adjusted than I was."

"You didn't know it was me," he said, his tone hard.

"I did. I know I did. How could it have been anyone else? I was a virgin, Cristian. Do you truly think I would have given myself away to a stranger?"

It was those words that softened his face, that brought the first evidence of doubt into his dark eyes.

"I wouldn't have," she continued, "you know I wouldn't have. I was so afraid of losing my parents. And I was afraid of marrying Raphael, but more afraid of scandal, of losing my security. I wasn't afraid of living my life without passion, because if that worried me, I would have left long ago. It was never about that. It was never about gaining experience. The thing that scared me most of all was going through life without knowing what it was like to be touched by you. Without being kissed by you."

"You may have convinced yourself now that you knew it was me, but I guarantee you, Allegra, nothing in me knew it was you."

"You didn't know," she said, her tone faintly mocking. "You didn't know that the woman standing by the cream puffs, who took your hand without hesitation, who looked to you like you were her salvation, was the girl that you sat across from at dinner so often for more than a decade?"

"No," he said.

She lifted her arms, curving her hands around his neck, lacing her fingers through his hair, forcing him to meet her gaze. Then, she pressed her lips to his.

# CHAPTER THIRTEEN

WITH EVERY KISS, every sweep of her tongue against his, every scrape of her teeth against his lips, she called him a liar. He was, she knew it. He had to be. Just as she was. She had been protecting herself for far too long, and she knew that it was the same with him.

She was so confident in it that she held nothing back as she continued to pour out her emotion on him, into him.

She wanted him. So much. More than just his body, more than just a marriage. She wanted all of him. Every broken, jagged piece, even if it might cut into her. Even if he might leave her wounded, marked. She wanted it all the same. And she was angry. Angry that she had come to this place where she was ready to hide nothing, to show every last piece of herself, and he still insisted there was nothing more for him to give. That he didn't know who she was that night. That she meant nothing special. That nothing in him had recognized *her*.

*Maybe it's true,* a voice inside of her whispered. *Maybe he didn't know.* Maybe you were never special.

She growled, rebelling against that voice as she kissed him deeper, tightened her hold on him. And he was powerless to resist the pull between them. He wrapped his arms around her, crushing her to his hard body, reversing the power structure of the kiss, claiming her, decimating her.

She was reduced. Reduced to nothing more than a quivering, *needing* thing in his arms. Her entire body crying out for all that he would give. Even if it wasn't enough. Even if it would leave her in a constant state of starving for more. She would take what he would give. Oh, in this moment, she would take whatever little thing he would give to satisfy her.

He pulled her top off over her head, exposing her braless state. He growled, raising his hands to cup her breasts, his thumbs teasing her nipples.

How she loved this. How she loved *him*. With every piece of herself. She didn't want to remain quiet. Didn't want to be appropriate or demure. Didn't want to behave. And so, she vocalized her pleasure. Thinking nothing of embarrassment, nothing much of shame. Because there was nothing to be ashamed of. Not in this moment. Not with him.

He called to the deepest, most secret parts of her, and brought them out into the light. Made her delight in them. Made her want to embrace them. United the pieces within her. How could he think that he would leave her broken? How had she ever feared this? That she would shatter her life, shatter herself by following her passion. No, this was being remade. This was finally being whole. And it was because of him. Because of this.

He lowered his head, drawing a tightened bud deep inside of his mouth, and she grasped hold of him, holding him to her, arching against him, relishing each and every moment of pleasure. Then he dropped to his knees, shoving her pants down her legs, leaving her completely bare to him, the light in his eyes starving, feral as he gazed upon her. He slid his hands up the backs of her legs, her tender thighs, moving them to cup her butt, drawing her up against his face as he lavished pleasure upon that aching, needy place with his wicked tongue and lips.

Cristian brought her pleasure she hadn't known possible. Made her want things, fantasize about things she had never thought to fantasize about before. He satisfied her and made her needier all at the same time. He had sprinkled dark magic upon her soul, and she knew that she would never again be the same. She didn't want to be.

Before she had been pale, she had been fashioned in the image that other people had created her in.

But now she was Allegra. Fashioned entirely from her passion for this man, for a desire, a love, that so deftly cast out fear it left nothing false behind.

She moved her hips in time with his ministrations, losing herself completely in the arousal that overtook her. She felt no embarrassment. There was no cause for embarrassment. Because this was safe. The place where they could express themselves without fear. After this, there would be words, and that was where the risk would come. But for whatever reason, Cristian seemed to be able to cast aside all of his reservations in these moments. With his body, he found honesty with hers. And so, she would be nothing less in return.

Each pass of his tongue over that tightened bundle of nerves sent her higher, further, her pleasure wrenched so tight, so intense down low inside of her that she thought it would shatter her. But when it did finally break, when her release washed over her like a wave, she found herself again, not broken, but brilliantly, perfectly her.

He wrapped his arms around her, brought her down to the floor, positioned himself between her legs. And then he thrust deeply inside her, arching his hips so that he went deep. So that he was fully seated within her, filling her, stretching her.

He was all around her. Above her, in her. His scent, the hard, heavy weight of him, the deep, intense burning in his eyes, threatened to overwhelm her.

He was everything to her in that moment. The very air that she breathed.

He reached down, cupping her face, kissing her as though it would never end. With such a deep, devastating tenderness that she ached.

The kiss that they were not able to have *that night*. Not without exposing themselves. That was what he gave her now. That kiss full of promise, full of need. That kiss, the meeting of mouths, that was somehow as intimate as his hard length inside of her.

When he began to move it was wild, with no restraint. And that was good. She didn't want his control. She wanted him undone, as she was. Wanted him to splinter and crack so that he would finally be free of that wall inside him. If she needed to be made whole, then he certainly did too. He needed to stop dividing up the pieces of himself. Holding back his very best in order to protect what had once been wounded nearly beyond repair.

She wrapped her legs around his lean hips, arching against him, urging him on. And she could feel him begin to lose himself. Could feel when he was brought straight to the brink, and when his hold on his control slipped.

He went over the edge, his big body shuddering as he found his release, and that, the sight of this man, this immovable man, completely undone by her, was enough to send her over too. They clung to each other, battered by the storm of their pleasure, rocked by it. She clung to him until it subsided, until she could breathe again. Until she could think.

And then, as the mist receded, as everything became brilliantly, abundantly clear, she spoke.

"I love you, Cristian."

Allegra's words hit him like a bullet straight to the chest. It was his greatest desire, his greatest fear, all playing out in front of him while he lay naked on the floor of his bedroom. He had been unable to get them to the bed that was only a few steps away. What did that make him? Who was he with her? What had this little witch done to him?

It was a question he had been asking himself from the moment he had looked at her and seen a woman, not a child. A question that had kept his tongue sharp in her presence, had kept his brain looking her over, trying to find anything he might be able to criticize. Something that might keep him from getting to the truth. That there was nothing to criticize. Because she was perfection to him.

The kind of perfection that could slip beneath his defenses and ruin everything he had built for himself.

"No," he said, pushing her away from him, moving to a standing position.

"Are you…telling me no? As though you have some control over my feelings?"

"You do not love me, Allegra."

"That isn't for you to decide."

"You don't," he said, "you don't know better. You are a child. A spoiled brat who didn't think marriage to a prince was enough to make a life. And so, you constructed some sort of fantasy out of making love with a stranger. And now, have continued on in that fantasy. As though your mistake, your transgression, is somehow the very thing that will rebuild your life. Don't you see? That is the imagining of a child." He spoke the words frantically, desperately trying to get himself to believe them as well. It made sense. Why would she want to believe that she had ruined her life by tying herself to him? She wouldn't. So of course she would tell herself it was love. She was young. Only in her early twenties. She knew nothing of the world. Nothing of the way things really were.

She certainly knew nothing of him. Not really.

"That's a fascinating story, Cristian. If being a duke

doesn't work out, perhaps you should go into creative writing."

"I know, no child wants to hear how young they are, but in this instance, I think it would be valuable for you to listen to me."

"For what purpose? So you can try to make me feel like I'm crazy? Like the last few weeks haven't happened? But even if you did, Cristian, it does not erase the realizations that I've had."

"Convenient realizations, I imagine."

"I knew it was you," she said, her tone hushed.

Those words, they were like an obscenity spoken in the church. Shocking, grating. He could not accept them.

"You didn't know it was me. Again, you weave very interesting stories for yourself when you find yourself in a situation that you can't control, one that you cannot change. Because you're trying to turn this into a fairy tale, and you're trying to give yourself a happy ending, but Allegra, with me there is no happy ending."

"You're so convinced of that?"

"I have seen it play out. How many endings do I need to see before you will believe I know the truth? My parents' marriage ended in nothing but tragedy and turmoil. My father drinking himself to death, my mother losing sight of herself completely. Taking off to party her way around Europe just to try and forget the sound of her son's bones shattering at the hands of her husband. And Sylvia? Ask about Sylvia's happy ending, Allegra. A fragile woman given to a man who knows only how to break beautiful, fragile things. Was there ever any other ending to be had? She wanted what I couldn't give her, and in the end that's what killed her."

"No," Allegra said, her tone soft. "You said yourself, she struggled with a variety of mental health issues..."

"And plenty of people go on to live lives in spite of

those issues. But my wife is dead. Why do you think that is? Because I wasn't the support system that she needed."

"It suits you to be a martyr, I see that. Because it allows you to keep people at a distance."

"Are you accusing me of having a convenient martyr complex? I was not aware there was such a thing."

"Of course there is. You are so convinced that you poison everything you touch, and it allows you to keep everyone away from you. So they won't see you. So they won't see that all you are is a hurt, terrified little boy." Her expression softened. "But of course you are. Why wouldn't you be?"

"Don't make the mistake of thinking that I'm some lost child you can save, Allegra. I saved myself. Grew into a man. And I grew hard. That is survival, and I do not regret it. However, it has made me the sort of man unsuitable to be a husband to a woman like you. It has made me the sort of man who should never be a deeply involved father to a vulnerable child. The best thing you could do is divorce me. The best thing you could do is divorce me and give our child a stepfather who can be the man that I can never be."

"You want another man sharing my bed? You want another man raising your child?"

"What I want and what is right are two very different things."

She studied him hard, her dark eyes seeing far too much. "Yes," she said after a long moment. "I do believe that's true. What you want is to hide. What is right is for you to let go of all of this and move on. Move on with me. Move on with our baby."

"I will do what I must to give the child a name. I will do what I must to provide the dukedom with an heir."

"But he's more than that. He will be. That's the simple truth of it, Cristian. You can try to distance yourself. You can think of it as nothing more than a theory right now. As nothing more than a carrier of your bloodline. But when push comes to shove, when the reality hits, you're going to have to face the fact that it's going to be a child. A little boy or little girl who will want their father."

"Not when I'm the father they have."

She shook her head. "You aren't going to hurt them. You wouldn't."

"You don't have to break bones to hurt somebody, Allegra. What would you think years of cold negligence will do? To you. To the baby."

"You aren't cold," she said.

"That's sex," he said, his chest aching.

"But it's where you tell the truth," she said. "At least when you're inside of me you're honest about how you feel."

"You have confused orgasm with emotion. A great many virgins have done it before you, so don't be embarrassed about it." He watched her respond to the words as though they were a slap. "I'm just really good in bed. It doesn't mean that I care for you any more than I have cared for any other woman I've had flat on her back. And trust me, Allegra, there have been a great many of them. I might have been celibate for the past few years, but I was no monk prior to my first marriage."

"Stop it," she spat. "I am starting to think that you actually believe this. But I don't. You're making excuses and you're calling them the truth. Throwing lies in front of honesty, and twisting it so that it's hard to tell which is which. You have yourself fooled, Cristian. But you don't have me fooled."

Each and every word was like a crack from a whip, lashing his skin, breaking it open, making him bleed. He wished... He wished that what she was saying was true. That it was so easy. That all he had to do was decide to move forward, and it would be so. But he felt like he was in chains, and no matter how he struggled he couldn't get free. And what sort of monster would bind a woman and child to a dungeon? They would have to meet him where he was, and he was in a place no one should ever have to go. He couldn't do it. Not to her, not to their future child.

"No," he said. "We will marry next week as planned. And when the baby is born we will divorce. We will not wait a moment after. He will be born within the bonds of wedlock, and that's the end of the discussion. But as far as you and I are concerned, there is nothing. I will not touch you. I will not kiss you. And I will not go to your bed."

"Cristian," she said, his name on her lips a raw, wounded sound. "Please, don't do this. You knew it was me. And I knew it was you. From the beginning. And that's why... That's why we couldn't. Because we knew that this is where it would end. But it can be more. It can be. You just have to be brave enough."

"Enough. I have had the bravery to get up in the morning with broken bones and face my father at the breakfast table. As a boy, I had that courage. If bravery were all it took then I would have been free a long time ago. But you want me to resurrect something inside of me that's dead. It isn't hiding. It's gone. And I'm glad that it is. I have never once regretted it." That lie burned. He regretted it now. More than she would ever know. "It is impossible. I have spoken. And the decision is made. You cannot force me to stay in a marriage I don't want."

"I wouldn't want to," she said, her words muted. She looked up at him, dark eyes full of tears. And he hoped that she would shed none of them. Because he wasn't worthy of a single drop. "I don't want to be with a man who doesn't want me. Ecstatically. Unreservedly. I had that future placed in front of me once, and I won't do it again."

"Good. Then we have an agreement." He turned away

from her, each beat of his heart making it feel like it was cracking. "It is, perhaps, for the best that I have some business to see to in Paris." He didn't. It was a lie. But he would go to his Parisian apartment and grant the two of them some space. "I will return before the wedding. In the meantime, feel free to allow your mother to torture the details of the event to her heart's content. It will make her happy."

"Yes," Allegra said, "it will make her happy." The heavy implication that it would in no way make Allegra happy. But, then, he had always known he never could.

"Get dressed," he said, his voice sounding rough to his own ears.

Something in her face changed then, infinitesimally. Barely recognizable. But he had a feeling he had made a mistake, and he didn't know quite what it was.

She nodded once. "As you wish."

And then, she set about obeying him. And he despised it.

In that moment, he saw that it was too late to extricate himself from Allegra's life without destroying something in her. Because the Allegra that she had been would have argued with him. And now, she simply complied.

He had never longed for a fight more.

# CHAPTER FOURTEEN

IT WAS HER wedding day, and Allegra knew that she should feel something other than a thundering, sick dread in her chest. But there was nothing else. Nothing but pain, nothing but nausea. She could blame it on morning sickness, but it wasn't that. She knew it wasn't. It was heartbreak. It was the very thing she had been trying to protect herself from since the moment she had looked at Cristian and truly seen him.

She hadn't managed to protect herself. She had tumbled headlong into an affair that was ill-fated. And as she looked at her wedding gown on the hanger, she wondered if, going back, she would make another decision if she could.

Being with him had changed her. Not in a surface way, in a bone-deep, indelible way that had shifted her cells, made her something else entirely. Something real.

She had a vague thought of that old story, *The Velveteen Rabbit*. Where the little rabbit had been loved until he was threadbare and worn thin. And only then had he been made real. There was supposed to be a lesson in that story that was encouraging, and she had always found it sad. That someone might love the color straight out of you, and only when you let that happen had you earned your value.

If that was the case, then she had passed that test with Cristian.

But, much like the story, it seemed that now she was a living, breathing creature, she would have to move on to an existence away from the one who had made her that way.

She tried to draw a deep breath, but found she was unable to. Her sadness was settled on her chest like a brick, heavy and uncompromising. She hated it. But there was nothing to be done.

She had to marry him. She had to marry him for the sake of their child. So that their child could inherit…what?

A father who had promised nothing but distance. To avoid a scandal she no longer cared about. To make sure he got a title and a castle that was reduced to nothing.

None of it had brought Cristian any happiness. Why were they acting as though it was necessary to give their child all of the same things that had never appeared to be more than a millstone to the man who possessed them now?

Standing there looking at her wedding dress, fighting with the sickness in the pit of her stomach, she had no idea.

There was a soft knock on the door, and Allegra turned to see her brother standing there. "Are you ready?"

When she saw Renzo, she nearly burst into tears. She had been holding herself together, being strong as a way of proving to her mother and father that she stood by the decision she had made, because the truest part of the rant that Cristian had subjected her to before he'd flown to Paris last week was that she was most definitely trying to pretend that none of this had been a mistake, for her own pride if for no other reason.

But in front of Renzo, the person who had always supported her, the one person that she had known would love her no matter what, she felt like she might crumble.

"I'm not ready," she said, indicating the shirt and pants she was still wearing, and her dress on the hanger.

"The wedding starts soon," he said.

"I know."

"Cristian is here. He has not run off, as you might have feared. He knows that I would hunt him to the ends of the earth, kill him and mount him on my wall." There was a dark note in Renzo's voice that left her in no doubt that he would do exactly that.

"There's no need," she said, trying to sound light. Airy.

"However," Renzo continued, "if you were to walk away from him, I would guess that you had a reason. And I would not chase after you and drag you back."

"Are you…suggesting that I jilt your best friend?"

"If you want to."

"*Want* has nothing to do with any of this."

"I don't want him to hurt you," Renzo said.

"It's a bit late for that."

"I feared as much." He took a deep breath. "There is much expectation placed on you, Allegra. But what is your expectation for your own life?"

"I'm having a baby. I need to do what's best for him."

"I've always thought that that was ridiculous," he said. "To pretend that a mother's happiness has nothing to do with the happiness of her children. That she must be so self-sacrificial so that they're well aware of what a burden they are to her. No, I have never thought that was the healthiest way to raise children. Our own mother is certainly no martyr."

Allegra laughed. "No. She isn't."

"She's strong. And even though I know she has imposed expectations on you that made things hard, you have seen her strength. Is that not what you would want your child to see?"

Allegra's stomach tightened. "I suppose."

"Be strong, Allegra. And make the life you want to

live. You don't want the example you give your child to be that they ended your existence. That they ruined you."

She thought back to Cristian. To how he felt about his father. About what he believed he had done to his father.

"No," she said, "I don't."

"If you don't walk down that aisle, I will be the last person to condemn you."

"It would disappoint everyone," she said. "Mother has said they'll disown me."

"She won't. Even if she did…that's no reason to go ahead with a marriage, Allegra. You're the only one who has to be married to Cristian. I know that's not something I would sign up for."

"For a few reasons, I bet," Allegra said.

"A few, yes." He took a deep breath. "This is *your* life, Allegra. You must live it in the way that makes you happiest." He paused, and for just a moment she saw a flash of pain in her brother's dark eyes. "Don't let mother and father decide for you. Don't let anyone decide for you. Your future has to belong to you. The alternative is a regret you don't want. Trust me."

He nodded once, then Renzo turned and left her there, standing and staring at the wedding dress. He was right about one thing. It was her life. As to happiness… That was a fleeting thing. She couldn't say whether or not loving Cristian made her happy. It certainly gave her times of great happiness. But it also hurt worse than anything else ever had. Felt more terrifying, more intense than any other emotion ever had. She wasn't certain that happiness was the name of the game at all.

But…love?

She wanted love. She couldn't marry Cristian only to divorce him. Couldn't live under the same roof as him when he was determined not to touch her. And what would that mean in terms of other women? Did he expect her to stay married to him, growing larger with her pregnancy by the day while he ran around with underwear models?

The pain that that thought brought on was like a knife stabbing through her chest. She couldn't bear it.

Loving Cristian wasn't easy. And she feared that when it came to that love she was a bit too far gone to turn back now. But she had choices and what she did with it. Exactly what she chose to subject herself to.

And Renzo was right. Their mother was no doormat. Nor was she a coward. She didn't live the life of a martyr. She had never been shy about saying what she wanted, and while that had put certain demands on both Renzo and Allegra, she sincerely doubted that a woman as strong as their mother would ever want Allegra to make decisions from a position of weakness.

Mostly, it was her life. And it was her love. And she could not, no matter what the noble thing was, no matter what most people might think of as the right thing, stand in front of hundreds of people and make vows to Cristian while he made them in return, if he didn't mean them. Every promise she made to him, she would keep.

She would love him, she would stay with him and she would forsake anyone else to be with him. But she could not get up there and have him lie to her. Not for honor. Not for bloodline. Not to keep their child from being labeled a bastard.

Allegra looked at the wedding dress one last time, and then, dressed in her casual clothing, she turned and walked out of the bedroom.

She wasn't coming. That much was clear. As Cristian stood at the head of the aisle and the music played, and the view in front of him remained abjectly brideless, he realized that she was not coming.

His Allegra, who had appeared so many times when

he'd asked her not to. Who had chased him down while he had been digging through the rubble in the *castillo*. Who had pushed him, and pushed him at every turn, was not coming this one time he had expected her to.

He looked over at his friend who was standing beside him in a tuxedo looking neutral.

"It seems your sister is absent," he said, keeping his tone soft. "You wouldn't know anything about that, would you?"

Renzo arched one dark brow. "You forget sometimes, I think, that Allegra is *my* sister. Meaning she most certainly has a mind of her own."

"What did she say to you?"

Renzo turned to him. "I think the more important question is what did you do to her?"

"I only offered to marry her."

"Yes, that's all," Renzo said, his tone dry. "You must have done something. Because if I know one thing, Cristian, it's that my sister loves you. That she has loved you since she was far too young to understand what a mistake that is. There is very little you could have done to make her abandon you on your wedding day. And so, I can only conclude that you must have done it. I applaud her for not showing up." Renzo turned back to face the crowd, but Cristian didn't do the same. Instead, he stormed up the aisle, ignoring the shocked ripple that ran its way through the crowd.

He stormed into the villa, knocking a vase off a table. It was probably a piece that had come from the *castillo*, priceless and unknowably old. And he didn't care.

"Allegra?" he shouted her name, even though she wouldn't answer, and he knew it. He shouted her name while he wandered the halls, his voice echoing back at him, as if to provide yet more evidence of the emptiness of the house. His house that was never empty, but was because his entire staff was outside waiting for the wedding to begin.

His house, which was never empty, but was now because his bride was not in it.

He went into her bedroom, and saw her wedding dress, hanging there. Mocking him.

Allegra was gone. And Renzo was right. It was his fault. He had pushed her away. He finally had. This one woman who had been so determined to reach the good in him had finally given up. He deserved it. If he knew nothing else, he knew that. He had never deserved to have her walk down the aisle toward him today, and yet he had wanted her to. He had shouted about divorce, about never touching her, but he had fully intended to claim her tonight, on their wedding night. Had fully intended to continue dragging her down into hell with him. Because he was weak. Because if he couldn't burst out from the prison that his heart was locked behind, then he was going to bring her into it with him. He was not strong enough to live life without Allegra. He was not courageous enough.

She had accused him of being a coward. He had rejected it. But now, he could see that it was true.

He thought back again, to that night in Venice. To that ballroom. And he let himself remember. Truly remember.

He had walked down the stairs, and that vision of perfect beauty had swam before his eyes. Dark curling hair over beautiful bare shoulders. He had seen her from behind first and a jolt of recognition had kicked him straight in the chest, a jolt that he told himself later was arousal.

She had shimmered. Burned. He had only ever known one woman who did that.

He knew it was her. Of course he had known. Everything in him had responded to her. He had been celibate for three years and not a single woman had ever called out to him except for Allegra.

He had told himself it was irritation, told himself it was anger. And then, that night in Venice he had told himself it was the excitement of being turned on by a perfect stranger.

He and Allegra had a habit of accusing each other of composing great works of fiction. They were both right. Both of them had written a story and removed each other from it. So that they could act without consequence, act without fear.

But, as surely as she had known, so had he.

It had always been her. *Always*. From the moment he had first recognized that she was a woman, it had been Allegra.

His entire being had cried out for her, for those things that he told himself he despised. Her innocence, her youth, her passion. He had told himself he hated it, because the only other option was that he loved it. And he could not allow himself such a thing.

The realization brought him to his knees now. Pain lanced him, stabbing him clean through. Of course he loved her. Of course he did. He always had. And only now, when it was too late, was he brave enough to call it what it was. Now that it had slipped through his fingers forever.

He loved this woman, this woman who carried his child, who was supposed to be his wife. This woman who he had broken, as he had broken everyone else he had ever cared about.

There was no fixing this. No fixing him. And in that moment the only place he wanted to be, was the place that had broken him.

# CHAPTER FIFTEEN

THE DRIVE TO the *castillo* was more familiar than he would like it to be. He would prefer that those childhood memories were not so indelibly burned into his consciousness. But they were.

As was the growing sense of dread he felt when the stone fortress came into view. A strange thing, to see it half-crumbled. To see its power reduced. He was here, because he wanted answers.

This was the place that had created him. This was the site that had formed him. He had decided, last he left, that it had no more answers for him, that it had no more power. But clearly, he was still allowing it to dictate his choices, so that was a lie. He parked the car, getting out and making his way toward the abandoned grounds.

There was nothing here. He knew that. Still, he wrenched off his suit jacket, and pushed his sleeves up past his elbows. Still, he walked toward the part of the place that was lying in a ruin.

Still, he dropped to his knees and began digging through the stones, digging as though he would find something. Something that meant anything.

There was nothing. He told himself that over and over again as he continued to dig.

He dug until his hands bled, until his heart felt raw and bloody, and hemorrhaging more with each beat.

And he found nothing. Because his cleaning crew was thorough. But still, he dug. Until finally, he found the edge of a piece of paper, sticking up from beneath the stone. Impossible, because it should be burned. He reached for it, shoving his hand through the rubble carelessly in his haste to grab hold of it.

A shard of scorched glass cut into his hand, slicing him deep. But the pain in his hand didn't match the pain in his heart or his head. So he ignored it. He tugged the paper out.

It was a picture.

The edges were burned and curling in on themselves. But the focus of the photo remained.

A little boy. About five years old, with dark hair and eyes, and a bruise on his cheek.

A bruise likely left there by his father. Cristian's heart seized tight.

A photograph of himself. He could not recall if he had ever seen one. He didn't go looking for these things, and he certainly hadn't ever sat down with his absent mother to pore over a past both of them wanted to forget.

He didn't go looking for pieces of the past. Never.

But there he was. The boy who had supposedly turned his father from the life of the party into a monster. The boy who had supposedly ruined his mother's life. Who had grown up to ruin his first wife. This boy whom his father had seemed to think deserved to be beaten because of his very existence.

Cristian was surprised to look into his eyes and find that he was only a boy. A child. A child that had been beaten with closed fists, who had been broken by a grown man. He could not fathom it. Staring at that little boy all he could see was innocence. An innocence he had never been able to attribute to himself before. It was a revelation. Stark and painful.

He let out a low, tortured sound.

It sounded more like a wounded animal than a man, but then, in that moment he felt more like a wounded animal than a man.

This was like looking at the truth for the very first time. Seeing something fully, being forced to face reality. If this boy wasn't a monster, then perhaps the man wasn't either.

There was innocence in this picture. Innocence abused. And he could truly look upon the boy he'd been and see the truth of it. See what he had been, and who the monster really was.

Looking at that little boy made him think of the child he would have. Of what he would see when he looked into those eyes.

He felt like someone had reached into his chest, grabbed hold of his heart and squeezed it tight.

He was having a child. A child that he had been planning on punishing for the sins of his own father. He would never have hurt his child physically. But he had been planning on depriving his child of his father because of the pain that Cristian had in his own past.

Yes, he was a coward. And he had been fully intending on making his child, making Allegra suffer for it. It had been easy for him to believe that because he despised himself so much, that because his opinion of himself was so low, that removing his presence from both Allegra's and his child's lives was a kindness. But he was hurting them.

On the heels of that realization, on the fresh pain it caused, came the first glimmer of hope he'd experienced in more years than he could count.

They would both need him. They would both want him. Allegra had made it clear that she wanted him.

She wanted him. Both the broken boy he had been and the broken man he'd become.

He had been foolish enough to turn her away. Had been cowardly enough to say no. To try to convince both of them that his love and his desire to be loved were dead.

That wasn't the problem. The problem was, he wanted it more than most. Not less. He had been starved of it, always. Had married a woman he couldn't love, and who couldn't love him in return. Had never pursued a connection with the one woman he had wanted. Until fate had taken charge. Until the perfect moment, the most convenient excuse, had presented itself and he had taken advantage.

He brushed his bleeding thumb over the picture, leaving a smear of red behind.

The monster had never been inside of him. He had just tried to make himself think so. Had, as a boy, been forced to fashion a beast inside him that was more terrifying than the one always lurking outside his bedroom door.

Had tried to force himself to believe it even as an adult. That something inside of him caused the devastation in his life, because the alternative meant bad things simply happened and he couldn't control them. That he was as helpless now to stop bad things, to stop Sylvia from taking her own life, as he had been as a boy. And he had despised that helplessness so much it had been more comforting to blame himself than to acknowledge he could not have stopped it.

But the very best protection the beast he had created provided him was keeping people far away, so that they couldn't hurt him.

But he had to let it go now. He needed Allegra more than he needed protection.

And as he acknowledged that, that wall inside of him, that wall that seemed to keep all of his emotion back, even when he wanted to let it free, crumbled effortlessly. Pain flooded him. Pain and need, fear and love. He might not be able to win her back now. It might be too late.

But he would give everything. He would lay himself bare for her.

He was ready, finally, to take off his mask.

# CHAPTER SIXTEEN

EVERYTHING HURT AND she was sick. It was as inglorious a situation as she had ever found herself in. She was hiding again, at the apartment in Rome. Because a girl had to take cover when she had broken an engagement to a prince, gotten pregnant with her brother's friend's baby, then jilted said friend at the altar, all in the space of a couple of months. She was of far too much interest to the paparazzi at this point. And most especially since she was tangled up in all of the happenings in Raphael's country at the moment.

He was marrying his commoner princess, who was visibly pregnant with his child, and it was all a little bit of a three-ring circus. Their sex scandals were inextricably linked. She, pregnant by another man, he, having impregnated another woman.

If only the world knew how desperately they did not care about each other. It might all be a little bit less interesting. But, then again, maybe not. Had all of this been happening to some famous reality TV family, she probably would have been reading about it with just as much interest. But it was her life. So, she found very little about it interesting or amusing. She just found it awful.

Additionally, she currently felt as though someone had shattered a glass and ground the pieces into her chest.

Heartbreak was terrible. So much worse than she had ever imagined. She had been smart to try to insulate herself from pain, really. Except, she hadn't even known how much something could hurt. Not really. She clearly had some sort of self-protective instinct that had been operating on an intelligent level, but, it hadn't truly known what it was trying to protect her from.

This was terrible. It hurt so bad she could barely breathe. Leaving Cristian was anything but simple. It might have been smart, it might have been right, but it felt like removing a limb, not just walking away from another person. Cristian was a part of her in a profound and deep way she wasn't sure she had truly appreciated until she had left him.

She was lonely. All the time. During the day, but especially at night, when she missed being held in his strong arms. Missed listening to him breathe. Missed feeling his heartbeat beneath her palm.

She loved that man. Even having left him, even knowing that he didn't love her back, she loved that man with everything in her.

It was terrible. And wonderful. Because even though she didn't have him, she still had all of the strength that being with him had given her. It was sort of magical, how loving him both destroyed and built her up, but, there it was.

"None of this feels magical," she grumbled, standing up from the couch and stretching. She walked across the room, checking her reflection in the mirror. She was wearing a white, loose-fitting top and a pair of stretch pants. Her pregnancy was beginning to show, and it was one of the very few things that made her smile today. Seeing the evidence of Cristian's and her passion beginning to become visible.

She would probably feel differently about it later.

Would probably fully realize what a struggle it would be to be a single mother. To know that Cristian was out there, but wanted nothing to do with the baby.

But right now, seeing the evidence of her pregnancy made her feel warm. It was her hope in the middle of all this darkness. She would take it, because she desperately needed some hope.

She heard a vague noise out in the hall, then the front door to her apartment burst open. She jumped backward, ready to defend herself against an armed intruder, or *worse*, an armed paparazzo.

But when she oriented, and focused, she saw that it was Cristian standing there. He was wearing a white shirt, the collar unbuttoned, the whole thing rumpled. There was blood on the sleeve, and on the bottom. His hair was a mess, as though he had run his hands through it a few too many times, and the black slacks he was wearing had certainly seen better days.

If she didn't know better, she would assume that he was still wearing the same clothes from the wedding-that-wasn't two days ago.

She looked at his hand and saw that it was bandaged, and that his knuckles were bruised and the skin on them broken.

"Cristian. What are you doing here? And what did you do to yourself?" Even now, she was concerned for his well-being. Even now, she didn't want him to be in pain.

"What?" He looked down at his hand, as though he had forgotten it was bandaged. "I cut myself," he said.

"Are you all right? Have you been drinking?"

"No. And also no."

"You're not drunk, but you're also not okay?"

"No," he said, his voice rough, fierce. He crossed the space between them, coming to stand right in front of her. The lines on his face seemed somehow more pronounced, the expression in his eyes wounded. Wild. "I am not okay. I have not been okay since the moment you left me standing there at the altar."

She cringed inwardly. "I'm sorry if I embarrassed you…"

"Who cares about my embarrassment? Damn my embarrassment. Damn my insufferable ego. I don't care about any of it. You could've jilted me in front of the world, in fact, you did, and I still wouldn't care for that. But you… I lost you. And that I cannot endure."

Traitorous, treacherous hope washed over her. "Cristian? What exactly are you saying?"

"I was a fool. Allegra, I was a fool. Of course I knew it was you. How could I not?"

"I…but you…"

"I know what you like to eat. And I know where you dream of vacationing. I know the slight curve of your lips when you're trying not to show that you're pouting on the inside."

"I don't pout," she whispered, her throat feeling tight, her chest heavy.

"You do," he said. "And you do it beautifully. Just as you're beautiful when you're holding in a laugh, or a smile. Or even better, when you don't hold them back at all. Of course it was you," he repeated. "How else do you think I could write whole menus for you, consisting only of what you liked. How else could I choose a gown for you that first night at dinner, when I claimed to be putting on a show for the media?"

She blinked, trying to stave off her tears, fully overwhelmed by this. By this brilliant, glorious evidence being set out before her, that he knew her. That he had always known her. Even when she was silent.

"When I walked down that staircase in that Venetian ballroom and I saw you," Cristian said, "facing away from me… The reaction that it created inside of me… It could only have ever been you. But I could not face that. Because I am everything you said I am. I am a coward. I have been afraid to embrace the feelings inside of me, and so I told myself they didn't exist."

"Cristian…"

"Allegra, why else do you think I threw Raphael in your path?" he asked, his voice low, rough. "Why else would I be so desperate to see you married to him? Why else did I pick at any behavior I thought might threaten that?"

"I just thought you… I don't know, because you like my parents so much…"

"Your parents mean a great deal to me, but it was never about them. It was always about you. I wanted you married off. Safe, and away from me because…because something in me always knew that I would lose myself and touch you when I had no right to do that."

"I used to stare at your ring and feel ill," Allegra confessed, her voice hushed. "Because you belonged to someone else and not to me." She looked up at him, her eyes full of tears. "Oh, Cristian, I always wanted you. I wanted to belong to you. It was never anyone else for me."

"I told myself I was protecting you," he continued, "with Raphael. And I do think that I believed it. But the only person I was really protecting was myself."

"What changed?" she asked, looking at the battered man standing before her, vulnerable, unmasked.

"I went back to the *castillo*. Looking for more answers. Answers I had told myself I wouldn't find. But I found them, Allegra. I found them."

"What did you find?"

"A picture of myself. When I was a boy. And I…" His voice broke. "I was not a monster. I was never a monster. I was just a child. And looking at my face, at the bruise where my father had hit me, I knew that I didn't cause any of that. I knew that it was him. It made me question everything. I told you that I had to become brave to withstand it, and that was the truth. I had to pretend that there was something dangerous in me, so that I felt I could fight back. So that I felt I could withstand. And later, I told myself it was all in me when the world fell apart and I couldn't control it. But I don't need those excuses anymore. Realizing that you loved me, enough that not being with me might hurt you? Realizing that you loved me enough that my withholding my love harmed you... How can I continue to see myself as worthless, Allegra? When someone such as yourself loves me? I may have destroyed it. I wouldn't be surprised if I had. I hurt you badly enough that you left me at the altar. But if you could still love me... If you could find it in yourself to try and give me another chance, then I would be... I would be humbled. I would be honored."

All of Allegra's breath rushed out of her. "Cristian, you idiot."

"Am I?" he asked, his dark eyes searching hers.

"Yes. I never stopped loving you. Ever. I didn't leave you because you destroyed my love. I left you because I love you too much to be married to you and have you not touch me. Cristian, there was no way that I could be near you every day and never have you. I couldn't do that to myself. I could no longer live my life that way. With everything stuffed down deep. I want to live loud. I want to live with my whole heart out in the open. I want to show my love for you, not just to you, but to the rest of the world. I just couldn't face going back into hiding. Not when you showed me how wonderful it is to live with passion."

"Allegra," he said, his tone rough, fierce. He pulled

her into his arms, cupping her chin and tilting her face up. "I always saw your passion. I always saw your fire."

"You hated it."

"I feared it. Because I knew it would consume me. But now I want nothing more. To be caught up in you, in this. I love you," he said, "I love you with everything in me. And I feel it," he said, pressing his hand against his chest, "I feel it like I have felt nothing else since I was a child. And it hurts. It hurts so badly I can barely breathe. This need that I have for you. It goes so deep I cannot see the end of it."

"Oh, Cristian," she said, pressing a kiss to his lips. "It's the same for me too."

"Be my wife. Not because you must, not because it makes sense, or because it will give our child a title. But because I love you, and you love me."

Allegra looked up at this man, the man she had once thought of as Death come to collect her soul, and she saw life. The rest of her life, shining brilliantly and beautifully before her. Then she smiled. "Yes, Cristian," she said, "I will marry you. For no other reason than that I love you. With all of my heart and soul."

# EPILOGUE

THE DAY THAT little Sophia Acosta was brought to the newly restored *castillo* directly from the hospital was the happiest day of Cristian's life. He had never imagined building a life in this place. This place that had housed so many of his past demons, but then, he had never imagined a life quite like this one.

With Allegra's love. With his beautiful daughter. With happiness. Free from the chains that had bound him in the past.

There were no demons here, not anymore. There were no nightmares. Only dreams.

There was only the bright, brilliant smile of his wife, the perfect, comforting warmth of his daughter's tiny body.

And a beautiful life he had never imagined he might have.

He wrapped his arms around Allegra, holding her close, looking down at her beautiful face, then down at the perfect, dark eyes of his new daughter.

"Thank you," he said, "for having the courage to take my hand in that ballroom, even while I was being a coward."

"Coward is a very strong word. There was some part of you that wanted us to be together. Some part of me. And they were stronger than fear."

"What was that, do you think?"

She wrapped her arms around him, resting her head on his shoulder. "It was love, Cristian. It was always love."

* * * * *

# SANTIAGO'S COMMAND

## KIM LAWRENCE

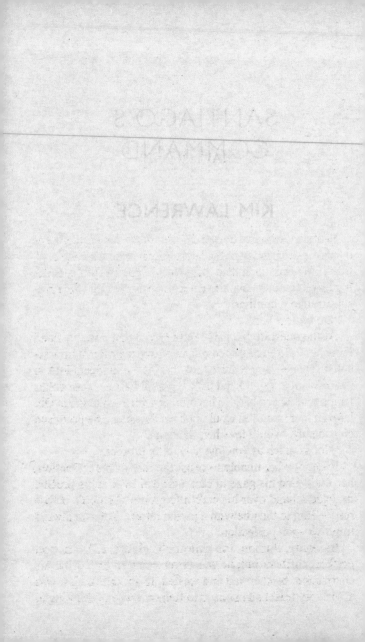

# CHAPTER ONE

'LUCY Fitzgerald…?'

Santiago, who had been half listening to his brother's enthusiastic description of the latest woman who was 'the one', lifted his head, the indent above his narrowed eyes deepening as he tried to place the name that seemed for some reason strangely familiar.

'Do I know her?'

At the question his half-brother, who had gone to stand in front of the large gilded mirror above the room's impressive fireplace, laughed. He took one last complacent look at his reflection, ran a hand over the dark hair he wore collar length and turned back to his brother with a white grin. 'Oh, if you'd met Lucy you wouldn't have forgotten,' he promised confidently. 'You'll love her, Santiago.'

'Not as much as you love *you*, little brother.'

Ramon, who, unable to resist the lure of his reflection, had swivelled his gaze to cast a critical look at his profile, dragged a hand over his carefully groomed stubble before responding to the jibe with a joking retort: 'You can always improve upon perfection.'

In reality, Ramon was philosophical that, effort or not, perfect profile or not, he was never going to have what his charismatic brother had and wasted. If not criminal, it was at the very least bad manners to Ramon's way of thinking to not even appear to notice the women who seemed more than willing to overlook his brother's imperfect profile—the slight bump in his nose was a permanent reminder of Santiago's rugby-playing days—as they sought to attract his attention by any, some not exactly subtle, means.

He angled his speculative gaze at the older man seated behind the massive mahogany desk. Despite the fact he wasted opportunities, his brother was no monk, but he was equally by no stretch of the imagination a player.

'Will you ever marry again, do you think?' Ramon regretted the unconsidered words the moment they left his lips. 'Sorry, I didn't mean to…' He gave an awkward shrug. It had been eight years since Magdalena had died and even though he'd been a kid at the time himself Ramon could still remember how awful the dead look in his brother's eyes had been. Even now a careless mention of Magdalena's name could bring it back. Not that he didn't have a constant reminder: little Gabriella was the spitting image of her mother.

Feeling sympathy for Ramon's obvious discomfort, Santiago pushed away the sense of crushing failure and guilt any thought of his dead wife always evoked and made himself smile.

'So this Lucy is making you think of marriage…?' he asked, changing the subject, fully anticipating his brother's horrified denial. 'She must be special,' he drawled.

'She is…'

Santiago's brows lifted at the vehemence in his brother's response.

'Very special. Marriage…?' A thunderstruck expression crossed Ramon's face before he directed a challenging look at his brother and added, 'Why not?' Ramon said, looking almost as shocked to hear himself say the words as Santiago felt hearing them.

Repressing a groan and taking comfort from the shock, Santiago struggled not to react to the challenge.

'Why not?' he drawled, struggling to keep the bite out of his voice as he added, 'Let me see…you're twenty-three and you've known this girl how long?'

'You were twenty-one when you got married.'

Santiago's dark lashes came down in a concealing mesh as he thought, *And look how well that worked out.*

Aware that too much opposition would just make his brother dig his heels in, Santiago gave an offhand shrug. Ramon's enthusiasms frequently cooled as quickly as they surfaced.

'Maybe I should meet this Lucy…?'

The beginnings of a belligerent gleam faded from his easy-going brother's eyes. 'You'll love her, Santiago, you'll see, you won't be able to help yourself. She's perfect! Totally perfect, a…' He moved his hands in an expressive curving sweep and gave a sigh. 'A goddess.'

Santiago raised an amused brow at the reverent declaration and, grimacing slightly, ran his thumb down the pile of correspondence designated personal that had been awaiting him on his return.

'If you say so.' His thoughts moving on, he picked up the top envelope and got to his feet, stretching the kinks from his spine as he walked around the big mahogany desk.

'You know I've never met anyone like her before.'

'This Lucy sounds…exceptional.' Santiago, who had never encountered a woman who was either perfect or a goddess, humoured Ramon.

'So you've no objection?'

'Bring her to dinner on Friday?'

'Seriously? Here?'

Santiago nodded absently as he scrolled down the page

he held, squinting to read the neat but microscopic tightly packed writing on it. The message it held was familiar: Ramon, his mother said, had messed up and what, she wanted to know, was he going to do about it?

His head lifted. 'You didn't mention you have to retake your second year.' A fact that his stepmother, without actually saying so, managed to expertly imply was actually Santiago's fault.

Maybe, he mused, she had a point?

Had the time come for some tough love? While he wanted his brother to enjoy the freedom he had missed out on after their father's premature death, had he been guilty of overcompensating and being too indulgent and overprotective?

Ramon shrugged. 'To be honest, marine biology isn't really what I was expecting.'

Santiago's jaw tightened as he scanned the younger man's face with narrowed eyes. 'Neither, as I recall, was archaeology or, what was it...ecology...?'

'Environmental science,' his brother supplied. 'Now that, believe me, was—'

'You're so bright, I just don't understand how...' Santiago interrupted, reining in his frustration with difficulty and asking, 'Did you actually go to any lectures, Ramon?'

'A couple...yeah, I know, Santiago, but I'm going to buckle down, really I am. Lucy says—'

'Lucy?' He saw his brother's face and added, 'The goddess. Sorry, I forgot.'

'A good education, Lucy says, is something that no one can take away from you.'

Santiago blinked. This Lucy didn't sound like any of the numerous females his brother had hooked up with to date. 'I'm looking forward to meeting this Lucy.' Maybe a good woman, someone who thought education was a good thing, was what his brother needed?

The jury was still out but he decided to keep an open mind.

When on her very first day at the *finca* Harriet's car had refused to start Lucy had said no problem and walked the mile into town. There had been a problem—not the distance, but the scorching Andalusian midday sun.

A week later Harriet's car was still sitting propped up on bricks in the yard, awaiting the part the mechanic had had to order, and the tip of Lucy's nose was still peeling, though the painful redness had subsided and her complexion had regained its normal pale peaches and cream glow.

Today she had not taken up Harriet's sensible suggestion of a taxi—she loved to walk—but she had chosen a more appropriate time to make the trip and, arriving early, she had managed to buy everything on Harriet's shopping list while it was still cool enough to enjoy the walk back through truly incredible scenery, but she was taking no chances. Lucy had plastered on the factor thirty and borrowed a shapeless straw sun hat from Harriet.

It was still only ten-thirty when she reached the footbridge across the stream that bordered Harriet's property, a single-story terracotta-roofed cottage that had the basics and not much else. It was the four acres of scrubby land that had attracted her friend. On retirement Harriet had decided to live her dream and start, to the amazement of her academic ex-work colleagues, a donkey sanctuary in Spain.

When Lucy had said she thought she was being very brave, her old university tutor had retorted she was simply following the example of her favourite ex-student. Lucy, who was not accustomed to being held up as a role model, had not pointed out that her change of lifestyle had not been one of choice, more of necessity.

On impulse she walked down the grassy bank by the bridge and slipped off her sandals. The first initial touch of the icy water against her hot, dusty skin made her gasp. She laughed with pleasure as she felt her way carefully over the smooth stones, wading out until the water reached her calves.

Pulling off the sun hat, she shook free her ash-blonde hair and, head tipped back to the azure sky, she closed her eyes to shut out the sun and sighed. It was bliss!

With a tightening of his thighs against leather and solid flesh Santiago urged the responsive animal out of the protective shadow of the pine trees where they had paused. His strong-boned features set in an austere, contemplative mask, he patted the animal's neck as it responded to his light touch and walked forward, hooves silent on the boggy patch of ground as they moved towards the fast-flowing stream.

Now he knew why the name had seemed so familiar.

The disguise of sexy angel was good but not that good, not for someone who possessed a once-seen-never-forgotten quality, and Lucy Fitzgerald definitely did!

She was not dressed in the sharp tailored red suit and spiky heels—four years ago that iconic image had been used again and again by the media—but he had no doubt that this was the same woman who had elicited universal condemnation from a morally outraged public.

She hadn't said a word to defend herself, but then that had been the idea; a word that broke the gagging injunction would have landed her in jail, a place that Santiago for one would have paid good money to see her end up!

An image of the tear-stained face of the wronged wife in the story drifted into his head, the brave face the woman put on not hiding the emotional devastation that presented a dramatic contrast to the cold composure that Lucy Fitzgerald had displayed under the camera lens.

It had been the sort of story that under normal circumstances Santiago would not have read beyond the first line—but for the timing. The situation of the advertising executive who had resorted to the courts to protect himself from Lucy Fitzgerald had borne an uncanny resemblance to the one he had at the time found himself in, albeit on a lesser scale.

In his case the woman—he barely remembered her name, let alone her face—who had sought to gain financially had been more opportunistic than ruthless, and of course not being married and caring very little what the world thought of him had made him a less vulnerable target than Lucy Fitzgerald's victim, who, instead of caving in to his mistress's threat of exposure, had instead sought an injunction to stop her speaking out.

Blackmail was the action of a coward and a woman like Lucy Fitzgerald represented everything Santiago despised. This was why, while the face of his own would-be blackmailer, a woman whom he had never even slept with, had vanished, the composed Madonna-like face that had hidden a dark heart of stone had stuck in his mind—his heavy-lidded glance dropped—as had her body.

*You and the rest of the male population!*

The silent addition caused his firm, mobile lips to twitch into a self-mocking grimace as his dark gaze continued to slide over the lush curves beneath the simple cotton top and skirt she was wearing. The woman might be poison, but she did have a body that invited, actually demanded, sinful speculation.

Of course she was all too…obvious for his taste, but it was easy now to see why his easily influenced brother had been so smitten, a case of lust not love.

Exert a positive influence!

He choked back a bitter laugh. His uncharacteristic and misguided optimism could not have been more poorly timed. Positive? If Lucy Fitzgerald was even a fraction as bad as her reputation, she was toxic!

Santiago felt a passing stab of nostalgia for the empty-headed, pretty but basically harmless party girls his brother had up to this point needed saving from…not that he had saved him. Up to this point Santiago had not ridden to the rescue, deciding that his brother would learn from experience. This, he reflected soberly, was an entirely different situation; he could not allow his brother to become a victim of this woman.

Had she specifically targeted Ramon?

Santiago, who did not believe in coincidence any more than he believed in fate, considered it likely; he could see how his brother would seem an easy prey to someone like her.

Did Ramon know who she was? Did he know about her history or at least her sanitised version of it where she no doubt became the innocent victim? He had no doubt that she could be very convincing and Ramon was obviously completely bewitched, though why bother raking up your sordid past when your victim had still been a teenager when the story had been big news.

A teenager!

Anger flashed in his deep-set eyes, the fine muscle along his angular jaw quivered and clenched beneath the surface of his golden skin. Not only was she a mercenary, corrupt gold-digger, she was a cradle snatcher. She had to be, what…? Doing the maths in his head, he scowled. Thirty, give or take a year or two?

Though admittedly, he conceded, reining in his mount a few feet from the riverbank, she looked younger, and for once in his life his little brother had not exaggerated. Lucy Fitzgerald was a woman that *goddess* could legitimately be used to describe. Poison to the core but breathtakingly beautiful, even barefooted and wearing a simple cotton skirt. On anyone else he would have assumed the transparency that revealed the silhouette of her long shapely thighs under direct sunlight was accidental, with this woman he was willing to bet that even her dreams were contrived.

As she remained oblivious to his presence Santiago took the opportunity to study the genuinely goddess-like attributes beneath the thin fabric.

There was plenty to study. She was tall and statuesque with long legs and a figure of iconic hourglass proportions. The woman oozed sex and Santiago felt a stab of annoyance as, independent of his brain, his body reacted with indiscriminate lust to the image.

As he watched she slid a hand under the neck of her top and wriggled to catch the bra strap that had slipped over her shoulder. The innately sexy action made her suddenly less pin-up and more earthily warm, desirable woman—very desirable.

As the sun caught her waist length hair, turning it to spun silver, Santiago realised that if he wanted to save his brother from this witch's machinations he would have to act swiftly. She was fatally beautiful.

One day Ramon would thank him.

The polished leather of his saddle creaked as he swung his leg over it and leapt lightly to the ground, his booted feet making contact with the stones with a metallic click.

Lucy jumped like a startled deer, instinctive fear showing in her blue eyes as she turned, seeing for a split second the tall, threatening bulk of a male figure outlined against the sun. The correspondingly massive horse beside him was drinking from the stream.

When the man spoke a moment later she had regained control, if not of her banging heart, at least of her expression.

'Sorry, did I startle you?'

*Only half to death*, Lucy thought, her eyes widening fractionally in reaction to the sound of his voice. The intruder spoke perfect English. He was not English though, she decided, picking up on the faint foreign inflection in his richly textured voice—a voice that was velvet over gravel.

Low in her belly things shifted slightly in response to the tactile quality in that deep voice. Shading her eyes, she gave a faint smile and moved her head in a negative gesture.

'I didn't know anyone… I didn't hear you.' She made a conscious effort to erase the frozen mask that her expression had automatically settled into, the same expression that had earned her the 'ice bitch' tag. It was a struggle; the defensive action was by now deeply ingrained.

There had been a time when she had been in danger of allowing her experiences to make her hard, cynical and—according to her mother—too scared to live. The worried accusation had shaken Lucy and she had been trying very hard of late not to assume the worst in any given situation.

Caution was another matter and in the circumstances seemed only sensible!

Arm crooked to hold back her hair from her face, she waded towards the riverbank, her gaze fixed on her feet to avoid stumbling on the rocky riverbed.

Reaching dry ground, she climbed the slight incline that brought her level with the stranger and close enough, thanks to the prevailing wind, for her nostrils to twitch in response to the scent of leather and horse. She kept her distant smile in place and tilted her head up to look at him.

It was a lot of tilting. He was extremely tall; broad of shoulder, narrow of hip and long of leg. She had an impression of power, raw and elemental. She lifted a hand to shade her eyes and her smile faded as, minus the direct dazzle, the man's face became more than a dark blur.

There was definitely nothing blurred about features that looked as though they had been freshly carved in bronze by the hand of an artist more interested in conveying a masculine ideal than reality. The rider's face, bisected by an aquiline, masterful nose, was long with a broad, intelligent forehead, strong square jaw and high, dramatically chiselled cheekbones. Her gaze drifted to his mouth and paused. It was wide and sculpted, the upper lip firm, the lower sensually full.

It was all jaw-dropping and deep-intake-of-breath stuff. Aware she had been staring and without the faintest clue of how long she had been standing there with her mouth unattractively open, she closed it with a snap and felt an embarrassed flush wash over her skin, struggling to maintain eye contact with the deep-set, heavy-lidded eyes that returned her gaze.

She was an expert at hiding her feelings, but this man took impenetrable to another level entirely. His obsidian stare was totally unreadable. His eyes were incredible; framed by thick ebony lashes that were long and spiky, they were densely dark and flecked with silver. They made her think of a starlit night sky.

Starlit skies…? She resisted the temptation to roll her eyes and thought, *Lucy, girl you need a sugar hit.* Sugar was not what her best friend, Sally—never afraid to call a spade a spade—had said she needed when she had told her she was off to Spain.

'The fact is, Lucy, principles are great and true love is nice and all—but in fairy tales! How about a compromise while you're waiting for your prince to climb your ivory tower? Enjoy a bit of head-banging sex with a sexy Spaniard. Let's face it, you won't be short of offers… God, if I looked like you…'

Lucy, who knew nothing about head-banging sex except

that it wasn't for her, pushed away the memory of the conversation, but not before her glance slid to the sensual contours
of the stranger's mouth. She found herself almost envying her
friend's pragmatic approach to sex as heat flashed through
her in a warm squirmy mess. She cleared her throat but it
didn't stop her voice sounding husky and breathless as she
said the first thing that came into her head.

'How did you know I was English?'

The last time she'd experienced this knee-sagging, heart-
thudding sensation the cause had been an earthquake that
had made the hotel rock and brought a nearby chandelier
crashing to the floor! Was this what people called animal
magnetism? Well, whatever it was he had it! And the earthy
aura of maleness was not something she would choose to
be this close to.

The stranger soothed his horse with a casual pat of his
hand on the glossy flank and raised a satiric brow as he allowed his gaze to sweep down her tumbling waist-length
hair in an unrealistic but eye-catching pale silvery blonde.

In all the pictures Santiago had seen she had worn her hair
in a puritanical elegant chignon that had exposed the swan-
like curve of her pale throat and the determined angle of her
delicate jaw. Her hairstyle changed, he presumed, depending
on what part she was playing, and he could see the tumbling
pre-Raphaelite curls appealing to his brother…actually appealing to any man.

'Your colouring is not exactly local…'

His glance moved over the delicate contours of her face.
Up close her pale creamy skin had an almost opalescent
sheen, the glow of roses on her smooth cheeks not the result
of make-up; astonishingly she wore none. Despite her fair
colouring her long curling lashes and arched feathery brows
were dark. A purist might say her lush, sensuous lips were
too full for her delicate features, but even the harshest critic

could have found no room for criticism with her eyes. Wide spaced and slightly slanted, they were an astonishing shade of dramatic blue, the electric colour emphasised by the black rim surrounding the iris.

'Oh…' Lucy lifted a hand to her head, tucking a strand of hair behind her ear as she gave a rueful smile, receiving in response a midnight stare. His expression was still shuttered but she was conscious of inexplicable hostility in his body language.

Was it personal or was he like this with everyone? Feeling increasingly antagonistic—the man's people skills could definitely do with some work—Lucy forced a smile as she admitted lightly, 'I suppose I do stick out a little.'

His dark eyes slid the length of her body.

The studied insolence in his stare brought an angry sparkle to her eyes. She fought the impulse to cover herself with her hands. Forget poor people skills—the man's horse had better manners than him.

'And you try so hard to fade into the background.'

A choking sound left her throat. 'Just what is your problem? I'm not trespassing, you know…but you probably are.' He had the look of someone who did not recognise boundaries.

'I am trespassing?' He looked amused by the suggestion. 'I am Santiago Silva.'

'Should I curtsy or bow?' So this was the man who was literally lord of all he surveyed, including the property that Harriet rented. From what her friend had told her, he was 'a great guy'. Odd—Harriet was normally a pretty good judge of character.

Placing a hand on a hip, oblivious to the sexually provocative style of her pose, she watched as his firm sensual mouth lifted at the corners in a smile that did not touch his hard eyes—they held the warmth of a diamond chip as he returned her stare.

'I had no idea we had such a famous—or should that be infamous?—visitor to the area, Miss Fitzgerald.' He saw her flinch and felt a stab of savage satisfaction as he thought, *Gotcha!*

## CHAPTER TWO

A FAMILIAR cold, clammy fist tightened in the pit of Lucy's stomach as she felt her expression freeze over. She cursed herself for being surprised that anyone would recognise her here in Spain; like they said, it was a small world and, with the advent of social networking, even smaller.

It didn't matter how many times she told herself that what total strangers chose to think about her was their problem, not hers, it still hurt, and it made her angry that the stares and contemptuous comments had the power to make her want to crawl away into a corner and hide, which according to some was exactly what she had been doing for four years.

Pride enabled her to lift her chin and train her level stare at his face. She was not going to hide any more; she had done nothing wrong. The gagging injunction was long gone; there was no longer anything stopping her telling her side. Nothing but the stubborn conviction that as the innocent victim she shouldn't have to explain to anyone; after all, the people that mattered had never believed any of the lies that had been printed about her.

'If I'd known how warm, charming and welcoming the natives were I would have made it here sooner,' she said, flashing him a smile of saccharine-sweet insincerity and having the satisfaction of seeing his jaw tighten in annoyance.

'And how long are you thinking of staying?'

'Why? Are you planning on running me out of town, sheriff?' she mocked, adopting a mock-Western drawl.

He responded to her levity with another stony stare. On the receiving end, Lucy found the level of his relentless hostility frankly bewildering.

*God, does this man need to get a life!*

Her story was old news and even if he believed she was as bad as they had painted her, which in truth was pretty bad, it hardly explained an antipathy that seemed…personal?

'I shouldn't joke—you probably can.'

She had the impression that all this man had to do was snap his fingers and the locals would be lining up to be part of a run-her-out-of-town posse, less a form of mob mentality and more mass hypnotism.

She wasn't seeing much evidence of it but it was clear the man exerted some sort of weird charismatic control locally… either that or there was something in the water. In the time she had been here Lucy had heard the name Santiago Silva with monotonous regularity in the area. You couldn't buy a loaf of bread without hearing someone sing the praises of this paragon, which, considering he was a banker—a fairly universally despised animal these days—seemed pretty amazing to Lucy.

Their comments had built an image of someone very different from the man standing there looking down his autocratic nose at her. He did not look remotely like the warm, caring person she'd heard described, but he did look every inch the autocratic feudal throwback who expected people to bow and scrape.

'You have met my brother.' He arched an ebony brow.

A mystified Lucy began to shake her head, then the penny dropped.

Her eyes widened. 'Ramon.' Who had rung the *finca* just before she left that morning inviting her to dinner at the *cas-*

*tillo.* Wow, was she glad she'd said no to this opportunity to meet his brother…the sort of social event nightmares were made of if this taster was any indicator! Stiff and starchy now, imagine how he'd look in a tie—besides beautiful. Lucy gave her head a little shake to dispel this image.

It was not so surprising she hadn't seen the connection straight off; Ramon had none of the autocratic arrogance of his unpleasant brother. He was actually a really sweet boy who had gone out of his way to help when they had been stranded in the clinic car park the day after she arrived. He'd been a hero, administering first aid to Harriet's ancient car.

Since then he had called twice at the *finca*, the last time, she recalled with a smile, he had helped her catch one of the donkeys before the vet arrived, falling flat on his face in the dust and dirt at one point and ruining his lovely suit. It was hard to believe he was related to this man.

'You will not meet him again.' The comment was delivered in a soft, almost conversational tone that was in stark variance to the menace it conveyed.

Lucy shook her head, genuinely bewildered by the turn this conversation was taking. Was this about her refusing the invitation to dinner at the big house? Had she committed some sort of social faux pas?

The possibility bothered her for Harriet's sake. Her friend had made a lot of effort to fit in so she felt her way cautiously. 'I won't?'

'No, Miss Fitzgerald, you will not.'

'Is Ramon going away?'

'No, you are going away.'

Lucy's patience snapped. 'Will you stop being so damned enigmatic and spit it out? Just what are you trying to say?'

He cut across her in a voice that felt like an icy shower. 'For someone who is clearly a clever woman you have not done your research. Until he is twenty-five, my brother has no access to his trust fund unless I approve it, and I will not. The lifestyle my brother enjoys now is totally at my discretion.'

'Poor Ramon,' she said, feeling sorry for Ramon but not totally sure why his brother should think the information was of interest to her.

'So you will be wasting your time.'

'My time to waste,' she responded, still without the faintest idea what this discussion was about.

The flippancy brought his teeth together in a snarling white smile. 'I suggest you cut your losses and move on to a more profitable...subject.'

Totally at sea now, Lucy shook her head. 'I haven't the faintest idea what you're talking about,' she was forced to admit.

Irritated by this display of innocence, Santiago twisted his expressive mouth in a grimace of fastidious distaste. Sensing his master's mood, the animal at his side pawed the ground and snorted.

Without thinking Lucy responded, moving forward, her hand outstretched to soothe the animal, only to be blocked by the horse's tall rider.

'He does not like strangers.' His concern was for his mount, not the stupid woman who clearly knew nothing about horses.

'Just now I'm identifying with him.'

Santiago was tempted to respond to the challenge gleaming in her blue eyes—the colour was so extraordinary it amounted to an assault on the senses. Instead, he made a decision. 'I want a quick resolution of this situation.'

The solution was not desirable—every cell in his body craved revenge and he was going to reward her but... He breathed a deep sigh, accepting that there were occasions when a man had to do what was necessary as opposed to what was right. He didn't have to like it though.

'If you leave immediately I will cover your expenses.' The resort hotel in the locality was aimed at the high end of the market as it was the only accommodation in the area, barring a couple of rural bed-and-breakfast establishments. He could not imagine the likes of Lucy Fitzgerald roughing it in some rustic retreat—it seemed safe to assume she was a guest at the hotel.

Lucy nodded solemnly and drawled, 'Generous…' Then gave a little laugh and angled a quizzical look at his face. 'But do you think you could give me a clue? I haven't the faintest idea what you're talking about.'

He clicked his tongue irritably. 'Move on, Lucy, you've done innocent and you give a first-class performance, but it tends to pall.'

She pulled herself up to her full height. In most company, even without shoes, that gave her an advantage, but not over this man. Ramon's brother was… Her narrowed glance moved up from his feet—the man was six four easy, possibly more and not an ounce of surplus fat on any of it. He was all hard bone and muscle and enough testosterone to light up the planet.

'My friends call me Lucy.'

'Of which you have many, I am sure,' he cut back smoothly.

Lucy grated her teeth. She had never considered herself a violent person but this man was making her discover new things about herself.

'Expenses and a one-off payment.' His lips curled. What was the going rate for a woman like her these days? 'But only,' he warned, 'if you leave immediately.'

'You want to pay me to leave where exactly?'

'The country and my brother.'

Lucy breathed in and played back the conversation in her head. She could almost hear the sound of the penny dropping. On the outward breath an explosive of anger dumped bucketloads of neat adrenaline into her bloodstream. Lucy saw red, quite literally, she blinked and, still seeing everything through a shimmering red heat haze, linked her badly shaking hands together.

'Let me get this straight. You are offering to pay me to stay away from your brother? I'm curious just how much—no, don't tell me, I might be tempted.'

He did and her eyes widened. 'Wow, you must really think I'm dangerous!'

A nerve pumped beneath the golden-toned skin of his lean cheek but he didn't react to her comment. 'This sum is not negotiable,' he emphasised. 'You must walk away—' He stopped, brows knitting into frustrated lines above his dark eyes. 'What are you doing?'

She paused and threw a look over her shoulder, sticking out one hip to balance the bag she had slung over the other shoulder. 'What am I doing?' She gave a laugh and fixed him with a glittering smile. 'I would have thought that was obvious, Mr Silva—this is me walking. I like walking but nobody has ever offered to pay me for it except for charity. Give me your number and I'll give you a bell the next time I do the marathon.'

He looked so astonished that this time her laugh was genuine.

Santiago watched her make her way up the dusty track, an expression of baffled frustration etched on his handsome face. He had pitched his offer high deliberately; he had allowed for the possibility she might try and negotiate the figure up, but her outright refusal had been an option he had not even considered.

With a gritted oath he vaulted into the saddle and turned his horse in the opposite direction to that she had taken.

It was not until his temper had cooled and he had slowed to a canter that it occurred to him that he had no idea what she had been doing there in the middle of nowhere. The only inhabited building within a two-mile radius was the place he had leased to the English academic who had started up, of all things, a donkey sanctuary.

It would be difficult to imagine two women with less in common, so ruling out that left—what…? Could she have been waiting for someone? In that lonely spot…no…unless… she had been meeting someone and they had required privacy?

By the time the horse had reached the *castillo* gates the conviction that he had stumbled onto a lovers' tryst, that she had been waiting for his half-brother, had become a firm conviction.

His brother was not behaving rationally. Santiago saw those electric-blue eyes in his head and he felt his anger towards his sibling subside. He doubted Ramon was the only man unable to act rationally around Lucy Fitzgerald, who was unable to see past her smouldering sexuality, the only man willing to ignore the truth in order to possess that body, but fortunately for Ramon he was not one of them.

Did she think she had won?

Beneath him Santana responded to the light kick of encouragement and broke into a gallop; to catch a thief one had to adopt the same ruthless methods they did.

Literally shaking with fury, Lucy made the last stage of her journey in record time. She paused at the *finca* door to compose herself. As satisfying as it would have been to vent her feelings on the subject of Santiago Silva, the last thing her friend needed right now was the news that her house guest had had a run in with him.

Harriet would feel obligated to defend her and she could not see that going down well with her feudal despot of a landlord, who would, she thought scornfully, quite likely feel perfectly justified evicting anyone who disagreed with him. He was just the type of small-minded bully who enjoyed wielding the power he had inherited!

No, the best thing all around, she realised, was not to mention the incident at all—and why should she? He had no idea that she was staying with Harriet and so long as she stayed out of his way and she didn't darken his doorstep with her presence—a treat she felt happy to miss out on—unless fate was very unkind she would never have to set eyes on the wretched man again.

Taking comfort from the knowledge, she took a deep breath, pasted on a smile and patted her cheeks. Her eyes widened as she felt the dampness there. God, Santiago Silva had achieved what a media army had failed to do—he had made her cry.

Harriet, normally uncomfortably observant, had not noticed the tear stains, which suggested that her white-faced friend was suffering a lot more than the mild discomfort she claimed after literally hopping out to the stables during Lucy's absence to check on an elderly donkey.

Lucy banned Harriet from attempting any more stunts and hustled her back to bed for a nap. The other woman looked so much better when she rose later that midway through the next morning Lucy suggested another nap and the older woman did not resist the idea.

Lucy decided to use the time to take hay to animals in the scrubby lower pasture. As she walked through the field buzzing with bees and chirruping crickets she became aware of a distant noise disturbing the quiet. As she distributed the feed to the animals who clustered around her the noise got perceptibly closer until... Lucy started and the animals ran at the sound of a loud crash followed by a silence that seemed horribly ominous.

Recovering her wits, Lucy dropped the hay she was holding and ran in the opposite direction to the agitated braying herd. Seconds later, panting, she reached the rise of the slight incline that hid the dirt track below from view and saw the cause of the explosive sound.

Her hand went to her mouth. 'Oh, God!'

One of the modern four-wheel quad bikes was lying at an angle, the front end in a ditch and the back wheels hidden beneath a tangle of scrub that the vehicle had dragged up as it slid off the stony path.

A quick scan revealed no immediate sign of the driver. Had he been thrown clear?

There was no time to speculate. Lucy hit the ground running, scrambling down the rocky incline and raising a cloud of dust from the dry ground. She reached the accident in a matter of seconds, though it felt like a lifetime. There was still no sign of the driver and she couldn't hear anything, but then it was difficult to hear anything above the thundering of her heart in her ears, even her own fearful cry of—

'Is there anyone...? Are you all right?'

'No, I'm not all right. I'm...' A flood of tearful-sounding Spanish preceded a small grunt that was followed by a deep sigh before the young voice added in flawless, barely accented English, 'I'm stuck. Give me a pull, will you?'

Lucy saw the small hand—a child's—appear from beneath the upturned quad bike. She dropped to her knees, her hair brushing the ground as she bent her head to peer underneath. The driver appeared to be a dark-haired young girl.

'It's probably not a good idea to move until—'

'I've already moved. I'm not hurt. It's just my jacket is caught—' The girl gave a small yelp followed by a heartfelt 'Finally!' as she dragged herself out from under the quad bike, emerging beside Lucy looking dusty, in one piece and with nothing but a bloody scrape on the cheek of her heart-shaped face to show for her experience—at least nothing else visible. Lucy remained cautious as the girl, who looked to be around ten or eleven, pulled herself into a sitting position and began to laugh.

'Wow!' Her eyes shone with exhilaration, a reaction that made Lucy think, *God, I'm getting old.* But then, though she'd had her share of her own youthful misadventures, they had had less to do with her being an adrenaline junkie and more to do with her need to please her father and compete with the legendary exploits of her elder siblings.

'That was quite something.'

'I'd call it a lucky escape.' Lucy got to her feet and held out her hand. 'Look, there's no reception here but I really think you should see a doctor to get checked out.'

The girl sprang to her feet energetically, ignoring the extended hand. 'No, I'm fine, I'm...' She stopped, the animation draining from her face as the condition of the overturned vehicle seemed to hit her for the first time. 'Is there any way we could get this back on the road, do you think?'

Lucy shook her head in response to the wistful question. 'I doubt it. I think you should sit down...?' *Before you fall down*, she thought, studying the young girl's pale face.

'Oh, I am in so much trouble. When my dad sees this he'll hit the ceiling. I'm not really meant to ride on this thing...but then I'm not really meant to do anything that is any fun. Do you know what it feels like to have someone act as though you can't even fasten your own shoelace?'

Lucy's lips twitched. 'No, I don't.' If she'd had a penny for every time her dad had said, 'Don't whinge, Lucy, just get on with it,' she would have been able to retire before she hit ten.

'That's why I'm home now, because my dad dragged me away from school. Not that I care. I hate school—he's the one who's always saying how important education is.'

Lucy, who thought so, too, adopted a sympathetic expression as the girl paused for breath, but didn't interrupt as the youthful driver continued in the same if-I-don't-get-it-off-my-chest-now-I'll-explode style.

'And Amelie didn't even have it!'

'Have what?' Lucy, struggling to keep up, asked.

'Meningitis.'

Lucy's brows went up. 'Your school friend has meningitis?'

'No, she doesn't have it, I just said so, and she's not my friend. I have no friends.'

'I'm sure that's not true.'

'It's true, and with a father like mine is it any wonder? He wouldn't let me go on the skiing trip and everyone was going and now, after the head told all the parents that there is no cause for concern, that Amelie didn't have meningitis at all, it was just a virus, what does he do?'

Lucy shook her head, finding she was genuinely curious to know what this much-maligned but clearly caring parent had done.

'Does he listen? No...' she said, pausing in the flow of confidences to turn her bitter gaze on Lucy. 'He lands his helicopter right there in the middle of the lunch break with everyone watching and whisks me off after giving the head an earful. Can you imagine?'

Lucy, who could, bit her quivering lip. 'That must have been dramatic.'

'It was mortifying and now he says I have to go back and there's only two weeks to the end of term.'

'What does your mother say?'

'She's dead.' She stopped, her eyes going round as she turned to face the vehicle hurtling at speed down the hill towards them. It came to a halt with a squeal of brakes feet away from them.

*I should have known,* Lucy thought as the tall, unmistakeable figure of Santiago Silva exploded from the driver's seat.

He had seen the overturned quad bike from the top of the hill seconds before he saw Gabby. In those seconds he had lived the nightmare that haunted his dreams. For a terrible moment he could feel the weight of his daughter's lifeless body in his arms the same way he had felt her mother's—it was his job to keep her safe and he had failed.

Then he saw her, recognised even at a distance the familiar defiant stance, and the guilt and grief were replaced by immense relief, which in its turn was seamlessly swallowed up by a wave of savage anger. An anger that quickly shifted focus when he identified the tall blonde-haired figure beside his daughter.

He should have known that she would be involved!

He approached with long angry strides, looking like some sort of avenging dark angel—the fallen variety. Lucy didn't blame the kid for looking terrified. She gave the shaking child's shoulder a comforting squeeze. Really, she should have guessed when the child had started talking casually about helicopters, but she hadn't. For some reason she hadn't thought about Santiago Silva as married, let alone a widow, or a father! It was still a struggle to think of him as any of these things, as was maintaining her smile as he approached.

Yesterday she had been conscious that where this man was concerned the veneer of civilisation was pretty thin; right now it was non-existent. He was scary but also, she admitted as she felt a little shiver trace a path down her rigid spine, pretty magnificent!

He swept straight past her, but not before Lucy had felt the icy blast of the glittering stare that dashed over her face.

She watched as he placed his hands on his daughter's shoulders and squatted until he was at face level with her.

'Gabby, you...' Torn between a desire to throttle his wilful daughter and crush her in a bear hug, he took a deep breath. Feeling like a hopelessly inadequate parent, he searched her face and asked brusquely, 'You are hurt?'

Even Lucy, who was extremely unwilling to assign any normal human emotions to this awful man, could not deny the rough concern in his deep voice was genuine.

'I'm fine, *Papá*. She—' the little girl cast a smile in Lucy's direction '—helped me.'

'Not really.'

For a moment his burning eyes met hers, then, a muscle along his clean shaven jaw clenching, he turned away, rising to his feet with a graceful fluidity that caused Lucy's over-sensitive stomach to flip.

'*Papá*...'

'Wait in the car, Gabriella.'

With one last look over her shoulder at Lucy, she walked, head down, towards the car.

Without looking to see if his daughter had obeyed, Santiago Silva began to speak into the phone he had pulled from the breast pocket of his open necked shirt.

Lucy's Spanish was good enough to make out that the conversation was with a doctor who was being requested to meet them at the *castillo*.

He might be an awful man but he was also obviously a concerned father. 'She wasn't unconscious or anything.'

Santiago closed the phone with a click and covered the space between them in two strides.

As he bent his face close to her own Lucy felt the full force of his contempt as he responded in a lethally soft voice,

'When I require your medical expertise I will ask for it. As for having any contact with my daughter...' He swallowed, the muscles in his brown throat visibly rippling. 'Do not attempt to make any contact or you will be sorry.'

Lucy's sympathy vanished and her anger rushed in to fill the vacuum it left. She didn't bother asking if that had been a threat—it clearly was.

Fighting the urge to step back, she lifted her chin to a pugnacious angle and enquired coolly, 'So, the next time I find her trapped under a grown-up toy she is clearly not old enough to get behind the wheel of, I'll walk by on the other side of the damned road, shall I, Mr Silva? That might be your style, but it isn't mine.'

'I know all about your *style* and I would prefer that members of my family are not contaminated by your toxic influence...but, yes, you did try and help my daughter, so thank you for that at least.'

It was clear that every word of the apology hurt him. 'Does it occur to you that your daughter wouldn't feel the need to break the rules if you cut her a bit of slack?'

He stared at her incredulously. 'You are giving me advice on parenting? So, how many children do you have, Miss Fitzgerald?'

She sucked in a furious breath. Where did this man get off being so superior? 'Well, if I did have one I'd make damned sure I wasn't too busy to notice she had driven off on a quad bike!'

The expression that Lucy saw move at the back of his eyes—so bleak it was almost haunted—made her almost regret her taunt, but she stifled the stab of guilt. She'd save her pity for someone who deserved it. He was a bully, used to people sitting and taking what he dished out.

Well, she wasn't going to take it, not from him, not from anyone.

'Stay away from my family or I will make you wish you'd never been born.' Without waiting for her response, he turned and started walking towards the car.

By the time she reached the *finca* Lucy was so mad she was shaking like someone with a fever.

'Lucy, my dear, what's wrong? What's happened?' Harriet studied the face of her ex-student with growing concern.

'Nothing, I'm fine. Don't get up,' she added as the older woman struggled to rise from her chair. 'You should have rested longer. You know what the doctor said about keeping your foot up to stop it swelling again.'

Harriet subsided back into her seat with a frustrated grunt. 'I'll stay here if you tell me what's wrong, Lucy.'

In the middle of pacing agitatedly across the room, Lucy paused, her fists in tight balls at her sides, her face coloured by two bright spots of anger on her smooth cheeks, and gave a high little laugh. 'Mr Smug Sanctimonious Creep Silva is wrong!'

Harriet looked confused. 'Ramon!' she exclaimed. 'But he seems a sweet boy, if a little full of himself...whatever has he done?' She had never seen the student she considered one of the brightest young women she had ever taught lose her air of serene calm. Even during the awful press witch hunt she had remained cool and aloof.

'Ramon...?' Lucy shook her head impatiently and took up her pacing. 'It's not Ramon, it's his brother,' she gritted.

'Santiago? You've met him...is he here?'

Lucy gave a grim smile. 'Oh, yes, I've had that plea-sure twice now.' She reached for the phone and punched in the number she had scribbled down on the pad beside it. 'Ramon...?' Lucy slowed her agitated breathing and took a deep breath. 'Dinner tonight...?'

When she told Harriet the full story her old tutor was

sympathetic but, to her annoyance, inclined to make excuses for Santiago Silva. 'He jumped to conclusions and that was wrong.'

'He virtually called me a tart and now today he flings out his threats!' Lucy raged. Even thinking about the man made her want to smash things. Nobody had ever got under her skin this way.

'Why not let me explain the situation to him, Lucy?'

Lucy's lower lip jutted mutinously. 'Why should I explain? He's the one in the wrong.'

'Gabby is the apple of his eye and very wilful. He's also very protective of his younger brother. I understand their father died when Ramon was just a boy, and Santiago was very young when he inherited the *estancia*. Reading between the lines, I get the impression that given half the chance his stepmother fancied herself as the power behind the throne, so to speak, which from what I know of her would have been a disaster,' Harriet confided. 'Santiago had to establish his authority from day one. Not easy for a young man, which might have made him a little—'

'Full of himself?' Lucy suggested acidly. 'The man needs teaching a lesson.' And *not*, in her opinion, people to make excuses for him just because he was rich and lived in some sort of castle.

'Oh, dear! You will be careful, won't you, Lucy? I've heard reports that suggested Santiago can be ruthless. I'd not given much credence to them, since successful men tend to engender jealousy and his reputation here is…well, I've never heard anyone have a bad word to say. Yet given what you've said…?'

Lucy smiled. 'I'll be fine.'

# CHAPTER THREE

DESPITE the fact she had been a successful model, Lucy had never been obsessed by fashion. This was not to say she didn't like clothes. Her lifestyle now meant comfort was the order of the day; heels were not much good when you were mucking out the stables! However, there were occasions when she got tired of her androgynous work clothes and sensible shoes and then she'd open the wardrobe and spend an hour or so parading around her bedroom in some of the clothes she had kept from her previous life.

It wasn't so much that she missed being a clothes horse, because she didn't; it was more she missed being, well...a woman!

And now, feeling the silky swish of a dress that had come from the designer in question's famous 'Marilyn Collection'—a gift, he'd said, because she had made him wish he were straight—Lucy had to admit the bright red dress really did do some amazing things for her figure, making her waist look tiny and her curves look lush.

She brushed her hands down the bodice and glanced in the mirror. The figure-hugging cut made the fabric cling to the long lines of her thighs when she moved. The effect was sexy and provocative, which seemed appropriate when what she wanted to do was provoke! Her anger felt strange when she'd spent the last four years trying to play down her looks and blend in.

An image of Santiago Silva's autocratic dark features formed in her head and the beginnings of doubt faded. Pursing her lips, Lucy gave her reflection a nod. The look was exactly what she wanted. Now, she told herself, was not the time for doubts.

'Wow, you look…' Ramon swallowed '…different.'

She arched a brow and, closing the door, followed him across the yard. 'Different good or different bad?' she teased.

Ramon laughed and opened the door to his low-slung car. 'Oh, definitely good, but it's lucky you didn't look like that the first time I saw you.'

'Why?' Lucy was curious.

'Because I wouldn't have dared approach you. You look way out of my league tonight, Lucy.'

'I'm still me.' Lucy felt uneasy, Ramon's appreciation bordering on reverence.

The sense of anticipation and righteous indignation she had begun the journey with began to fade by the time they reached the massive gates of the Silva *estancia*, replaced by a growing sense of unease and guilt.

What the hell was she doing? This was a crazy idea! She glanced towards Ramon and thought, *Not just crazy—cruel.* In her determination to score points off the awful brother she had not paused to consider the consequences of her actions. Not for one second had she considered the hurt she might be inflicting on the nice brother.

The sense of shame grew until she couldn't bear it another second.

'I can't,' she muttered under her breath as she reached for her seat belt. 'Stop!'

Ramon responded to the shrill screech and hit the brake,

jerking Lucy, who had freed herself from the belt, into the windscreen.

'*Madre mia*, are you all right?'

Lucy rubbed her head and leaned back in the seat. 'Fine,' she said, dismissing his concern with a shake of her head and then regretting it, she had the start of a headache.

'What's wrong?' Ramon cast a questioning look at her tense profile. 'I could have slowed down, all you had to do was ask,' he joked lightly as he wound down the window. 'That was quite a bang you took.'

'It's nothing.'

'So, other than my driving, what's the problem?'

Lucy looked at Ramon and read concern in his handsome face. She bit her lip, feeling more guilty than ever. She took a deep breath. There was no way she could continue with the charade so it was best to come clean now.

'No, I'm not all right—I'm a total bitch!' Not as much of a bitch as Santiago Silva thought she was, but it was a close thing.

Ramon looked annoyingly unconvinced by her emotional claim.

'When I rang you it wasn't…it was a mistake. I'm sorry. I know I let you believe, but the—I'm not interested in you that way…'

Ramon did not display the shock she had anticipated. 'I did wonder… So, you don't fancy me?'

She flashed him a grateful look and shook her head slowly. 'I really am sorry.'

'Are you sure you don't fancy me?'

This drew a laugh from Lucy, who begged, 'Please don't be nice to me! I feel awful enough as it is.'

'Relax, I'll survive. It's not as though I haven't been knocked back before…' He paused and grinned. 'Actually I haven't. I'm wondering why…?'

She shook her head.

As Ramon sat there looking at her in silence for the first time she saw some family resemblance, a likeness to his brother, not so much in the individual features, more the tilt of his head and his hairline...hairline! She frowned. She had only met him the once and the encounter had lasted minutes but weirdly the details of Santiago Silva's face were burned into her brain.

'So why did you ring me and say you'd changed your mind?'

'I was angry and I wanted to punish...'

'Me?'

'No, of course not. The thing is I met your brother and he—he made me mad.'

'Santiago made you mad...?' Ramon echoed in astonishment.

Ramon saw the anger in her sparkling expressive eyes before she tipped her head tightly. 'Yes.' He grew curious. This was not the usual impression his brother made on women.

'When did you meet Santiago? What did he do?'

Lucy rolled down her window and took a gulp of fresh night air redolent of pine. 'I met him yesterday and then again this morning...' For a split second she considered telling him the truth, but held back. What was it about that wretched man that turned her into some sort of petty vengeful cow?

It wasn't as if people had not thought and said worse about her. Why had his assumption got to her this way? Just thinking about him made her skin prickle.

'It...it was something and nothing, really,' she admitted, rubbing her arms as if she could rub away the memory. 'He recognised me yesterday. You don't know, but a few years ago I—'

'Oh, the super-injunction stuff, you mean.'

Lucy stared at him in astonishment. 'You know about that?'

Ramon, who was adjusting his tie in the rear-view mirror, turned his head and looked amused. 'Of course I know about it, Lucy.'

'But how?'

He waved his mobile phone at her. 'I punched in your name, though actually,' he admitted, 'I was checking out your age on the off chance…not that I have a problem with an older woman,' he added quickly. 'In fact, but well, never mind. Imagine my surprise when I got not only your age but the other stuff, too.'

'Oh!' Lucy said, feeling foolish for not anticipating this possibility. It was impossible to have secrets when all someone had to do was punch in a name and your life—or a version of it—appeared on a screen.

'So all this…' the expressive downward sweep of his hand took in the silk that clung like a second skin to her body '…is for Santiago's benefit, not mine.'

His brother sounded more philosophical than annoyed by this discovery, but Lucy was horrified by the suggestion.

'Of course not!' She almost bounced in her seat in her enthusiasm to deny the suggestion. Then as she examined her conscience she added, 'Well, not in that way.'

'So what did big brother do to make you so mad? Threaten to have you arrested for corrupting a minor? Have you framed for a felony? Pay you to leave the country?'

Lucy looked away quickly, but not quickly enough.

Ramon's joking expression vanished. '*Dio*, he did, didn't he? Santiago tried to pay you off?'

'He…sort of,' she admitted, feeling reluctant to tell tales.

'I don't believe it,' Ramon breathed, looking stunned.

'I understand your brother wanted to protect you. It's only

natural.' She stopped and thought, *Why am I defending the man who is clearly a total control freak?*

'Will you do me a favour, Lucy?'

Lucy quashed her instinct to say anything out of sympathy. 'That depends,' she responded warily.

'Go through with your plan to teach my big brother a lesson.'

For the first time Lucy heard anger in his voice and realised that it was aimed, not at her, but his brother.

'I'm sure he thought he was doing the right thing…'

'You're still defending him?'

'No, of course I'm not,' she replied indignantly. 'I think your brother is the most…' She became aware of Ramon's expression and stopped.

'He's really got under your skin, hasn't he?' he observed.

Lucy adopted an amused expression and lied. 'It takes more than your brother to get under my skin.'

'You won't deny that he needs teaching a lesson…?' She nodded—how could she not? 'So why not give him a night to remember? Why not? You're all dressed up and nowhere to go. Please…for me?' he coaxed. 'Or if not, for good old-fashioned revenge? I'm tired of Santiago always thinking he knows what is best for me. For once, I'd like him to treat me like a man. I know he means it for the best and I know my mother gives him a hard time and blames him every time I mess up, but it's humiliating and…'

'You want to teach him a lesson.'

Ramon nodded. 'He's gone too far this time and he's involved a friend. What'll he do the next time—lock me in my room? I'd just like to be the one doing the manipulating for once, so he knows what it feels like.'

Lucy sighed. 'I'm probably going to regret this…'

* * *

'My God, it's a castle.' Lucy sat awestruck in her seat as Ramon stood by the open door. 'Enormous!' she breathed, staring at the intimidating edifice lit by strategically placed spotlights. 'As in national monument enormous...is that tower Moorish?'

Ramon cast a negligent look over his shoulder. 'I think... yeah, it's big,' he agreed.

She started to shake her head. 'I can't do this.'

Ramon grabbed her arm and hauled her out. 'No, you're not going to chicken out now. It was your idea, remember.'

The impetus of his tug made her stagger into his arms. 'A terrible idea!' she muttered in his ear, drawing a laugh from Ramon.

'Are you not going to introduce me to your guest?'

The voice as smooth as silk made the hairs on the back of her neck stand on end. The only thing that prevented her jumping away from Ramon was the hand in the small of her back.

'Of course.'

Ramon loosed her but as she pulled away grabbed her hand.

Lucy took a deep breath, the surface of her skin prickling in a weird response to the sound of his voice. 'Good evening.' She turned her head as Santiago Silva emerged fully from the shadows.

Her already rapid heart picked up tempo as she struggled to hide her reaction, not that he could be unaccustomed to attracting awed stares.

He was, she admitted, pretty awesome and she was staring.

She struggled to direct her gaze past him, but like a compass point returning north her eyes zeroed back to the tall, rampantly male figure dressed in a beautifully cut dark suit teamed with a white shirt he wore open at the neck. The informality went skin deep; he looked exclusively and every inch the autocratic patrician occupier of a castle.

He inclined his dark head, the courtesy of the gesture doing nothing to disguise the predatory gleam in his hooded eyes.

She was no adrenaline junkie but she imagined it might feel this way to jump out of a plane with nothing but a parachute. Actually maybe not even the parachute, she thought, moistening her dry lips with the tip of her tongue.

The nervous action drew his dark gaze to her mouth.

Lucy swallowed and felt a flicker of apprehension. Harriet had warned her that this was not a man to be messed with and she was messing. Was she mad or just...? She swallowed, suddenly identifying the emotion mingled in with the trepidation as *excitement*... Yes, clearly she was mad!

Santiago recognised the surge of molten anger he felt as he watched them, but refused to acknowledge the accompanying emotion as being related in any way to jealousy. He was not jealous of his brother; he was furious! Furious that Ramon could be so stupid; frustrated that he could not think above waist level; that he could not see past the stunning beauty of the woman in his arms.

He, on the other hand, could compartmentalise, think past the painful level of his arousal. She really was the embodiment of sin, he decided, swallowing hard as his burning glance moved over the undulating curves of her body. She was sheathed in a tight red dress that would probably and legitimately in his opinion be illegal in several countries.

'Lucy, this is my big brother, Santiago...Santiago, this is Lucy.'

Ramon pushed her forward with a pat on her bottom that under other circumstances Lucy would have objected to, and she found herself taking a stumbling step towards Santiago. Recovering her poise and covering her growing anxiety behind a plastic smile, she took a second, more graceful step, murmuring a good evening and ignoring the voice in her head that was counselling she run in the opposite direction.

Her half-extended hand fell away as Santiago met her midway. Bending down towards her—not something that happened a lot when you were five ten in your bare feet— he planted his hands on her shoulders.

The light touch concealed a strength that she felt as strongly as the brush of his breath on her cheek. Steeling herself for an air kiss, she stiffened, gasped faintly and closed her eyes as his mouth, his lips, lightly touched her skin.

Feeling the responsive quiver run through her body, he smiled and bent in closer.

'Great work,' he admired. 'Though you might want to rethink the dress—it's a bit obvious—but the husky sexy voice, nice touch, I like it…'

The blue eyes winked wider in protest. 'What? Husky, sexy? I wasn't…'

She stopped, remembering just in time her role of heartless courtesan, and produced a wide, brilliantly insincere smile as she whispered back, 'In my experience—'

'No doubt vast.' His nostrils quivered in response to the fragrance she wore. It smelt of something light, floral and very feminine.

'You have no idea.' A joking comment made by her solicitor drifted back into her head. 'The only way we can legally clear your name is to produce a medical certificate saying you're a virgin.' He had never appreciated the black irony. 'In my experience there is no such thing as too obvious when it comes to men, and if you think that was sexy… watch and learn…'

She let her voice trail away significantly and had the satisfaction of seeing a muscle along his hard jaw clench. She lifted her chin, turning a deaf ear to the voice in her head that was screaming warnings about playing with fire. Instead of lowering the temperature she raised it several degrees, responding to the anger she saw reflected back at her in the dark surface of his eyes with a slow 'cat got the cream' smile.

The guiding hand that then slid to her elbow was not this time light, but she refused to give him the satisfaction of reacting to the biting, bone-crushing grip of his fingers. With Ramon walking on the other side of her, he steered her towards the sweep of stairs that led to the massive porticoed entrance.

Feeling more frogmarched than guided, she lifted the ankle-length hem of her skirt as gracefully as she could and took the first step up.

*It's never too late to run.*

# CHAPTER FOUR

THE door pushed wider and a figure appeared at the top of the stairs. For a moment Lucy thought it was a child, then as she stepped into a shaft of light thrown by one of the spotlights that illuminated the building Lucy realised it was actually a young woman.

She was petite and wand slim, her slender curves almost hidden by the long black fine-knit silk sweater teamed with black leggings she wore. Not a look many could have pulled off, but this girl did!

Ramon, with an exclamation of welcome, pushed past Lucy. 'Carmella!'

As she watched the two embrace Lucy was very aware of dark eyes watching her like the hawk Santiago reminded her of—it wasn't just the nose and the hauteur, but the predatory ruthlessness. She schooled her expression into serene neutrality and considered the situation objectively—or as objectively as was possible when your body was humming with an uncomfortable combination of antagonism and a heart-pounding awareness that made her skin prickle. The wretched man set every nerve ending in her body on edge. She longed to put some distance between herself and the weird electrical charge-negative he exuded. God, even her scalp was tingling!

Presumably the presence of the tiny creature with the

slow dark eyes and slender graceful body had been invited as the competition. She was definitely a dramatic contrast, the more so because the young woman wore flat leather pumps as opposed to Lucy's four-inch spiky heels!

Coming level with the younger woman, Lucy immediately felt big, blowsy and clumsy next to this delicate creature who emerged from Ramon's embrace looking flustered.

'Lucy, this is Carmella—she's like the little sister I never had. What are you doing here, Melly?'

The girl looked towards Santiago, who said smoothly, 'Does there have to be a reason?'

Conscious of the hand on her elbow, Lucy performed the move she had been mentally rehearsing. It went flawlessly. 'Oh, I'm so sorry.' She tossed a look of sparkling insincerity up at the man whose foot she had just ground with four inches of spiky heel. It had to have hurt, but other than a grunt of shocked pain he had sucked it up like a real tough guy.

Santiago acknowledged her apology with a slight tip of his dark head and a white wolfish grin that carried a promise of retribution.

Conscious of a fizz of excitement in place of the more appropriate trepidation, Lucy lowered her gaze.

'I'm so clumsy,' she trilled.

Clumsy! A laugh locked in the back of his throat, Santiago sucked in a sharp breath through flared nostrils. The last thing in the world anyone would use to describe this woman would be *clumsy.* Her every move was imbued with a sinuous, sensual, seductive grace. Yes, she might represent everything he loathed and despised, but even with the overkill of hip swinging she was the epitome of grace.

After a struggle Lucy broke her gaze free of his dark, compelling, almost hypnotic stare and, reckless excitement still humming through her body, turned with a smile to the girl.

'Hello, Carmella.' From the way the little brunette was looking at Ramon it seemed doubtful that she felt very sisterly towards him. Poor girl, she was clearly crazy about Ramon and his brother could not be unaware of the fact, yet it hadn't stopped him using her to provide a distraction. He obviously didn't care whose feelings he trampled so long as he got what he wanted. Lucy's blood boiled when she thought of all the casualties he must have left in his wake.

Ramon was right: it was about time someone gave him a taste of his own medicine.

'Carmella is a ballet dancer,' Ramon said, switching to English as the two broke off their conversation.

'Back row of the corps de ballet,' the girl corrected, looking embarrassed by the accolade.

The conversation had taken them through a hallway of epic cavernous proportions. This place was not what anyone would term cosy, but it was impressive. Had the circumstances been different she would have been bombarding her host with questions about the history of this fantastic building.

'How interesting,' she said, meaning it. She had had ballet classes herself until it became obvious that she was not built on the right scale.

Santiago, who had been speaking in a softly spoken aside to a dark-suited individual who had silently materialised, murmured, 'Thank you, Josef,' before turning back to them. 'It appears our meal is ready. So, what do you do, Lucy?'

Caught off guard by the addition, Lucy blinked. It took her a second to recover her poise and resist the compulsion to say, 'Live off impressionable boys.' Lucy didn't know how she managed to suppress the words hovering on the tip of her tongue.

'I manage to keep busy.'

'And you're staying at the resort hotel? I just love the spa there,' Carmella enthused.

'Isn't that where you usually get your dinner dates, Ramon?' Lucy teased, forgetting for one moment her role. 'Actually, I'm staying with a friend.' She broke off and swallowed a gasp. The room they had entered had the dimensions of a baronial hall complete with tapestries that were probably priceless on the stone walls; all that was missing was someone playing a lute in the minstrels' gallery. The candles on the table, heavy with silver and gleaming crystal, had been lit. A person would need a megaphone to speak to a person sitting at the far end of the table.

'How…cosy,' she murmured sarcastically.

'Friend?' Santiago angled his question towards his brother, not Lucy, pulling out a chair for Lucy at the table and ensuring that several feet of antique oak separated her from Ramon. Not that he would have been surprised if the woman had slithered across the surface to latch onto her prey.

An image flashed into his head of her lying across the table in a silvery pool of her own hair, the slinky red dress pulled up to reveal her long legs, one arm lifted in supplication. He froze the frame before it progressed and deleted it, but not before his temperature had risen by several degrees.

Three pairs of eyes swivelled his way as he cleared his throat; he turned his head sharply to block out the blue. 'What friend?'

'Harriet Harris,' Ramon supplied.

His brother's expression was openly sceptical as he turned to Lucy, looking at her accusingly from dark brows that had formed an interrogative straight line.

'The Cambridge don…?'

She would have been amused by the proof of his snobbish prejudice had her normally lively sense of humour survived the trauma of the evening.

'Yes, that's right,' she said, thinking, *Sorry for stepping out of the box you've put me into.* Her scorn increased. Presumably in his world she and women like Harriet occupied separate universes.

'How do you come to know Harriet Harris?'

'She was my personal tutor when I was at Cambridge.'

She had the satisfaction of seeing shock he could not conceal chase across his lean features. 'You were a Cambridge student?'

She nodded, still smiling, counted to ten, but she was unable to hide the growing antagonism that revealed itself in the sparkle in her electric-blue eyes.

'You graduated?'

He sounded as though discovering that Martians had landed was a lot more probable. At that moment Lucy, who habitually played down her intellect—bad enough being head and shoulders above your contemporaries at school without being a swot—would have happily shoved her certificates down his throat if she had them to hand.

Ramon saved her from replying to this continued interrogation. 'She came to the rescue to help Harriet.'

'To the rescue once again,' he drawled, drawing a puzzled look from his brother. 'From what does Harriet need rescuing?' The local community had initially been wary of the Englishwoman who had moved here two years ago. She was still considered eccentric for her alarming multicoloured hair and her devotion to the donkeys she provided a sanctuary for, but she had endeared herself by learning the language and integrating with the local community.

'She's broken her leg.'

*'Dios!'* he exclaimed, displaying what, had it been anyone else, Lucy would have considered concern. In his case she attributed his reaction to a pathological need to be in

charge. The man was a total control freak. 'Why did I not know of this?'

Yes, a control freak of epic proportions!

'And why did Anton not inform me?'

Lucy didn't have a clue who Anton was but he had her sympathy. God, working for Santiago Silva would be like working for some feudal warlord... Of course, a very good-looking feudal warlord, she conceded, her eyes drifting over the length of his long greyhound-sleek, lean, hard body and one with very good hygiene—the scent of the cologne he used mingled with warm male showed a tendency to linger in her nostrils. She gave her head a tiny shake and looked away.

'Is she in hospital?'

His manager dealt with the everyday burden of the estate but Santiago was not an anonymous landlord. He made it his business to know all his tenants and took an active interest in the village, just as his father had done. He took the responsibility that came with his role here seriously and he got a lot from it.

When you worked in finance it was easy to lose sight of the human face behind the columns of clinical figures, but here he saw firsthand how decisions made in a boardroom could affect people's lives. This was not to say he didn't get a buzz from what he did, but the estate and the people who lived and worked on it kept him grounded.

*Duty* might be an unfashionable word but it was deeply ingrained in Santiago. Even so, the early days had not been easy. When still grieving for his father he had found himself expected to step into his shoes—and they were big shoes to fill. He'd been living with Magdalena in the city when his father died. She had been really supportive and it had seemed natural to ask her to move with him to the *castillo*. He had not anticipated she would take the request for a marriage proposal but after the initial shock he had thought why not?

It would happen eventually. Now he recognised that it might very well not have happened, that had things been different they would have eventually drifted apart.

'Only for a day. She's at home now. And don't blame Anton—when he left for his cousin's wedding I think maybe I told him I'd tell you when you got back,' Ramon admitted with a rueful grin.

One sable brow lifted. 'Maybe?'

'All right, I said I would, but no harm done,' he added cheerfully. 'Lucy is helping Harriet until she gets back on her feet.'

Santiago's glance slid from his brother to the woman sitting to his left. Was Ramon joking? Did his brother seriously think this woman would do anything that risked chipping her nail varnish? His glance slid automatically to the hand that held the goblet, though she appeared not to have touched the wine it held.

His sneer faded as he registered the fingers curved lightly around the stem. They were long and shapely but the pearly nails were neither long nor painted; they were trimmed short and unvarnished. With a tiny shake of his head he dismissed the incongruity. Short nails did not make her any the less useless when it came to manual labour, and donkeys might be appealing to look at, but they were high-maintenance animals, not to mention deserving of their stubborn reputation.

'She couldn't be in better hands,' Ramon continued.

The words brought an image of his half-brother enjoying the ministrations of those hands, except it wasn't his brother he was seeing... Santiago stiffened. 'I doubt very much if Miss Fitzgerald—'

'Oh, that's so formal. Please call me Lucy.' Maintaining the saccharine sweet smile was making her facial muscles ache.

Santiago, who could think of several things he'd like to call her, smiled back.

As their eyes connected black on bright cornflower-blue, clashed and remained sealed Lucy was seized by a determination not to be, on principle, the first one to look away. The effort of following through with her childish self-imposed endurance race brought a faint sheen of moisture to her skin. In the distance she was vaguely aware of Ramon and Carmella's voices as they laughed and chatted, the sound softer than the sound of the blood that pounded in her ears.

On the other side of the table Ramon knocked over a glass. The sound as the crystal hit the floor was like a pistol shot. It was hard to say which one of them looked away first but all that mattered to Lucy was that the accident had splintered the growing tension. A silent sigh left her parted lips as Lucy squeezed her eyes closed, just glad that she had broken that nerve-shredding contact.

'Speak English...' She heard Santiago reproach the young couple who were exchanging laughing comments in Spanish. 'Lucy will be feeling excluded.'

As if that wasn't the idea, Lucy thought, opening her eyes and switching to her less than perfect Spanish as she said, 'No problem. I need the practice.'

She saw a spasm of annoyance move across his face as he turned his accusing stare her way. 'You speak Spanish?'

Assuming his irritation stemmed from the fact blonde trollops in his world were not allowed to speak any language but avarice, she chose to reply in English.

'A little.'

'More than a little. She also speaks French, Italian, German, and...Gaelic...?' inserted Ramon from across the table.

Lucy nodded, impressed that he had remembered.

'Not just a pretty face and perfect body...' he added, with his eyes trained on her bosom. 'She has brains, too... Do I know how to pick them or do I know how to pick them?'

He smiled sunnily at his brother, inviting his admiration before rising from his chair to give access to the maid who had come to remove the broken glass.

'Quite the linguist.'

'My family is quite…cosmopolitan.' A massive understatement—the Fitzgerald clan was spread across the globe. 'Actually Ramon is being kind. My Spanish really is pretty basic,' she admitted in a burst of honesty, forgetting for a moment that her character did not do self-deprecating or honest.

She almost immediately retrieved the situation and invited his anger by dropping her voice a sexy octave. 'I'm hoping to improve my vocabulary considerably during my stay.' She produced a close approximation of the look she had used to sell everything from shampoo to insurance as she looked at Ramon from under the sweep of her fluttering lashes, feeling just as silly now as she had back then when the photographers had asked her to smoulder.

'And Ramon is such a good teacher.'

It wasn't just the open provocation, it was the fact that he was not immune to the effects of her husky purr that fanned his smouldering anger into full-blown flames.

Her glance swivelled sideways in response to the sound of a cut-glass goblet coming down with a crash on the table. Catching the edge of Santiago's thunderous glare, she thought, *You haven't lost it, Lucy.*

'So are you, *querida.*' Across the table Ramon picked up the cue, fixed his eyes on her bosom and added throatily, 'I'm learning a lot from you.'

For a moment Lucy was in danger of slipping out of character. She bit her quivering lower lip and brought her eyelids down to hide the laughter sparkling in her eyes. Ramon was getting into his role a little too enthusiastically. If he didn't watch himself his brother was going to smell a rat. She somehow doubted he'd see the funny side.

Was there a funny side?

She reached for her glass and drained the contents. If anyone noticed her burning cheeks she could blame the alcohol, for heartless seductresses did not blush.

'It's always a pleasure to teach a willing pupil.'

Worried that this might be over the top, too, she slid a surreptitious glance towards the man sitting beside her. He was totally still…still as in 'a volcano about to explode' still. She needn't have worried, he seemed only too happy to believe she was a total trollop.

'So do you have a big family, Lucy?'

Lucy smiled. Carmella seemed blissfully ignorant of the undercurrents swirling around the table. 'Vast. I have nine siblings—my father had three wives.' Her own mother was his last.

'Presumably not all at once.'

Lucy clenched her teeth and bridled at the amused contempt in Santiago's voice. The man was the most smug, self-satisfied creep she had ever met. Plan or no plan, while she was willing to stomach his insults and digs when she was the target she would not tolerate him insulting her family, who had rallied around protectively when she'd needed them.

It was true that when he was alive Lucy had had her share of disagreements with her father, culminating in the massive argument that had ended with her leaving home rather than follow the course in life he had chosen for her.

Determined to show she could make it alone, Lucy had started modelling, her intention being to make enough to fund her degree. She hadn't anticipated for one moment that she would have the sort of incredible success she had enjoyed…though actually the world of modelling had never been one she enjoyed, however much she'd loved the freedom making that sort of money gave her.

It still did. Her father had been right about one thing—she

had inherited his financial acumen, though not the buzz he spoke of that came when you had nailed a deal. The investments she had made at the time had weathered the global downturn and enabled her to live comfortably off the income.

The thing that mattered was that when she had needed him her dad had been there, as had all her family, and she wasn't about to sit by and let this man look down his nose at them.

'And do you share your father's attitude to marriage?'

'According to my mother I'm very like him.' She shrugged and, dropping her role of seductress, added with quiet dignity, 'I can't see it myself, but I really hope I share both my parents' values.'

Did he look taken aback by her reply? It would seem she had imagined it because when he replied it was with that now familiar nasty smile that made her fingers itch with an uncharacteristic desire to slap his smug face.

'I'm sure they are both proud of you.'

Clearly there was more to Lucy Fitzgerald than met the eye. He'd been so confident removing her from Ramon's life would be easy that he hadn't even bothered spending five minutes researching the details of the scandal—a fundamental error. His mistake was that he'd been treating this problem differently from those he encountered in his business dealings—he'd made the error of letting it become personal.

If she had weaknesses beyond greed, he would discover them, though of course it was inevitable that greed would be her downfall.

He suddenly saw the headline under a photo of her shielding her eyes from flashes as a man helped her into a blacked-out limo, and experienced a eureka moment.

'Your father is Patrick Fitzgerald!'

The accusation drew a grunt of amazement from Ramon, who forgot his besotted act as he stared at his brother. 'You didn't know?' He suddenly grinned and taunted, 'I thought you knew everything.'

'Who is Patrick Fitzgerald?' Carmella asked.

Ramon laughed. 'Melly doesn't read books, do you, angel? Just celebrity magazines.'

The girl kicked him under the table and he laughed, snatching away her plate that held a bread roll, teasing, 'Careful, you might put on an ounce looking at it. Seriously, Lucy's dad had a finger in many pies—he was a bit of a legend actually—but he was about the most powerful publisher on the planet... He was—' He glanced towards Lucy.

'My dad died last year,' she explained to Carmella. 'He'd been retired for a while.'

Santiago continued to feel annoyed with himself for not making the connection sooner. He had not met the man, but Ramon was right—in financial circles he had been pretty much a legend, a man who had started the publishing house that had become the biggest and most successful in the world and still remained in the hands of the same family today.

He felt an unexpected stab of sympathy for Fitzgerald, who had been known to guard his privacy jealously. It must have been hell for him to see his daughter publicly humiliated and her sordid secrets shared with the world, and of course it was always the parents' fault—a universally accepted premise that every parent was conscious of.

Santiago had lost count of the sleepless nights he had spent second-guessing his parenting decisions and Gabriella was not even in her teens yet. As a man who could afford to indulge his own child, Santiago knew only too well the pitfalls that were out there for a father who did not want his love of his child to ruin her.

If the results were anything to go by, Patrick Fitzgerald had fallen into every pitfall there was. If the man had still been around he might have rung him to ask him how he brought up his daughter so that he could do the exact opposite.

God knew what motivated a woman like Lucy Fitzgerald, but apparently it wasn't money after all. His eyes drifted in her direction just as the maid who had been making a discreet exit with her dustpan paused by Lucy's chair.

'Oh, I am so sorry, miss…your lovely dress. I'll…'

Lucy glanced without interest at the splash of blood stains on her dress and rose to her feet. 'Forget the dress—your hand!' She removed the dustpan from the girl's hand, put it down on her seat and took the injured hand in her own. 'Your poor hand.'

She grabbed a clean napkin from the table and pressed it to the small laceration still oozing a little blood on the girl's palm.

'No, miss, I'm fine, just clumsy.'

'You're not fine…'

Santiago found himself the focus of an accusing icy blue stare that could not have been more condemning had he taken a knife and cut the girl himself.

'It must have hurt like mad and she didn't say a word.' The girl's silence was obviously a symptom of an atmosphere of oppression in the workplace, she decided.

She turned back to the girl, the frost in her eyes warming to concern. 'Look…sorry, I don't know your name?'

'Sabina.'

'Well, Sabina, I think your hand needs cleaning—there might be some shreds of glass in it—and it needs dressing.'

The girl looked confused and Lucy turned to her fellow diners with an expression of exasperation. 'Will someone help me out here?' Her Spanish did not stretch to a translation.

It was Santiago who reacted first. Pushing aside his chair, he moved across to the timid-looking maid and spoke to her in Spanish. Lucy listened, unable to follow the rapid flow of words, noticing how different his voice sounded when he spoke to the girl, how kind and gentle.

Whatever he said made the girl smile and look less terrified. Across the table Ramon added something that drew a weak laugh from her.

Lucy was still holding the napkin to the wound but the girl was staring with starry-eyed devotion up at Santiago. Lucy bit her lip and looked away. Was there a female on the planet who didn't think he walked on water? She thought, *Am I the only person who sees him for what he is?*

'You can let go now, Miss Fitzgerald.'

Lucy started as the sound of Santiago's deep voice jolted her out of her brooding reverie.

'Josef will take over from here.'

'What? Oh, yes, of course.' She nodded to the sober suited solemn-faced man standing at her side and removed her hand from the makeshift dressing. 'You need to apply pressure.'

'Josef is more than capable, Miss Fitzgerald.' Santiago's dismissive glance swept across her face before he turned back to the girl, his manner changing as he spoke to her softly before she was led from the room by the older man.

'Perhaps you would like to clean up, Miss Fitzgerald?'

She glanced down to hide her hot cheeks, mortified as her body reacted with dramatic tingling awareness to the critical clinical stare directed at the smears of blood on the upper slopes of her breasts.

She could see his point, a little blood could go a long way and the smears did look awful.

'And obviously you will send me a bill for the cleaning.'

Actually he was just realising that nothing about this woman was obvious.

She had had an expensive dress ruined and, obviously, spoilt, self-absorbed materialist that she was, there should have been tantrums. But no, what did she do? Go all Mother Teresa on him! And he'd seen her face—her concern was either genuine or she was the best actress he had ever seen.

So maybe she was not all bad, but her redemption was not his business. Saving his brother was.

For Lucy the faint sneer in his voice was the last straw. She could almost hear the sound of her control snapping as she turned on him, eyes blazing, bosom heaving.

'I can pay my own bills. Do you think I give a damn about the dress? I...' She stopped, horrified to feel the prick of tears behind her eyelids. 'I'll go wash up!' she blurted, making a dash for the door.

# CHAPTER FIVE

Outside the room Lucy had composed herself enough to ask for directions to the bathroom when she was approached by a staff member in the bewildering baronial hallway.

In the decadently appointed bathroom she had been directed to, Lucy stood with her hands under the running water, waiting for the desire to cry her eyes out to subside.

Finally feeling marginally more composed, she looked at her reflection in the mirror above the marble washbasin. The lighting above it emphasised the waxy pallor of her oval face; she didn't even have her bag with her to make running repairs to her make-up.

With a deep troubled sigh she set about sponging the smears of blood from her skin and clothes.

Reluctant to leave the marble lined sanctuary, Lucy stood with her back against the cool wall. She shook her head, still totally bewildered. She had no idea what had been going on in there, didn't have a clue why she had blown up that way.

Her efforts to analyse what had happened and why were hindered by the fact that every time she felt an answer to the puzzle was in reach, the image of his dark face and sleek body rose in her head, effectively blanking everything else.

*What is your problem Lucy?* He was *meant* to think she cared more about dresses than people, that had been the idea, so why had she reacted that way?

She had no idea how long she had been standing there before there was a tentative tap on the door. It was followed by a voice calling her name.

'I just wondered—are you all right, Lucy?'

Lucy straightened her shoulders, took a deep sustaining breath and opened the door. An anxious-looking Ramon, who was standing directly behind it, took a step back.

'I'm fine,' she said, forcing a smile as she emerged. 'Sorry about that but I've never liked the sight of even a speck of blood.' She stopped and shook her head and looked at him with eyes dark with emotion. 'I'm fine with blood, Ramon, but not your brother. I can't do this...over the years I've developed a thick skin but somehow he manages... I'm tired of being judged,' she finished with a weary sigh.

Ramon shook his head and looked remorseful as he enfolded her in a comforting bear hug. 'God, no, it's me. I shouldn't have asked you to do this. It's my problem, not yours, and to be honest I wasn't expecting Santiago to be quite so...' His hands slid down her arms and stayed there.

Standing in the loose circle of his arms, Lucy gave a shrug. 'And you thought I could take it? I thought so, too,' she admitted. 'I really don't care what your brother thinks of me,' she hastened to assure Ramon. 'But this stopped being my idea of a fun evening when he started making snide remarks about my family.'

'I understand,' Ramon said.

Lucy was wondering a little uneasily about the inflection in his voice when he reached out and touched her forehead. 'God, you're going to have a bruise there,' he said, touching the discoloured area that was developing on her forehead. 'You really took a bang.'

Santiago stood in the minstrels' gallery, his unblinking stare trained on the couple below, tension vibrating in every taut fibre of his lean body as he listened to the buzz of their soft voices, unable to make out the words, but you didn't need words to see the intimacy in the way they stood close together.

When his brother touched her face tenderly he turned, biting back a harsh gasp as he felt something kick hard and low in his belly.

'I'll try and stay in character,' Lucy promised Ramon. 'But after tonight that's it.'

She returned to the dining room with some trepidation, but the rest of meal passed relatively uneventfully. Their host showed little inclination to make conversation other than a few passing asides to Carmella, which should have been a good thing but turned out not to be.

Lucy was painfully conscious of his eyes following her and spent the entire meal waiting for him to pounce, so tense that every bone in her body ached with it.

And of course she did what she always did when she was nervous: she babbled like an idiot until the sound of her own bright chattering voice was giving even her a headache. Afterwards she didn't have a clue what she had been talking about, which was probably a good thing.

Santiago excused himself before coffee was served and Lucy used his absence to make her own hurried exit. Outside, it was a beautiful night. She released a long sigh and breathed in the fresh night air almost dizzy with relief that the ordeal was over.

Just behind her she was conscious of Ramon pausing to speak to the man who had emerged from the house but the effort of translating what they were saying was beyond her.

She was struggling to think anything beyond the fact that she was escaping from this place and that hateful man; she wanted to forget the entire evening had ever happened.

And she would—tomorrow she would go back to doing what she had actually come here to do. God knew why she had ever got involved. It wasn't as if she hadn't been insulted before, but she had never lowered herself to her persecutor's level; she had always maintained her silence and the moral high ground.

Anyway this was not her battle, it was Ramon's. If he had issues with his brother he could sort them out himself.

'Wait in the car.'

Lucy automatically extended a hand to catch the keys he threw her. 'What?'

'Phone call. It's urgent and no one can find Santiago. I'll be back in a minute,' Ramon promised, following the sober-suited man back indoors.

*No one knows where he is.* She glanced back at the building; golden light spilled from the windows making her think of eyes watching her.

'Seriously paranoid, Lucy.' Her laugh had a hollow sound as she turned her back on the building, unable to shake the feeling that the man they couldn't find was in one of those windows watching her.

She shivered and told herself it was the chill in the evening air. Despite this she did not follow Ramon's suggestion and take shelter in the car. Instead Lucy wandered away from the brooding presence of the sombre fortified house.

She had walked some way across the manicured lawn when she found herself drawn towards the sound of water and discovered, not the pond she had expected, but a river.

She walked out onto the wooden bridge and, leaning her arms on the rail, gazed down into the dark water. Her expression was pensive as her thoughts drifted, the memories of the evening revolving in her head. If not the worst night of her life, it had been right up there.

On the plus side—her brow puckered as she struggled

to come up with one, other than the fact the night was over and if she ever saw Santiago Silva again she would leg it in the opposite direction. She was hanging up her scarlet-woman hat.

Trailing a hand towards the water, she leaned farther over the rail, following a leaf caught on the current, running to the opposite side as it disappeared from view to follow its progress.

Santiago, who had followed her from outside the house, watched as she leaned forward. The lust that lay coiled in his belly morphed into alarm as she leaned so far over the rail that she appeared in danger of toppling in. This woman seemed oddly drawn to water and bridges.

'If you're planning on jumping in don't expect me to leap in and save you.'

Lucy started as if shot, took a hasty step backwards and found herself staring at Santiago. He was looking mean, moody and, if she was honest, totally magnificent in the moonlight.

She took a deep breath and lifted her chin as he stepped onto the bridge.

'Relax, I don't need saving. I'm not on the lookout for a white knight.' Which was just as well as he definitely did not meet the criteria...all that dark brooding stuff made him far more likely to be the bad boy.

'That wasn't an offer.'

'And it so happens I swim like a fish.' She felt no guilt for playing up her ability.

'Just as well, given your affinity for water. I keep finding you knee deep.'

She extended a leg, displaying a dry and slightly muddied shoe. 'I wasn't paddling, but I'm a Pisces so maybe that's it, and I wasn't going to jump.'

'No...?'

'You sound disappointed.'

His grin flashed and faded as his dark glance slid down her body. Lucy was disgusted with herself for being unable to control the flash of heat that engulfed her body. Dear God, all the man had to do was look at her and she started acting like some sort of hormonal teenager.

'If I throw you into the water will you sprout a tail and swim away?' It was true, she did look like a particularly sultry mermaid in that dress with the cloud of silvery hair, a siren capable of luring men to their deaths.

And her intended victim was Ramon. His brother's life might not be in danger but his heart was, and he would save Ramon from this woman's clutches by whatever means possible.

And if money was not a lure he would have to think of something that was…and if it required that he used himself as bait it was a sacrifice he was willing to make.

*You're a saint, Santiago*, admired the sardonic voice in his head.

Lucy inhaled and straightened her shoulders. Her fingers tightened on the wooden rail, her defiant pose perilously fragile as he walked towards her. It was utterly mystifying how a man as big as him could move so silently, like some big jungle cat stalking his prey.

The analogy sent a shiver sliding down her spine as she watched him approach, the golden-toned skin of his throat and face very dark in contrast to the dazzling white of his shirt.

You didn't have to like the man to be utterly riveted by the way he moved and nobody could fail to be aware—in an objective way—of the aura of raw, earthy sensuality he exuded.

Lucy bit her lip and felt her shaky composure develop a few more cracks as he paused, his hand on the rail, a few feet away from her. She looked at his fingers only inches away from her own and tightened her grip, easing her hand back surreptitiously. She had a nasty feeling that if he touched her even lightly those cracks she was aware of would split wide apart.

'Do I make you nervous, Lucy?' he asked, staring at the blue veined pulse point that was throbbing at the base of her throat.

'You'd like that, wouldn't you?'

When he responded to the breathless accusation with a slow smile that said he knew exactly how his presence made her feel, her heart hammered against her ribs. She found herself hating him more than ever. It was weird but she had never felt this sort of violent animosity towards anyone, not even Denis Mulville, who had made her a hate figure out of sheer spite.

'Do you always lurk like that?' She pressed a hand to her breastbone, hating the fact she still sounded breathless because, yes, he made her nervous...not excited, because that would be stupid.

'I'm not lurking. It is my habit to take a walk before I go to bed.'

'Then don't let me stop you.'

'From walking or going to bed?'

'You followed me, didn't you...?' Lucy felt pretty stupid for not seeing the obvious and smelling a set up. 'You planned...' she moved her hands in an expressive fluttering motion and fixed him with a blue accusing glare '...this.'

'Such piercing insight,' he drawled, drawing a hissing sound of rage from between her clenched teeth. 'I did warn you what would happen if you came near my family.'

'So how is Gabby?'

'Back in school.' Gabby had assumed the day-early return was part of her punishment and Santiago had seen no reason to disabuse her of this notion. At least she was safely out of reach, though he doubted that his daughter would have found the scent of this woman's perfume quite so disturbing.

*Sure, Santiago, you're so 'disturbed' that you can't think above the waist. Admit it like a man—you want her so bad you can taste it.*

'Lucy's changed her mind—she's coming!' had been the words that had greeted him on his return that morning, making it pretty conclusive that his threats had backfired big time and Lucy Fitzgerald had lost no time calling his bluff—only he didn't bluff, as she would find out.

'I thought we could have a private little talk...' Not this little talk—Santiago was annoyed with himself for losing focus.

'We don't have anything to talk about and, for the record, I don't like being played. How did you know—' She stopped, feeling stupid. 'There wasn't an important call, was there?'

'Of course there was a call...and I imagine it will take a good thirty minutes.'

'Imagine or know!'

He met her angry glare with a lazy, insolent smile. 'What's the problem, Lucy—you can dish it out but can't take it?'

Her chin went up at the challenge. 'Dish it out?' she echoed, her blue gaze falling from his. 'I don't know what you mean,' she denied, thinking, *He knows...* The realisation that he had seen through their act was, she realised, almost a relief. She expelled a long sigh—no more pouting! With all the sexy stuff she hadn't felt like herself all evening— 'herself' being cool, blonde and in control.

This evening she'd been blonde and continually on the edge of losing any semblance of control. This man pressed all her buttons and made her feel the victim's rage she had thought she had conquered long ago.

She felt a twang of guilt, which turned into pity for Ramon—she could not imagine his brother seeing this as a bit of harmless fun.

'I am presuming that the overacting this evening was for my benefit?' An image of her stroking his brother's arm, a relatively innocent action if it had been anyone but this woman, drifted into his head and he snarled, 'Ever heard of subtlety?'

Lucy's head lifted and she read the contempt and anger etched in the sculpted lines of his hard-boned face.

'I presume this was to drive up the price.'

Her eyes widened—so he didn't know.

He saw her reaction and gave a thin smile. 'Another language you speak fluently...money.'

It occurred to Lucy as she sucked in a breath that she had played her part a bit too well—he was looking at her with a level of loathing that she struggled to be objective about.

'And did it work?' she wondered, hiding the stab of irrational hurt that threatened to make her well up behind her amused smile. The opinion of a self-righteous jerk, she reminded herself, was no reason to feel bad. In fact the time to worry was when a man like him started approving of you.

'No, there is no extra money on the table—there is no money.'

She pursed her lips into a pout and took what she hoped came across as a fearless step towards him. Thrusting one hip out, she planted her hands on her thighs and fixed him with a smile that deepened as she heard the distinct sound of his teeth grinding.

'Pity...still, sometimes the satisfaction of a job well done is reward in itself.'

'I have no idea if some bad experience turned you poisonous or if you were just born that way because, to be frank, the nature-nurture argument does not interest me.'

Inside seething, Lucy adopted an air of amused interest, watching the muscles along his strong jawline ripple.

'And I can take anything you can throw at me.' Brave

words, or should that be reckless? Lucy just hoped they would not come back to bite her.

'We'll see, shall we...?'

Sheer stubbornness made her retain eye contact. It saved running the risk of not being able to look away. His black stare had a disturbingly hypnotic quality.

Her pounding heart drowned out the lonely cry of a hunting owl overhead. The atmosphere was suddenly thicker than the thick emerald-green moss that grew along the riverbank, the moss her heels had sunk into as she'd walked to the bridge... Lucy felt as though she were sinking now. She swallowed past the constriction in her throat and, doing her best to look amused, met his black stare. He probably got some sadistic kick from seeing people squirm. No, she thought, there was no 'probably' about it.

She was aware that anything she said now might be construed as a challenge...and he was obviously a man who could not resist any opportunity to prove himself superior. He was pathetic, she told herself, though actually *pathetic* was about the most inappropriate term imaginable to describe the man standing there. He oozed a raw masculinity. There was something raw and elemental about him that made her traitorous heart skip a beat and her mouth dry and her knees weak.

A lot of other things were going on that she didn't even want to think about right now. *Deep breaths, Lucy...deep breaths.*

He held her eyes with a steady stare and watched the colour in her face fluctuate. Her skin fascinated him, so creamy he wanted to feel it to see if it felt as soft and satiny as it looked. He wanted to feel her naked underneath him. He had wanted it from the moment he had set eyes on her and, damn her, she had known it.

His chest swelled. He had never wanted a woman this

much in his life, so badly that he could taste it. He wanted to taste her so badly that... He embraced his anger just to stay in control.

Lucy sucked in a deep, wrathful breath and blurted, 'You are one manipulative—'

He moved so fast that it seemed that one moment he was standing several feet away, the next he was beside her with his finger poised a whisper away from her parted lips. She felt the pressure building inside and felt totally helpless to do anything about it.

'Think very carefully before you continue, Lucy. I am not my brother and I am not in the habit of turning the other cheek.'

'You mean you haven't mastered meek—imagine my amazement,' she drawled, slapping his hand away and taking a shaky step back.

Her heart was beating so hard it felt it might explode from her chest; the simple act of drawing air into her lungs required conscious effort... The musky scent of his warm skin lingered tantalisingly in her quivering nostrils.

He laughed. The sound was not unattractive; actually nothing was unattractive about him but his personality.

'Whereas you have.'

She gritted her teeth in response to the silky sarcasm of his retort and wrapped her arms around herself.

His brow furrowed as he watched her shiver. 'You're cold.'

He faked solicitude well, but Lucy recognised this new tactic for what it was—an attempt to soften her up. She knew that she was not the sort of woman who brought out the protective instincts in the opposite sex. She was not small or delicate and she did not consider this a bad thing. She had never envied the fragile little creatures that made men feel macho and strong.

'Look on the bright side—I might get pneumonia and die. Problem solved.'

A spasm of impatience tightened the hard contours of his jaw. 'Do not be stupid.' But she wasn't, anything but; the evening had proved that he had underestimated Miss Lucy Fitzgerald.

For 'stupid' Lucy translated 'anyone who didn't act as though his every word was engraved in stone'. She watched as he began to shrug off his jacket. The shirt he wore underneath was white with a subtle silver stripe and in the moonlight it was possible to see the lean shape of his body beneath it as he held out the jacket towards her.

She lowered her gaze but not before her insides had dissolved.

'You've got to be joking.'

His face was in darkness now, but bands of moonlight fell across his body. 'You find old-fashioned courtesy amusing.' His hand smoothed the contrasting silk lining of the jacket he had shrugged off.

'In the light of the fact you've spent the entire evening being as rude as hell to me…yes, actually, I do!'

Lucy planted her hands on her hips, her breasts under the red silk heaving as she glared up at him. 'You know something—I feel sorry for you!'

'Is that a fact?' he drawled, sounding bored. 'I suppose it's too much to hope you are not going to tell me why I am an object of pity in your eyes?'

'Because people like you—'

'People like me?'

'Sorry, I forgot, there are no people like you—you're special,' she drawled, sketching speech marks in the air. Her mocking smile faded as she added in a voice that shook with contempt, 'But actually you're not. Living in a castle and having pots of money makes you lucky—not special.'

'And you were born on the wrong side of the tracks forced to live off your wits? I don't think so,' he drawled.

Lucy blinked, but recovered quickly. 'I don't live in a castle.'

'And the Fitzgeralds are paupers, I suppose?'

Her blue gaze grew frosty. 'Leave my family out of this,' she warned fiercely.

This display of protectiveness struck him as ironic. 'Like you did? Did it ever occur to you to consider how your actions would affect them? How do you think they feel when they see you use your body and beauty as a weapon?'

Lucy laughed, finding the accusation particularly ironic when she was standing here struggling to control her breathing. *If only!*

'What can I say? I'm a shallow and superficial person.'

'You're…' He lunged without warning and grabbed her by the waist, the other hand went to the nape of her neck, his fingers pushing into her hair as he pulled her into him.

Panic made her struggle but then his mouth was on hers and her resistance melted, *she* melted; the arm banded around her narrow waist took her weight as she went limp.

He sank his teeth into the plump fullness of her lower lip, sighing as she moaned. The heat of his body penetrated the silk of her dress…nothing she was feeling was like anything she had experienced before.

'I really want to taste you.'

His smoky voice shivered through her body, awakening an answering need deep inside her. Using what strength she had to force her heavy lips open, she looked up at him with passion-glazed blue eyes.

'Yes,' she breathed huskily. 'Please.'

He kissed her deeply, his warm lips seductive, his probing tongue shockingly intimate, but it was the contrast of soul-piercing tenderness and ravenous hunger of the carnal assault on her senses that drew a series of soft moans from Lucy's throat.

Overwhelmed by the need his touch awoke, she wound her arms vine-like around his neck and kissed him back hard, meeting his tongue with her own.

The shocking rock-hard imprint of his erection as it ground into her belly excited her incredibly, making her gasp and moan, giving herself over totally to the wild hunger in her blood as the passion generated between them burned hotter. His mouth demanded more and she struggled to give it.

His hands moved down her body, moulding her against him, as Lucy's hands slid over his shoulders feeling the hard ridges of muscle through his clothes feeling the racing of her pulse, feeling his heartbeat, the two sounds becoming one.

The desperation of their soft moans and murmurs grew more frantic and uncontrolled until finally Santiago pulled back.

It took a few seconds for sanity to return. When it did the shocking realisation of what she had just done hit Lucy. She stood staring at him as she shook her head in denial, unable to accept the need he had awoken inside, the confusing tangle of emotions that the kiss had shaken loose.

He said nothing. The shadows across his face accented the strong planes and fascinating hollows. Just looking at him made her ache to touch him. 'You think that proves anything?' she challenged.

'It proved that we'd be pretty sensational in bed.'

She gave a scared little gasp and just ran.

When Ramon returned she was waiting in the car. He was terribly apologetic about the wait and didn't seem to notice anything unusual about her silence.

# CHAPTER SIX

'RELAX,' Ramon recommended as Lucy looked nervously over her shoulder. 'You won't see him.'

That assurance was the only reason she was here—that and Ramon's promise of a ride on a pure-bred Arab, which she had been unable to resist.

Though she'd managed to do so until Ramon, correctly interpreting her reluctance, had promised his brother would not be there. 'So there's no need to be nervous.'

Her pride stung, she had retorted hotly, 'Your brother does not make me nervous. I simply find him...' At a loss to explain even to herself the way the man made her feel, she finished lamely, 'He won't be there.'

'No chance,' Ramon had promised, coaxing, 'Come on, the least I can do is give you the ride I promised. You've fulfilled your side of the bargain and, yes, don't worry,' he soothed, predicting her interruption, 'I know you don't want to carry on with our plan... You are sure about that?'

'Quite sure.'

'Pity, I was having fun. Oh, well.' Ramon gave a philosophical shrug. 'It's not all bad—you really got to Santiago.'

*Not nearly as much as he got to me.*

'Did I?' she said, getting hot as she thought of his hard, lean, ardent body pressing her...his warm breath... She sucked in a steadying breath and thought, *Keep it together, Lucy. The man kissed you—big deal!*

'Well, he was as rude as hell to you.'

'I assumed that was normal for him.'

Ramon shook his head. 'Big brother is always polite even when he's mad as hell. He has this way of letting you know you've messed up without raising his voice.'

'I feel so special.'

'You still sure you don't want to carry it on?'

'I don't. Sorry, Ramon, but I'm here to help Harriet and that doesn't leave much time to make myself a sitting target for your delightful brother's insults.'

Actually she did have time, as Harriet had pointed out when she had heard Lucy knock back Ramon's offer to go out.

'I appreciate what you're doing, Lucy, but even convicted prisoners are allowed time off for good behaviour and, besides, you're giving me an inferiority complex. The place has never looked so immaculate.'

Lucy had allowed herself to be persuaded…perhaps a little too easily?

'Ah, well…but it's all good. You made such an impression that no matter who I date is going to seem an improvement, so it's win-win for me.'

Lucy's lips quivered. 'I'm so glad to have been of help.' The sarcasm passed over Ramon's head. 'You are sure your brother won't be around?' She wasn't scared of bumping into him, it was simply a matter of common sense. She hated spiders so she wasn't going to wander into a room where she might encounter one.

'I told you Santiago rides before anyone is up. He's already done half a day's work before breakfast. The man's a machine, not human—he might not even sleep at all.'

Lucy did not share the admiration in Ramon's voice. 'Or maybe he can't sleep because he has a guilty conscience?'

The spiky comment drew a laugh from Ramon. 'Most people think Santiago is one of the good guys.'

Lucy snorted.

'That's Santiago's horse, Santana,' Ramon said as she walked to the stall containing the massive magnificent black stallion she remembered from her first meeting with Santiago… Was that really only four days ago?

It seemed like a lifetime ago.

The animal rolled his eyes, showing the whites as Ramon caught the hand she had extended to the animal and pulled her back. 'Not a good idea. He's a bit unpredictable.' *Like his master*, Lucy thought, remembering that kiss again and shivering. Jaw clenched with the effort, she pushed the memory away.

A few sleepless nights ago she had finally decided to cut herself some slack, realising that the only reason she had kissed him back like some sort of sex-starved bimbo was because she was—the sex-starved bit anyhow. She had been living the life of a nun and that was not normal or healthy.

When you thought about it, their kiss had been inevitable. It had certainly not been some life-changing experience, just the result of bad timing and hormones.

It had made her realise that what she needed was some balance in her life, and while she was not about to sign on with a dating agency or start attending speed-dating evenings—both suggestions from helpful family members—she was not going to actively avoid the possibility of a relationship. Rather, as her mum poetically phrased it, she was going to put herself out there.

If Friday night had proved anything it had proved she did after all have a libido. Her full lips twisted into a bitter smile—it was just a pity that she didn't have good taste!

She shook her head and tuned back in time to hear Ramon say, '…and not very fond of anyone but his master. Now how about Sapphire?' He drew Lucy towards a chestnut pure-bred Arab filly several stalls away from the black stallion. 'She's a lovely girl with very good manners.' Ramon held out his hand to offer a treat to the horse.

'She's lovely,' Lucy agreed, patting the animal. She placed a hand to her stomach as another of the cramps that had started an hour or so earlier made her catch her breath. The pain passed and she forgot about it as her attention strayed to the animal in the stall. 'Have you ever ridden Santana?'

Ramon laughed and shook his head. 'Santiago would have my skin if I tried. He doesn't share. You really have a way with horses.'

'My father bred racehorses as a hobby—we all ride. He put me on the back of my first horse when I was two and led me on a thoroughbred when I was six.' She broke off as Ramon lifted a hand to his head. 'Are you all right?'

Ramon shook his head. 'Fine, fine…I just need…' He flashed her a tight half smile and said, 'I'll be back in a minute. Tomas here will look after you.'

The groom Ramon hailed smiled and saddled up both horses, and when he realised that she knew what she was doing, left her alone.

'Abandoned,' she said, burying her face in the filly's neck.

She patted the gentle filly, who was tethered beside Ramon's mount—a good-looking Arab—and, pushing up the sleeve of her shirt, glanced at her watch.

'Great!' She gave a hissing sound of frustration and stomped up the aisle between the stalls. What was Ramon doing?

At this rate she would miss out on her ride altogether. She had left Harriet some sandwiches for lunch, but if her bored friend was left alone too long she knew that she wouldn't be able to resist starting the round of chores without her and probably put back her recovery several weeks in the process.

She was half tempted to take the pretty filly out alone and— The sound of hooves connecting with the wooden panel of a door interrupted her chain of thought.

'Hello, boy,' she said, walking to the stall where the stallion was pacing restlessly up and down. The animal pawed the ground and rolled his eyes. Lucy smiled and held out a hand fearlessly towards him, murmuring softly.

With a whinny the animal came forward, bending his head towards her as he pawed the floor.

'My, you're a handsome boy,' she soothed, finding it easy to identify with the animal's restless impatience. 'You need a run, don't you? So do I,' she added with a sigh. 'Have you been neglected? I wish I could…' She stopped, a slow smile spreading over her face as she thought, *Why not?*

Despite any number of answers surfacing in response to her silent question, the reckless idea took hold until by the time she had saddled the animal she had rationalised her decision to the point where she was actually doing the horse's true owner a favour—a beautiful creature like this needed exercise.

She did not doubt her ability to handle him: she had grown up around horses, she was a better than good rider and she had a natural affinity for all animals.

Her confidence seemed justified as she walked the animal around the exercise yard a couple of times before taking the path that Ramon had said led to a great gallop over open ground.

'We are a school, not a prison. We do not chain our girls to their beds and I can assure you our security is more than adequate. However, if a girl wants to run away…well, it is hard to prevent her.'

Santiago was not impressed by the logic and even less by what the school deemed an appropriate punishment for the crime. He clenched his jaw and struggled to moderate his response, aware his own school days had coloured his views of the educational world.

At seven he had been sent away to a school where bullying was endemic and the teachers had turned a blind eye to the activities of a group of sadistic pupils.

'Is not excluding someone who has tried to run away rather playing into her hands?' It certainly seemed to Santiago that the only lesson his daughter had learnt was run away and they sent you home as a punishment, which was exactly where she'd been heading when they'd caught up with her at the bus station.

A bus station where she had rubbed shoulders with… His hand bunched into fists as he brought this line of thought to a screaming halt.

His blood ran cold when he thought of his eleven-year-old daughter wandering around alone in a city. Gabby might think of herself as very grown up, and in some ways she was, but in others his daughter was very young for her age, something he was glad of, but it made her vulnerable.

'Gabby's behaviour has been unacceptable—'

'I find it unacceptable that you apparently have no idea why my daughter felt the need to run away.'

'Teenage girls—'

'My daughter is eleven.'

'Of course and as you know I was not comfortable with her skipping a year…a bright girl, of course…but…' Combating his growing irritation, Santiago tuned out the rest of a speech that when condensed read 'not my fault'. His tone cold and clipped, he finally interrupted.

'So Miss Murano will accompany her on the train.'

'Yes, and you will arrange for her to be picked up at your end?'

Santiago, who intended to pick his errant daughter up himself, grunted an affirmative and put the phone down.

He was leaving his study when he almost collided with his head groom. The man was so incoherent that it took him several minutes to make sense of what he was saying. When he did he experienced a flash of blind fury.

'So the English lady took out Santana and she headed which way?'

Santiago hit the ground running, no longer keeping his anger in check but releasing it to keep the nightmare images floating in his head at bay... This was not happening again.

It could not!

His brother's horse was fortuitously saddled and waiting in the yard. Santiago loosed the rein from the post it was looped over and, vaulting into the saddle, dug in his heels. The animal responded to the urgency and leapt responsively forward.

As they galloped onto the trail Santiago planned the words that would annihilate her. He was visualising the humility he would see in her attitude before he eventually wrung her lovely neck when his own horse, his mouth flecked with white, his black mane flying, galloped past.

An icy fist clenched in his chest and the images of retribution evaporated. He soothed his own spooked mount, sternly checking the animal's desire to follow the stallion, and rode on. The scene that met his eyes when he emerged from the forested strip was his worst nightmare.

He dismounted, leaving the animal to graze as he ran to where the still figure lay, dread clutching in his belly.

# CHAPTER SEVEN

It was happening again.

Not déjà vu, more a waking nightmare.

His face was like carved granite as he made himself look at her. Her face was pale; she looked like an effigy carved from ice.

She would be growing cold and there would be blood. He remembered the blood in his dreams; he saw it often. Saw the scarlet flecks on her mouth and knew it was his fault because Magdalena, sweet, gentle Magdalena had been trying to impress him.

Lucy heard the crunch of footsteps on the hard ground getting closer as she lay there, her chest burning as she tried to replace the air the fall had knocked out of her lungs. It hurt, but it was nothing more than she deserved, she decided, furious with herself for making such an amateurish mistake. Anyone could fall, but to let go of the reins when you came off…now that was stupid!

She waited for another of the painful stomach cramps to pass—this one was even more painful than the one that had hit her when the horse had stumbled—before she prised her eyelids apart and saw the shiny Italian leather shoes. She didn't need to go any further up the leg of grey tailored trousers… She knew who was standing there.

Of all the people who could have discovered her in this ignominious position, it had to be him.

The surge of intense relief Santiago had felt when he saw her blue-veined eyelids flutter against her pale waxen cheek was submerged by the equally strong blast of white-hot fury that rapidly succeeded it. When she began to move his entire body shook with the effort of keeping his feelings in check, feelings that had been shaken loose by the sight of her seemingly lifeless body.

'Keep still!' he yelled, fighting his way through the memories that crowded in on him and forcing himself to think here and now...think potential spinal injuries?

Ignoring the terse instruction—did the man have to make everything sound like an order?—Lucy, determined not to lie there like a stranded fish while he looked down at her with disdain from an Olympian height, pulled herself up into a sitting position.

She clamped her teeth over the groan as the effort of the simple action caused a fine layer of cold perspiration to break out over the surface of her skin.

The immediate problem was breathing.

'Just winded...' she rasped between gasps, her voice barely audible as she struggled with the fastener of the helmet, then, exhausted by the effort, she lay it in her lap.

Santiago's dark eyes moved from her pale trembling fingers to the cloud of silver-white hair that, released from the confines of the helmet, spilled down her back unbidden. The memory of feeling those glossy strands sliding through his fingers like silk surfaced... He pushed but the tactile memory lingered so inexplicably strong that his fingertips tingled.

Lucy plucked a piece of grass from her once pristine white shirt, very conscious of the angry figure who towered over her. Why didn't he say something...? Finally unable to stand the simmering silence any longer, she croaked, 'I've got grass stains on my shirt.'

With a snarl of disbelief, Santiago dropped down into a crouch beside her.

'Grass stains!' he ejaculated, taking the helmet from her trembling fingers and resisting the growing compulsion to press one of her slim white hands between his palms. This woman did not need comforting, she needed therapy.

Needed kissing.

'*Por Dios!* If you can't say anything sensible, shut up!'

Lucy, who could not have said anything even had she wanted to, swallowed past the aching emotional occlusion in her throat and clamped her teeth down on her trembling lower lip.

'This thing…' His voice faded as he laid the helmet to one side with exaggerated care. He inhaled and levelled a burning glare at the top of her blonde head as he fought for control. 'This thing probably saved your life. You were lucky.' It was not always the way… His heavy eyelids lowered partially, concealing the bleakness in the dark depths as the brutal inescapable images played in his head.

For a moment the silence hung between them, broken when Lucy gave a strangled sob she turned into a cough before pressing her face into her cupped palms. 'Don't dramatise,' she mumbled, unconsciously repeating the phrase her father had always said when she became overemotional as a child.

That brought his head up with a jerk. 'Dramatise!' He swore in his native tongue and sucked in a wrathful breath as he dragged a hand over his ebony hair. 'You want to see dramatic…?'

She lifted her face, her slightly dazed electric-blue eyes connecting with his, and Santiago lost track of his train of thought. Despite the tough-guy act she looked as he felt, and the petulant rebuttal seemed to have exhausted her. All the fight was gone, leaving her looking defenceless and vulnerable and several million miles away from the seductress his brother needed saving from.

With her defences stripped away her luminous beauty shone through: perfect bone structure, flawless skin… It was hard to look at such perfection and remain unmoved. As he stared he felt his anger drain away, leaving him feeling as if his armour had been stripped away… He felt suddenly exposed… He pushed away the thought. The only thing that was exposed was her inability to think beyond her own instant gratification.

Lucy sat there, her breath coming in painful uneven rasps, chin on her chest, her eyes lifted to the man squatting casually on the balls of his feet beside her. As always, he gave off the impression of elegant good taste overlaid by an aura of raw sexual magnetism that always made the details of what he was wearing secondary. Today it was an outfit more appropriate to the office than riding—a pale grey suit, crisp white shirt and silk tie, all classic and tasteful.

As their eyes connected the anger that was rolling off him hit like a physical force.

'You shouldn't be moving,' Santiago snarled, thinking in the same breath he had to stop her before she caused permanent damage and it would serve her right if she did.

Practically speaking, if she chose to ignore him, short of flattening her with a rugby tackle and pinning her to the ground—an image that his imagination tended to linger unhealthily over—Santiago recognised that all he could do was watch.

'Just because I'm saying something doesn't mean it's the wrong thing to do, Lucy.'

Lucy blinked, horrified to feel the sting of hot tears behind her eyes. She was proof against his insults but the unexpected gruff gentleness she heard in his voice sliced through her defences like a hot knife through ice cream.

She bit her quivering lip, held up a hand in mute appeal and husked a breathless plea. She couldn't cry—her tears would be something else for him to curl his lip contemptuously at. 'I just need a minute…to get my breath back.'

Santiago opened his mouth to speak, then closed it again and tilted his head sharply in acquiescence before rising to his feet in one fluid motion. He walked away feeling an urgent need to put some distance between them.

Running one hand over his jaw, he reached for his phone with the other. The woman, he decided, punching in a number with unwanted viciousness, was amazing. Considering the circumstances, he had been bloody restrained and yet with one look from her swimming blue eyes she managed to simultaneously look like some innocent virgin and make him feel like a bullying tyrant—it was quite a skill.

In the periphery of her vision Lucy was conscious of him pacing a few feet away while speaking tersely into a mobile phone. When he dropped down beside her once more a few moments later her breathing was normal and more importantly she was no longer on the brink of a teary outburst.

'Better?'

She nodded in response to his abrupt enquiry and said in her head, *Suck it up Lucy, keep it together.*

Santiago remained sceptical. The alarming rattle had gone, but her breath still seemed to be coming rather fast; she was almost hyperventilating.

Aware that it might appear he was staring at the heaving contours of her full breasts, which he was, but with total clinical objectivity—not everyone might get the objectivity—Santiago dragged his gaze clear.

'Your leg.' For the first time he saw the damage done to the well-worn jodhpurs that clung to her hips and the long lines of her magnificent legs. Along the outside of the right leg the fabric was torn, from thigh to ankle it gaped, revealing a section of bare skin.

His fingertips barely brushed her calf before she snatched her leg up. 'It's fine—a graze.' With a dismissive shrug she tucked the limb underneath her and concentrated on the pain in her calf to stop herself thinking about how much she had wanted him to touch her.

Perhaps she had had a knock on the head?

Friday night it had been the glass of wine, or so she had told herself through the long, sleepless, guilt-racked night that had followed, and now it was a bang on the head—what excuse would she have the next time she found herself craving this man's touch?

*There isn't going to be a next time.*

He arched a sardonic brow and shrugged. 'If you say so.' The doctor might have other thoughts. The groove above his nose deepened as he glanced down the track—where was the doctor?

'I do,' she said firmly.

As he replayed the phone conversation of moments before in his head the oddness of Ramon's response to his request to call for a doctor struck Santiago for the first time.

'Good idea,' his half-brother had said without asking why or for whom medical assistance was required.

Hand on the back of her neck, she angled a cautious look at Santiago's face. She knew the lull in hostilities would not last; this reprieve was definitely only temporary. Even when she hadn't ridden off on his favourite horse he couldn't open his mouth without being snide and cutting.

Now she actually was in the wrong the comfort of the moral high ground was a dim and distant memory... *Oh, God.* She took a deep breath and thought, *Take it like a man, Lucy. Bite the bullet and when you run out of clichés, apologise.* She closed her eyes and thought, *What the hell was I thinking?*

She hated admitting she was wrong at the best of times, but admitting it to Santiago made it a hundred times worse. She could take his anger—it was the knowing she deserved it that she struggled with.

Crazily, with all the legitimate things she had to stress about, it was the irrational one that was giving Lucy the most problems. She knew he couldn't read her mind—he just liked to leave the impression he was all-seeing, all-knowing—yet she couldn't shake the conviction that he was going to look at her and know she had spent the last few nights fantasising about him.

'Did Santana run home?' she asked in a small voice.

Santiago's head jerked towards her, his silent anger more articulate than a stream of abuse.

Unable to take her eyes off the errant muscle that was clenching and unclenching spasmodically in his cheek, in the face of his fury she leapt to the obvious conclusion. She began to shake her head in denial.

'Oh, no, he isn't injured…!' The thought of being responsible for an injury to that beautiful and expensive animal… God, no wonder he looked as if he wanted to throttle her. 'He's…' Her blue eyes widened in her milk-pale face as she whispered fearfully, 'He's not dead, is he?'

'Would you care if he was?'

A sound close to a whimper emerged from her throat and Santiago, who never had been comfortable with kicking someone when they were down, took pity on her obvious distress.

'I have no idea how Santana is,' he admitted, before adding with a scowl, 'But he was so spooked when I saw him that it will probably take a week for him to calm down and an army to catch him.' He lied, well aware that the animal would have gone straight back to his stable.

'I'm so, so sorry.'

'For stealing a valuable horse, for proving you can't handle anything bigger than a donkey or for getting caught?'

Her blue eyes flew wide. 'I didn't steal anything!'

He arched a brow at the protest. 'Tell that to the police.'

She regarded him in horror. 'You wouldn't call the police.'

He smiled and arched a sardonic brow. 'You think?'

Was he serious? Lucy refused to let him see that his threat had scared her. 'I think you're a total bastard.'

'Not illegal last time I researched the subject.' He gave a nasty smile. 'Unlike horse stealing.'

'I wasn't stealing your horse, I was just…riding him.'

'Why?'

She blinked, struggling after the fact to explain even to herself the impulse that had made her take the horse out. 'Why not?' She shrugged.

'So this is a case of anything Lucy sees and wants Lucy has to have even if it belongs to someone else?' Didn't she understand that a person could not have anything they wanted? There were rules, like the unwritten one that said a man did not muscle in on his brother's girlfriend—did it count when you'd be saving your brother from a terrible fate? Did the unwritten rule stand when the brother in question didn't possess your own ability to keep your sexual appetites and your emotions separate from a terrible fate?

Lucy saw where he was going with this. 'Ramon doesn't belong to anyone else, even though you went out of your way to make it seem like he does.'

Santiago's scowl deepened. He had thrown Carmella, with her crush on Ramon, into the mix hoping she would offer a distraction with her youth and innocence. He was ready to admit that his plan had failed miserably and he felt guilty for using the kid.

'But Denis Mulville did.' What chance would any wife have if Lucy Fitzgerald decided she wanted a man?

At the name Lucy's face lost any colour it had regained. The condemnation on his face was nothing new. She had seen similar expressions on the faces of virtually everyone she met four years ago, and some of those faces had belonged to people she had considered friends.

At the centre of a storm of ill will Lucy had felt every cruel word and jeer until she had taught herself not to care about the opinion of others. People could and would think what they liked, but so long as she knew the truth that was all that mattered…at least in theory.

Reality meant that there had still been nights when she had cried herself to sleep and days when she had longed to put her side of the story, but she had maintained her dignified silence even after the gagging order was lifted.

Not once had she yelled at one of her accusers—'I never slept with the man. He was a creep!'

As she did now, ironically to someone whose good opinion meant nothing to her, someone who dismissed her words with a contemptuous shrug.

There was a chance, Santiago thought, that she told the literal truth—a man who got her in bed would not be likely to fall asleep!

'How did you justify breaking up a family?' A hissing sound of disgust issued from between his clenched teeth as he dragged a hand through his ebony hair. 'Do you tell yourself that he wouldn't look at you if he had a happy marriage? That there wouldn't have been an affair if the marriage hadn't been in trouble to begin with—isn't that what the other woman always says?'

'You tell me! You seem the expert on the subject.'

She broke off, wincing as she experienced a stomach cramp a lot sharper than any of the previous ones. She closed her eyes and gritted her teeth. If she threw up in front of this man the humiliation factor would be off the scale.

Lucy lifted her head, breathing through the pain.

'What's wrong?'

'Nothing!' she snapped.

The beads of perspiration that had broken out over the pale skin of her brow suggested otherwise.

'I know I shouldn't have taken the horse, but I was waiting for Ramon and Santana obviously needed exercise and you hadn't bothered to exercise him...'

'So this is my fault?'

The note of fake comprehension caused the spots of dark colour on her pale cheeks to deepen. 'No, but—'

'But you,' he cut back in a hard voice, 'saw an opportunity of scoring points because I warned you off—'

'No!'

'Then I can only assume you wanted my attention. You didn't have to steal my valuable horse in order to get that—if you wanted to be kissed all you had to do was ask.'

She looked at him with simmering dislike. 'Not in this life!' she pronounced with an emphatic shake of her head. She swallowed and pressed a hand to mouth.

'What's wrong?'

'I'm feeling a bit nauseous,' she admitted, thinking about Ramon's abrupt departure and wondering if the two could be connected... They had shared that smoked salmon sandwich...?

'Let me look in your eyes,' he said, taking her chin in his fingers.

'I don't have a head injury.'

His fingers fell away. 'Do you remember what happened?'

'Of course I remember what happened—I came off.'

'Got thrown.'

'All right, got thrown,' she gritted, thinking, *Go on, rub it in why don't you?* 'That's why I lost control when he got spooked by that little pig.' Actually it had been quite a large pig.

To hear one of the dangerous wild boar that lived in the woods dismissed with a disgusted grimace made him blink.

'I'm a good rider. I've been riding all my life.'

'And have you been falling off all your life?'

Struggling to combat the rising nausea, Lucy wiped the rash of damp off her forehead, managing to lift her head and fix him with a glare. 'I suppose you have never fallen off.' She pressed her hand to her mouth and thought, *Please do not let me throw up in front of him.*

The annoyance died from Santiago's face as he studied her pale features. 'You look terrible.'

And she felt terrible.

'Do you feel faint?'

At that moment she would have accepted a graceful, aesthetically pleasing swoon, but it wasn't an option. 'No, I don't feel faint, I feel...' She clapped a hand to her mouth, jumped to her feet and sprinted across the clearing. A few yards away she fell to her knees.

'You all right?'

She shrugged off the hand on her shoulder and got to her feet, unable to meet his eyes. 'Obviously I'm not all right.' The nausea was much easier to cope with than the humiliation of the situation... God, she wanted to die; he had actually held her hair away from her face!

Santiago was the very last person in the world she would have expected a display of such thoughtfulness from, or, for that matter, expected to possess such a strong stomach.

'Did you hit your head...lose consciousness?' Her creamy complexion was tinged with a greenish hue and she was

visibly swaying like a young sapling in a breeze… Sheer
bloody-minded stubbornness, he suspected, was the only
thing keeping her upright.

'No, I…I was already…' Losing track of her rebuttal, her
voice faded to a whisper as her eyes half closed.

Convinced now he was dealing with a concussion at the
very least, Santiago was moving in to catch her when she
opened her eyes, directing her wide-eyed cerulean stare directly at his face.

'It wasn't the fall. I've been feeling…off most of the morning.' Her brow furrowed; it was hard in retrospect to recall
when it had started. Post smoked salmon, definitely.

The confession sparked his dormant anger into life. 'Of
all the selfish…stupid…!' he blasted. 'So let me get this
right—not only did you steal a horse you could not handle
simply to thumb your nose at me, you did so while unwell.'

Lucy, who had been on the point of offering a shamed
apology, lost all urge to admit she'd been wrong.

'I didn't know I was going to be sick…' Wincing at the
unattractive whiney note in her voice, Lucy reached for the
scarf she had wound around her neck that morning, intending to tie back her hair with it, and found it was gone…

'What is it now?' He watched cautiously as she bit her
quivering lip and hoped she was not about to start throwing up again, though he conceded it was preferable to tears.

It was bizarre. He had always considered himself an even-
tempered man, certainly not someone prone to mood swings,
but with this woman he could feel a strong compulsion to
throttle her and two seconds later an equally strong compulsion to offer her a shoulder to cry on.

'I lost my scarf…' She stopped as he looked at her as
though she had gone mad and added, 'And I wasn't trying
to thumb my…' Her forceful declaration came to an abrupt

halt, she swallowed and thought, *My God, wasn't that exactly what I was doing?*

Something about this man made her want to score points: his aggressive sexuality, his self-righteous attitude, his smug conviction he was always right—no, actually, it was everything!

'I shouldn't have taken the horse…the biggest horse,' she tacked on before she could stop herself.

And once she'd begun it was impossible to stem the flow of words that spilled from her.

'The one that nobody else can handle, fastest, shiniest car…biggest bank balance…oh, and let's not forget the Olympian-class smug superiority. Do you ever stop competing? It's nothing short of a miracle that Ramon isn't riddled with insecurities.' She ran out of steam, dismay gradually seeping into her expression as she realised what she'd just said.

'Shiniest car?'

Her eyes fell.

'Is that how you see me—a boy with his toys…?'

She saw him with no clothes on, or she had in her erotic, shameful dreams. She closed her eyes and groaned. 'Oh, just call the police. I'll go quietly.' Sitting in a police cell had to be preferable to enduring his company.

'Don't worry, I am not going to call the police.'

She choked on her relieved sigh when he tacked on, 'I'll sack the groom. It was his responsibility and rules are rules.'

Her horrified blue eyes flew to his face. 'You wouldn't…' She stopped as she encountered an ironic look.

'And with my word being law and my reputation as a despot being at stake I need to make an example of someone,' he delivered straight-faced.

'Very funny. Oh, God, I'm going to be ill again.'

# CHAPTER EIGHT

'THERE'S no point waiting.'

The decision made, Santiago slid an assessing glance towards the woman who was now sitting with her back propped against a tree trunk looking very much like a wilting exotic flower. The last bout of vomiting had left her very weak.

Admiration was something he had never imagined he would feel about Lucy, but, you had to hand it to her, she did not complain.

She might be putting on a brave front but, guts or not, there was no way in the world she could make it under her own steam...but with his support she could sit in the saddle in front of him and they could be back at the *castillo* in a matter of minutes. They would be now if he hadn't assumed that help was on its way.

Santiago turned, clicking his fingers as he did so to bring the horse to him...only there wasn't a horse to bring. Ramon's gelding was nowhere in sight.

The expression on his face when he realised that the horse had wandered away would have made her laugh on any other occasion.

He swore softly under his breath.

'We've both lost a horse.'

His withering gaze swung her way. 'Thank you for pointing that out. It is most helpful.'

Head tilted to one side, he fixed her with a narrow-eyed assessing glance until Lucy, feeling increasingly self-conscious by his unblinking regard, snapped crankily. 'What? What's wrong?'

'I was just considering the options...'

Presuming he was about to share the details, she was taken totally by surprise by the abruptness of the action that followed his terse explanation. Lucy was so shocked that she offered no resistance when he almost casually lifted her into his arms—just a scream.

A moment later she managed a breathless, indignant, 'What are you doing?' Other than displaying strength that Lucy—who was not by anyone's standards a small woman—struggled hard not to find impressive. However, she had never had a single fantasy about being rescued and swept into the strong arms of a man—any man.

Especially not *this* man!

'Not wasting further time hanging around.' For assistance that seemed to be taking a long time coming.

Or asking permission before treating her like a sack of coal, she mused, giving a second shrill yelp as he moved, striding across the open ground towards the forest trail.

Lucy stared at his ear and held herself stiff, noticing the way his hair curled around it into the nape of his neck... strong neck. It was mid-morning but she could see the beginning of stubble on his jaw and cheek. It would feel... She paused mid-thought and gasped.

'I don't want to know!'

'Know what?'

Lucy's eyes fell away guiltily. 'Know how long it will be before you drop me.' Pleased with her quick recovery, she lifted her gaze just as he loosened his grip for a split second but enough to make her react instinctively out of self-preservation.

She grabbed him, one hand sliding under his unfastened jacket, the other around his neck.

'Breathing would be nice.'

There was an embarrassing delay before her brain, busy processing details like the warmth and lithe hardness of the warm male body she was crushed up against, reacted to his dry comment.

'Very funny,' she drawled, loosening her grip but not all the way—he was almost jogging now and the next time it might not be a joke. 'Will you put me down? This is ridiculous.' Almost as ridiculous as her reaction to a bit of muscle.

'Look, I'd love to argue the toss with you, but frankly I need all my breath. You're a lot heavier than you look.' Her weight was not the problem, but the soft yielding nature of the warm body that seemed to fit naturally into his was. Lucy Fitzgerald was not a woman who had sharp angles; she was not a woman that a man could be close to and not think about naked.

It was an image that Santiago, whose normal iron control when it came to such matters was at that moment absent, struggled to erase. In fact, he was struggling to think beyond the surge of hormones that made him want to lay her down on the warm mossy ground and… The sound of his harsh inhalation was drowned out by Lucy's indignant gasp.

'Are you calling me fat?'

The growl of desire growing low in his throat turned into an amused snort as, appreciating the irony, he quirked his lips into a twisted smile. He had called her many things that were worse, but it was the suggestion that she was overweight that rattled her.

'I may not be a skinny—'

A stone too heavy, according to the man from Hollywood who, at the height of her notoriety, had dangled the female lead in a new film with the proviso she lose that stone. It had

clearly not even crossed his mind, or for that matter her ju-
bilant agent's, that Lucy would say thanks but no thanks to
the chance of being the love interest to one of the industry's
most bankable stars.

'Sorry, but I can't act,' she had said to soften her refusal.

This, it had turned out, was not an obstacle and her ability
to look good in very little apparently more than compensated
for this minor deficiency. The scandal attached to her name
had apparently been deemed box-office gold.

'But I'm not about to starve myself so men like you can
feel macho hauling me around.'

*'Dios mio!'* He stopped dead and angled an astonished
stare at her indignant face.

As their eyes connected the amused exasperation in his
expression vanished, as did any temptation to defend himself against the accusation.

In his arms Lucy could feel his chest lifting as though
standing there were putting more stress on his heart than jogging along had; her own heart was fluttering like a trapped
bird in her chest cavity.

She told herself it was her weakened state that made her
tremble, unable to admit even to herself it was being the
focus of his febrile gaze that had sent her nervous system into
shocked overload. As for the impression that the air around
them was literally shimmering with a heat haze—that was
obviously a result of dehydration or fever.

'You have a perfect body and we both know it.'

Turning his attention abruptly back to the trail ahead, he
picked up pace—not a cold shower but the next best thing—
and wondered about the shock in her face. Such a reaction
seemed bizarre considering she was a woman who traded
on her looks and sensuality.

Silenced by the abrupt assessment, Lucy was almost glad
when the nausea and stomach cramps took her mind off the

molten stream of desire that had turned her into a breathless bundle of craving and reduced her brain function to zero.

When a short while later, or it might have been a long time, Lucy had lost track, he asked, 'Are you sulking?' Lucy thought it wise to warn him.

'No, I don't feel very well...' Her eyes were closed as she spoke but she could feel his dark gaze on her face.

Presumably she looked terrible because he started jogging faster. There was no way, she thought dully, that he could keep up this pace for much longer even if he was incredibly fit.

'Nearly there,' he murmured close to her ear. 'Hold on.'

'God, don't be nice to me,' she begged, wondering what alternative universe she had slipped into where Santiago made her feel safe and cared for. 'Or I'll cry.'

Tears would have left him unmoved but the plea touched him. He could not think of another woman he knew who would prefer to be yelled at than give in to tears. 'Shut up or I'll drop you.'

Lucy sketched a weak smile and forgot to hate him. 'Thank you. I suppose I am being very ungrateful.'

'Yes.'

'I'll try not to throw up on you...it's a beautiful suit,' she heard herself say, and wondered if, despite the fact she felt freezing cold, she had a fever. 'God, I'm never sick!' she groaned, vowing to show more sympathy in future to people who were physically more fragile than she was.

She was now and the sight of her poor pale face made him complete the last leg of the journey in record time.

By the time they reached the stableyard there was no question of it being illicit lust that made Lucy cling to him; she wasn't even aware that she was groaning softly into his shoulder.

He looked around the deserted yard, which normally at

this time of the day was a hive of activity, and felt his frustration grow.

He cut between the buildings built around a quadrangle and across the lawn, ignoring the burning of his shoulder muscles, spurred on by the soft moans of the woman he carried.

He walked straight through the massive double doors of the front entrance and into the vaulted hallway. It was empty. He opened his mouth to yell when Josef appeared. Normally insouciant Josef's eyes widened when he saw his boss with a semi-conscious woman in his arms.

'Where is my brother?'

'With the doctor. He's rather unwell.'

'Ramon is ill, too?' Santiago closed his eyes. Two invalids on his hands, one literally, and an errant daughter to collect from the station. When they spoke of it never raining but pouring, his was presumably the day they were referring to.

'Can I help with the young lady, sir?'

'No, you can get Martha and the new girl…Sabina, and ask them to come to the west-wing suite…inform the doctor he is required there and have the helicopter ready to take off in thirty minutes. Gabby is coming home early.'

Josef waited as he reeled off the instructions and then, with a nod, vanished. A man of few words, Josef; Santiago liked that about him.

'You're so pretty.'

Lucy blinked and pushed her way free of the last layers of sleep. The figure standing by the window came into focus. To her relief, it was not a hallucination—unless hallucinations spoke and wore braces.

She blinked at the small elfin features of Gabby.

'Thank you,' Lucy replied, easing herself carefully up on one elbow and turning her curious gaze around the room.

She had not been that interested in her surroundings the previous night when Santiago had brought her in here and relinquished her to the care of the doctor and the two women who had stayed with her during the night.

One of them had spoken perfect English, the other was the sweet girl who had cut her hand, both had been incredibly kind.

'I thought you were in school.'

'I ran away.'

Lucy was weak enough to feel a fleeting moment of sympathy for Santiago.

'What time is it?'

The furniture in the room that was massive enough to lose the enormous four-poster she was lying in was dark and heavy and looked like museum pieces. The stone walls were covered with tapestries and portraits of severe-looking historical persons. The personal touch of an arrangement of garden flowers in the gleaming copper bowl set in the empty cavernous fireplace filled the room with their scent and lightened the general museum-style gloom.

'It's two o'clock.'

Lucy was startled. She had fallen asleep in the early hours. 'Why didn't someone wake me?' She brushed her hair from her face and struggled to tear her eyes from the portrait of a hatchet-faced woman in a jewelled turban. The eyes looked spookily familiar, an ancestor presumably of the present incumbent. Clearly hauteur was not a new Silva characteristic, any more than the masterful nose.

'They said to let you and Sara sleep.'

Lucy yawned and dragged her attention back to the girl. 'Sara?' Her brow crinkled. Was she meant to know the name? At that moment she was struggling with her own.

'She's one of the maids. She ate some of the bad salmon that was for the cook's mother's cat, too.'

Struggling to follow this information overload, Lucy moistened her lips with her tongue—they felt dry and cracked—and recalled the smoked salmon and cream cheese bagel that Ramon had produced when she had said she couldn't possibly go riding until she had had her breakfast.

'I haven't eaten either but not to worry, I have it covered,' he had said, producing the breakfast treat wrapped in a linen napkin.

When she had laughed and conceded he had thought of everything she hadn't known that had included food poisoning! Could he have escaped unscathed?

'Ramon?'

'Oh, Uncle Ramon was much worse than you.'

'But he's better now?' Lucy was just relieved that Harriet, who she had cooked breakfast for before she went out to attend to the donkeys—six a.m. was not a time of the day that Lucy personally felt happy eating—had not shared the breakfast.

'I don't know. Ramon was really sick. He had to go to hospital.'

'Hospital!' Lucy exclaimed in alarm.

She nodded. '*Papá* said it serves him right for raiding the pantry.'

Gabby took a seat on the brocade bed cover using the crewel-work curtains that draped the bed for leverage.

Lucy discovered that she was wearing a long white Victorian-style nightgown in a fine, exquisitely embroidered fabric. Her memory of how she came to be wearing this period-looking piece was sketchy, but she was sure—almost—that Santiago had not been involved.

Having delivered her, he had immediately made himself scarce and she didn't blame him, though… Her brow furrowed. She did have a vague recollection of hearing a deep male voice and feeling cool fingers on her forehead at one point during the night, but that might have been part of a dream.

Running the flat of her hand down the gossamer-thin floaty sleeve of the nightdress, she lifted her gaze to find the child watching her. Santiago's daughter was a pretty little thing with a roundish face, big dark eyes and a cupid's bow mouth and dimpled cheeks—did she look like her dead mother?

'That's mine off Aunt Seraphina. Awful, isn't it? She always buys me stuff that's massive for me to grow into, but I never do.' The little sigh made Lucy smile—clearly the size thing was an issue with her.

'*Papá* says it's good to be petite but what does he know? He's a man and ten feet tall…' she grumbled, adding enviously, 'Like you. Is your hair real…not extensions?' She viewed the silken skein that framed Lucy's face with a mixture of curiosity and envy. 'I'd like to bleach my hair but *Papá* would kill me. It might be worth it, though,' she added with a grin. 'And who knows? It might be the final straw and they'll expel me this time.' She caught Lucy's quizzical look and added, 'I hate school.'

The description made Lucy think wistfully of the time when her own father had seemed the biggest thing in the world. She repressed a smile.

'The hair is all my own,' Lucy admitted, reaching for the water on the bedside table and taking a sip. Her throat felt dry and raw. 'Well, your *papá* is right—there's nothing wrong with being petite. I always wished I was.' But it was never good to be different and at this girl's age she had towered above her contemporaries.

'*Papá* is right…? Can I have that in writing?'

Lucy slopped water all down the front of the borrowed nightdress and turned to see Santiago standing framed in the doorway.

The sight of his tall dynamic figure sent a wild rush of energising adrenaline through her body. Dressed in a white tee shirt and jeans, his slicked wet hair suggesting he had just stepped out of the shower, he oozed a restless, edgy vitality.

He also looked sinfully gorgeous and Lucy didn't have the energy or for once the inclination to go through the entire 'sexy but not my type' routine… She was hopelessly attracted to him. Just sex, she told herself, drawing back from deeper examination of the tight knot of emotions lying like a leaden weight behind her breastbone.

'What are you doing here?' she quivered accusingly.

He arched a brow and said mildly, 'I live here.'

She flushed and heard the words *king of the castle* in her head as she followed the direction of his quizzical gaze. It led to the silk-covered pillow she was clutching to her chest like a shield.

Lucy had no recollection of grabbing it and equally she had no intention of letting it go, though as shields went it was about as effective as a feather in a storm against the illicit lust that hardened her nipples to thrusting prominence beneath thin, fine fabric.

'I didn't wake her, *Papá*, honest, did I?'

Santiago levered his tall lean frame off the wall, not ten feet but muscle packed, and very impressive.

'No, I was awake,' Lucy lied, and received a beam of gratitude in return.

'What is this—a conspiracy?' He appeared faintly amused as he turned to the child and added, 'Run along, kiddo, you are already in enough trouble and Miss Fitzgerald is tired.' He turned to Lucy and said, 'The doctor is with the maid who was sick, too. I just called by to let you know he'll be here when he's finished with her.'

Tired… Miss Fitzgerald, he thought, his hooded glance

skimming her paper-pale face, looked like some Hollywood version of a sexy vampire—fragile but deadly.

Once he started looking it was hard to stop. She was the most dramatically beautiful woman he had ever seen. A bare scrubbed face only emphasised the crystal purity of her perfectly symmetrical features; the skin, stretched tighter after her sleepless night, across the beautiful bones was satiny smooth; her sleepless pallor and the dark smudges made the colour of her eyes appear even more dramatic than usual.

It was a major improvement to the way she had looked the night before. Last night she had looked... Struggling to hold onto his train of thought, Santiago narrowed his eyes in concentration and broke contact with her sapphire stare.

The muscles along his angular jawline quivered as he recalled the attitude of the doctor, who turned out to be not the family friend but a locum who seemed barely shaving, standing in. The man, having already called an ambulance for Ramon, had seemed inclined to underplay the severity of Lucy's condition.

To Santiago it had seemed logical to err on the side of caution and he had been far from convinced by the doctor's assertion that staying where she was and reviewing the situation tomorrow was the best course of action in Lucy's case.

He had been proved right and Santiago had been ready to admit as much this morning. The doctor deserved an apology and he respected the fact the other man had not rolled over and said yes sir—a response that Santiago encountered all too often.

The doctor's response to his apology had been a good-natured shrug.

'I've been called worse and threatened with worse,' he'd said. 'Though not from anyone who looked quite so capable of carrying through with the threats,' he'd admitted with a rueful roll of his eyes. 'It's hard for people to be objective when they are emotionally involved.'

Santiago had been midway through assuring the man that he was not in any way emotionally involved with the patient, that in point of fact he barely knew the woman, when he had realised that, the more he protested, the more he sounded like someone in denial.

He had let the subject drop.


'She's been asleep for hours and hours.' Gabby relinquished her perch on the bed but only took one step towards the door before her curiosity got the better of her. 'And the doctor says that no one can catch anything. You're not…contagious…?' She glanced towards her father, who nodded. 'And all we need to do is maintain…' Again the glance.

'Basic good hygiene.'

'Basic good hygiene. Did you really ride Santana?'

Lucy's eyes flew guiltily to Santiago and she discovered with a little shocking thrill that he was staring at her. Guilty heat poured into her face. 'I…it was a…mistake.'

'And you fell off?'

*Take it like a man, Lucy*, she told herself. 'Yes, I fell off.' Some people might call it bad luck and some, she thought, flashing a glance to the silent man before her, might call it what I deserved.

'Did it hurt?'

'Not much.'

'But you didn't die. I'm glad.'

Amused by the solemn little girl and her apparent fixation on the gruesome details of the accident, Lucy smiled and said, 'It was nothing.'

'People do die falling off horses,' the girl replied matter-of-factly. 'My *mamá* did.'

Lucy's horrified intake of breath sounded loud in the silent room.

# CHAPTER NINE

'SHE was dead when *Papá* found her—'

This casual revelation drew another exclamation from an unprepared Lucy before Santiago, his deep voice calm and wiped of any hint of emotion, cut across his daughter.

'Gabby, leave Miss Fitzgerald in peace. You can interrogate her later.'

Lucy's eyes flew to his face. In profile his expression was veiled, nothing other than the suggestion of tension in the muscles along his firm jaw to suggest they were discussing a tragedy.

Tears started in her eyes as an empathic shudder ran through her body...to lose his wife in a senseless accident and to discover her body... A bone-deep chill settled on Lucy as she realised what he must have thought when he found her... *Oh, God, to have it all brought back...and I thought he was overreacting!*

He was a tough man, but even steel had weaknesses.

The horrid realisation that she had been the catalyst for bringing back heaven knew what sort of nightmarish memories made her feel like an utterly selfish... And it was her fault and why...?

She had known it was wrong and she had done it anyway.

'But, *Papá*, I...' The girl met her father's eyes and gave an exaggerated sigh. 'All right, but I was only—'

'Say goodbye to Miss Fitzgerald, Gabriella.'

'Goodbye, Miss Fitzgerald,' she trotted out obediently.

'Goodbye, Gabby.' No mystery why Santiago's parenting skills veered towards the overprotective!

The child threw a half smile at Lucy over her shoulder before she left the room, dragging her feet with exaggerated reluctance.

Lucy half expected him to follow his daughter out, but instead Santiago moved into the room, closing the door behind him.

'Your wife died…' Lucy began awkwardly. 'The circumstances…I didn't know…'

His shoulders lifted. 'There is no reason you should know.'

Subtitles were not required to read the silent addition of *back off*!

'So you are feeling better?' His eyes touched the purple smudges beneath her eyes. 'The lab results on Ramon have confirmed the strain of bug… You have been relatively lucky. They have kept him in to rule out any complications.'

Her eyes widened in alarm. 'Complications?'

'Apparently there have been rare cases when the kidneys are affected. It is only a precaution. The doctor will be here to see you shortly. In the meantime just ring the bell.' He nodded to the old-fashioned arrangement above the bed and Lucy visualised it ringing in the nether regions of the place—she had no intention of using it or of staying in bed.

'In the meantime I am instructed to tell you to take plenty of fluids.'

It would be a brave person who instructed him to do anything. 'That's very…kind of you.' *Kind* was not a word she had ever imagined using in relation to this autocratic man but he had been, and she had not exactly been grateful. 'But totally not necessary. I'm fine. If someone could bring my clothes—' holding back her hair with one hand, she pulled back the covers '—I'll—'

'You're weak as a kitten,' he said, placing a finger on her chest that sent her back against the pillows. Pulling back the bed covers, he leaned in to tuck them around her, affording Lucy a smell of the soap he had used mingled with the warm male smell of him.

'You can't keep me here against my will!'

He nodded his head. 'True, I can't, always assuming of course that I would want to.' His amused glance travelled over her rigid figure, making Lucy painfully aware of how awful she must look… Several steps down from dragged through a hedge was clearly no temptation…not that she wanted to tempt him.

He took a step back and nodded towards the door. 'Feel free to go back to the *finca* if you wish.' Bowing his head, he made a sweeping gesture of invitation.

Suspicious of the easy victory—why the sudden climb down?—she viewed him through narrowed blue eyes and didn't move.

'I'm sure Harriet will drag herself out of her own sickbed to look after you.'

'Harriet!' In the act of tossing her hair back in defiance, Lucy froze, her beautiful features melting into a horrified mask of dismay. She had not given her friend a single thought.

Though tempted to torment her a little more, he soothed, 'Do not worry.' She looked ready to leap out of bed there and then, which would probably result in her collapsing. She looked, he decided, as weak as a day-old chick. 'Harriet is being taken care of. A man is seeing to the animals and a girl from the village is helping out in the house.'

'You did that?'

'Harriet is my tenant. It is my responsibility… Had I

known of her accident I would have arranged for help until she was on her feet.'

'And I wouldn't have come. We would never have met.'

Santiago contemplated the afternoon sun that was pooling on the dark wood beneath his feet and grunted. 'In a perfect world,' he agreed, thinking how much simpler his life had been a few short days ago.

He had said many worse things to her but strangely this hurt more than any of the others. It was not even a rebuke, it was just a rather obvious statement of fact—she had caused him nothing but trouble, had gone out of her way to do so.

'You're crying?' Santiago had always had a cynical attitude to female tears. At best they were irritating, at worst manipulative. His usual response was to walk away or ignore them.

For some reason he found himself able to do neither.

'No!' she said, sounding insulted by the suggestion. 'I'm fine.' She sniffed, sticking out her chin and looking anything but. 'And I'm sorry to have been a nuisance and put everyone to so much trouble.'

He shrugged. 'I think that as my brother poisoned you it was the least we could do.'

Lucy's eyes went wide as she blurted the question that she couldn't get out of her head. 'She wasn't riding Santana, was she?'

Santiago tensed, his body stiffening before he vented a hard laugh. 'Magdalena was afraid of horses.' It turned out that she was more afraid of his bad opinion. 'All horses. She would not have gone into the same stable as Santana. The mare she was on broke a leg in the fall and had to be put down.'

'But if she was afraid—?' She broke off, colouring. 'Sorry, it's none of my—'

'You want to know why my wife was riding if she hated

horses?' His voice was harsh. 'It is a fair question,' he conceded with a tight nod of his dark head. 'She went out riding because I said she should conquer her fears. I told her she should suck it up and stop being pathetic.'

His thoughts flew back to the incident that had preceded the tragedy; over the years he had replayed it innumerable times.

It had been Gabby's birthday. The previous day he had cleared his calendar to be part of the celebrations, cancelled a series of important meetings and had been feeling pretty smug about taking his paternal responsibilities seriously. Apparently he took his husbandly ones, in light of the subsequent events, much less so.

Magdalena was a great organiser and the party had been a big hit for everyone except his daughter, who had spent the day watching wistfully as her friends clambered on the bouncy castle and sat on the back of the placid Shetland pony while it was led around the garden.

When he had asked her if she wanted a turn she had shook her head. 'It's very dangerous. *Mamá* says I might get hurt.'

When he had carried her onto the bouncy castle her terrified sobs had been so pathetic that he'd had to remove her. He had known then that situation could no longer be ignored.

That evening he had confronted Magdalena, too angry to be tactful or gentle, accusing her of infecting their once-fearless daughter with her own insecurities and fears… He had shouted her down when she had protested that it was her duty to protect her child from danger.

'Danger! You think a lollipop represents danger,' he had mocked angrily. 'I will not have our daughter grow up to be a woman who is afraid of her own shadow.'

'A woman like me?'

The silence had stretched—they had had this conversation before, or a version of it, many times, and it was at this point where he rushed in to comfort her, but this time he had held back. He had previously told her everything would be all right and the situation had not improved; if anything it had deteriorated.

So Santiago, still angry with himself as much as her for allowing the situation to continue, had hardened his heart to the appeal in her eyes, ignored her quivering lip and said angrily, 'Yes.'

When they had married Santiago had been convinced that with his support and freed from her parents' oppressive influence his timid wife would blossom. He had seen himself as the noble hero Magdalena had thought him.

His lip curled into a contemptuous smile. He had thought it would be easy but in those days he had imagined that love could conquer all, that he could mould Magdalena into the woman he had known she could be.

In reality the gentle timidity that had originally drawn him to her and aroused his strongly developed protective instincts had begun to irritate him.

In retrospect he could see that his disenchantment had begun after Gabby had been born. He had always believed that a mother should be a strong role model for a daughter, but it had seemed to him that the only things Magdalena was passing on to their child were a lack of confidence and a whole host of phobias.

'She was doing what she thought I wanted,' he told Lucy now. *And you are having this conversation why, Santiago? And with the woman your brother is sleeping with, of all people.* 'Magdalena wanted to please me and it killed her—I killed her.'

*And you,* she thought, *have been punishing yourself ever since...* This was a side of Santiago Silva that she had never seen. Part of her way of coping with this man was listing him under the heading of inhuman—the suggestion he had normal vulnerabilities made her feel uneasy.

'If that were true you would be in prison,' she offered in a level voice. 'It was a terrible tragic accident,' she added, refusing to offer him the condemnation he appeared to be inviting.

'Accidents cannot be predicted.' And neither, it seemed, could her response—he'd thought he could have relied on her to take advantage of the chink in his armour.

The self-loathing in his voice made her wince. 'What do you want me to say—that it was your fault?'

'I do not wish you to say anything.' She could have legitimately asked why he had introduced the subject, but she didn't. After a quick glance at his face she reached for the crystal water jug, not anticipating the weight of it. Her wrist trembled, sending an ice cube skidding across the polished surface of the bedside table.

With a grunt Santiago took it from her hand, his fingers brushing hers. The contact was light but the response of her nerve endings was anything but… It zigzagged through her body like an internal lightning bolt.

'Let me—you'll have the place drenched.'

She watched from under her lashes, nursing her still-tingling fingers against her chest as he filled her glass with a steady hand.

'You have a lovely daughter,' she said, turning the conversation into a less painful topic. 'She is back home?'

'An extended summer break. My lovely daughter has been excluded from school…again. However I'm sure my daughter's schooling is of no interest to you.' Women who were ruled by self-interest were rarely interested in any subject that did not directly affect them.

*Self-interest has her living in a primitive farmhouse, acting as unpaid labour and nursemaid?*

Santiago turned a deaf ear to the contribution of his objective self. He hadn't figured out what her endgame was yet, but he was confident that it would in time become clear just what lay behind this apparently altruistic act of helping out a friend.

The blue eyes turned to him were not uninterested; they had softened with what appeared genuine sympathy. 'She's unhappy?'

His jaw tightened in response to the combination of the probing question and the overflow of empathy aimed his way. This was the reason he did not open up, not even to his own family. After Magdalena died there had been far too many who had viewed him as a tortured soul they could save—it was not a role he had any intention of adopting.

'She is spoilt.' His tone signalled the subject was closed. The message was not ambiguous, but Lucy either didn't pick up on it or chose not to.

'Perhaps she doesn't like school...?' Even as she made tentative suggestion she was anticipating a frigid 'mind your own business' response—it didn't come.

'Like? Life requires we do things we do not like.'

Did she not think that he didn't want to protect his child from everything in life that could hurt her? Following his instincts would not prepare her for what life would throw at her. Of course he was concerned that he had the balance wrong, that he was going too far, being too tough...

Habits, he brooded darkly, were notoriously hard to break and he had spent the early years playing the bad-cop parent to Magdalena's good cop in an effort to achieve some sort of balance.

His frustration found release in his snarling addition.

'Duty may be an alien concept to you...'

Lucy let go of the pillow she was clutching in front of her as an energising flash of anger brought her bolt upright in bed. 'Yes, well, let's just pretend for the moment that I have a vague idea of what it means.'

'I hated school also, but a person does not run away from things they hate… It is habit forming.' And Santiago was not about to allow his daughter to develop this habit.

Lucy was unimpressed by the logic. 'Is that from the same book that says what doesn't kill you makes you stronger? Has it occurred to you to ask her why she runs away?'

He slung her an impatient look. Did the woman think he was stupid? 'Of course I have asked her.' He gritted his teeth and delivered a white clenched smile. 'And I find myself reluctant to take advice on parenting from someone who is hardly a role model for any young woman.'

Lucy's expression froze over. 'Well, I'll try not to infect her with my…' She stopped and took a steadying breath. 'I'm sorry to have put you to so much trouble,' she added with frigid formality. 'Not you personally, obviously, but your staff. Everyone has been very kind.'

'As I told you—it was the least we could do.' Actually the least would have been not fighting with her while she was whacked with exhaustion and ill.

That silent addendum was pretty implicit in her blue eyes.

And it was true, Santiago acknowledged. He had felt her getting close and the irony was he knew he only had himself to blame. He had opened the door and invited her to stamp around in her size fives in his head and then he had reacted instinctively to push her away as hard and brutally as possible.

'How is Ramon?'

'I'm visiting him this afternoon,' he told her coldly.

'Will you give him my love?'

Santiago's face was a mask of contempt as he looked down at her and snarled, 'No, I will not!'

She recoiled from the anger in his reply. 'Fine, I'll do it

myself when I get out of here and don't worry—it will take an earthquake to keep me here a second longer than necessary!' she yelled after his retreating back.

# CHAPTER TEN

WHEN the doctor called a few minutes later Lucy was feeling so wretched that she was not surprised when he said that the bug she had contracted was a particularly virulent strain. In fact, she almost retorted—yes, the Santini Strain!

Lucy, who had been hoping for permission to leave, was dismayed when he announced he wanted her to stay in bed until the next day and after that he would review the situation.

In the event, she did not feel much like getting out of bed. She slept a good deal of the time, waking on one occasion during the early evening to find Gabby perched on the end of her bed.

She knew that Santiago would be furious if he found her there and, as the girl began with, 'Don't worry, *Papá* has gone to the hospital to see Uncle Ramon,' it was pretty obvious that the child had been warned not to visit.

She was saved from having to shoo the child away by the arrival of Josef, who came with one of the rehydration drinks that the doctor had instructed she take through the evening.

He left taking a reluctant Gabby with him.

The next morning Lucy was feeling better and would have welcomed a visit from Gabby to stop her replaying every conversation she had ever had with Santiago in her head over and over. She had improved on many of her responses and never made others.

When he arrived she was able to assure the doctor that she had spent a comfortable night; there were some things you didn't tell anyone, even your doctor, and the dreams that she had woken from hot, sweaty and shaking the previous night came under that heading!

After a medical twenty questions he pronounced himself happy for her to go home if she managed a light lunch with no ill effects.

Lucy would have loved to have explored the fascinating building, but she reluctantly passed on the opportunity, keeping to her room to avoid the possibility of running into Santiago, and he did not seek her out—not that she had expected him to. He might have been avoiding her, but it was equally likely that he had forgotten she was there. With this self-pitying reflection she made herself consume a portion of the light lunch that was served on a silver tray.

Another night in this place was not an option.

'I feel so bad about Lucy.'

His brother looked like death warmed up and in deference to his weakened condition he had not brought up the subject uppermost in his mind, but now that Ramon himself had introduced it Santiago found himself unable to hold back.

'For God's sake, Ramon, I know you're bewitched by the woman and I admit she is…compelling…but—'

Ramon waved the hand attached to an intravenous drip. 'But I'm not sleeping with her.'

He saw his brother's expression of disbelief and gave a weak smile.

'Oh, don't get me wrong, I would if I could, or rather if *she* would. She isn't interested in me. I found out about you warning her off and I… The truth is I'm fed up of you trying to run my life. For God's sake, Santiago, how am I meant to learn from my mistakes if you never let me make any?

'I knew you'd got it into your head that poor Lucy is some sort of dangerous femme fatale and I wanted to…' he took a deep breath, there were some advantages to being at death's door—his brother couldn't hit him '…teach you a lesson.' He waited for a reaction and when there wasn't one added crankily, 'For God's sake, say something. I'm dying here.'

'You're not sleeping with her?' If Ramon was not, then he… Santiago's chest swelled as he released a deep sigh. 'Good.'

'That's it—good?'

Santiago's lips curved into a slow smile as he bared his white teeth and confirmed softly, 'Very good.'

Very good that he no longer had to feel jealous of his own brother. That he no longer had to rationalise his determination to keep Ramon out of Lucy's bed and finally that he no longer had to pretend that Lucy's bed wasn't exactly where he, Santiago, wanted to be.

What was not good about the anticipation of enjoying sex with a beautiful, experienced woman? He would satisfy this hunger and get Lucy Fitzgerald out of his system.

A few hours later, staying that extra night was looking like a real possibility. Drumming her fingers on the table top in the small salon she had been seated in to wait for transport, Lucy glanced at her watch.

She was deciding to give it half an hour before she took matters into her own hands and called a taxi when the door opened. She half rose and then sat down heavily, the eager expression on her face fading to one of almost comic horror.

'I didn't expect to see you still here.' Santiago stood there looking down, arrogance and hauteur etched in every angle and plane of his incredible face. 'I thought nothing short of

a natural disaster would keep you here a second longer...'
That and Josef, who could always be relied on to rise to the
occasion. The man, he decided, deserved a raise. He'd said
do not let her leave but Josef was more subtle.

Lucy flushed and got to her feet. 'I'm still waiting for the
car,' she explained in a small stiff voice. 'Josef said it won't
be long.' That had been two hours ago.

He elevated a sardonic brow.

'I'm sorry if I've overstayed my welcome...' She walked
towards the door, back ramrod stiff.

'Sit down.' He sighed.

Responding to the pressure of the hand on her shoulder,
Lucy sank back down into her seat, her breathing coming
quicker as she combated the electrical tingle caused by the
light contact.

His eyes brushed her face and for a brief moment she saw
something in his dark hooded stare that made her stomach
lurch, then it was gone—if it had ever been there...? Lucy
had started to mistrust her own senses when she was around
him.

She concentrated on not panting—pretty much a give-
away as he walked across the room to the bureau, pulling
the heavy stopper off a decanter sitting there. He poured a
finger of the liquid into a glass and proceeded to toss it off
in one swallow, then he reached for the decanter again.

He refilled it before looking directly at her. 'Is that what
I said?'

'No,' she conceded, noticing that he looked relaxed...yet
those tensed bunched muscles in his neck told a different
story. 'But—'

'Are you this defensive and prickly with everyone or is it
just me?' He ground the words from between clenched teeth
as he covered the bottom of another glass. 'Do you think I
am not capable of saying what I mean?'

She thought of saying she didn't drink spirits, but decided the stuff might be of some medicinal benefit so after a pause she took the glass he held out to her. She nodded graciously before she held it to her nose and breathed in the fragrance.

'I'm sure you're totally capable of…' She stopped, losing her train of thought as her gaze met his. A comment from a deeply in lust acquaintance popped into her head: 'God, I can't look at him without thinking how incredible he'd be in bed.'

At the time Lucy had struggled to imagine what that would be like.

'I'm…cautious with people,' she blurted, drawing his curious stare to her face.

She lowered her eyes but continued to watch him over the rim of the glass, thinking, *Not cautious enough with you.*

She should, she realised, have run in the opposite direction the moment she saw this man. Instead she had spent her time inventing reasons to be around him, telling herself she was a victim of circumstance, when in reality she had been a victim of her libido.

*So just add me to the list of women that have made fools of themselves to catch the eye of Santiago.*

*Cautious* struck him as an interesting choice of word and one that he would never have applied to someone who seemed to act first, think later.

She had lectured him on parenting, stolen a valuable horse without thinking and now, it turned out, been part of a conspiracy to teach him a lesson. 'So I'm not special.'

If only, she thought as he shrugged off his jacket and draped it around the back of a chair. His innate elegance as always sent a shimmy of sensation down her spine. Her fascination with him—with everything about him—showed no sign of diminishing. If anything it became stronger. He was like an addictive drug in her bloodstream. *Look but don't inhale, Lucy,* she told herself, *and never, ever touch!*

Lucy followed him with her eyes while he loosed the tie he wore around his neck; she had never imagined she could get pleasure just from looking at a man.

'I was just catching up with my emails,' she said, nodding to the machine on the table, adding, 'Josef said it would be all right. Harriet doesn't have internet access, and I was hoping to see you,' she lied.

'I'm flattered.' He selected a chair, pulled it a little closer to her and lowered his long lean frame into it with another display of riveting fluid grace.

'I was hoping you had news of Ramon.' As their eyes met Lucy had the horrid feeling he could see right through her lie; she felt terrible because she actually hadn't thought of Ramon once this evening.

'Second best again.' He sighed. 'You know how to put a man in his place.'

The prospect of becoming Lucy's lover excited him as nothing had in a very long time. She challenged him and not just with her incredible looks. She was the most stunningly beautiful creature he had ever seen, but he had discovered that Lucy had an intellect to match her beauty. All that and the woman ate him up with her hungry eyes... She literally trembled with lust when their hands brushed. All the bloody restraint he had been displaying was killing him.

His concentration was shot to hell; he couldn't focus on anything; in short he had lost his edge and the cure for his problems was within tantalising reach. He blinked to clear the image of her, magnificent and naked, straddling him, flashing through his head. Lost his edge...? Hell, at times it felt as if he had lost his mind!

While she was obviously not the two-dimensional scarlet woman the media had painted her, she clearly had a past, but then who didn't? He did not require every woman he took to bed to be a blameless virgin. In fact had such a female existed such attributes would have immediately put her off-limits, not to mention bored him senseless.

The last thing Santiago was looking for at this stage in his life was a woman who had been waiting for the 'right man'; he was nobody's right man.

He had tried denying the existence of this strong attraction—it hadn't worked. He had tried waiting for it to pass—it hadn't. That just left working through it...the third was by far the most attractive option.

'I've had an interesting conversation with Ramon.'

Lucy tensed at the seemingly casual comment. Her guilty conscience was making her jumpy—if Ramon had come clean about their fake romance, Santiago would have come in here breathing fire and retribution.

The knowledge made her relax slightly.

'How is he?' she asked, matching his casual tone as she sat back in her seat, leaning her elbows on the wooden arms of the chair.

'They are discharging him at the weekend.'

Her relief was genuine. 'Great!'

'So you can take up where you left off with the big romance.'

'I wouldn't call it a big romance...exactly...' she muttered, dodging his gaze and taking another gulp of the brandy—too much too fast. She choked as it hit the back of her throat and settled in a warm glow in the pit of her stomach.

'No? What would you call it?'

'It's hard to say,' she admitted, sidestepping the issue.

Santiago laced his fingers and, resting his chin on the bridge they made, smiled at her. 'Try.' His voice was not smiling; neither were the eyes fixed like lasers on her face.

She slung him an irritated glance, compressed her lips and

crossed one ankle over the other. 'We're not in a long-term relationship, all right?' she snapped without looking at him.

'And have you ever been—with anyone?'

'The odds are not exactly stacked in favour of lasting relationships, are they?' The sad fact did not stop her being a ridiculous optimist and believing that there was someone out there for everyone, just sometimes they missed one another.

The reply would only have displeased a man who was looking for long term and he wasn't. 'So you are not looking for anything permanent.' All good, he told himself.

*Show me a woman who says she isn't and I'll show you a liar*, she thought. 'Permanent requires making concessions and I'm not good at that.'

'So you don't believe that there is someone out there who will complete you…a soul mate…?'

Was that what his pretty wife had been, his soul mate?

Lucy lifted her gaze, bright smile in place the moment their eyes meshed. Her smile guttered as she searched his face and her eyes widened.

'You know.'

'Know what?'

The display of fake ignorance drew a growl from Lucy.

'Ah,' he drawled. 'You are referring to the fact you haven't actually slept with my brother, that there is no steamy affair.'

In retrospect Santiago could see that he should have guessed the truth sooner, and would have had his judgement not been clouded by sexual jealousy. He had watched them together, seen them flirt and fought a desire to rip them apart. If he'd been thinking straight he might have seen past the window dressing to the lack of chemistry.

Her chin went up. 'Not yet.'

'Not ever!'

He acted with bewildering speed and zero warning. One minute he was lounging in the chair several safe feet away, the next he was right there, pulling her out of her chair and drawing her body up against his hard, lean front.

She opened her mouth to ask him what the hell he thought he was doing when he took her face between his big hands, framing it with his fingers, resting his thumbs in the angle of her jaw as he tipped her face up to his.

The rampant wild hunger in his glowing eyes drew a raw whimper from her aching throat.

His eyes were like a dark flame as they moved across her face. 'You're so beautiful.' His powerful chest lifted in a silent sigh as he shook his head in an attitude of disbelief. 'I keep looking for a flaw but there isn't one.'

Lucy trembled, weak with lust and longing as she stared up at him with passion-glazed drowning blue eyes. 'What is happening?' she whispered.

'I think you know.'

Her stomach quivered and clenched as his long fingers speared deep into the single skein of her hair, lifting it off her neck to expose the smooth lines of her throat.

Her head went back as his warm lips nuzzled the wildly beating blue-veined pulse spot at the base of her throat. The moist contact sent a fresh slug of frantic desire shuddering through her trembling body.

Her even white teeth clamped along the quivering curve of her full lower lip and her heavy lids drifted closed as he moved up her throat, his lips barely touching her skin, the light contact blitzing a tingling, erotic trail of sensation.

His lips brushed her cheekbone, her ear, then, lifting his head, he touched the cushiony softness of her full lower lip, dragging his thumb across the outline before he bent his head. Slowly he fitted his mouth to hers, but when the kiss came it was not slow, it exploded, searing, not gentle, but rough, raw and hungry. Swept away on a swirling tide of elemental need, she reached up her arms, circling his neck as she met the darting intrusion of his tongue with her own, the taste of him exciting her unbearably.

As they kissed his hands were on her body, sliding down her spine, cupping her bottom, pulling her up and against the rock-hard bold imprint of his erection.

'You've been waiting for this.'

She looked into the silver lights shining in his dark eyes and felt dizzy. 'Yes,' she admitted, thinking, *I've been waiting for you.*

Nostrils flared, he breathed in the scent of her hair. 'I want to wrap myself in this,' he said, letting the pale strands slip through his fingers. 'I want to be inside you.'

The throaty admission sent a jolt of sexual longing through her body and the need inside her rose until she could barely breathe, think... 'Take me to bed, Santiago?' she whispered, simultaneously shocked and excited by her own boldness. 'Please.'

The febrile glitter of passion in his dark eyes made her tremble while for several heart-stopping moments he searched her face, then nodded. Taking her hand, he walked towards the bookcase, then, pressing a hand to a panel, stood to one side as a large section swung open.

'A secret door!' she gasped.

'Hardly a secret, but it is useful.'

Lucy entered the secret space and found herself, not in a traditional dark and gloomy room but surrounded by limestone walls that gleamed in the electric light that shone from sconces. All the way up the spiral stone staircase a heavy red rope strung to the wall provided handholds.

How many women had he taken up these stairs? Lucy wondered as she began to climb the stone spiral staircase concealed inside the wall, the growing sense of anticipation making her heart beat hard.

She shook her head and pushed the thought away. Forget

the others—this was her night. At the top Santiago reached over her shoulder and pressed a panel, the door this end opened into a massive panelled room.

'My bedroom,' he said, watching her face. 'And my bed,' he added.

His dark intense gaze didn't leave her face for one second as he led her across to the carved oak bed that took pride of place. He peeled back the plain white bedlinen and deposited Lucy on the bed.

Not sure she'd ever get used to being picked up as though she were small and fragile, Lucy pulled herself up on her knees, swaying as the mattress beneath her moved.

She pushed her hair from her eyes and looked at him. 'Santiago...?'

He responded with a grunt of acknowledgement and continued to strip off his clothes.

'I need to say something.' Need, not want. Nobody on the brink of having sex with— 'Oh, God!' she gasped as he fought his way successfully out of his shirt, having sent the buttons scattering noisily across the floor.

There was not an ounce of surplus flesh on his hard body to hide the perfect muscle definition. Every individual muscle in his torso was perfectly delineated beneath his satiny gold skin.

Moist heat flashed between her thighs, but she felt a tremor of fear. He was magnificent. Certainly not the sort of person to whom you wanted to admit: 'I'm not great in bed but I'll do my best.'

'Look, I'm not...there's something you should know about me—'

This time the distraction was even more severe. Having kicked away his trousers, he was walking to the bed wearing just a pair of boxers that were totally inadequate to disguise the level of his arousal.

A pulse of sexual longing slammed through her body.

'We have all done things we are not proud of.'

Oh, God, he obviously thought the thing she wanted to get off her chest was more along the lines of 'my night of passion with a football team', not 'I'm actually a clueless virgin'.

He arranged himself beside her, long, sleek and incredible, and slid his hand inside her shirt. 'No, really—' The rest of her protest was lost in his mouth, then a second later gone...as his tongue stabbed deep into her mouth and she thought, *I can do this!*

It felt natural...easy and wildly exciting to kiss him back, touch his skin, taste... 'Oh, God, I want to taste you.' Fascinated by the fluid-looking ripple of muscle under his satiny skin, she reached out, spreading her fingers across the ridges of his flat belly, and felt him gasp.

*'Dios Mio!'* he groaned, tipping her onto her back and almost simultaneously slipping the buttons on her blouse with dexterity that suggested a lot of practice.

*Just as well one of us has*, said the practical voice in her head.

'You will,' he promised throatily. He buried his face between the soft swell of her warm breasts, pressing them together as he slid the straps down her shoulders, peeling back the lace cups to expose the rosy peaks of her breasts.

When he applied his tongue to first one rigid nipple and then the next, Lucy pushed her head deep into the pillows, exposing the long line of her white neck as she let out a low keening cry.

Her reaction drew a deep masculine growl of appreciation from his throat. *Madre di Dios*, she was so exquisitely sensitive!

One hand resting on her rapidly rising ribcage, he removed her bra completely, freeing up her magnificent breasts. The visual impact brought flashes of colour to the high contours of his cheekbones.

His hands were shaking as he removed her skirt and finally the little lace pants underneath. While he did so he was conscious of her passion-darkened eyes watching him from under her half-closed eyelids; the sexual tension crackling in the air around them was explosive.

A muscle in his lean cheek clenched as his hot glance slid over her silky pale curves. She was the epitome of all things feminine, there was not a sharp angle in her lovely body.

'You are a goddess,' he breathed.

Lucy shook her head. She did not want to be a goddess—they got put on pedestals. She wanted to be held and touched.

'No, I'm a woman.' *Your woman*, she said silently in her head.

The first skin-to-skin contact was overwhelming, a total sensory overload. Her hand slid to the tight curve of his buttock, hard under the boxer shorts he still wore.

Taking her hands captive, he rolled her onto her back and, pinioning them lightly, he knelt over her.

He released her hands as he moved down her body, touching her with his fingers and lips and tongue until all her skin was burning and tingling. She had no idea how long this sweet torment went on, but he seemed to know exactly where and how to touch her, to bring her to a point where there was only Santiago and mindless pleasure. The two were the same in her head.

'This is so…' She writhed, her head flung back, her arms curved above her head as he kissed his way damply down her stomach, still caressing her aching breasts as he moved lower. The hot, liquid throbbing ache between her legs had become almost unbearable when she felt his fingers slide along the silky skin of her inner thigh. She stiffened and felt rather than saw his questioning gaze.

'Is something wrong?'

Heart thumping a wild tattoo that vibrated through her body, she opened her eyes, her greedy gaze sliding over the gleaming muscled contours of his sleek, powerful body.

She looked at him and thought, *Nothing at all. I want this...* She had never wanted anything more than she wanted this...him...now.

In reply she shifted slightly and let her thighs part.

The symbolic invitation wrenched a low feral moan from his throat as he slid the shorts down over his hips.

Her awed gasp of, 'Oh, my goodness!' drew a fierce grin from Santiago, who kicked away the shorts.

Holding her eyes, he took her hand and curved her fingers around the satiny hard column of his erection.

Her blue eyes flew wide then as her fingers tightened. Heat spread through her body and she closed her eyes to intensify the tactile sensation.

'Enough!' Primitive hunger burning through his blood, Santiago took her hand in his and touched her, sliding his fingers across the engorged nub. Her wild cries of delirious pleasure deepened the level of his arousal.

Unable to resist the primitive fire burning in his blood, he could no longer fight the need to bury himself inside her, to feel her tightness around him.

Kissing her, he settled over her, nudging her thighs farther apart with his knee as he slid between them.

'Look at me.'

Lucy was looking at him when he drove deep into her.

She was too involved with what was happening to her own body, the incredible sensation of being filled and stretched, to register his hoarse cry of surprise.

She responded instinctively to the slow erotic movement of his body, rising to meet him, pulling him deeper, wrapping her long legs around him to hold him close to her core, sinking into herself with him.

The sensations were incredible, the pleasure so intense, so sweet, that it brought tears to her eyes. They slipped unchecked down her cheeks.

Swept along on a wave of sensation that was both exhilarating and terrifying in its intensity, she hung onto him, loving his weight pressing her down, loving his hardness filling her—loving him!

'Let go, let go...*querida*,' he urged between the kisses he pressed on her parted lips.

Lucy nodded in agreement even though she had no idea what he meant, then she did.

It felt like falling weightless through space. She had no control over the intense pulses of wild pleasure that spread out through her body like golden arrows; she just gave herself up to them and let it happen.

She was in the centre of this firestorm of hot sensation when she felt his hot pulsing release inside her.

# CHAPTER ELEVEN

'THIS isn't possible?' Though his skin was still hot and slick with sweat Santiago's face was very pale as he rolled away.

Not willing to lose the skin-to-skin contact so soon, Lucy looped her thigh across his hip and scooted in closer until they lay side by side again. She lay her head against his hair-roughened chest, running her finger around the flat, pebble hardness of a male nipple.

Lucy lifted her head in protest as he caught her hand and pressed it into the pillow.

'Lucy, will you stop that? I'm trying to…' He stopped. She looked like a lovely wanton angel lying there. How the hell was it possible that he had been her first lover…? A frown pleating his brow, he tried to join the mental dots but no matter which route he took nothing became clearer.

'You're trying to what? Work out why someone took out an injunction to stop a blackmailing bitch selling her sordid kiss-and-tell story when the bitch in question was a clue-less virgin?'

The muscles along his jaw tightened as Santiago ran his hand down her smooth thigh, dragging her in closer. 'Do not use that word.'

'Which one—bitch or virgin?' He did not smile back. 'All right, it isn't complicated, but it is long. I won't bore you with the details.'

'Bore me.'

His tone did not invite debate so she took a deep breath and launched reluctantly into her explanation.

'I did a charity catwalk show and I was introduced to Denis Mulville. He was an advertising executive working for one of the sponsors.

'Long story short, he made me an offer that he thought I couldn't refuse—I did.' She gave a shudder. The man with his horrible wet mouth, fake smile and fake tan had turned her stomach, but she had not realised at that time that he was dangerous.

'He was persistent, flowers and gifts, et cetera, but I sent them back and ignored him, assuming at first that he'd lose interest. Then things got a bit nasty—nobody says no to Denis Mulville apparently.' She felt the tension in Santiago's body and lifted her head. 'Nothing physical, just texts, emails, that sort of thing. Not threats, just suggestions—it was all quite subtle, not nice.'

Santiago, who had struggled to control his feelings while she had laid bare the bones of a story that made his blood boil, swore savagely under his breath. Not nice, a classic example of British understatement, but he was not British and there was nothing understated about the murderous rage hardening inside him.

'The man stalked you,' he said flatly. 'How was it the injunction was against you?' The world had condemned her and he had been only too eager to jump on the bandwagon taking her guilt as a given. He sucked in a deep breath, self-disgust tightening like a fist in the pit of his belly as he thought of the things he had said.

'His final revenge. I wouldn't sleep with him so he invented an affair, confided in friends—actually it seemed everyone knew about it except me. He laid the groundwork so when he claimed later that I was trying to blackmail him he was believed.'

Santiago swore. 'What happened to innocent until proved guilty?'

You did not, he told himself, have to care about a person to care about an injustice—and caring had nothing to do with admiration or respect. After all, how could you not respect someone who had risen above something that would have destroyed many? And she had done so with incredible dignity, not lowering herself even once to the level of the creep who had tried to destroy her.

'This wasn't a trial, it was an injunction. The same rules do not apply,' she told him quietly.

*'Madre di Dios!'* he grated, burying his face in her fragrant hair as he pulled her into his arms, dragging her body across his.

Lucy sighed as she pushed her face into the angle between his shoulder and chin.

'His identity was protected but not mine—my name was out there, and the best bit was I wasn't allowed to say a word... It was a total gagging order. I couldn't defend myself against anything they decided to write about me.' She rolled onto her back and grabbed a pillow, hugging it to her chest as though it would protect her from the memories.

As he listened to her relate the story in that flat little voice Santiago felt the tightness in his chest increase to the point where he could barely breathe past the outrage he was experiencing. How could she seem so calm, so lacking in bitterness after what had happened to her?

'But the same order protected his name, though of course everyone knew. You've got to hand it to him—it was the perfect revenge...almost poetic when you think about it. Now if I'd really been thinking on my feet I'd have told him I was gay.'

Santiago was not fooled by her laugh. 'He did this because you refused to go to bed with him.'

'Like I said, poetic.'

'Poetic it is…the man is…' He snarled a savage oath and said a word that was not in Lucy's vocabulary, one she was guessing she would not find in many dictionaries, either.

'He's petty and vindictive and not actually worth wasting my life thinking about.' Lucy had lost count of the number of times she had told herself this.

'But when the injunction was lifted…? You were free to speak then…?' This aspect puzzled him. Why hadn't she shot the bastard down in flames when the opportunity came to expose him to the world for what he was?

If it had been him he would have served up justice with a smile on his face and a figurative sword in his hand. Never mind a pound of flesh, Santiago would have claimed the whole worthless carcass!

Lucy tilted her head in acknowledgement as she pushed the pillow under her head. 'Oh, sure, I could have made a fortune with my story.' Despite her joking tone she had received offers. The mocking smile curving her lips vanished as she added sombrely, 'What would have been the point of resurrecting it?'

The dull thud pounding like a metronome in his temples, grappling with the information, the knowledge of what she had been through and come out smiling the other end…he felt a fresh stab of shame when he thought of how he had judged her… How many other people had done the same?

'Besides, everyone that mattered already knew I'd done nothing wrong. My family were great. They stood by me. I know it was hard for them reading that stuff about me, especially since Dad and I hadn't talked in three years, but when—'

'You were estranged from your father? I thought that the Fitzgeralds were tight.'

'We are but that doesn't mean we don't have our fallings out. Dad had plans for me but I wanted something different. With Dad there was only one way and that was his so...'

'He threw you out?' Santiago frowned. As a father he could never imagine a situation where he would deliver an ultimatum that would run the risk of him losing his daughter.

She nodded, seeming to him remarkably philosophical about the past.

'That's why I was modelling to begin with. My dad brought his kids up to be independent and strong, or that's his version of it.'

'Not your version?'

The question drew a rueful laugh from Lucy. 'No, more yours. I sometimes struggled to conform.' And frequently failed completely.

His dark brows hit his hairline. 'You're suggesting I'm like your father...?'

The startled offence in his voice dragged a laugh from Lucy. She ran a hand down his muscled flank and pressed a kiss against the centre of his hair-roughened chest.

Santiago's mind struggled to stay on track as his lust stirred into life.

'I suppose you have as much in common as powerful men with principles do.'

'So you think I have the odd principle.'

'You're not all bad,' she admitted huskily.

'So what was your father's version of strong?'

'Never admitting you're wrong even to yourself...oh, and tears are definitely out, and, well, actually I think his method of teaching his children to swim about sums up his attitude to parenting.'

Santiago's brows lifted. He knew the man by reputation obviously, but... 'Not seriously...?'

'Yep, he threw us in the deep end of the pool and we either sank or swum.' Santiago looked shocked so, anxious to dispel any impression that her father had been a monster, she added hastily, 'Not that he'd have let us actually drown. He threw us a lifeline if necessary.'

'And was it necessary with you?' He found himself seeing her as a kid trying to please her father, trying to keep up with her older siblings.

'No, I got to the side, after a fashion.'

'And what doesn't kill you makes you stronger...?'

The reminder of her earlier comment made Lucy grimace and grin.

'Or in your case fearless.'

Lucy heard the grudging admiration in his voice and thought, *If only you knew*. If he got to know the real Lucy he would be very disappointed, but no problem because he wouldn't.

'I get scared,' she admitted.

'When were you scared?'

'I was scared stiff of being awful in bed.' This was weird—after years of successfully boxing up her feelings she was leaking information like a sieve.

He ran a finger down the curve of her cheek and felt her tremble. His lips curved upwards into a smile that left his eyes dark and burning. 'You weren't.'

She lowered her eyes, suddenly feeling shy, which was crazy after what they had just shared.

'I get that after the Mulville guy you might have been wary of getting involved, but before surely there were boys... men?' It still made no sense to him that a woman who was so sensual should come to his bed a virgin.

'I dated when I was young but my dad scared them off.'

'The idea of Gabby bringing home boys brings me out in a cold sweat.'

She laughed and tossed a pillow at his head. 'You want to start worrying when she doesn't bring them home.'

He grinned back, looking so handsome that her heart flipped and skipped a beat. 'You have a point.'

'So didn't you have men queuing round the block when you were a model?' His dark glance made a leisurely journey from her soft lips to her full, firm breasts and back. He swallowed. 'I find that very hard to believe.'

'Actually you'd be surprised, but, sure, I dated a little. The thing was, it usually turned out that the guy wanted a trophy girlfriend to parade in front of his mates and I didn't fancy being anyone's arm candy. In my experience the nice guys assume you are unattainable when you're a model or brainless. I once thought of seeing...' She flushed a little as her eyes fell from his. 'But I chickened out. It all seemed so... clinical. That probably sounds stupid to you.'

Santiago thought of the woman he had shared a bed with this time last year and could not remember her face; she probably couldn't remember his. For a moment he almost envied Lucy. 'No, not stupid.' Just untarnished and idealistic—the sort of woman who could be hurt... He pushed away the thought.

There had been no coercion. She had wanted this as much as he had...so why couldn't he shift the vague sense of guilt?

'Besides, it was no problem.' She had simply assumed she was not highly sexed. 'Probably because I didn't know what I was missing.' Now she did, but it remained hard to imagine doing what she had with Santiago with any other man.

'And now you do.'

Lucy nodded, her eyes darkened to midnight-blue as she gazed into his face... The emotional ache of longing in her throat increased as she greedily absorbed the strong lines and planes of his proud patrician features.

'I've never been anyone's first before…' Cool and spiky on the outside and smouldering and sensual on the inside. The idea of being her second, third and fourth pretty much consumed him. He had never experienced the sort of rampant, relentless hunger he felt when he looked at Lucy in his life before. It was a chemical reaction, quite arbitrary, but it was easy to see why people who found themselves in the grip of such relentless passion mistook these feelings of lust for love.

Happily he was not in danger of making this mistake.

'Well, I'm glad you were mine—you made it very good for me.'

'We do seem…compatible…?'

Lucy nodded and wondered where this was going.

'You are here for a while?' She tipped her head. 'There is no reason that we should not continue to be compatible?'

'Sex, you mean?' How did that work—did they compare diaries? The cold-blooded approach made her uneasy. Casual sex had never really appealed to her, but she was not about to knock back the chance of having Santiago show her what she'd been missing. She was totally hooked and deeply in lust with him.

'You are looking for more?'

Despite the wariness she saw in his eyes, she resisted the temptation to say what she knew he wanted to hear, what a girl in her position was meant to say. Instead she responded with as much honesty as possible—total honesty would have meant admitting she would take anything he was willing to give, but she still had a modicum of pride.

'I don't know what I'm looking for, but I suppose that after this…' Her glance slid to the tumbled bedclothes as, unable to keep the wistfulness from her voice—what woman did not want to be wooed?—she added with a laugh, 'Dates and flowers would be kind of...' she felt his eyes on her face and shrugged '...not exactly required with someone as easy as me.'

His lips thinned in displeasure. 'I would not call you easy, Lucy. And I do not date, and for the record I have not given any woman flowers since my wife died.' The thought brought a familiar stab of guilt; flowers could not compensate for a total selfish lack of interest in a person.

Her amazed violet-blue eyes flew to his face. 'You mean you haven't done...this since— God, no, of course not,' she muttered, breaking off in embarrassed confusion.

For some inexplicable reason she kept blurting the first thought that came into her head, no matter how foolish...and it didn't get any more foolish than the suggestion of Santiago Silva living the life of a monk!

He looked faintly amused. 'No, I have not been celibate, that is not in my nature. I have had lovers but none who require or expect dates or flowers.'

Again before the thought was fully formed it leapt from her lips. 'You don't mean you sleep with...?' She stopped, this time blushing vividly.

Reaching out to touch the curve of her cheek, he felt her shiver. A woman had never responded to him the way she did. Smiling, he shook his head. 'Sleep with...' He stopped, a look of startled realisation spreading across his face as he caught her drift.

His hand fell away. 'I have never had to pay for sex, Lucy,' he said, not sure if he was insulted or amused by her comment.

'I'm not saying you would have to—obviously you could have anyone you wanted.'

Right now he wanted her—right now.

'I just thought you might...I read this story once when after the hero's girlfriend died he only slept with prostitutes because that way he didn't think he was being unfaithful to her memory…and I'm babbling, aren't I?'

Her comments had inadvertently made him think of the expensive parting gifts his secretary gift-wrapped at the end of a relationship, gifts that had not been unappreciated even though the recipients, women successful in their own right, had all been more than capable of buying their own jewels.

Did Lucy have a point?

'I am not looking for anything permanent, Lucy.'

Her eyes widened. 'God, no, of course not. I never thought that…you…I…that this was…'

'Come here and I will show you what I mean.'

There was nothing even faintly cold about the smouldering glow in his eyes. Lucy stopped talking with relief and gazed at him. 'Oh, yes, please!'

A week later there had been no diary comparing but a lot of sex, although the previous night had been the first time she had stayed over. Not because he had asked her to stay but because she had fallen asleep and woken at five.

It had taken all her willpower to resist Santiago's very persuasive argument to stay longer, but she had and he had not looked at all happy when she had dragged on her clothes and rushed back to the *finca*, dropping a hasty kiss on his lean cheek as she'd left.

She wasn't sure why it seemed so important to her for Harriet not to know she had spent the night; it wasn't as if she were ashamed. After all, having casual sex was not a crime and the older woman was no prude. And Harriet had to have known something was going on with Santiago because, it didn't matter how discreet you were, in a small community like this there were no secrets.

Even so the older woman had not brought up the subject. Perhaps she'd been waiting for her to do so? Lucy mused.

But what was she meant to say? She was not in a committed relationship. She could not talk about Santiago and say 'we'; they were not a couple. She had assumed that they were exclusive for the duration of the affair but it had not, she realised, been spelt out.

Should she bring up the subject? she wondered as she walked across the yard to the stable block. The idea of Santiago even thinking about other women while he was with her made her feel sick to the stomach... The thought that he could be with another woman and then come to her... Hand extended towards the stable door, she froze and closed her eyes, shuddering through a wave of intense nausea as her hand closed into a white-knuckled fist that left the imprint of her neatly trimmed nails in the skin of her palm.

The nausea was real; happily the knife she felt plunging in her chest was not...though, God, did it hurt! Lucy lifted her chin. She hardly recognised the emotions she was feeling... Hell, she hardly recognised herself. She took a deep breath and stepped into the shadowy coolness of the stable. She would, she decided, bring the subject up when she saw him.

The intention was forgotten the moment she heard the plaintive cry. She ran down to the end stall. The animal lying there in some distress bore little resemblance to the one some sixth sense had made her fetch in the previous evening from the pasture. Though she was not due, the heavily pregnant jenny had obviously gone into labour early and even to Lucy's inexpert eye it looked as if things were not going well.

Lucy dropped down beside the animal, making soothing noises and feeling totally useless as she made a cursory examination of the animal before she ran back into the house to ring for the vet. She struggled to maintain her calm in the face of the reply she received from the man's wife.

'So when are you expecting him back?'

Lucy, tapping her feet impatiently, gritted her teeth when

the answer proved frustratingly vague. Explaining the situation again, she asked that the vet call back as soon as possible.

'Whenever that might be,' she muttered to herself as she set the receiver down. Her hand lifted to her hair, sliding her fingers into the silky mesh. God, what was she meant to do next? If Harriet had been there...but Harriet wasn't there. A neighbour had taken her for her physio appointment and she wasn't due back for another hour at least.

An hour could be too long, Lucy thought...

She had punched Santiago's private mobile number into the phone before she had even consciously registered what she was doing.

'I don't know why I'm ringing—you're probably busy and—'

The pleasure Santiago felt at the sound of her husky musical voice—he had never imagined that a woman's voice could give him so much pleasure—was swiftly replaced by anxiety as he registered the uncharacteristic panic in Lucy's tone.

'I am not busy,' he said, closing his laptop as he glanced out at the distant helicopter that was at that moment disgorging suited figures, black blobs in the distance. He had flown them in for the meeting he had already cancelled twice because he was working his schedule around his love...sex life.

The mental correction smoothed the indent between his dark brows. A sex life he could handle; a love life was too high maintenance.

The chemistry between them was so strong that he had been confident that the fire would burn itself out quickly, but if anything it was stronger than it had been. And despite the combustible raw quality of their lust she still managed to make him laugh in bed and, even more amazingly, out of bed, but then Lucy was, as he was discovering, an incredibly smart woman and unlike the other smart women he knew she seemed remarkably undriven.

Lucy swallowed. 'I don't know why I'm ringing you,' she admitted, 'but I didn't know who else and you...' She stopped, thinking, *Whenever I feel bad or am in trouble your voice will make me feel better...* Was that part of being in love?

Her knees sagged and she sat down heavily. Luckily there was a chair there to break her fall. *Oh, God, Lucy, you idiot!*

'I am glad you did. Now take a deep breath and tell me what is wrong.'

*Other than the fact I've fallen in love with you?* she thought, before taking the suggested deep breath and laying the facts out in a voice that showed a marked tendency to tremble... Her voice never trembled.

How could she be in love with someone she didn't even like a lot of the time, someone she had originally hated? Admittedly she'd never been indifferent to him, for Santiago was not a man who inspired indifference. Respect, yes, and admiration; she had seen this with her own eyes. And she admired him, not because he was rich or powerful, but because he was a man who wanted to be a good father, a man who cared for his younger brother, a man who set himself impossibly high standards and all the time there was that deep sadness she sensed in him... Would he always pine for his lost wife and feel responsible?

The tension that had been holding every muscle in his body rigid loosed its vicious grip as Santiago listened.

'A donkey...this is about a donkey?' A tidal wave of relief washed over him as he banished the images of Lucy in peril that his fertile imagination had conjured.

The suggestion of laughter in his voice brought an angry sparkle to her eyes. 'Are you laughing at me?'

'Not laughing, no…I will be there in less than five minutes.'

Lucy put the dead phone down. As always Santiago was not a man who used two words when one would do, but on this occasion she felt his promise had been optimistic.

She had not allowed for his innovation or his access to expensive toys, she realised as she watched a helicopter put down on a flat area several hundred metres from the *finca*.

Santiago, looking devastatingly handsome, dark and exclusive in a silver-grey suit and dark red silk tie, strode across the meadow to join her.

He did not waste time with small talk.

'Show me the way.'

Inside the stable Santiago took off his jacket, unclipped his watch and rolled up the sleeves of his white shirt to reveal his strong hair-roughened forearms before dropping down in the straw beside the animal.

He ran his hands over the animal, speaking in a soft soothing voice.

'Her name is Bonnie,' Lucy supplied.

'As in Bonnie and Clyde?'

Lucy tipped her head in acknowledgement. 'You look like you know what you're doing,' she said, impressed by the competent way he was gently examining the animal.

He lifted his head and delivered a heart-stopping white grin.

'I'm all you've got so let's hope so, *querida*.' He had seen horses delivered and had helped himself as a boy, but not for years. 'I'm assuming a horse is much like a donkey. Lucy, I need some water and soap.'

She nodded and went away, coming back a few moments later with what he had requested. 'Is there anything I can do?'

'I'll let you know. She's done all the hard work—she just

needs a little help, don't you, girl? I think I should be able to free the legs manually.'

Taking this as a request to keep out of his way, she took a few paces back as he stripped off his shirt and plunged his hands and forearms into the bucket of water.

Lucy lowered her eyes and stared at her hands. She needed a manicure, she thought, extending her fingers, but not as much as she needed a little self-control. Her lustful appreciation of his beautifully muscled back was wildly inappropriate considering the circumstances.

'It's a boy.'

With a gasp Lucy looked up in time to see the new mother nudge her damp baby and begin to clean him as he staggered to his feet.

Tears sprang to her eyes. 'Oh, that's so beautiful.'

'Yes, very beautiful.'

Something in his voice made Lucy turn her head. She discovered that Santiago, who was drying his hands on his very expensive jacket, was looking not at the newborn but at her. She felt the warmth bloom in her cheeks as her tummy went into a deep dive.

She brought her lashes down in a protective sweep to hide the emotions she was struggling to contain. 'You were brilliant. I'm really grateful.'

He tilted his head. 'I do my best.'

Santiago's best was in her experience better than perfect.

'But actually I did little.'

Other than leave a dozen high-powered executives standing watching as he had jumped into the helicopter they had just vacated and ruin a suit in reaction to her plea for help, said the voice in his head.

'It was very chivalrous.'

The women who had shared his bed, the ones he told upfront that the only female he altered his schedule or put himself out for was his daughter, might have called it something else.

Santiago's acknowledgement stopped short of speculating what word his previous lovers might use to describe his actions.

Lucy watched as he pulled on his shirt. On anyone else she might have described the dark ridges along his high cheekbones as a blush but this was Santiago, she reminded herself, dismissing the idea.

'I'm just glad I came back this morning when I did,' she said, her brow puckering as she recalled how close she had come to remaining in bed with Santiago. Where he was concerned her willpower went out of the window.

He stopped fastening his shirt and stared at her. Conscious as he did so of the tight knot of smouldering resentment and dissatisfaction that had lingered in the pit of his belly all morning loosening. 'So you were concerned about the animal—that is why you would not stay.' He had never had a woman refuse an invitation to remain in his bed, but it was not bruised ego or sexual frustration that had made him unable to dismiss the incident—he had virtually begged. Santiago knew his dissatisfaction went deeper.

Accepting now that the root of the problem was he no longer wanted casual, hard for him to think let alone say, the question remained: if a fling with Lucy did not satisfy him, what would?

This was uncharted territory for Santiago and he wanted to sort out his own feelings before he shared his thoughts with Lucy—bring it into the open and there was no going back. Others had paid for the mistakes he had made in the past and he would not allow that to happen again.

*It's called scared*, mocked the unsympathetic voice in his head.

On the way to his face Lucy's eyes travelled over the

golden expanse of his deeply muscled chest. Things deep in her pelvis quivered as she fought the urge to touch his skin. 'I told you.'

'Did you?' he husked, lifting a strand of silver pale hair from her cheek and watching her bewitching blue eyes darken before he bent his head to touch his lips to the exposed curve of her neck.

Lucy shivered and clung, pressing her face into the angle of his shoulder. 'Yes, I explained.'

'I couldn't have been listening. It is possible, I think,' he slurred against her mouth, 'that I had my mind elsewhere.'

'I wanted to stay,' she admitted as she emerged breathless from a deep, drowning kiss. 'But I…'

He took a deep breath and pulled back from her. 'I know you have made a commitment to your friend and I respect that.' That did not mean it didn't frustrate the hell out of him. 'But the situation will not always be this way. When the plaster is off and you are a free agent…'

Lucy's heart rate escalated. 'Yes…?' she prompted.

'Then we will review the situation.'

The anticlimax was intense… She'd anticipated warm and loving and got a bucket of cold and clinical right in the face, and it was all her own fault for allowing herself to harbour unrealistic expectations because she had fallen for him. That was mad but a fact, and trying to convince herself that he felt the same way would be compounding the insanity.

'Great, I can hardly wait,' she flung carelessly over her shoulder as she picked up the bucket and stalked away, head high, hoping to prove that she could do cold and clinical, too.

Frowning heavily, he caught up with her at the door.

Lucy reluctantly responded to the heavy hand on her shoulder and turned back.

'Have I done something to annoy you?'

Refusing to meet the dark eyes searching her face, Lucy shrugged carelessly, knocking his hand from her shoulder. 'Not a thing.'

Cursing under his breath, Santiago followed her out into the yard. He stopped short, almost colliding with Lucy, who had stopped dead.

'I don't believe this,' he heard her mutter.

'I think in military terms they call this a three-pronged attack.' In personal terms they called it too many people, he thought as he watched his daughter emerge from his estate manager's Land Rover, the vet from his car and Harriet from the neighbour's MPV.

He managed to restrain Gabby until after the vet had examined the new mother and baby and pronounced both to be fit and well. She then dragged Lucy back into the barn. Santiago, who would have liked to drag Lucy back in the barn himself, though not to visit the donkeys, watched as he fielded the seemingly innocent questions being tossed at him by an avidly curious Harriet, questions that made it clear that Lucy had not discussed their relationship with her friend.

Didn't women tell each other everything? He had certainly always operated on this principle, never confiding in bed anything he did not want repeated, but it appeared Lucy was an exception.

He excused himself as quickly as he could politely do so and went back to retrieve his daughter.

Gabby was perched on the rail around the animal stall, watching with starry eyes the newborn foal and mother. Sometimes the overwhelming love he felt for his daughter hit him, rendering him speechless, like a bolt from the blue. This was one of those times—it made all the sleepless nights of worry worth it.

Lucy sensed his presence courtesy of the hairs on the back of her neck before Gabby did. The expression in his beautiful eyes as he watched his daughter brought a lump to Lucy's throat... She felt almost an intruder on a private moment, but before she could look away he turned his head.

Their glances locked.

'That's what I want to be.'

The sound of Gabby's happy voice broke the spell that had held Lucy mesmerised. She realised her hands were shaking and pushed them into her pockets, watching as Santiago ruffled his daughter's hair and teased, 'A donkey?'

Gabby rolled her eyes. 'No, a vet, silly!'

'I'm sure you can be anything you wish, but for now I think we should be getting back and leaving mother and baby in peace.'

'Must we?'

'We must.'

Gabby sighed. 'All right.' She ran to Lucy and hugged her.

Not sure what Santiago's reaction to this spontaneous display of affection might be, she didn't look at him as she hugged Gabby lightly back. Did her undefined role allow for such familiarities?

'And you will come to dinner tonight, won't you?'

This time Lucy did look at Santiago, hoping to convey with her helpless expression that this had not been at her instigation.

'I invited Lucy to dinner,' Gabby announced importantly.

'So I see.'

Lucy could read nothing in his expression. 'I think I'm—'

Santiago's drawl cut across her. 'Good idea.'

'It is?' she said, startled.

Santiago delivered one of his silky smooth smiles. 'I wish it had been mine...' His experience of relationships that involved anything more than sex was rusty, to put it mildly. 'Then shall we say seven for half past?'

Her thoughts spinning in circles of speculation, Lucy nodded. 'Fine.'

'I really like Lucy,' his daughter confided as they walked across the yard.

*So do I...* His forehead pleated in a frown. 'You do know that Lucy has a life of her own—that she won't be here for ever, Gabby.' A life that did not involve him.

'Why?'

'Well, because...' He stopped. 'She just does.'

Beside him Gabby skipped. 'But not for ages yet.'

'No, not for ages yet.'

When she arrived for dinner at the appointed time it was Josef that showed her into the salon and poured her a glass of wine. She was nursing it when Gabby bounced in.

'I need your help!' she said dramatically.

'So you had an ulterior motive for your invitation.'

'This is serious—I'm talking about my future!'

'Sorry,' Lucy said with suitable gravity.

'I hate my school.'

'You mentioned.'

Gabby frowned at the interruption. 'And I don't want to go back next semester. I've been doing some research and I think this is the solution.' She dropped a glossy brochure in Lucy's lap. 'It's only a half-hour drive, five minutes by helicopter and I could be a weekday border.'

'You seem to have it all sorted.'

'They have an excellent academic record plus a brilliant art department, which is important because that's what I'm going to be, if I'm not a vet...but we won't tell *Papá* that bit yet. Just emphasise the academic stuff and tell him that I miss him like mad, 'cos I do.'

'We...?'

'Well, you really, he won't listen to me but he—'

'Oh, no, Gabby, I'd love to help but I can't. This is between your dad and you. He wouldn't like it if I got involved.'

Gabby's bottom lip began to quiver. 'Please,' she said, channelling beaten puppy.

'I wish I could, Gabby, but you should talk to your dad.'

'What should she talk to her dad about?'

Lucy closed her eyes and swore softly under her breath. This was getting to be a habit—she was going to put a damned bell around his neck!

His daughter snatched the brochure from Lucy's lap and threw it at her father. 'I know you'll say no, but just so as you know my life is *ruined*!' On this quivering note she ran from the room.

'What was that about?' Santiago asked, picking up the brochure. His frown deepened as he read the title page. 'How did she find out about St Mary's?'

'Find out?'

'St Mary's is one of the two schools I've whittled it down to. Well, it was obvious the other place didn't suit Gabby,' he said in response to Lucy's look of surprise, 'so I've been looking at alternatives and this one is close enough for her to be a weekly border.'

'Sounds perfect,' said Lucy, biting her quivering lip. 'How's the art department?'

'Exceptional as it happens. What,' he asked, walking up to take Lucy by the shoulders, 'was all that about?'

'Girls that age have hormones.'

*'Dios!'* He gulped, looking horrified.

'Nothing a little talk can't smooth over.'

'Later. You are looking very lovely this evening.' His eyes

were slow to rise from her cleavage. 'And I, too, have hormones.' His hormones were telling him to rip off her clothes and throw her down on the rug. His appetite for her remained unquenchable. 'We're not eating for a while...' he murmured.

Lucy was already shaking with desire. 'You have to go and talk to Gabby.'

He sighed and dragged a hand through his hair, casting one last wistful look at her mouth. 'I know...I always seem to say the wrong thing.'

The rueful confidence made her lips twitch. 'You're a great dad, Santiago,' she said, wondering how she could ever have thought otherwise.

'I am?'

She nodded. 'And Gabby is lovely, but she will make mistakes and it won't automatically be your fault.'

Aware that he was watching her with an odd expression, and wondering if he was about to warn her she had stepped over the invisible line she was always conscious of when it came to Gabby, she was amazed when he said, 'One day you'll make a great mother.'

*But not for your children!* The strength of her sadness was almost incapacitating.

'Wish me luck and remember where we were.'

'Good luck.' She managed to hold back the tears until he had left.

When he returned her smile was in place until he kissed it away.

Lucy emerged from the kiss feeling beautifully ravaged and breathless and, as it turned out, not at all hungry—for dinner at least.

Instead, she took his hand and without a word led him to the secret panel and her own personal stairway to heaven.

# CHAPTER TWELVE

'GIANNI and Miranda. It's a family wedding.' Lucy regarded the top of his dark head with frustration. 'Have you been listening to anything I have said?'

Santiago closed the lid of his laptop with slow deliberation and turned his narrow-eyed stare towards the figure by the window. Her attention was directed to the dog who had thrown himself down at her feet.

'That animal should not be indoors. You encourage him.'

Lucy patted the animal and pulled a face. 'Rules are made to be broken.'

'Rules are there to make things function smoothly.' She smiled and for a moment he forgot to breathe. She was backlit by the sun shining in through the window; the light picked out the silver highlights in her glorious ash-blonde hair and he felt his chest tighten... She was the most beautiful and desirable woman he had ever seen.

'So you are leaving this morning?' he said slowly. For the past week he had been convinced that there was something she was hiding from him. Was it this trip, he speculated, and if so why?

His brows twitched into a dark line of disapproval. He was already not in the best of moods as a direct consequence of Lucy spending the previous night, not in his bed, but at the *finca*. This surprise she had dropped on him did not improve it, though it did reveal why she had refused to stay the night. Presumably she had been packing for her trip, a trip she had not even mentioned until it was imminent. His frown deepened in direct proportion to his suspicions.

'I'll be back on Friday before the big day.'

'Big day?'

'Harriet has the plaster off next Monday and we planned to celebrate.' The bottle of champagne was on ice and after that there would be no reason for her to stay.

It was something that on a day-to-day basis she tried very hard not to think about. After all, why ruin the pretty near-perfect present? Since that day weeks ago now there had been no mention of the 'review'. Lucy knew from something Ramon had let slip before he left that Santiago ended all his relationships with a gift... Was his review shorthand for some shiny piece of bling? If so she would, she decided, throw it back at him.

'So soon?'

She couldn't leave.

Half of him resented the pressure to face up to his feelings, yet half of him welcomed the push. He had spent the past weeks enjoying the present and dodging the issue of the future. A future he had never imagined sharing with a woman and now, forced by her shock announcement to do so, he was horrified to realise that he could not imagine a future that did not have Lucy in it.

Losing Lucy would be like losing a limb, losing a vital part of him...the better part!

'So soon' had been pretty much Lucy's own reaction when she had seen the day circled on the calendar.

'Not soon—it's almost two months.'

Two months of going to sleep with her in his arms, hearing her voice every day and night. The thought of not...

Santiago took a deep breath, every fibre of his being rejecting the idea utterly.

A silence followed her words.

*What did you expect, Lucy?* she mocked herself. *That he'd suddenly discover that he couldn't live without you...? That he'd beg you to stay with him?*

She knew that for Santiago this had only ever been about sex. It had started out that way for her, too, but she could have sworn that over the past weeks it had changed, yet he never acknowledged the fact while she had foolishly allowed herself to dream and hope.

'I think Harriet will be relieved. She's resorted to throwing things on the floor to make it seem homely. She calls me a neat freak.' Her laugh sounded almost realistic.

'You are getting better,' he murmured. 'You no longer leap out of bed after we have made love to neatly fold your clothes.'

*Do not read anything into it,* cautioned the voice in her head, *but he said made love, not had sex.*

'At what?' she challenged.

He arched a brow and she blushed, drawing a husky laugh from him. 'I sometimes forget that you were...still deep down I think you remain the blushing virgin.'

Her eyes fell from his as she tried to hide her disappointment. 'I really should get going.'

'You are back Friday?' he repeated, thinking, *That gives you two days to get your act together, Santiago. Two days of hell without Lucy.*

She nodded.

'Two days—it hardly seems worth it.'

Lucy stared—unbelievable!

This from the man who had flown to Australia the previous week, spent two hours at a meeting and had flown all the way back, according to him because he had a heavy schedule that week.

His heavy schedule had not stopped him spending all but one of those nights with her and he had not seemed tired. She pressed a hand to her stomach, feeling the deep muscles clench and quiver. The earthy memory of the afternoon he had returned still had the power to make her skin prickle with heat.

She had been standing in the stables at the *finca*, leaning on her broom, feeling a glow of satisfaction as she surveyed the results of her labours, when she heard the creak of the large double doors banging closed. Her first thought was, *They need oiling.* The next was less practical.

As she turned and saw the tall figure whose massive breadth of shoulder seemed to fill the doorway her broom fell with a clatter to the floor. Her hand extended in a fluttery gesture to the silent silhouette.

'Santiago?'

'You were expecting someone else?'

In a state of shock, she was incapable of hiding her delight in seeing him. With a cry she ran towards him. Santiago strode to meet her halfway, swinging her off her feet. As their bodies collided his ravening mouth crashed down to claim her lips.

'Now that is what I call a satisfactory hello,' he growled when they came up for air.

She searched his face. 'You look tired.' Tired but utterly perfect, she thought as her sweeping scan took in the lines of strain bracketing his mouth and radiating from the corners of his incredible eyes.

He lifted a hand to his jaw and grinned. 'Now you know why I never let you see me without my make-up on.'

'Funny…' Lucy's shriek was in the nature of a token protest as he carried her over to the bales of sweet-smelling hay stacked in an empty stall. Her heart was thudding with anticipation as he laid her down and knelt beside her.

'This really isn't appropriate, Santiago...'

'The mouth...incidentally a delicious mouth,' he husked, nipping the full pouting curve of her lower lip. 'The delicious mouth is saying one thing, yet the eyes are saying another... Admit it—you want me here and now.'

If he ever knew how much she was in serious trouble. 'I'm working—'

The rest of her protest was muffled by his mouth as it moved with sensuous silken pressure over her parted lips.

'I thought you liked me being inappropriate...?'

The hand that lay on the juncture of her thighs rubbing her through the denim of her jeans was extremely inappropriate; it was also marvellous. 'I do...' she admitted with a throaty sigh. 'I do, but someone might come in and...'

He had shrugged off the suggestion, looking amused. 'What if they do?' There was no amusement in his dark eyes as he held her eyes, just predatory intent that sent her pulse rate through the ceiling. Without a word he yanked her up into a sitting position, then, taking the hem of her light cotton sweater in one hand, peeled it over her head in one smooth motion. Slinging it over his shoulder, he continued to stare at her with that same soul-stripping, hot intensity as he unfastened the clip that held her hair at her nape and sank his long fingers into the shiny filaments, spreading the soft silky mesh around her face.

Lucy shivered, not because the air was cold on her skin, but because his eyes were hot.

'Nice,' he approved, transferring his scrutiny to the pink lace bra she wore. 'But this is so much nicer,' he added, clicking the front fastening and taking a sharp audible intake of breath as her full, firm breasts sprang free from their confinement.

He bent his head and with a groan took one tight pink nipple into his mouth, causing pleasure that bordered pain to rip through her body.

She sank her fingers into his hair and kept his head there against her breasts until they fell back together on the hay.

It had been barely thirty-six hours since they had had sex, yet as they tore at each other's clothes, their mutual hunger amounted to ravening starvation. He took her as if she were the last drop of water in a desert and he were a man consumed by thirst, driven by it.

And Lucy wanted to be devoured. She wanted to give him what he wanted...to surrender to him and the need thundering through her veins.

Nobody had intruded during the frantic coupling and when later that night she had pointed out his apparent immunity to jet lag he had slid her beneath him in the bed and growled thickly, 'You are my cure for jet lag.'

'Is this something you really need to attend?'

The sound of his cranky voice dragged Lucy back to the present. 'I want to attend. Family is important to me.'

His jaw tightened. *And I am not?*

Shock rippled across Santiago's lean face, drawing the skin tight across his perfect bones. He was jealous that she preferred to spend time with her family than him.

She watched, puzzled, as he began to slide the items he had just removed from his briefcase back into it, his expression abstracted. 'I hope you enjoy yourself,' he said, sounding strange to Lucy.

She nodded, struggling to sense his mood. 'I hoped that you would sort out some help for—'

He cut her off with a wave of his hand. 'Obviously.' She had not even come to say goodbye; she had come to arrange Harriet's care.

'So you are close to this...Gianni?'

She smiled, her face softening. 'Yes.'

'Relative—so what is this Gianni? First cousin?' Santiago had tuned into the affection in her voice and taken an instant dislike to this unknown man.

She was puzzled by the glint in his eyes when he said Gianni's name. 'No, actually he's my nephew, though he's older than me. His dad is my eldest brother. He's marrying the girl who is house-sitting for me.'

When Gianni had spoken of Miranda, the stunning petite redhead she had left in charge of her menagerie, Lucy had heard the pride and love in his voice. Her good wishes had been genuine but tinged, if she was honest, with envy.

'It turns out I'm a matchmaker.' It was only her own love life she had problems with.

'So this is something of a whirlwind romance, then?'

Previously Lucy might have agreed with him, but now she knew that when a person fell in love it was not about timing or intention or even desire for it to happen—it just happened. 'That kind of depends on your definition of whirlwind.' She picked up her bag, began to move towards the door and stopped, turning back. 'Actually I was wondering…there are some seats on the flight and my invite is for "and friend"…?'

He arched a brow and looked at her, saying nothing, and Lucy thought, *Help me out here, will you?* 'Would you like to come?'

There, she'd said it, after spending the last week wondering if she should, and now she had and why not? It was no big thing if he said no.

Who was she kidding? It was a massive thing if he said no! If he accepted, this would be the first time they had been seen in public together as a couple… Were they even a couple? Actually she didn't know, that was the problem and, worse still, she had let the kernel of hope creep in. She had allowed herself to think of a future where they were together.

*And you based that on what, Lucy?* Sure, she stayed the night here sometimes, she even had a toothbrush in his bathroom and a drawer for her clothes, but it was all casual.

The intimacy, the luxury of not thinking before she acted or spoke, did not extend beyond the bedroom or wherever else they made love. Obviously the sex was incredible, sublime, and under his skilled tutelage she had discovered a passionate part of herself she had never dreamt existed, revelling in the world of sensory pleasures that had opened up to her.

But she was only different up to a point. She had never been able to separate the physical from the emotional and that hadn't changed. For a short time she had, out of a sense of self-preservation, refused to recognise the obvious. She was only able to give herself without boundary or reservation because while she had fallen in lust with him that lust had fast turned to love.

Santiago was the love of her life and the knowledge made her feel more vulnerable than she ever had before. Even at the height of the scandal she had been able to retain an objectivity and respond with a cool restraint to the insults that came her way. With Santiago that was impossible; she felt as though she were stuck in the middle of an emotional quicksand with no way out.

'You are inviting me to this wedding—today.' Santiago's veiled eyes fell from hers.

*Well, you wanted to know, Lucy.*

Only she hadn't known it would feel this bad!

A look was worth a thousand words—was that a saying or had she just made it up? Well, if someone hadn't said it they should have, she decided as she forced a smile.

It had been a calculated risk but she had always known

that this might be his response. She had taken the risk and
now she had to live with it.

'Fine, no problem, don't worry about it. It's short notice,
I know, and you're busy.' There, she had not made a scene,
she had given him a get out. *Which,* Lucy thought, *is very
grown-up and civilised of me.*

She didn't feel grown-up.

'I did not say no.'

She smiled and thought, *But you're going to.*

Santiago flicked his cuff and glanced at the silver-banded
watch that circled his hair-roughened wrist. 'Give me fifteen minutes.'

Without waiting for her reply, he walked through the open
door of his study and closed it behind him.

He had recovered quickly but she had seen the shock on
his face. The humiliating memory of it was going to be difficult to erase. Presumably he needed fifteen minutes to
polish the details of an excuse… She saw no reason to hang
around to hear it and give marks out of ten.

# CHAPTER THIRTEEN

LUCY spotted a space on her third circuit of the overflowing airport car park. With a sigh of relief she drove forward, intending to back into the space when the guy in the car behind her zipped neatly into it.

Lucy, her temper fizzing, jumped out of the car just as the other driver got out. She opened her mouth, but her protest died as the man gave a shameless 'all's fair in love and parking spaces' shrug.

'Oh, what's the point?' she asked herself.

About to get back into the car, she registered that the line of vehicles that had followed her were now honking their horns. She thought, *What the hell?* And, grabbing the bag containing her wedding outfit off the front passenger seat, began to walk away from the car as fast as her legs would take her—Lucy had very long legs.

She had gone a few yards when she was hailed by a uniformed figure who came running up behind her, warning breathlessly that her vehicle would be towed if she left it illegally parked.

She paused, then turned and, with an expressive shrug of her own, tossed the car keys to the official.

His jaw dropped as he caught them.

Lucy waved cheerfully and shouted, 'Feel free.' Before,

shoulders straight, her head held high, she walked confidently down past the rows of legally parked vehicles.

What was the worst they could do—arrest her? Actually they probably could, but only if they could catch her, Lucy thought, breaking into a jog as she reacted to the reckless buzz of angry defiance in her head.

She would get to this wedding if it killed her—or got her a criminal record. Despite her unease nobody stopped her and she reached the terminal with time to spare—not much, admittedly, but she had made it.

Now the pressure was off and she had reached her goal the adrenaline buzz and anger that had got her this far receded. The anticlimax left her feeling horribly flat, which was probably the reason that when she was one off the head of the line and the departure board showed the one thing that could stop her now she burst into loud sobs.

'Sorry…sorry,' she said to everyone who stared at her as she struggled to subdue the mortifying sobs. 'It can't be delayed,' she said when she reached the head of the line.

The woman, unmoved by Lucy's tear-stained face and wobbly voice, shook her head and, professional smile in place, recited, 'I'm afraid that—'

'No, you don't understand,' Lucy cut back, struggling to contain her frustration. 'It can't be delayed. I have to be there for this wedding…' She stopped. The woman was not listening, she was already looking beyond her, but other people were still casting curious glances her way wondering, presumably, who that madwoman was, or maybe they recognised her?

Lucy blew out a breath, hitched her bag higher on her shoulder and shoved her hands deep into the pockets of her designer jeans. She struggled to control the paranoia…. *Just because you're paranoid doesn't mean someone isn't follow-*

*ing you*, mocked the voice in her head, and the same premise was true of staring and judging.

*Let them*, she thought, lifting her chin. If she had learnt one thing over the last few weeks it was that she had spent the last four years hiding away under the pretence of embracing a simple life. Well, no more—Santiago might be ashamed to be seen in public with her, but she was not going to hide any more… No more skulking in corners—after all nobody could hurt her more than he had. The fact that she had laid herself open to such hurt did not make it any less painful.

Reacting with a brilliant smile and the approved level of meek obedience a person was expected to display in an airport, Lucy straightened her shoulders and, head high, moved away, mentally doing the arithmetic… How delayed could the flight be before she missed the wedding? The answer was not good news. Her window of opportunity was pretty narrow…an hour and a half, two at the most.

Lucy knew she should ring home and warn them she might be late, but that would be admitting defeat and she wasn't ready to yet. What she needed was some coffee. A caffeine hit would make the world look a less unfriendly place.

She had almost reached the coffee outlet when she caught sight of her reflection in a full-length plate-glass window and stopped, a choking sigh of horror escaping her lips. If people were staring it had little to do with her notoriety and everything to do with the fact the mascara that hadn't formed the comical panda circles around her eyes was smeared in streaks down her cheeks.

She pulled a tissue out of her pocket and began scrubbing at her face, tilting her head to see the results in the glass—not great. Coffee, she decided, scanning the area for the nearest ladies' room, would have to wait until she had managed some urgent running repairs on her make-up.

She had just located the sign she was looking for when

she saw them. They were a prosperous-looking couple, the woman in pearls and Chanel-style suit, presenting a picture of understated elegance but very much the supporting act next to the thick-set silver-haired man looking distinguished in a double-breasted suit and dapper waistcoat.

Shock detonated inside Lucy's head like a bomb, wiping out everything except panic. Her feet nailed to the spot, she stood there shaking as she fought off a wave of faintness, while a disembodied voice in her head screamed—*Run!*

She wanted to respond to the voice but she physically couldn't. She just stood and waited, the awful sense of inevitability lying like a heavy cold stone in the pit of her stomach.

The woman saw her first...Barbara. Lucy had always wondered about her. Did she know the true nature of the man she lived with and simply chose to ignore it? Or was she genuinely ignorant? You read of cases where women lived with men who made a mere serial adulterer look pleasant and claimed they had had no clue, that the man they knew was kind and loving.

There was no question that the woman had recognised her. She coloured visibly through the smooth matt make-up and tugged at her husband's sleeve. Speaking in a loud voice, he ignored her interruption at first, then when he did give her his attention there was impatience in his handsome face.

The woman spoke, stabbing a finger towards Lucy. Too far away to hear what she was saying or even see her face, Lucy could sense her agitation from where she stood. After a few seconds the man's head lifted, his gaze following the direction of his wife's pointing finger.

Then they were walking towards her, the wife trailing a little behind her husband, perhaps less eager for the confrontation.

The scene could have been lifted from one of Lucy's recurrent nightmares except instead of wearing pyjamas and fluffy slippers she had mascara streaked all over her face like warpaint. To Lucy's overheated imagination the crowds seemed to part for the swaggering, self-important figure.

Then as suddenly as a switch clicking Lucy was no longer nervous or ashamed. A weird sense of calm settled over her. She was still shaking but now it was with anger. She had allowed this man to steal part of her life, but no more.

Heart thudding, she took the initiative and strode towards them with purpose. Conscious of her mother's advice of 'it's not what you wear, it's the way you wear it,' she lifted her head, and, hearing a photographer's voice saying, 'Work it, Lucy, give it some attitude, baby,' she put an extra sway into her hips.

Control had been taken away from her once but she was about to take it back. Easier without mascara panda eyes, perhaps, but she was working with what she had, and she had a body. A body that until now she had appreciated on a purely 'it works' level, yet now thanks to Santiago she knew possessed a feminine power.

*Panic* was not a word or an emotion that he had time for, but when Santiago had come out of his study and found her gone he had experienced something that felt uncomfortably like it. Not that this was surprising…not a word, not a note, nothing. She had vanished.

Fifteen minutes, he had said—was fifteen minutes too much to ask for? His jaw clenched as his initial panic was rapidly replaced by a slow simmering fury. He had spent those requested fifteen minutes rearranging a high-powered meeting that had taken weeks to organise in the first place. Bankers had travelled from several continents to attend and he stood the risk of causing massive offence, not to mention a mountain of ill will, by cancelling.

But he had.

And why? Because he had recognised a turning point in their relationship. Santiago knew about turning points—he normally managed to walk before they occurred. He had seen this one coming but he had made no attempt to avoid it, although he'd assumed he would of course choose the fork marked 'I don't do relationships'.

Then she had asked him, not just for more, but to meet her family. It was almost in his mind a public declaration of intent and, instead of telling him to run away, his instinct had pushed him towards it.

In his experience *things* in life were generally simple, it was *people* who complicated things. However this situation, when you stripped away the detritus, amounted to one simple question, or at least the answer to that question: was he willing to lose her for ever? To push away the woman who had removed the wall of cynicism around his heart brick by brick? She was an infuriating, frustrating mixture of toughness and vulnerability and the idea of living a life she was not part of scared him more than anything in his life had. Just admitting it to himself gave him a sense of purpose, a feeling of liberation.

He had vowed never to put himself in a position where he was responsible for another person's happiness but suddenly that responsibility no longer seemed like a burden, it seemed like a privilege.

No longer afraid to take that step off the cliff in the dark, which essentially was what love was, he had finally faced down his personal demons only to find that the woman who had inspired him to take that leap hadn't bothered to hang around and wait for him.

Had she set out to anger him? What other conclusions was he meant to draw when he discovered that to top it all she had taken a car from the garage?

Her selection of vehicle was not wasted on him. It was

the powerful new addition to his collection, a sports model he had made the mistake of describing as not a woman's car... The comment had elicited an 'anything you can do I can do better' tirade, which he had endured with relative good humour because, as he'd admitted to Lucy, she was probably right.

He did not dispute her ability, but this did not alter the fact that he had no intention of providing the means for her to break her beautiful neck.

As he drove the route to the airport he tensed with each successive hairpin bend he negotiated, half expecting to come across the tangled, twisted remains of the car. He never did, so presumably she had managed to get to the airport in one piece. Once he got hold of her that might change, he thought grimly.

It turned out, when he reached the airport, that his car had also made it unscathed. There didn't seem to be a scratch on it, though the fact it was clamped and sitting behind a tow truck made it hard to be positive about this.

For the first time since he had started this pursuit he smiled, then he laughed, making a passing group of tourists turn and stare curiously.

He pointed at the disappearing tow truck. 'That's mine!'

The explanation caused the group of tourists to quickly move on.

Inside the terminal building Santiago was deciding where to begin his search when he saw the couple, recognising the pair from the articles he had read. A split second later he saw Lucy herself. Her tall, blonde-headed figure was not one that got lost in a crowd. The relief he experienced in that moment was quickly followed by a rush of protective concern as he assessed the situation.

He was moving forward to intervene when he saw Lucy straighten her slender shoulders and advance towards the couple looking like a queen, head held high. Her hair swishing like a silver halo around her beautiful face, she radiated confidence and purpose, a sexy avenging angel. He experienced a wave of pride mingled with lust. Lucy Fitzgerald was many things but a coward was not one of them.

Santiago hesitated, torn between a desire to applaud and an equally strong need to rush in and protect her. He forced himself to stand back.

'Well, well, this is a blast from the past…you're looking good, Lucy.' Feeling the lascivious eyes move over her body like grubby hands made Lucy shudder.

'Denis, don't…come away, she's not worth… I don't know how she has the cheek to be seen in public!'

Denis Mulville cast his wife a look of contempt before turning back to Lucy. 'No hard feelings, Lucy.'

Lucy looked at the hand extended towards her and gave an incredulous laugh. 'Go away, you pathetic little man. There is nothing you can say or do that could harm me.'

Denis looked utterly astonished by her response. His good humour vanished in the blink of an eye, replaced by an air of narrow-eyed menace. As he took a step towards her, pushing his face up close to hers, Lucy grimaced with distaste. The man smelt like a distillery; he had clearly been drinking heavily… It took all her willpower to hold her ground and not retreat from the glittering malice aimed her way.

'My, my, you really have come down in the world,' he slurred. His eyes dropped, his sneer growing more pronounced as he took in her jeans, casual open-necked shirt and flat shoes. 'Not so special now, are we, Miss I'm-better-than-everyone-else? Bitch…I showed you.'

'Denis, please…'

The agonised plea from his wife fell on deaf ears, or at least very drunk ears.

He looked around the crowded terminal and raised his voice. 'Stuck-up little bitch thinks she's a cut above—'

'That is because she is.'

The cool voice cut across the toxic bluster and caused Denis to stagger back drunkenly. He blinked, then seemed to Lucy to shrink as he took in the size and quality of the man who had come to stand beside her.

Lucy gave a sigh of relief and relaxed into the strong arms that came up behind her back.

'And who might you be, friend?'

'I am not your friend and I am the man you should be thanking. If one is going to be knocked out cold in a public place I think it is always far less humiliating if the person striking the blow is a man, not a woman...' His austere expression melded into a tender smile that took Lucy's breath away as it was directed at her.

'Yes, I know, *querida*, that you can handle it, but I think possibly he does not. And a man likes to feel needed.' He felt her tremble and pulled her in closer to his side, fitting her curves into his angles. His voice dropped to a low threatening rumble as he pitched the addition for the other man's ears only. 'If you do not close your filthy mouth I will close it for you.'

'You can't talk to me like that,' he blustered.

Pale except for the twin spots of colour on his fleshy cheeks, Denis's face glistened unhealthily with a layer of sweat.

Santiago arched a sardonic brow. 'But as you see I can. To clarify matters, because I have no wish to continue this conversation any longer than necessary, that is not a threat or even a promise, but simply a fact.'

He turned from the older man, who was opening and closing his mouth like a fish coming up for air, and turned to Lucy, his manner altering again dramatically.

'The private jet is on standby. We have, I think, a wedding to go to...' He nodded towards the unhappy-looking woman and said curtly, 'Madam, you have my sympathy.' Before, a hand in the small of her back, he guided Lucy away.

'Good girl,' he said without looking at her, adding as she began to turn her head, 'Don't look back.' For the first time in a long time Santiago wasn't. His eyes were fixed firmly on the future. 'Just smile.'

'I wasn't going to look back and I don't feel like smiling.' She felt like throwing up.

'Well, you should feel like smiling. You just faced your private demon and spat in his face. You came out on top, Lucy.'

Her eyes widened. 'I did, didn't I? Where are we going?'

'Pay attention, Lucy...private jet?'

'But you weren't serious?' It had been a nice touch and she was grateful that he had played along. 'What I don't understand is how you got to be here just when you did.'

'I'd like to claim psychic powers but actually it was luck and of course a few speeding fines.'

He stopped, turning her around to face him. 'Why do you think I'm here, Lucy?' he asked quietly.

Her heart skipped several beats as the rest of the room, the noise, the crowds, all vanished. There was just Santiago and his warm wonderful smile, his expressive eyes saying things that she could not allow herself to believe.

'Don't look at me like that.'

Santiago rolled his eyes. 'Are they handing out double firsts to idiots at Cambridge these days? For an intelligent woman, Lucy Fitzgerald, you can be monumentally stupid at times.' His hands tightened around her forearms and the mockery faded from his eyes. 'You're shaking like a leaf.' He swore through clenched teeth and gritted savagely, 'I knew I should have throttled the little bastard.'

She flickered a look up through her lashes at his clenched profile. 'It's not him, it's you.'

Santiago swung back to her, a look of shock stamped on his dark features. Frowning, he hooked a finger under her chin, drawing her face up to him.

She was too shell-shocked to think of a lie. 'You make me shake when you touch me.' She winced, half expecting to see his eyes light up with sardonic mockery. They did light up—they blazed, but with a male predatory satisfaction that sent her sensitive stomach into a dive. 'I can't help... Ouch!' she yelped as a passer-by slammed a heavy case into the backs of her knees.

'Sorry!'

Santiago snarled something rude under his breath and sent a murderous glare towards the retreating figure.

'Calm down, it was an accident and no harm done. I'm fine.'

Santiago's dark expression softened into a rueful smile as his glance settled on her upturned face. 'I am not,' he admitted. 'This place, it is impossible...' He stopped, shook his head and, taking her hand in his, said firmly, 'We will continue this conversation when we are in the air.'

'There is really a plane on standby?'

'Yes.'

'Does that mean you are coming to the wedding with me?'

'Am I still invited?'

She struggled against a smile as she imagined the reactions of her family, who had been trying to hook her up with a man for years. They might just break out into spontaneous applause. 'Oh, yes, you are still invited.'

'Then what are you waiting for? It is considered bad manners to arrive late and upstage the bride.'

'Oh, I wouldn't do that. Miranda is beautiful,' Lucy delivered, breathless as she trotted to keep up with Santiago's long-legged stride.

The comment drew a laugh from Santiago. 'And you of course are speaking as someone who is a little homely and plain.' At his most dry, he shook his head. 'Taking humility a little too far. Lucy, you are the most beautiful woman in any room at any time.'

The tribute made Lucy stumble and cast an uncertain look at Santiago's lean, autocratic profile. 'I doubt if Gianni would think so.'

'*I* think so,' he ground out forcefully.

Opening the door to the VIP area, he stood to one side and captured her wide sapphire gaze as she walked past him like a sleepwalker. Helpless to fight the knife thrust of sexual hunger, Santiago shot out an arm just as she had entered the room, then, pulling her back towards him and standing in the doorway, planted a the kiss on her parted lips so hard it bent her body in a graceful back arch.

Then as if nothing had happened he pulled her upright. Her world was spinning, people were staring, and who could blame them? Santiago was straightening his tie as though he had not just ravished her in public… Shaking off the daze, she touched her lips, feeling well and truly ravished but also indignant that he had made such a public spectacle of her.

'Please do not distract me, Lucy, we are on the clock here.'

Lucy's jaw hit her chest. '*Me* distract *you*—' she began, but he was dragging her in his wake and she had a struggle catching her breath, let alone talking.

As soon as the jet lifted off Santiago unclipped his seat belt and stretched his long legs in front of him.

'Now, that conversation we put on hold.'

Lucy regarded him, her sapphire stare steady but wary. She tugged at the open neck of her shirt… Santiago anywhere made her feel breathless. In the confined space of the admittedly luxurious aircraft cabin his brooding presence was pretty much overwhelming.

'Why did you not wait for me? I asked for fifteen minutes.'

'I assumed…'

He arched a sardonic brow. 'You assumed?'

'I assumed there was no point. I didn't think you meant it…I thought…' She threw up her hands in frustration and ran her tongue across the outline of her dry lips. 'There didn't seem much point waiting when you were obviously going to say no.'

'Obviously.'

The sarcastic drawl brought a flush to her cheeks. 'Well, how was I to know?'

'Possibly by doing me the courtesy of waiting.'

'All right, I'm sorry I didn't wait but I didn't think you'd say yes.'

'Then why did you ask me?'

Her eyes fell from his. 'Family weddings when you're an almost-thirty-year-old woman who doesn't have a partner can be pretty dire, people looking sympathetic or worse, trying to get you off with their nephew or brother or recently divorced best friend.' The lie came easier because it was essentially true even though it had nothing whatever to do with her reason for asking him.

'So you invited me to stop you looking like a sad loser? You really know how to make a man feel special, Lucy,' he drawled.

She lowered her gaze and sucked in a deep breath, looking at her fingers clenching and unclenching in her lap. 'All right, I invited you because it's what you do if you have a boyfriend…' Even saying it made her feel ridiculous. She left a space for his laugh and when it didn't come she added, 'I know you're not my boyfriend but we do have…' *Sex, all we have is sex. You're making a fool of yourself, Lucy.* But he was here—that had to mean something…didn't it? 'I suppose I wanted more.'

'So do I.'

Her eyes flew to his handsome face. 'You want more?' she repeated, feeling her way cautiously. 'More sex or…?'

'I have no problem with more sex,' he conceded with a flash of his hard wolfish grin that sent a corresponding stab of lust humming through her body. 'However that is not what I meant.' He looked serious now. His muscular shoulders lifted in a shrug but his grave eyes remained fixed on her face. 'This surprises you?'

'Yes, I thought… It always seemed that you avoided being seen in public with me. I mean, I know my reputation is pretty toxic and—' Her voice broke and she bit her lip. 'So it is pretty understandable.'

Santiago had sat there, his body tense, his face set in a mask as he listened, fighting the urge to interrupt, but the little crack in her voice snapped his restraint.

*'Por Dios!'* He surged to his feet, looking even taller and more commanding than normal in the limited confines of the luxurious cabin. 'Yes, I did avoid taking you out.' The admission made her wince. 'But it was not shame that made me avoid public places…' He shook his head, his expression reflecting his disbelief that she could think such a thing as he dropped into the seat beside her. 'Not shame, just selfishness. The time we had together was so limited. You spent more time with the damned donkeys than me. When we were together I did not want to share you with other people.'

Shaken as much by the raw intensity spilling from him as what he had said, Lucy, who had been bright red as he spoke, was deathly pale as she stared at him, her wide blue eyes glimmering with unshed tears.

Unable to fight the need to touch her any longer, he turned

in his seat, drawing her hands into his lap. Turning them over, he rubbed his thumb across the small calluses on her palms. The light contact sent the muscles low in her pelvis into quivering spasms.

'You walk into a room and you light it up.' The husky throb of his voice made her tremble. 'People are drawn to you—your warmth, your beauty, your genuine interest in them. *Por Dios*, ashamed?' He gave a raw laugh, the pretence of control gone as he stared into her face. 'I know that when you are beside me I am the envy of all men.'

Tears trickled out of the corners of her eyes and she sniffed, dragging her hand from his to dab them, pushing the tendrils of hair back from her face and tucking them behind her ears with trembling fingers.

'I am not an easy man to live with…'

He was asking her to live with him!

'But you are a strong woman.'

'Is that a polite way of saying stubborn and hard-headed?'

'It is a way of saying not like Magdalena.'

Lucy swallowed at the blunt pronouncement, her eyes filling. She felt the raw pain reflected in his tortured expression in the depths of her soul.

'And you won't let me get away with bullying you.'

Unable to bear the self-loathing in his voice, Lucy laid a finger on his lips. 'Please don't say such things,' she begged. 'I hate it and it's not true. Magdalena had problems that were not of your making and her death was an accident,' she told him fiercely. 'A cruel random act of fate.'

She could see in his eyes that he didn't believe her. He would always, she realised, carry the guilt, though with time and maybe with help from someone… The well of love inside her rose up so intense that she could hardly breathe—she wanted to be that someone there for him.

Santiago's chest swelled as he looked into the fierce blue

eyes raised to his. They swam with tears she struggled to hold back as he framed her beautiful face with his big hands.

'Did you really think I would ever let you leave me?'

The emotion in his voice made the fist of longing lodged in her chest grow heavier. She had never known that love could feel like a physical thing...that it was even possible to love someone so much it hurt.

'I would be a madman and, besides, Gabby would never forgive me. She is already imagining the impression you will make on the other girls when you arrive on parents' night.'

'Oh, God, I'm sorry!' Being in a relationship that extended outside the bedroom was one thing, but she could only imagine how the commitment-phobic Santiago would have reacted to his daughter marrying him off.

His brow furrowed. The way Lucy's mind worked remained a mystery he doubted he would ever solve. 'Sorry?'

'I'll have a word with her if it helps. Young girls often fantasise.' Older girls, too.

'You think it fantastical that my daughter thinks of you as a mother?' he asked, sounding strange.

Lucy struggled to read his expression. 'I think it's lovely of her,' she admitted huskily. 'And I'd like to be a friend to her but—look, I know this is none of my business, but maybe—'

'None of your business? Of course it is your business!' He slapped his hand down hard on his chest and gritted, '*I* am your business. And Gabby, she has friends, she has a father—she needs a mother. I was hoping to be able to tell her that she will have one...?'

It took a few seconds for her to register what he had said. Lucy went ice cold. 'Is that a proposal?'

Outrage made her voice quiver and shake. Not the response he had anticipated or hoped for.

'Is that a no?'

'You're asking me to marry you to give your daughter a mother! Too right it's a no!' she yelled back, furious, because with the cold-blooded proposal he had trampled all over her precious dreams. 'When I marry I want a man who—' She bit her trembling lip and scrunched her eyes closed, forcing tears from the corners. 'I want a marriage that gives me more than a ring. I'd prefer a fling than a cosmetic, convenient arrangement.'

'Fling! What are you talking about? I'm not asking you to marry me because of Gabby. I'm asking you to marry me because I love you!' he bellowed.

Her eyes flew open. Paper pale, she dabbed the stray tears from her cheeks. 'You love me?' she whispered, thinking if volume was any indicator he did. She was amazed no one had come running to see what was happening but she assumed they had been instructed to leave them alone. She didn't imagine many people who worked for Santiago ignored his instructions.

'Why else do you think I asked you? Cancel that question. Next time you'll probably get it into your head that I'm asking because you match my hair and tie?' It seemed safer to leave no room for error, Santiago decided as he took her in his arms, drawing her warm soft body into his and feeling the anger drain from his body.

His smile made her heart turn over.

'You love me...?'

'With all my heart, *mi esposa*...with all my heart.'

She shook her head. 'This doesn't seem real.'

He bent his head and fitted his mouth to hers. Lucy gave a sigh as she pulled back whispering, 'I love you, Santiago.'

When they came up for air she was sitting on his lap and had no idea how she'd got there—being there was enough. Being with Santiago was enough, it was everything.

When Lucy tore herself away from him to change she

found her dress hanging freshly pressed, waiting for her. Slipping it on, she smiled at her reflection. The shift with the ruffles around the neck was a shade paler blue than her eyes. It clung, emphasising the curves of her hourglass figure.

When she returned to the cabin Santiago was in a dark lounge suit, the jacket unbuttoned to reveal a grey tie dark against his immaculate white shirt. He looked sleek and sophisticated and utterly gorgeous.

His face lit up when he saw her. 'Nobody will be looking at the bride. You look absolutely incredible.'

Tears of emotion flooded her eyes. In her opinion all eyes would be on her handsome fiancée. 'God, please don't make me cry.'

'You wish me to be nasty to you?'

Lucy gave a watery laugh. 'About us—do you mind if we don't tell my family today?'

He stiffened, the look of wary hurt in his face bringing her rushing to his side. 'It's not that I don't want to tell them—I do want to,' she declared enthusiastically. 'To yell it off high buildings! It's just today is Gianni and Miranda's day. I wouldn't want to steal their thunder.'

His face cleared and he drew her to him. 'Of course you don't, because you are a kind, thoughtful person with the tendency to put other people's feelings above her own, combined with a desire to steal my prize possessions.'

Her eyes went round as she stepped back and gave a guilt-stricken gasp. 'Your car! I forgot. I'm not sure where it is actually. I sort of…double-parked. There might be a fine…?'

'I will bill you,' he promised.

Hand in hand they left the plane, then Santiago handed her into the waiting limo.

Arriving with Santiago at her side was the proudest moment of her life. He went out of his way to be charming and members of her family who commented on him all said the same thing: *a keeper, Lucy, don't let him go.*

Lucy, who had never cried at a wedding in her life, had tears rolling down her cheeks during the simple ceremony in the flower-decked village church. When the couple exchanged their vows Santiago, who held her hand tight all through the ceremony, looked suspiciously misty-eyed himself.

Like many of the other guests they drifted outside where a band played music and people danced under the fairy lights strung through trees.

The band began to play a slow number and Santiago pulled her into his arms.

'You can dance,' she discovered.

He smiled. 'This was a beautiful wedding.'

'It is, and everyone loves you.'

He stopped circling and tipped her face up to him. 'There is only one person whose love I need.'

'You have it, oh, you have it,' she promised in a voice that throbbed with emotion.

Without warning he let out a war cry and picked her up, twirling her around until she begged to be put down.

Back on terra firma she turned her loving eyes on the man beside her. Lucy's heart swelled with love as she looked at him. 'I don't think any day could be more perfect than this,' she said huskily.

'Our wedding day will be.'

'Don't put your hat away, Maeve—it looks like another Fitzgerald wedding to me.'

Lucy turned with a smile to the aunts walking past and shook her head. 'No, not a Fitzgerald wedding, Auntie Maggie, a Silva wedding, but don't advertise it until this one is over.'

'Why, darling,' her aunt retorted, 'you two have been advertising it since you walked in holding hands and why not? Ain't love grand!'

'Extremely grand,' Santiago agreed, his eyes on his bride-to-be.

\* \* \* \* \*

# LET'S TALK

*Romance*

For exclusive extracts, competitions
and special offers, find us online:

 facebook.com/millsandboon

 @MillsandBoon

 @MillsandBoonUK

**Get in touch on 01413 063232**

# JOIN US ON SOCIAL MEDIA!

Stay up to date with our latest releases, author news and gossip, special offers and discounts, and all the behind-the-scenes action from Mills & Boon...

 millsandboon

 millsandboonuk

f millsandboon

*It might just be true love...*

# MILLS & BOON

## MODERN

# Power and Passion

Prepare to be swept off your feet by sophisticated, sexy and seductive heroes, in some of the world's most glamourous and romantic locations, where power and passion collide.

Julia James
Bianca's
PREGNANCY
SCANDAL
MILLS & BOON
MODERN

Jennie Lucas
Chosen as the
SHEIKH'S ROYAL
BRIDE
MILLS & BOON
MODERN

Kim Lawrence
A WEDDING
of the
ITALIAN'S DEMAND

Sharon Kendrick
The
SHEIKH'S
SECRET BABY
MILLS & BOON
MODERN

Eight Modern stories published every month, find them all at:

## millsandboon.co.uk/Modern